"STAND BY
FOR EVASIVE MANEUVERS,
MR. CHEKOV . . ."

Spock shoved the throttle control to maximum. The G-forces squeezed them back into their seats.

"Damn." Chekov glanced up from his scanner. "They're still closing on us. They were built for this . . . we weren't."

Spock replied by yanking the throttle back, cutting their speed to a standstill. The pursuing Chorymi ships rushed past.

Chekov grinned wickedly. "Good move, Mr. Spock."

"Not good enough, I'm afraid," Spock replied. The tactical screen showed the dogged Chorymi fighters hadn't given up. Within seconds they were back in weapons range, and fired another volley.

Spock and Chekov felt the shuttle take two hits at the stern. A muffled explosion shook the ship, and the cabin lights flickered . . .

Look for STAR TREK Fiction from Pocket Books

Star Trek: The Original Series

Star Trek: The Next Generation

A STAR TREK® NOVEL

DEEP DOMAIN

HOWARD WEINSTEIN

POCKET BOOKS

New York   London   Toronto   Sydney   Tokyo

This one's for Lynne Perry
With thanks for letting me Trek to other worlds while keeping one foot
in this one

An *Original* Publication of POCKET BOOKS

POCKET BOOKS, a division of Simon & Schuster Inc.
1230 Avenue of the Americas, New York, NY 10020

ISBN: 0-671-70549-0

First Pocket Books printing April 1987

10 9 8 7 6

POCKET and colophon are registered trademarks of
Simon & Schuster Inc.

Printed in the U.S.A.

Author's Notes

FLASHBACK: October 1984. I'd just gone on a whale-watching cruise off the Massachusetts coast with my friend T. J. Burnside. We visited humpbacks and dolphins in the wild, and discussed late rumors about *Star Trek*: despite the success of *Star Trek III*, it seemed there might not be a *Star Trek IV*. Dismaying, to say the least.

Next day, I got a call from a science fiction acquaintance, asking if I could come in and meet with Leonard Nimoy that afternoon. If *S.T. IV* got made, he would be directing it, and he was preparing by holding a series of brainstorming sessions with various writers and scientists around the country, stirring up new ideas for the next film. So, could I come in and chat? *You bet!*

It was fun meeting Leonard for the first time, and a challenge to come up with suggestions that might be useful. I got over being nervous in a few minutes. He wasn't at all nervous about meeting me. Following that session, I thought I might have a chance to submit a story outline for the movie, so I quickly wrote one based on some of the notions we'd discussed.

As it turned out, Leonard and Harve Bennett had already decided on a basic story involving time travel, so I set mine aside. But it didn't go to waste—it evolved into this book.

If you saw *Star Trek IV: The Voyage Home,* you might've spied my name near the end of the credits, under "The Producers extend special thanks to—" So I guess I helped 'em a little. And I loved the movie—my compliments to all the chefs responsible for *S.T. IV.*

Partly because they originated in the same pot of ideas, *Deep Domain* and *S.T. IV* share some common ground, though the different approaches will become obvious as you read this novel. But both focus to some extent on marine life (though that's *not* a whale on the cover; it's an

v

Akkallan triteera, recognizable by its triple-fluked tail). Both touch on themes of co-existence with other species and ecological responsibility. And they attempt to do what science fiction does so well—make us take probing looks at our own world. It's the only one we've got and we're *not* taking very good care of it.

Hardly a week passes without horrific headlines about chemical spills polluting water and air, man-made noxious potions punching holes in the atmospheric ozone that protects us from cancer-causing rays of the sun, acid rain reducing forests to lifeless sticks of wood and killing streams that once teamed with fish. . . .

You don't have to be an environmental crazy to get the point: If we turn our beautiful planet into a sludge-encrusted cesspool with brown air and crunchy water, we ain't got no place else to go. If you're sitting there thinking, *But I never dump toxic wastes into the ocean, so why's he busting my chops?* I'll tell you why.

Not doing rotten things just isn't good enough anymore. As we used to say, before "social activism" became dirty words, *"If you're not part of the solution, you're part of the problem."*

Yes, I realize we can't all go out in small boats and stop illegal whaling by interposing our bodies between explosive harpoons and the whales at which they're aimed. Or go out and intercept barrels of radioactive garbage before they sink to the bottom of the sea. Or physically wrest deadly weapons from the fingers of poachers intent on butchering endangered rhinos for their horns and elephants for their tusks.

But if it outrages you to know that gentle mountain gorillas (perhaps a few hundred remain in the wild) are murdered and their hands cut off to be made into *ash trays* for tourists, there's something you can do. Simple but vital.

First, you can help other people understand the importance of these issues. And, for a very few bucks, you can contribute to one of the fine organizations dedicated to protecting Planet Earth and its many life forms (including we humans, who often seem too dumb to protect ourselves *from* ourselves). Three that I personally recommend: Greenpeace, the Cousteau Society, and the World Wildlife Fund. All are reputable and devoted to preserving our world. If you can't locate an address (check your school or public library), then write to me c/o Pocket Books, 1230 Avenue of the Americas, NY, NY 10020. Send a stamped, self-addressed envelope and I'll send the info you'll need to contact them.

Whatever you do, please don't leave it to the other guy. We all have it in our power to make the world a little better, or at least keep it from getting worse. We won't always succeed— but unless we try, we can't *possibly* succeed.

Before I forget, special thanks to Julia Ecklar (for Russian advice), Bob and Debbie Greenberger, Ann Crispin, Debby Marshall, Mom and Dad, George Takei, Walter Koenig, Eddie Egan, Dave McDonnell, Cindi Casby, Tom Roberts, Sharon Jarvis, Liz Hartman, Dave Stern—and, of course, Mail Order Annie.

Howard Weinstein
December 1986

Historian's Note: Those who have avidly followed the exploits of the U.S.S. *Enterprise* and her crew should note that this mission takes place in the years following the events related in printed and audio-visual reports of the *Enterprise*'s encounter with V'ger, circa Stardate 7412.

Chapter One

"WHERE THE HELL are the damn cops?"

Dr. Cynthia McPhillips bit off each word with barely restrained rage. She ran a hand through her dark, short-shag hair and watched droplets from the mist outside trickle down the large bay window of the Federation science outpost on Akkalla.

Dr. Naw-Rocki reacted with a quizzical expression as he joined McPhillips at the window. "Cops," the seven-foot-tall alien echoed. "Unfamiliar word. Neology? Or perhaps colloquialism?" His multifaceted amber eyes blinked expectantly, and he smoothed his blue-green, downy skin.

"Old Terran word for police or security forces."

"Ahh, understanding," Naw-Rocki said in a voice incongruously prissy for a being of his size. "Assistance certainly required for our return to dwelling."

They heard the door to the lab open, and Dr. Enzo Piretti, the third member of their team, came in. He shrugged out of his rain gear, grabbed a towel and rubbed his white hair and beard, which offered stark contrast against his deeply tanned skin.

McPhillips occasionally envied his color, even though she knew it was largely a product of Mediterranean genes. Sunburn was hardly a concern on Akkalla, and she'd grown tired of seeing her own ashen complexion in the mirror each morning. She'd also had her fill of humidity-frizzed hair and thought now and then that she'd like her next duty station to be someplace truly arid.

"Any interesting data on the instruments, Enzo?"

"Yeah, boss. Big surprise—it's raining," he said.

1

"Thanks. I hadn't noticed. We've been here four hundred and three days. It's rained all or part of three hundred and eighty-nine of 'em. But who's counting?"

"That's the news from the back," Piretti said. "What's going on out front?"

"See for yourself," McPhillips said in disgust, waving toward the mist-coated glass.

Piretti stepped forward to see a line of perhaps a hundred Akkallans positioned atop the massive seawall protecting the stretch of shore from high tides and heavy surf. They effectively blocked the path leading from the science station to the slip where the researchers' mag boats were moored. Many carried signs inviting the Federation researchers to leave the planet as hastily as possible, condemning the offworlders as sinners, or warning of unpleasant fates awaiting them if they lingered on a planet where they were obviously not wanted. Empty-handed protesters pumped hostile fists into the air with growing fervor.

Piretti whistled. "Getting worse every day."

Naw-Rocki nodded solemnly. "First time departure has been obstructed."

"That's why I called the Grolian Guard. I want some official protection for us, or there'll be hell to pay when the *Enterprise* gets here," said McPhillips.

"So where *are* our friendly neighborhood Grolian Guards, anyway?" Piretti asked.

"Damned if I know. I called twice. If we don't see some results in about five minutes, I'm going to call again. I'm building up to a real good blowup." She began pacing in front of the window, always keeping her eye on the scene outside.

Piretti sat back in a recliner at his desk. "What a group. A seventy-year-old Italian—"

"Descended from Roman emperors," Cynthia McPhillips interjected.

"Hey, I swear it's the truth!"

"Uh-huh."

"—a seven-foot blue-green guy from Rannica III, and a woman ecologist in charge who's spent the past year fighting with every Akkallan authority every day and twice on Sunday," Piretti finished. "And what do we have to show for our four hundred and three days?"

2

"Survivalness," Naw-Rocki said wryly.

"Something to be said for that," Piretti agreed.

"We've got nothing to be ashamed of," McPhillips said. "We would've had a lot more to show if the damn government didn't put us on a short leash."

"But is that going to be enough when the *Enterprise* gets here to evaluate us? Do we get our extension, or do we get yanked home?" Piretti wondered. "Maybe it's better if we leave with the starship, considering—" He jerked a thumb toward the crowd outside.

McPhillips shook her head in frustration. "Dammit, Enzo, we're so close to confirming this new life form. I know it's not what we came to study, but it's damn exciting. I'd hate to lose the chance to follow the trail."

"Y'know what gets me, Cindy," Piretti said. "What made the Akkallan scientists and the students from the Collegium hate us so much?"

Naw-Rocki raised a spindly blue-green finger. "Probable speculation: government disinformation."

"Can't argue with that," said McPhillips. "Where else could the entire Collegium get the idea that we were conspiring *with* the government *against* them? On a world where the government controls every medium of communication, keeps offworlders in separate compounds, and won't let us even talk to the native scientists . . . *dammit!* If only we could've worked together . . ."

"Things I won't miss about Akkalla," Piretti said, pausing to consider. "The weather, the government . . . the weather . . . umm, the weather."

"Naw, tell us again what the weather's like on your planet."

The towering alien allowed his eyes to slip closed in a moment of fanciful escape home. "Perpetual choice. We modulate patterns completely."

Enzo laughed. "That settles it—I'm headed for Rannica III as soon as the *Enterprise* gets us out of here. I just wish we hadn't been outta direct touch for so long." His smile faded.

Cindy McPhillips widened her brown eyes in feigned amazement. "What? But the Publican's office assured us that all our messages were relayed to the Federation Science Council on the government subspace channel. And they

3

swore they gave us all the messages sent to us. Don't you believe them?"

Enzo Piretti growled a skeptical-sounding response in Italian. McPhillips wished she knew the language, but the tone was more than enough to make his feelings clear.

"We never should've let 'em close down our subspace transmitter," he said.

"Negative choice in that matter," Naw-Rocki said. "A common vernacular expression exists on Rannica. I find it somewhat appropriate."

The others waited several moments for him to share the Rannican maxim, but Naw-Rocki just moved the tip of his pointed tongue along his lips, which they knew by now meant he was thinking.

"Well, you gonna tell us?" Piretti prompted. "And is this one gonna make any sense to us, or is it gonna be like most of the others you come up with?"

"This is cause for hesitation—attempting most applicable translation." He took a deep breath, then decided to try what he'd come up with. "When mastig says, 'Don't worry, I may not consume you until later'—worry. Oh, mastig is like, uhh, your legendary dragon. Existence, however, confirmed."

"Mildly appropriate," said McPhillips. "You're getting the hang of English, Naw."

The downy alien smiled. "Appreciation expressed."

"Well," McPhillips said, "we've only got two more days to teach you, assuming the *Enterprise* is on time."

Enzo shook his head. "And would we know if she wasn't gonna be? I doubt it."

McPhillips leaned on the window sill, admiring the chiaroscuro of the Akkallan sky, a work painted by nature from a palette of grays ranging from glowering to silvery, clouds that all at once swirled with the fury of storms and floated gently on the mildest of mists. "You know, this can be a really beautiful planet, in spite of everything." She glanced at the wall clock. "Their five minutes are up. I'm calling the damn Grolian Guard office again."

She stalked toward the communications panel.

"Cindy, arrival," said Naw-Rocki.

Out in the lagoon, a pair of sleek silver police cutters cruised up to the dock extending from the seawall, searchlights slicing the gloom of twilight, loudspeakers broadcasting a warning for the protesters to disperse. The three scientists watched as the path was slowly cleared. Within a few minutes, a guardsman dressed in lightweight gray body armor and clear helmet entered the lab. Cynthia greeted him with a snarl.

"It's about time you got here. We've been under siege for an hour—that's three of your hexos. I had to call for help twice. We're representatives of the United Federation of Planets, of which Akkalla is a member. I expect better protection for the duration of our stay."

The guardsman remained at polite attention, then spoke through the mouthscreen in his helmet. "The only way to completely ensure your protection is to place you and your science team under house arrest in a secure facility."

"You mean prison," said Piretti. "And I get the feeling your Publican would like to do that anyway—and not for *our* protection."

"I'm not a policy setter or a magister or an overlord of the Continental Synod," the guardsman said simply. "I'm just doing my job. And if you're ready, we'll escort you to the residential compound."

Dr. McPhillips glanced at her friends. "We're ready." As they followed the guardsman down spiral metal steps and out into the damp evening, Enzo Piretti whispered to his colleagues, "I hope the *Enterprise* can find us when she gets here. She may not, if we're in prison by then . . . or dead."

"All right, Sulu, who's this one great love of your life?" asked Lieutenant Seena Maybri. Her tall, foxlike ears perked sharply, and her gray saucer eyes narrowed, losing their natural innocence for a moment, replacing it with a suspicion that Lieutenant Commander Hikaru Sulu, chief helmsman of the starship *Enterprise,* had been teasing her for the past half-hour of their lunch together. She turned away petulantly to stare out the wide viewing port of the observation deck, missing the smile that played across his lips—the smile that would have confirmed her suspicion.

"Ahh, the impatience of youth," Sulu said in sage tones.

She glanced back, but by then he was poker-faced again. "Oh, I'm not that young—and I'll bet there never *was* any great love."

"When your brother Sahji wrote to ask me to look after you, he never told me you were so cynical." He slumped back into deep couch cushions and pouted.

Maybri's slender shoulders and ears drooped in unison. "Oh, don't look hurt, Sulu. You're too old to get away with that. So stop it—it doesn't work with me—and besides, you know I can't stand it when you look hurt."

It had indeed worked, and his face brightened. "So you want to hear the sad story?"

"No, I do not."

"Well, do you want to know her name?"

She hesitated, wanting to say no and yes at the same time. Instead she said nothing. Sulu jumped into the breach.

"Well, okay then, if you really don't want to—"

"Tell me her name," Maybri said, her whispery voice as insistent as it ever got.

He hesitated. "Wellll, it's not exactly a her . . ."

Her foot tapped impatiently, and Maybri's skin began shading from normal pink to the deep red displayed by Erithians under stress. The color almost matched her uniform jacket. "Then what is it?"

"It's an it."

"The love of your life is an it. My brother warned me Terrans can be rather strange. Now *tell* me—this is your last chance."

Sulu dipped his head, and she lowered her own to see if he was hiding a smirk. "Chocolate," he said quietly.

Maybri cocked her head like a confused puppy. "The love of your life is a food substance?"

This ended Sulu's self-control. He let out a short burst of machine-gun laughter, enough to fill the lounge area and cause other crew members to pause in their own quiet contemplations and conversations. Sulu's trademark laugh was as infectious as any space plague, though with fortunately more pleasant effects—smiles spread throughout the deck.

Sulu reined in his laughter, though he continued to be amused by Maybri's attempt at looking stern. Her color faded back to pink again, and her ears settled at half-mast. Her feathery hair fluttered the way it often did when she was distracted. She shook her head as if at a small child telling tall tales. "A food substance . . ."

"Solid ambrosia," he corrected.

She shrugged. "We've managed without it on Erithia."

His oriental eyes widened. "You've never had any? We'll have to remedy that." His voice lowered to a conspiratorial pitch, and he reached inside his tunic, taking out a small morsel which he carefully unwrapped. "I happen to have a secret cache of the best chocolate in the galaxy. It's from Shoratoa IV. Don't tell anybody." His eyes darted from side to side, scanning for spies. Then he snapped off a chunk and placed it in her palm. "Don't chew it—savor it."

She did as she was told, swishing the piece around in her mouth. She swallowed and looked at him blankly. "So?"

"That's all—so?"

She shrugged again. "I guess it's an acquired taste. How did you acquire it?"

"I think it was prenatal. I just always loved chocolate. There's an old term for people like me: chocoholic."

"What was the sad story you threatened to tell me?" she asked dubiously.

"Hey, I was telling the truth. The sad story was, loving chocolate more than life itself made me, uh, a tad on the chubby side. When I was kid, I got two nicknames hung on me: Hefty Hikaru and Sizable Sulu."

Maybri laughed. "Obviously those don't apply anymore. What happened?"

"Human children can be cruel, and it got to me. I had too much pride to keep being the butt of everybody's jokes—so I got interested in sports to prove myself. Not only did I turn out to be a fencing and track star and get lots of girls—which is very important to teenage boys—I also lost lots of weight."

"No more Sizable Sulu." Maybri's delicate lips pursed thoughtfully. "Are all Terrans this odd?"

Sulu grinned. "No odder than you Erithians, though your brother always said that came from living on a desert planet."

"Did I tell you I got a subspace call from him last week?"

"No. How is he and where is he?"

"He's fine, he's temporarily assigned to Mars Base, and he said to say hello to you. He really appreciates your being my surrogate big brother. I do, too."

Sulu spread his hands. "That's what friends are for.

Y'know, I haven't seen Sahji in . . . God, it must be over five years."

Sulu grew pensive as he turned toward the viewing port. Outside, in the profound blackness of deep space, the stars danced like lights on a distant shore. "That's the one bad thing about spending your life in space, making warp-speed jaunts around the galaxy. You get to miss people at home, people who'd be just a transporter beam or a shuttle hop away if you were on the same planet as they were."

With a supportive touch, Maybri reached out to rest her hand lightly on his. "I guess I'm too new at this to feel that way. Two months out, everything's still so exciting I don't notice anything else."

After an awkward silence, the young lieutenant licked her lips. "Uh . . . could I have another piece of that chocolate substance?"

Sulu's eyes lit like a preacher about to baptize a convert. "Aha—I knew you'd be hooked."

"Who said anything about hooked? I'm just doing what any good scientist should do—repeating an experiment and comparing the results."

"Uh-huh." He broke off another dark shard and gave it to her.

With a measuring look, she held it inches from her face. "Kind of a small piece, Sulu."

"Like I said, hooked."

Her eyes widened in protest. Before she could defend herself, the intercom whistled and Communications Officer Uhura's precise voice came from the speaker. *"Lieutenant Maybri, to the briefing room, please."*

"Maybri here, Commander Uhura. Do you know what it's about?"

"Something to do with your assignment at Akkalla. Admiral Kirk has some changes to discuss with the landing party."

Maybri frowned. "Thank you. On my way." She stood in place for an extra moment, then noticed Sulu had stepped next to her.

"Don't look so worried," he said.

Her hair fluttered, betraying her nervousness, and her skin tone began darkening again. "I can't help it. I keep expecting Admiral Kirk to discover that somebody made a mistake and I don't really belong on a starship as my first duty post."

"Of course you do," Sulu said, placing a friendly arm around her shoulders. "To begin with, there aren't that many biologists qualified to deal with unusual ecologies. And you're rated as one of the best."

"But that's book learning and computer simulations." She gestured weakly out the viewport toward the dusting of stars. "Those are real planets."

"And you're a real biologist. A strange one from Erithia, maybe, but a good one."

She forced a smile, and they left the lounge together, headed for the nearest turbolift. The doors slid open, then shut behind them. "Deck 6," Sulu said. The lift hummed and accelerated smoothly through its maze of shafts and tubes.

"Oh, I hope I haven't been bumped for someone more experienced," Maybri said softly. "Akkalla is my favorite sort of planet."

"What's that?"

"Ninety-eight percent water. Aquarian worlds are just the most interesting!"

"How does someone from a planet that's mostly sand get interested in water worlds?"

"Change of pace, I guess," she said brightly.

The lift module opened on Deck 6, and they stepped out. "Hey, Sulu?"

"Yeah?"

Chewing her lip nervously, she sidled up to him. "Um, do you think I could, uh—"

"Yes," he said with a tolerant half-smile, "you can have a whole chocolate bar all to yourself."

She blinked in surprise. "How did you know that's what I was going to ask?"

"Like I said, hooked."

With a satisfied gait, he strolled the other way. It wasn't until he was out of sight that she heard his reverberating laugh. "Hooked," she mumbled, shaking her head.

Charging around a corner, Maybri gasped as she barely avoided slamming full-steam into Dr. McCoy. She stuttered an apology and felt her skin shading toward its darkest red.

9

McCoy smiled reassuringly. "No harm done. An old ship's surgeon should know to stand aside when there're young officers on the loose. I think we're headed to the same place." He paused. "You know, Lieutenant, that skin darkening of yours is rather unusual."

Her color had begun fading back to normal, but now it hovered at a medium hue. "It's also a big pain," she blurted.

"How do you mean—unless it's something you'd rather not talk about . . ."

She sighed as they continued walking toward the meeting. "It's not that. It's just that, well, how would you like it if every time you were under stress, or some stimulus was causing your body to produce extra heat, everyone could tell just by looking at you? I feel like a neon tube fish from Spyrion VII. And I feel so *different* from everyone else on board."

McCoy gave a professional nod. "But you didn't feel that way back home on Erithia?"

"It wasn't unusual there."

"Yes."

"Well, y'know, we humans can tell a lot about each other's reactions just by looking."

"Not like this," Maybri said glumly.

"Maybe not to your eye, because you're not used to it. But I can look at any human on this ship and I can detect stress, embarrassment, excitement. Don't even need my tricorder."

Maybri's glumness shifted to interest. "Really? How?"

"Blushing, perspiration, darting eyes, rapid respiration, dry lips—lots of ways. So, y'see, you're no more of an open book than the rest of us are."

"Maybe," she smiled. "But I still wish I didn't blush quite so vividly."

They arrived at the briefing room. Chekov, Spock, Chief Engineer Scott, and Admiral Kirk were already seated. Kirk cleared his throat. "Let's get right to it. Starfleet has ordered a change in our current mission. An emergency situation has developed on Vestra 5, and we're the ship assigned to help. Mr. Spock?"

The Vulcan science officer inserted a data cassette into the computer console at his end of the table, and a chart of the Vestran system lit the main viewscreen on the wall.

"The Vestran star system is located in Sector R-973, with only one inhabited planet. Vestra V is Class M, with a civilization development level of point nine, Type A—"

"For the noncomputers among us," McCoy said, "how 'bout a translation into English, Mr. Spock?"

Spock's eyebrow raised just slightly. "Rudimentary interstellar spaceflight capability, advanced technological culture, society presently at peace. Vestra 5 is not a member of the Federation, but nearby Federation planets do have extensive trade and other relations with it. In fact, Vestra has been invited to join the Federation on two occasions, with the most recent negotiations eleven solar months ago."

"What're they hesitatin' about?" asked Scott.

"Seems the Vestrans are the independent sort," Kirk said. "They just aren't sure about any alliance. But the vote was closer the second time, and the Federation feels the next vote'll turn things around. They *want* Vestra as a member, and that's why our mission is so important. Spock, explain the emergency, please."

"Aberrational weather patterns have caused severe drought conditions in the planet's primary farming regions. The pattern has persisted for three years now, and despite massive irrigation projects, attempts at meteorological modification, and stringent water conservation, they have been unable to reverse a serious reductive trend in agricultural output."

McCoy scratched his nose. "In other words, they're facin' starvation."

"I believe that is what I said. As a result, they have asked the Federation for humanitarian assistance." Spock touched a computer key, changing the viewer image to a star chart indicating an essentially linear course between the starship's present location, Starbase 18, Vestra V, and finally the Akkallan system. "Quantities of food, seeds engineered for rapid germination and growth in arid environments, and techno-agricultural teams are now being gathered at Starbase 18. Our original course had us bypassing starbase by point six three light years. However, we are the closest ship, and we can easily divert. We will then proceed directly to Vestra to deliver the aid."

Lieutenant Maybri glanced quickly at the other officers, all considerably senior to her. She wondered if it was her place to ask questions, but she spoke up before thought could lead to timidity. "Sir, what about our assignment at Akkalla?"

"The Science Ministry still needs the evaluation in a hurry. They've got deadlines on setting next year's budget, and they've got to know what projects warrant continued funding. So, when we dock at Starbase 18, Mr. Spock'll take a scout shuttle to Akkalla and start the evaluation. The *Enterprise*'ll rendezvous with the evaluation team as soon as we're done at Vestra 5."

"You said 'evaluation team,' sir," Maybri said. "I'd like to volunteer."

"Sorry, lieutenant. Mr. Spock will be taking only one other crew member along—Mr. Chekov."

The young Russian reacted with slight surprise. "Thank you, Admiral. I was beginning to wonder why I was included in the briefing."

Kirk chuckled. "Did you think I was planning to ignore your request to get back into sciences a bit more?"

"I didn't really know, sir."

Chekov happily followed the Vulcan out, and Maybri watched them go, looking not at all pleased. Her skin began darkening, but she kept quiet.

"While we're on the topic, why *am* I in on this briefing, Jim?" asked McCoy.

"Because I'm going to need you on Vestra, Bones."

"Crop failure, irrigation, reseeding? I'm a doctor, not a gardener."

"We don't actually know how bad the medical situation is. Starfleet should have more for us when we get to starbase. But the plan is for us to take a large medical team to work with local health authorities on combating the complications brought on by malnutrition. You'll be supervising."

"My favorite activity, Jim. I'm sure there'll be tons of reports—"

"Sorry, Bones. The bureaucracy demands its due."

McCoy shook his head ruefully. "We may have replaced paper, but we'll never escape paper*work.*"

"Scotty," Kirk said, "it's up to you to make sure we've got room for all the supplies and equipment. Once we're orbiting Vestra, we've got to be efficient. We'll be making use of all shuttlecraft, and we'll be beaming people and

12

crates all over the planet. I need you to keep things organized."

"Aye, sir, we'll keep on top o' everything."

As Scott headed toward the door, McCoy got to his feet. "Am I dismissed too, Jim? Or do you have some other bureaucratic torture you'd like to inflict on an old country doctor?"

Kirk raised a thumb. "Get out of here, Bones. Lieutenant, you're—"

"Sir," she said, cutting him off, "I'd like to have a word with you in private, if you don't mind."

"Fine. Now's as good a time as any."

McCoy ambled out with Scott. "If anybody needs me, I'll be in sickbay—sharpening pencils."

"What's on your mind, lieutenant?" Kirk asked when they were alone.

"The evaluation team chosen to go to Akkalla, sir."

Kirk's lips tightened. "Are you questioning my judgment, Lieutenant Maybri?"

Now I've done it, she thought, certain she was turning the darkest shade she'd ever been. *Insulting the admiral. There goes any chance I ever had for fieldwork. I'll be locked in a lab until I'm a hundred.*

"Relax," Kirk said, amusement twinkling in his hazel eyes as his expression softened. "I was just testing your resolve a bit. You're allowed to question the judgment of any superior officer, as long as you've got a good reason to back it up—and you don't get any notions of mutiny."

"Well, sir, it's not that I'm questioning your judgment, exactly. It's just that I'm very knowledgeable about planets like Akkalla," she said, managing to push a little forcefulness into her voice. "I've done a lot of preparation for the original evaluation, and I believe I should still be going . . . sir."

Kirk leaned back and crossed his arms. "Another thing you should realize, lieutenant. Superior officers don't *owe* anyone any explanations for command decisions. But that doesn't mean you shouldn't ask. At times you may get one—like now, for instance. Chekov is going because he has broader experience than you do. My choice is no reflection on your abilities or record. In fact, your friend Sulu made sure I knew just how fine your Academy record is."

Maybri closed her eyes in embarrassment. "I'll kill him."

Kirk grinned. "Don't—I need my senior officers to give me their judgments, the benefits of their experience. Based on everything I've heard about you, I'd like to think you might be one of those senior officers in the future. At any rate, I know this was going to be your first field assignment, and I know you're disappointed, but it's only a delay, not a cancellation. You'll have your chance to tackle Akkallan ecology once the *Enterprise* finishes up at Vestra. Meanwhile, I think Spock and Chekov could use your help in programming their evaluation sequence. That's an order, Maybri."

"Yes, sir . . . and thank you."

"Dismissed."

Kirk watched her go, eagerness in every step. When the door shut behind her and he was by himself, he thought about all the eager young officers he'd had under his command—Chekov, Sulu, Uhura, Reilly—more names than he could recall. He'd watched those young officers come through their baptisms of fire, seen coltish exuberance tempered by hard-won wisdom. Kirk also thought about the officers who'd died under his command. Those names he would never forget. He could still visualize every letter he'd ever had to send to a home world where a grieving family waited, seeking a reason for something that seemed senseless. . . . *Sorry to inform you of the death of . . . A fine and dedicated officer who made the ultimate sacrifice in support of our shared quest for knowledge and peace. I share your loss, and wish you comfort in your time of grief . . .*

With a chilled shiver, Kirk shook himself free of the specters, though just for the moment. The older he got, the more easily they came to call on his subconscious.

"I don't want to write any more letters like that," he said softly. Then, almost without thinking, he found himself caressing the cold surface of the table, seeking solace from the heart of the *Enterprise* herself, the gallant lady who'd been his partner through so many trials. He knew he was trying to use her to fill a cold, dark place in his own heart, a space he'd discovered only recently. Or perhaps it had always been there, and he'd only lately been able to admit to the existence of that small spot of emptiness.

Why should it be there? he asked, aware it was a question only he could answer.

James T. Kirk had become virtually everything his destiny had promised. On balance, given the chance to live life over again, he'd follow the same course. Still, there was that empty corner inside, a hidden sanctuary he wasn't yet able to summon the courage to enter. But he'd peeked, fleetingly, long enough to glimpse a message written there in ghostly relief. *Home,* it said. *Maybe it's time to go home . . .*

Perhaps soon, but not yet. For now, there was work to do. Jim Kirk left the briefing room and headed for a chamber where he never felt the emptiness—the bridge of the starship *Enterprise.*

Chapter Two

CAPTAIN'S LOG—STARDATE 7823.6:

As Chief Engineer Scott oversees the transfer of equipment, supplies, and personnel from Starbase 18 to the *Enterprise*, Science Officer Spock and Lieutenant Chekov are outfitting the science scout shuttle *Cousteau*. They'll be departing before we will, headed for Akkalla, where they'll begin reviewing the work done over the past thirteen months by Dr. Cynthia McPhillips and her team. Akkalla is of great scientific interest because of its unusual ecology. It's one of only a handful of worlds with a surface almost completely covered by water yet also having developed a normal variety of flora and fauna, including intelligent humanoid life. It would seem a routine assignment, easily handled by two of my best officers. But we have been made aware by Starfleet Command of certain potential problems. First, although Akkalla is a Federation member, it's been a troublesome one, with a government leaning substantially toward the authoritarian. Second, I'm concerned with the fact that there's been no direct contact with the McPhillips science team, only messages relayed through the Akkallan government. Official Federation protests against this Akkallan policy have had no effect.

THE STARSHIP HUNG in a synchronous orbit about one hundred miles from the large space station that housed Starbase 18. The station was shaped somewhat like a rather odd dumbbell, with spacedock modules on either end of a long central cylinder, where twenty decks of habitable work space and living quarters were located. Each docking module had room inside for up to a dozen ships of various sizes, with other vessels in numerous parking orbits outside. But traffic patterns were rarely that heavily filled in this sector, and at present the *Enterprise* was the only ship of any great size in the vicinity.

Kirk drummed his fingers lightly on the arm of the command seat. With his crew doing their jobs, he found himself in the unenviable position of simply waiting. He checked the chronometer on his control panel, then pressed the intercom button.

"Bones, how's everything going?"

McCoy came into view on one of the overhead screens. *"Everything isn't going at all,"* he said with mild sarcasm. *"I don't know what's going on down there, Jim, but base seems incapable of beaming people and cargo at the same time. So until they're finished filling our holds, no personnel are transporting up. So I'm just cooling my heels."*

"Oh." Keeping McCoy on, Kirk contacted the ship's lower cargo section, which appeared on a split screen with the picture from sickbay. The cargo levels were bustling with activity. But Scott was nowhere in sight. "Mr. Scott, progress report, please?"

After a few seconds' lag, Scott lurched into view, wiping beads of sweat off his forehead. *"Aye, sir. Scott here."*

"Dr. McCoy says base won't beam personnel until they're done transporting cargo."

Scott's eyes widened, and he gritted his teeth. *"I don't believe it. That's what they were supposed to be usin' the shuttles for. The plan was t'do it at the same time. Y'd think they were havin' a bloody picnic down there instead of doin' work. D'y'want me to call and knock some heads together?"*

"Looks like you've got enough to keep you busy. Finish up with the freight. We'll take care of the problem up here."

The cargo deck faded from the screen, leaving McCoy on visual. *"Marvelous operation they've got going over there, Jim."*

"Yeah, well, I think we'll have this straightened out in a minute. Stand by, Bones. You'll have guests any time now."

The screen went blank, and Kirk turned to his communications officer. "Uhura, tackle the bureaucratic maze, please."

She tapped her earpiece with a manicured fingernail. "I'll clear it up, sir."

"Kirk to *Cousteau*. Progress report, Mr. Spock?"

The Vulcan's voice came over the speaker. *"Spock here. We have just completed final prelaunch checklist."*

"Mr. Spock," Chekov broke in. *"We have launch clearance."*

"Thank you, Mr. Chekov. I presume you heard, Admiral."

"Yes. Good luck, Spock. I hear the *Cousteau*'s a good ship."

"Do you have any idea yet when we can expect to rendezvous with you at Akkalla?"

"At the moment, I don't even know when we're leaving here. But I don't think it'll take more than two or three days."

"We should be well along in our evaluation by that time."

"Good. We'll see you then, Spock. We'll be in touch if anything unexpected comes up. Kirk out."

Spock and Chekov sat side by side in the contoured seats of the science shuttle.

"All moorings cleared, Mr. Spock," Chekov said as he handled the navigation controls with a sure touch.

On the broad curved viewscreen in front of them, Spock and Chekov watched as the docking bay's great doors engaged and began sliding ponderously aside, gaping like a whale's mouth. When the opening was wide enough, the red blinking lights along the ends of both doors changed to steady green. A female voice came over the *Cousteau*'s speaker.

"Cleared for departure, Cousteau. *Take good care of the rowboat, Commander Spock. Remember, she's only rented. Bon voyage."*

"Thank you, Starbase Control," Spock replied. "Mr. Chekov, take us out."

"There she is," Uhura said, adjusting the viewscreen angle so the bridge crew could watch their colleagues leaving. The *Cousteau* was sky blue, with leaping dolphins emblazoned on her flanks adjacent to the ship's name and registry number. Constructed especially to explore watery worlds, it was capable of landing on water as well as land

and could even submerge and operate as a submarine. So it wasn't surprising that, like animals nature had intended for life in the seas, the science craft seemed ill at ease anywhere else.

Chekov changed the craft's attitude and flew directly past the *Enterprise*. Both ships winked their running lights in salute.

"Mr. Chekov, set course for Akkalla, warp three. Engage when ready."

"Course already laid in, sir. Warp three."

He gripped the throttle with a firm hand and moved it ahead. The science shuttle's warp drive kicked in, and with the familiar rainbow effect it blasted into hyperspace.

Spock knew why he'd been placed in charge of assessing the work of the Akkallan science outpost. He was, after all, the *Enterprise* science officer, he had both command and hands-on science experience, and he'd previously done this sort of rating of independent projects as well as evaluating the starship's own science departments. His assignment by Kirk was, in fact, the logical thing to do. But the Vulcan couldn't help feeling vaguely uneasy. As a Vulcan, he based his judgments only on demonstrable, objective findings by the science team under scrutiny. Data were entered into the computer program Spock himself had designed for just such tasks, a program deemed so effective at providing a sound system for measuring scientific endeavors that it was used throughout Starfleet and the Federation.

Subjectivity was all but eliminated from the process, and the conclusions reached were inarguable, built strictly on statistical analysis. And with Vulcans and other rigorously rational races, the results were accepted without question or quarrel. Unfortunately, in Spock's opinion, there were many more intemperately irrational beings to deal with than rational ones. And with those, any remotely negative ratings invariably elicited displays of damaged, prideful ego. Spock had faced similar distasteful situations often enough to prefer avoiding evaluation duties altogether. But half a lifetime as a Starfleet officer made him all too aware that certain onerous tasks were part of the service.

The *Cousteau* was a small spacecraft, but it could accommodate a maximum crew of eight, so it seemed roomy with only two aboard. Guidance computers were on automatic, and Chekov was taking his sleep period in the aft cabin. Alone, Spock used the quiet time to review all data on the McPhillips team and Akkalla itself. He popped a cassette into the computer and scanned the readout at high speed.

McPhillips, the ecologist in charge, was from Earth, born on the Irish coast and raised in Hawaii. She'd studied at the University of Hawaii Marine Biology Department and Cetacean Communications Center, got her doctorate there, then received her first Federation science grant. For the past seven years, she'd proven quite adept at writing proposals and obtaining funding for ecological studies that had taken her to four very different planets around the galaxy: one unnamed world where life was just being born in the nutrient-rich ooze of primordial seas; Kochev's Planet, a chilled fossil reaching the end of its existence in the feeble light of a dying ember of a sun; Ra-Menae III, the only habitable planet in a rare trinary star system, where giant shell-encased creatures dominated in an otherworldly version of earth's age of dinosaurs; and, finally, Akkalla, the water-covered planet that allowed McPhillips to return to her first love, marine ecology.

Interestingly, McPhillips was younger than her colleagues. Dr. Enzo Piretti, born on the Italian isle of Sicily, was seventy-three. Dr. Naw-Rocki, the only non-Terran of the group, was one hundred and thirty. But he was a Rannican, where life spans commonly reached three hundred. Cynthia McPhillips was only forty, but she was so highly regarded in her field that she'd had her pick of colleagues for this study.

As for Akkalla, it was the third planet of six in its system. The second planet, Chorym, also harbored intelligent life. In fact, the Chorymi were more advanced, having developed interplanetary spaceflight capability. But they'd made it very clear on several occasions that they had no inclination whatever toward becoming part of the United Federation of Planets.

Spock found himself questioning the logic behind the Federation's unstinting effort to get as many planets as possible to become members. Privately, he believed more attention should be paid to quality of applicants than to quantity. Granted, there was a certain security in having the

Federation flag fly in all corners of the galaxy. It made adventurism by Klingons, Romulans, and a host of other less powerful antagonists somewhat less likely. But certain planets, no matter that they'd sworn to abide by the codes of conduct of the Federation Charter, simply didn't seem able to fit in comfortably.

Not that Spock wanted to alter the way any particular worlds chose to conduct cultural and societal affairs. After all, he subscribed wholeheartedly to the Vulcan IDIC philosophy: infinite diversity in infinite combinations. But *combination* was a key word, and in order to be successful, or at least feasible, any combination had to include a tolerance and acceptance of differences in other parties. Some worlds seemed unwilling to make tolerance a two-way proposition.

And not that he had any easy answers. To the contrary, Spock had none. But he would have been more sanguine about the whole political process had Federation Council leaders shown more open recognition of the need for discussing organizational inadequacies.

He often wondered how his father had managed to be a diplomat for so many years, having to confront so regularly the illogic inherent in political relationships. Yet Ambassador Sarek's reputation was one of nearly imperturbable restraint and patience. Spock admired his father for that, though he was quite certain his own temperament would never lend itself to similar accomplishment, not in the diplomatic field at any rate. No, scientific evaluation assignments were as close as he cared to get to walking that fine line between truth and tact.

The computer beeped at him, indicating that the data cassette had ended. On the viewscreen above the paired pilot seats, a blue-gray globe had come within visual range. It had ice caps at both poles, and much of the planet was shrouded by clouds. There was a single major land mass, an uneven continent straddling the equator, with mountains rising up along a north-south line like a spine and jagged coastlines studded with bays and inlets. Rivers criss-crossed the island continent like veins on a leaf, with many feeding or originating at numerous lakes of all shapes. There were a few islands of varying sizes in both northern and southern polar waters, others lying just off the western continental coast, and some scattered far off the mainland. But the dominant feature of this world was the endless sea.

"Akkalla, I presume," Chekov said, wiping sleep from his eyes as he climbed up to the control cabin. "It really is all ocean. I've never seen a planet with so little land surface. Easy to see why they never developed air travel there."

"Indeed. The continent has an eminently navigable river and tributary system. It is approximately equal in size to your Australian continent."

"And I thought we had a lot of water on Earth."

"Yes," Spock agreed. "Seventy point eight-five-three-one percent by a recent calculation, taking into account glacial melting and silt buildup in the larger river delta regions. That is among the higher water-to-land ratios in the known galaxy."

Chekov gestured at the screen. "But nothing compared to Akkalla. Ninety-eight percent—"

"Ninety-eight point six-one-one, Mr. Chekov. We must maintain maximum accuracy in our data."

"Aye, Mr. Spock," Chekov sighed, silently chastising himself for dispensing with the decimals.

"Would you care to fly manual final approach?"

Chekov grinned. "As a matter of fact, I would. Flying this vessel is very different from the *Enterprise.*"

Spock's long fingers flipped a pair of toggles and disengaged the automation systems. "Very well, lieutenant. The ship is yours. Take us in."

Their destination was Tyvol, the mainland capital set on the shore of Havensbay, a well-protected harbor on the northwest coast, with three rivers flowing through the city and emptying into the bay. Tyvol also had an extensive canal network.

The *Cousteau* was still some distance away, and the planet's rotation was carrying the continent out of view. The other side of Akkalla was a stunning sight—just a few small outcroppings of land rising from a vast blue-gray sea, probably the tips of submerged mountains and volcanoes. They looked like forgotten scraps left behind after the planet was created, lonely and lost.

"Not much to see on this side of the world," Chekov said.

"Nothing apparent, but oceans are noted for hiding things of great interest, Mr. Chekov. Your own planet's history is replete with examples of surprises yielded by the oceans' depths only after decades or centuries of exploration."

"That's true. I remember reading about that fish they found in the twentieth century after they thought it was extinct for millions of years—"

"The coelacanth," Spock said.

"Perhaps a survey orbit or two would be a good idea then, sir?"

Spock nodded. "Set coordinates, please."

Chekov tapped the keys of the navigation panel, and the *Cousteau* heeled over to its new course.

"Computer," Spock said, "begin full scan of planet, including cross-sectional scan of ocean and categorization of life forms."

As the survey craft swung into orbit, it accelerated to exceed Akkalla's rotational velocity, starting on the night side but rapidly approaching the line of demarcation between night and day on the continental side of the world.

Chekov frowned and put one hand up to his communications earpiece. "Sir, I'm receiving a message."

"Source?"

"The planet—an Akkallan government channel." The Russian flipped a switch, routing it to the cabin speaker. They heard an official-sounding female voice.

"To unidentified spacecraft intruding on Akkallan orbital territory—you are warned to turn back immediately. Do not approach—repeat—do not approach. The Akkallan government is not responsible for your safety if you proceed past this point."

Spock activated the comm system. "To Akkallan government—this is Commander Spock of the Federation science vessel *Cousteau*. We are on a scheduled approach and request clearance. We—"

The voice interrupted, repeating its message: *"To unidentified spacecraft intruding on Akkallan orbital territory—you are warned to turn back immediately. Do not approach—repeat—do not approach. The Akkallan government is not responsible for your safety if you proceed past this point."*

"Presumably an automated broadcast," Spock said, his eyebrow elevated. "Set comm system for the government contact channel previously authorized."

23

"Aye, sir."

To be on the safe side, Spock reduced their speed while Chekov punched in the local frequency. The speaker came to life again with the now-familiar warning: *"To unidentified spacecraft intruding on Akkallan orb—"*

As abruptly as it had started, the message was cut off, sliced by static. Chekov winced as he yanked out his earpiece with one hand and decreased the volume with the other.

Spock glanced at him. "Did you break contact?"

Chekov shook his head. "No, sir." He replaced the earpiece carefully and tried to pick up the automatic warning again, to no avail. "It's being jammed, Mr. Spock."

"At the source?"

"No, sir. Something between the broadcast station and us." Chekov tried other channels. "All communications are inoperative, sir."

The *Cousteau* drifted forward, into Akkallan daylight. In the sudden glare of Akkalla's sun, they saw something that shouldn't have been there—a half-dozen spaceships. Five were insignificant insects buzzing around the sixth, a giant vessel nearly the size of a starship. Its configuration was totally different, though, with no grace to its form. Utilitarian, ugly, lumbering, it had a wide, blunt bow, a dome on top, stubby protrusions on its lower flanks, and a tapered area that swept back before flaring into a squared engine housing. The housing had small thrusters on all sides and a matched pair of main engine nozzles at the stern.

The five escort ships, each smaller than the *Cousteau*, were shaped like sculpted diamonds, longer at the bow and truncated behind. By the way they were arrayed in protective formation around the larger ship, Spock judged them to be fighters of some sort.

"Mr. Spock, those ships are doing the jamming."

"Switch scanners, Mr. Chekov. We will need as much information on those vessels as possible."

The other spacecraft were moving purposefully in the same direction as the *Cousteau* and had not yet noticed the newcomer behind them. "Reduce speed," Spock ordered. "Pace them."

"Aye, sir."

"Computer, is there sufficient data for identification?"

24

"Affirmative. Ships registered as Chorymi military fighters accompanying harvest ship."

The Vulcan's eyebrow arched again at the word *military*. "Fascinating. There is no record of hostility between Chorym and Akkalla."

"No, sir. In fact, I remember reading that there have been a number of treaties of peaceful cooperation between them."

"Then why a Chorymi military convoy—and why were we warned away by a message evidently triggered automatically by our approach? Recommendation, Mr. Chekov?"

"Continue to maintain our distance, but follow the ships and see exactly what's going on."

Spock nodded. "I agree." He adjusted the viewscreen to maximum magnification, and the huge mother ship filled their field of vision. "Full power to deflector screens, Mr. Chekov."

"Aye, sir." As Chekov diverted reserve power to the ship's defensive shields, the cabin illumination dimmed and the emergency lights blinked on. The yellow alert indicator flashed on the overhead instrument console.

The convoy slowed and entered a polar orbit around Akkalla. Spock nudged the *Cousteau* into matching orbit as the Chorymi ships moved into position high over a vast stretch of Akkallan sea.

"Most interesting," said Spock. "Their course seems deliberate. Analysis, Mr. Chekov?"

The Russian's fingers skipped over several keys at the science console. A second later, sensor data appeared on the small screen to his right. "They're in geosynchronous orbit, six hundred kilometers above the surface, approximately five thousand kilometers off the coast, and six hundred north of the equator."

"And sensors indicate they are scanning deep into the sea itself. They appear to be searching for something in particular. Divert one-quarter of our sensor capability to scan the same region."

"Aye, sir." Chekov peered into his science station scope while commanding the computer to switch scanner targets. Then he felt the ship change course and gain speed, and he looked up.

"Whatever it is they seek, it seems they have found it,"

25

Spock said as he guided the *Cousteau* to follow, though still keeping a discreet separation. "Any data yet, lieutenant?"

"Yes, sir. I'm getting overwhelming life-form readings from that part of the ocean. There's so much there it's almost impossible to analyze."

"Recorders at maximum. We shall examine the data later."

The Chorymi convoy was diving toward Akkalla, as if making an attack run at the planet surface. The *Cousteau* trailed behind, a faint pink glow curling around the small ship as it encountered the first diffuse particles of the atmosphere's upper fringes. Their angle of descent was steep, and Chekov concentrated on the sensors as the Chorymi spacecraft began sweeping curves, using atmospheric friction to help reduce their speed.

"Altitude one hundred thirty kilometers. Speed eight thousand kilometers per hour," he said.

The coral glow enveloping the *Cousteau* deepened to fiery orange, and the ebony darkness of outer space began to change from inky indigo, with the stars still visible as unwavering pinpoints, to cobalt, then azure. The stars blurred, then gave way to the power of the Akkallan sun. Below, a cottony floor of clouds seemed to rush up at them—and with a sudden thump and shudder, they broke through the thick shroud and into a grayness that stretched to every horizon. Rain spattered across the viewscreen and the image of the giant Chorymi ship that loomed before them.

"Altitude five kilometers," Chekov continued. "Four . . . three . . . two . . ." The Russian stopped and took a startled breath. "Mr. Spock, there are ten surface vessels converging on the same spot!"

He initiated a computer search for any communications from the spacecraft or the surface vessels. "The surface craft are Akkallan patrol boats—and the Chorymi spaceships are *definitely* not welcome."

Chekov's face twisted as he read the computer's instant sensor report. "This is impossible. I've never seen such a powerful magnetic flux artificially generated. It's—it's coming from the mother ship."

Spock leaned over to glance at the same readout. "I see it, Mr. Chekov. It appears to be creating an energy field around it. I would surmise that we are about to find out why the Chorymi convoy is not welcome."

The ocean churned with increasing violence, jolting the Akkallan ships as they raced along. High overhead, the dark bulk of the Chorymi mother ship continued its precipitous drop. The Akkallan cutters had sharply streamlined silhouettes, all curves and angles, decks completely enclosed, but they were having increasing difficulty slicing through the ever higher seas. Even worse, the waves rose in no normal pattern, rearing suddenly, cresting and swirling all at once. The closer the invading spaceships got to the water, the more turbulent the seas became.

"It stopped." Chekov's voice was a stunned whisper. "It's—it's just hovering."

On screen, the monstrous vessel had indeed paused, a thousand meters above the crashing seas, like a ship becalmed in the eye of a tempest. But it was a tempest of the spacecraft's own creation, and the Chorymi ship was quite clearly immune to all its violent effects.

From the ocean below, the Akkallan defenders launched surface-to-air rockets, each cutter firing missiles in pairs. With their contrails twisting like angry snakes, the rockets homed in, and the diamond-shaped Chorymi fighters broke their geometric formation to engage in battle. Two tackled the incoming projectiles with pulses of blue flame spitting from their bellies as cannon pellets picked off the missiles soaring up from the ocean.

The remaining trio of fighters arced high over the mother ship, then banked into a dive to strafe the Akkallan patrol boats. The new attack was too much for the boats, already floundering in the waves, and they broke off their abortive defense. Survival became their first order of business.

Spock called up an infrared image of the area directly around and below the big Chorymi vessel. Tightening red coils whipped about a blank core, with orange and yellow tendrils like the arms of a whirling galaxy. Splashings of green and blue measured the much cooler temperatures of the seawater farther from the center of the disturbance. The patterns changed even as they watched, and the Vulcan's eyes narrowed with deepening interest. "Most ingenious."

"What is it, sir?"

"The large craft is actually manufacturing an intense miniature hurricane." Spock pointed at features on the infrared chart. "Their energy field has somehow produced a ripple in the prevailing winds, which trapped moist air at sea level. Such air contains energy in the form of latent heat absorbed from the sun. When this vaporous air is drawn up, it cools, condenses, and warms surrounding air molecules, which also rise, in turn drawing additional air up. The Coriolis force caused by planetary rotation directs winds converging at the center of this rapidly developing low-pressure system, imparting a counterclockwise spiraling."

"All that just to fight off the Akkallan surface ships?"

"I suspect they have another purpose, although it was an effective air-to-sea weapon."

"What are they up to?"

It wasn't long before they witnessed the next phase of the Chorymi raid. The huge craft tipped slightly forward and dropped inexorably toward the ocean. The unnatural squall grew more and more violent, the fury of the blow spreading and tossing the Akkallan boats like toys.

Then the lower part of the harvest ship's prow yawned, resembling the mandible of some nightmarish beast lowering to eat.

"Mr. Spock, barometric pressure dropping in the vicinity of the spacecraft."

"Indeed. Still dropping?"

Chekov blinked in disbelief. "Affirmative. It's—it's down to zero at the eye of the"—he wasn't sure what to call it, then finished with a shrug—"the storm." He held his breath for a moment, then sat back and looked at Spock's hooded eyes. "Negative pressure."

A funnel of seawater gathered and surged from the ocean's surface, freed of gravity's constraints by the Chorymi energy field. With a cyclonic spin, the vortex weaved uncertainly, seemingly anchored. The harvest ship dipped even farther until it was barely above the frothing waves. The waterspout widened suddenly and was sucked into the gaping maw of the giant vessel as it crept forward, swallowing vast volumes of Akkallan ocean.

Of the overmatched patrol cutters, three had been swamped. The others fought to escape the pull of the alien

28

energy field and the storm it had generated. The sleek boats vaulted towering whitecaps, only to be battered by cross-swells crashing in from all sides.

"Analysis of the contents of that water funnel, Chekov."

"Seawater, trace elements, and . . . thousands of life forms, ranging from microscopic to creatures up to twenty-five meters long, the size of whales."

Unconcerned by the destructive forces set off in its wake, the harvest ship earned its designation by skimming the roiling waves and vacuuming up thousands of tons of water. Spock and Chekov could see torrents cascading out of the ship's mouth through grates on the ventral surface of the jaw.

"It has a filtration system," Chekov said, reading the scanners again. "The water coming out of the bottom is free of life forms. They're being held inside."

The big vessel made two more long sweeps, and then, like a sated leviathan, the harvest ship took a leisurely path to higher altitude, making a wide turn as its escort fighters returned to regroup for the voyage home. And they spotted the *Cousteau* for the first time. Two of the small angular craft peeled away from the harvest ship and streaked directly toward the previously unnoticed spectator.

Spock quickly opened a communications channel—and got a shriek of feedback. "We're still subject to their jamming. Probably interference caused by the energy field."

"Which means we can't tell them who we are."

"Correct. Stand by for evasive maneuvers."

The science shuttle held its course, then ducked sharply, causing the Chorymi fighters to zip directly overhead. Spock rolled up into the desirable position of having their attackers flying away from the shuttle at high speed. He had to assume they'd be back but hoped they didn't consider this unidentified quarry worth much of a chase. "Mr. Chekov, calculate the most direct course to the Akkallan mainland."

None too delicately, Spock shoved the throttle control to maximum intra-atmospheric speed, and the G-forces squeezed them back into their seats.

"Damn." Chekov glanced up from his scanner. "They're closing on us. They were built for this . . . we weren't."

Spock replied by throwing the *Cousteau* into an evasive

29

spiral, taking care to keep relatively on course toward the Akkallan capital of Tyvol. The first burning blue streaks of Chorymi cannon fire sizzled past the shuttle's flanks, and Chekov flashed the tactical readout on Spock's display screen.

The fighters were still closing on their tail.

Suddenly, Spock yanked the throttle back and cut their speed to a standstill. The pursuing Chorymi ships rushed past, trying to duplicate the maneuver long after it was too late.

Chekov grinned wickedly. "Good move, Mr. Spock."

"Let us hope it was good enough." Spock spurred the shuttle back to top speed as the engine whined in protest. The Akkallan continent was in sight, its flat shores protected by a string of volcanic islands rising up from the sea.

But the tactical screen showed the dogged Chorymi fighters hadn't yet given up. They were back within weapons range, and they fired a second volley. Spock threw the *Cousteau* into a spin, but not in time. He and Chekov both felt the shuttle take two hits at the stern. A muffled explosion shook the craft, and acrid smoke seeped up from the lower deck, burning their eyes. Cabin lights flickered, then steadied at a low level when Chekov cut the main engines and patched in emergency battery power. They could smell the chemical foam of the automatic fire control system from the rear compartment.

Just as they were expecting to be finished off, the aggressor blips on the tactical grid veered away to catch up with the rest of their fleet, which was already nearing the upper atmosphere on its way back home. Chekov acknowledged this providential twist of fate by letting out a very long breath.

"We're lucky, sir. I thought they were going to blow us out of the sky for sure."

"Vulcans do not believe in luck, Mr. Chekov. And even if we did, I would be forced to question your conclusion. Our main engines are inoperable, and our batteries are damaged, as are our navigation and guidance systems. We may not have sufficient power to reach the mainland—"

Chekov brightened. "But this ship can land in the water."

"We do not know the extent of structural damage. The

30

ship may not be seaworthy. If we set down in water, we may sink."

Chewing on his lip, Chekov regarded his senior officer silently. *Well,* he thought. *We Russians are supposed to be fatalistic.* "I will go below and check our survival gear."

"A constructive idea. I shall attempt the best possible landing."

As he clambered out of the cockpit area, Chekov paused. "Even though you don't believe in it, good luck, sir."

"As we have seen, Mr. Chekov, luck is a relative term."

Relatively speaking, their luck held out, though it took their combined technical skills to guide the ship manually and ditch it within sight of an island off the coast of the continental mainland. With landing skids stretched forth prayerfully, the *Cousteau* hit the water and skipped like a flat stone before settling.

Chekov hit a console switch, and they heard a hydraulic grinding, followed by a vacuum-release hissing. "Auxiliary flotation devices deployed."

Spock made a quick check on the external environment via ship's sensors. "Temperature thirty-three Celsius. Humidity eighty-one percent."

Chekov's lip curled disapprovingly.

"Such readings are to be expected," said Spock. "We have landed at an equatorial latitude."

"Russians," Chekov sighed, "were never meant to live in a rain forest."

"We shall make every effort to keep our stay here as brief as possible, lieutenant. Now, we are approximately one point two-six kilometers from the nearest land. Our best course of action appears to be abandoning ship."

"I guess so, sir." Chekov gave a grudging nod. "I'll go below and get the life raft ready. I'll also anchor the ship so we can find her when the *Enterprise* gets here."

"I'll gather what we need here."

The younger officer unstrapped his safety harness and climbed out of the cockpit. He paused at the hatch. "I knew she'd be seaworthy."

Spock busied himself packing data cassettes as well as old-fashioned maps and charts in waterproof packs. Then

31

he heard bootsteps climbing up the ladder from the lower deck and turned to see Chekov with a dubious expression on his face. He was soaked up to his knees.

"She's not quite as seaworthy as I thought, Mr. Spock."

"How bad is it?"

"I couldn't find the leaks, but water's coming in from somewhere. She may not be afloat for very long. But everything else is ready. The raft is packed and on the winch."

The Vulcan handed two packs to Chekov and took two himself. With one last look around the cabin, they made their way through a cramped midship passage to the open exterior hatchway. The inflatable life raft hung on its cables, and they stepped in. Chekov touched the remote control switch, and the winch assembly lowered them three meters down to the waves. With a nod from Spock, he released their last mooring lines, and the raft floated free of the science shuttle, which was now listing slightly to starboard. Again using the remote, Chekov sealed the hatch.

The life raft had a small motor, as well as watertight compartments containing food, medical kits, tents, tools, and devices they'd need for survival. Spock opened one seal and withdrew a pair of tricorders—and phasers.

"Navigator's discretion, Mr. Chekov. Head for shore, and we'll take stock of our situation."

"Aye, sir." He opened the throttle wide and grasped the rudder handle, aiming for the mountain island facing them across the expanse of sea. "Maybe we'll find dancing girls in grass skirts who'll greet us as conquering gods."

"Doubtful. Our purpose would be better served by finding residents capable of guiding us to Tyvol on the mainland."

"Well, why not wish for both?"

The beach stretched like a narrow grayish apron around the island. With the raft riding the crest of a low wave, Chekov cut the motor and let the surf push them up on the coarse, gritty sand. Before the undertow could take hold and tug them back, he and Spock jumped out into knee-deep water and caught the mooring cords, beaching the inflatable out of reach of the salty fingers of breakers rolling in and foaming on the shore.

Though the beach seemed to form an unbroken rim as far as they could see, at least a mile in either direction until the coast curved back, it was a shallow strip, and lush forest crept toward the water's edge. High tide might cover the sand altogether, judging by the seaweed and flotsam washed nearly all the way to the foliage. It was clear they wouldn't be able to camp right along the shore.

The humidity made its presence felt with every breath of dank air. They stripped off their uniform jackets and bunched their shirt sleeves up around their elbows. Up in the sky, the clouds parted and the sun burst through.

If the Russian wasn't genetically suited for equatorial weather, neither was Spock. His home planet was certainly known for its ovenlike heat, but Vulcan was also dry as a parched streambed.

Considering the likely tidal path, they hauled the raft to the top edge of the sand and lashed it firmly to a pair of sturdy tree trunks curving high over their heads. Wherever their reconnaissance might take them, they wanted the only means of water transport they had to be there when they came back. Spock scuffed the toe of his boot down into the sand, turning up a greater concentration of darker grains below the surface level.

"Volcanic."

"All these islands are volcanoes, aren't they?"

"Affirmative. Built up by thousands of years of eruptions. Volcanic material produces high-nutrient soil once it breaks down."

"Do you think this one is extinct?"

Curiosity raised the Vulcan's eyebrow, and he picked up a tricorder, scanning the island and forest. They stepped back for a better look over the trees. The mountain's gently sloped cone wore a coat of green along its base, then faded into mist. "I am reading some signs of activity—heat release, movement of magma deep within the core."

Chekov looked worried as Spock continued.

"But no indications of recent—or imminent—eruptions."

Spock came back and sat on the soft side of the raft, pulled out a data cassette, and inserted it into the tricorder. According to their charts, the island was known as Shilu. It was the largest of a string of six, about seventy miles across,

33

and it consisted essentially of one five-hundred-thousand-year-old volcano called Shiluzeya. Last known eruption two hundred years ago, now classified as dormant, but definitely not extinct.

Shilu was about a hundred miles from the continental coast and nine hundred miles from Havensbay, the protected harbor where the capital city was located. Since the raft's motor was fueled by hydrogen that it got directly from seawater, there was no limit to distances that could be sailed in the tiny craft. And navigation wouldn't be hard, just a matter of following the coast. But the lifeboat was not fast, and they had no idea what conditions they'd be facing out on the water. In all likelihood, it would take them longer to reach Tyvol than for the *Enterprise* to get to Akkalla from Vestra V.

The only certainty at that moment was the time of day, perhaps three hours before nightfall, too late to do any further traveling. The decision on their next moves could wait until morning. For the present, Spock decided they should scout the forest slightly inland, then return to the beachfront, and spend the night there, near the raft.

With tricorders held high and phasers in hand, they ventured through the curtain of ferns and vines and into the rain forest. The ground was spongy, a carpet of dead leaves and rotting wood, cushioning their footfalls and allowing them to move in near silence. But the sounds of footsteps would have been overwhelmed in any case by the music cascading from the leafy canopy above, a symphony of screeches, whistles, chirps, grindings, and howlings. While their ears and tricorders registered unmistakable imprints of life, the animals might well have been invisible, hidden as they were in the treetops. The only visual hints of their existence came when an occasional vine could be spotted swinging with leftover momentum after some creature had used it to sweep from one tree to another.

Once they'd penetrated the outer fringes of dense, ground-hugging vegetation, they found their way unobstructed. The branches of the tallest trees effectively screened out direct sunlight to the forest floor, preventing much growth around the tree trunks themselves. Chekov looked up at bright rays filtering through, shimmering in the dimness, with insects flitting like tiny dancers in spotlight beams. The darkness made it noticeably cooler than it had been on the beach. The still air carried the sweet scent of fresh humus, which was constantly being replenished by dead foliage falling from above to decompose rapidly in the moist soil and enrich the living trees, completing the rain forest's cycle of life.

Graceful arches formed by intertwined boughs and ethereal dappling painted on the ground by flickering sunbeams gave the forest the feel of a natural cathedral.

"There's so much life up there." Chekov's tricorder registered the activity they could hear but not see.

"Yes. When rain forests are part of a planet's ecology, they are often the most densely populated habitat. On your planet, rain forests were being destroyed at such an accelerated rate in the twentieth and twenty-first centuries that fully half of all known plant and animal species disappeared within a thirty-year period. It was ironic indeed that, at a time when many of humanity's great scientific minds were studying the extinctions of antiquity, their fellow Terrans were causing a mass extinction to rival the most devastating ever produced by nature."

"I wish we could see some of the animals here."

"Perhaps we can." Spock pointed to something shadowed between two stout tree trunks, and they approached cautiously. It was a bower, carefully woven from vines, twigs, grass, and leaves, built to a height of five feet. Chekov aimed a small flashlight at the leafy structure, and they spotted a foot-high opening at the base. Suddenly, a lethal-looking beak sprang out, snapping savagely. Chekov and Spock were momentarily startled and didn't move as the beak's owner emerged—a three-foot-tall birdlike creature with eyeballs waving on short stalks, huge talons on its toes, and gray-green skin that looked like a rumpled coat. It shrieked as it charged to within a few feet of them, and they retreated hastily, phasers ready just in case. But as soon as they scrambled away, the creature halted its advance, evidently satisfied that it had staked out its territory in no uncertain terms. It fluffed its coat and waved its beak in their direction with a bullying cockiness. With a few more snaps for good measure, the creature strutted backward toward its lair and disappeared inside.

"A fascinating specimen," Spock said.

"From a distance," Chekov decided, flashing a doubtful look at Spock.

With phasers on their lightest utility setting, it didn't take long for them to cut away some of the bushes and undergrowth at the edge of the rain forest. When they were done, they had a flat spot of ground large enough for a two-man sleeping tent and a cooking area. While Spock constructed the tent, Chekov popped open the compact stove.

Preparation didn't take long, and Spock was soon nibbling on a vegetable stew. Chekov ate cold borscht and a meat-filled croissant. Between bites, the Russian started absently humming a dirgelike melody, eliciting a fractional arch of Spock's eyebrow.

"Dinner music, Mr. Chekov?"

Chekov grinned. "Just remembering songs we used to sing around the fire at Youth League campouts." He leaned back on a tree, hands folded behind his head as he reminisced. "Ahh, summers in the Caucasus or on the Black Sea. Cooking decadent western marshmallows . . ."

"Marshmallows? I am not familiar with them."

"Really?" Chekov leaned forward. "Well, they're . . . uh . . . it's hard to describe them. They're sort of little cylindrical puffs of sugar and air." His fingers formed a rough approximation. "And you stick them on the end of long forks or just twigs, and you hold them over the fire. A real fire works better than one of these."

"And then what happens?"

"They turn golden-brown and crisp on the outside, and they start to melt inside. And then you eat them directly off the stick, or you try to pull them off without having them fall apart. They're very sticky and rather messy, I suppose."

"And yet you find these marshmallows a pleasurable food item?"

"Yes, we do."

"Based on the ingredients you mentioned, they are not nourishing."

"No. But they taste so good, we would eat so many of them . . . sometimes we'd get sick."

Spock cocked his head as he considered the facts. "It would seem they serve no useful dietary purpose."

"No, sir. But . . . I wish we had some now. Then you'd understand."

"Perhaps, but I tend to doubt it. The attractive elements of many human preferences are not readily apparent to Vulcans."

"Don't Vulcan children ever sleep out under the stars and sing songs around a campfire?" Chekov asked with an expansive gesture. After he said it, it occurred to him he'd have a hard time picturing the scene he'd just described.

Spock thought for a moment. "We sleep outdoors during the *kahs-wan,* the ten-day survival test of maturity Vulcan children must pass according to ancient custom. But that is not, as humans would classify it, fun." Then he shook his head. "No, we never sing songs around a campfire . . . although, at the hottest time of summer, Vulcan youngsters might accompany their tutors outside to enjoy the cool evening air."

Chekov clapped his hands together. "Now we're getting somewhere! Do they look up at the stars and the Vulcan moons?"

"Yes, now that I recall."

"Are you *sure* they wouldn't sing songs?"

"Quite certain, lieutenant."

"Then what would they do?"

"Their tutors would quiz them about quantum mechanics and astrophysics."

Deflated by inescapable reality, Chekov sank back against the tree. "I should have known."

Suddenly, a searing light flashed into his eyes, and he tried to shield his face. At the same time, he and Spock both reached for the phasers on their belts. But they froze when a deep voice boomed, "Hold still—hands on your heads—drop to your knees."

Instead, Chekov tried to stand, reaching again for his phaser. He was rewarded with a stinging blow to his chin, strong enough to stagger him.

Spock was aware that there were two separate light beams, one shining on his face and one on Chekov's. Their intent was to blind, to prevent them from seeing their assaulters. The beams held steady as rough hands enforced the order to kneel and took their phasers and communicators. The voice came from another angle. That meant he and Chekov were outnumbered at least five to two. Bad odds. Time to assess the situation, not to act without knowing the exact circumstances of their apparent capture.

Footsteps scuffed the ground . . . the rustle of fabric as someone spread the tent flaps open and hastily searched inside . . . voices conferring in rumbling whispers, too faint even for Spock to hear clearly . . . Chekov's breathing, first rapid, then growing calm as he gained control over his fear . . . sounds floating in from the darkness.

Powerful hands locked under Spock's arms and dragged him to his feet. The light beams raised to stay on target. He could tell Chekov had also been hauled up from his kneeling position. Except for the couple of orders barked at them, there'd been no attempt at purposeful communication. Too little information about their foes to make any reasonable assessments of their likely fate. Spock judged it unlikely that he'd be killed just for speaking, and any reaction he might evoke would be of some use in gauging their status.

"Our vessel was disabled at sea. We—"

He was silenced with a fist to the midsection, doubling him over more out of surprise than pain. The punch wasn't that hard, and he straightened quickly. The commanding voice spoke again, snarling this time.

"You keep quiet unless you're told otherwise."

Finally, the lights were aimed at the ground. Spock's vision cleared almost instantly—five people, three men and two women, dressed in camouflage outfits to match the colors of the rain forest, baggy pants gathered at the ankle, arms bared to the shoulder, sandals, hair in close-cropped unisex style, utilitarian rather than fashionable, framing young faces hardened by experience. Except for one face. The leader was much older, old enough to be father to the other four. And his expression was the hardest of all, the stone-set jaw, the glint of fanaticism in the eyes, like a knife blade reflecting a pinpoint flash just before it slashes for blood.

"You're prisoners of the Cape Alliance," said the leader. He was a thin man with weathered features and a raw-boned strength. "Got anything to say for yourselves?"

Spock measured the man with a probing gaze. "As I attempted to explain, we were forced to seek shelter on this island when our vessel was disabled. We are not your enemies, sir."

"I'll be the judge of that."

"Obviously. However, since you clearly occupy a position of leadership, you bear the responsibility to be a fair judge, weighing all relevant facts prior to passing sentence."

"You've got a brave tongue, considering your predicament. What's your name?"

"Spock. This is Chekov. Do you also have a name?"

"I do. It's Zzev."

"May I ask what the Cape Alliance is allied against?"

"The Publican of Akkalla and his illegal government. Enough questions from you, Spock. You give me some answers. You're no Akkallan, with those ears. Vulcan?"

Spock replied with a silent nod.

"Where's your ship?"

"It was approximately one kilometer off shore when we abandoned it."

"How were you damaged?"

"We were observing the altercation between your defense forces and the intruder convoy from Chorym."

"Not *our* defense forces, Vulcan," Zzev sneered. "We've got no love for this planet's Paladins. Tell me, how did they do?"

"They were rather soundly beaten—something of a mismatch of firepower."

Zzev snorted a short, mirthless laugh. "That's an understatement. But it serves them right. They invited the Chorymi to harvest our seas to begin with. Now that the harvests have turned into raids, there's not a damn thing Akkalla can do to stop them."

"You are not then allied with the Chorymi either?"

"We hate the Chorymi, Vulcan. Though it's hard to fault animals for following their natures, I suppose."

One of the younger rebels had gone off to rummage through the life raft and returned carrying a maroon uniform jacket. Zzev snatched it and growled, "Starfleet officers, eh? That answers my question about where you two came from. You've got something to do with that Federation science station, don't you—and don't lie to me—"

"We are members of the crew of the starship *Enterprise*, here to evaluate the work of the Federation outpost to—"

"A whole starship of Federation slaysharks gathering for the kill. Well, they're going to be in for a surprise when they get here. So will the Publican . . . and at least we know what crime to charge the two of you with. Tie them up."

Two of the others moved to bind Spock's and Chekov's hands behind them.

"I tell you, we have committed no crimes," said Spock.

"You and your friend here are charged with conspiracy."

"Conspiracy with who?" Chekov blurted.

"With the Publican, to keep the truth from the Akkallan people. If those scientists of yours sided with us instead of him, we wouldn't be outlaws now."

"But our scientists do not take sides in local disputes," Spock said.

"More Federation lies, Vulcan. We may be hunted as traitors now, but once the Publican is overthrown and we take control of the Continental Synod, we'll see a few differences on this planet. So—your starship's coming here. You two may be pretty valuable commodities, so we'll keep you alive for the time being. But if you're worthless sea scum, you'll face the revolutionary court. And I can tell you now, the sentence is going to be death."

The rebel band moved into the forest, then picked a spot to rest for a couple of hours. As the first streamers of sunrise bled across an indigo sky, they started a long hike up the gently sloped flank of the Shiluzeya volcano. For purposes of cover, they stayed under the forest's leafy canopy most of the way. But twice they came across geologic zones that reminded them that the island they were on was actually a giant volcano. These were rifts in the mountainside where lava had bubbled forth from deep within the planet's molten core. Early in its history, Shiluzeya had been a simple crack in the planet's crust. Over millions of years, undersea eruptions had built up sufficient material to create an island with enough altitude to rise up above sea level.

The rifts allowed streams of lava to creep down toward the sea, and the old lava the rebels and their captives crossed was hardened like rough black pavement now, with golden highlights marbling its mottled surface.

It was almost dark by the time the guerrillas followed the downturn of a gulley and approached a cave entrance burrowed into the mountain.

"Are we going in there?" Chekov asked the young blond woman who was escorting them.

"That's our base on this side of the island."

The Russian swallowed hard, his pulse racing. His palms turned cool and clammy, but the way his hands were bound behind him made it impossible to wipe them off. Sweat-soaked from the heat and humidity, his face blanched to chalk white. The thought of going deep inside a mountain, hands tied, no way to protect himself, no idea when—or if—he might emerge, had his stomach doing gymnastics and his legs transforming to rubber. Spock noticed as they paused at the entrance.

"Mr. Chekov, are you quite all right?"

"Never better, Mr. Spock. Why—why do you ask?"

"Your complexion."

Chekov's dry lips parted into a wan imitation of a grin. "It's—it's just that caves aren't my favorite places."

"Indeed. Perhaps I should request that we be permitted to remain outside."

Before Chekov could reply, a scrabbling sound from the trees nearby snared the attention of the rebels, who dove for cover behind boulders and trees, shoving their Starfleet captives unceremoniously face-down onto the moist ground. One of the young men pulled his sidearm and fired at a target barely glimpsed in the shadows beyond the clearing. The weapon flashed with a blunt report. Spock's eyes were able to follow the streaking bullet as it weaved around tree trunks and found its mark. The target screeched and thrashed briefly, then tumbled to the ground.

The entire incident had taken a total of perhaps three seconds. While Chekov and Spock waited, still flat on their bellies in the dirt, their blond escort cautiously side-stepped toward the victim. The others covered her from protected positions.

She bent down. "Dead. But not a Paladin." When she straightened, she held a small corpse up by one of its legs.

Zzev shined his flashlight in her direction. "What is it, Ttrina?"

She came back to the group, displaying a small, furry primate with veinous flaps of skin stretched between its arms and legs. "Just a glider."

"We'll cook it," said Zzev.

Chekov's stomach lurched as Spock helped him to his feet, and he weaved unsteadily. "They seem a little jumpy, sir. I don't think this is the time to complain about the accommodations. I'll be all right."

Two of the younger rebels led the way into the cave, painting the rock walls with roving light beams. Spock and Chekov were pushed in next, with Zzev and the others just behind. At intervals, the leaders paused to ignite chemical torches mounted on the cave walls. The torches crackled as they cast quivering shadows out past the group.

"Claustrophobia is not an unusual problem, Mr. Chekov," Spock whispered. "Although I am somewhat surprised that the symptoms do not manifest themselves within the confines of a small spacecraft."

Chekov tried to coax some saliva into his mouth, where he was certain alkaline tufts of fuzz had taken root. "It's not—not claustrophobia. It's—it's just caves. One summer, on one of those camping trips I told you about—"

"The ones with the marshmallows."

"Da. Some older children told me they wanted to show me something scary, but they thought I wasn't brave enough to go with them. I said I was, and they said they'd only take me if I went blindfolded."

"Did you?"

Chekov nodded. "They took me into a cave, left me standing in the middle with my eyes still covered. Then they crept away—and at the last second, they threw a rock and scared all the bats off the cave ceiling. The bats flew right past me and . . . well, I was almost the first eight-year-old in the history of the Youth League to have heart failure. Ever since then, I haven't liked caves very much."

"But you are now an adult, Mr. Chekov. Is it not time to overcome childhood obsessions?"

"Logically, yes. But we humans aren't ruled by logic."

"So I have observed."

The narrow passageway broadened into a triangular chamber with a vaulted ceiling soaring overhead. A half-dozen torches were lit, revealing a cavern like a cathedral, with crystalline stalactites hanging down and stalagmites rising up from the cave floor like magical columns. In the central part of the grotto, stalactites dripping down had formed ornate pagodalike pillars, wide at the bottom, then spiraling up into the darkness. Water droplets splashed in atonal harmony.

Judging by its contents, this particular cave was indeed a regular guerrilla base. In addition to the chemical lights in wall brackets, the main chamber had simple metal-framed cots, cooking implements, and supplies in sealed containers. Spock quickly scanned the cavern, absorbing and cataloging every detail. Then he turned back to see how Chekov was coping. The Russian seemed considerably calmer.

"This cave has some amenities, lieutenant. Remember that irrational fear is a construct of an undisciplined intellect."

"I know that, sir."

"In fact, I would estimate that the cave itself presents less of a danger to us than our captors do—unless, of course, this volcano reactivates while we are inside, emitting toxic gases which would kill us within five seconds, or erupting and adding molten lava flows to the manufacture of the gases."

Chekov's only response was an extremely dubious look.

Chapter Three

CAPTAIN'S LOG—STARDATE 7825.9:

We've completed our relief mission at Vestra, and the disaster control team left behind has begun helping the Vestrans battle the effects of prolonged drought. Although the crisis is far from over, the aid provided by the Federation came in time to prevent wholesale death, and the prognosis is hopeful. The *Enterprise* is approaching Akkalla, where Science Officer Spock and Lieutenant Chekov have already begun the evaluation of Dr. McPhillips's ecological survey. Upon arrival, we'll finish that task, and I'll pay a courtesy call on Publican Abben Ffaridor, leader of the Akkallan government. I anticipate no problems.

"We never heard from your people." Cynthia McPhillips's face filled the small viewer over Uhura's communications console, reflecting the austerity of someone accustomed to stress.

So much for my optimistic log entry, Kirk thought. "You've been there at your lab the past two days?"

"According to our usual schedule, yes. Besides, your people know how to reach us at the residential compound."

"Mr. Spock had that information. I know Starfleet and the Federation science people have had a hard time getting directly in touch with you. Do you think Spock could've had the same problem?"

McPhillips shrugged. *"Admiral, anything's possible here. We've got some real horror stories to tell you. As for your people, your guess is as good as mine."*

44

"I don't plan to guess, doctor. I plan to find out," Kirk said, more sharply. "Let us know if you hear anything. We'll be in touch. Kirk out."

"How in hell could they have disappeared without a trace, Jim?" McCoy paced the upper level of the starship's bridge, behind the command seat.

Kirk turned first one way, then the other. "Bones, stay in one place."

The surgeon halted, grasping the curved railing with both hands as he leaned forward. "Where *I* am isn't the problem. Where are Spock and Chekov?"

"First, let's find out where they aren't. Uhura."

"Still hailing on direct channel D-7, but there's nothing—not even static."

"Sulu, do a full sensor sweep of the planet. Look for anything that might fit the configuration of the survey shuttle."

"Sir, there's an awful lot of Akkalla that's not land."

"I'm aware of that. If they had to make a forced landing, let's hope they were able to make it on terra firma. Search dry land first. Start with the main continent and move out in concentric circles from there."

"And what else are you planning to do, Jim?" asked McCoy, hovering over Kirk's shoulder.

"Make my courtesy call on the Publican." Kirk swiveled out of his seat and moved to the turbolift. "Care to join me?"

"I better go. You may need me to help cut through the diplomatic double-talk."

"No interplanetary incidents, please, doctor."

Kirk and McCoy beamed down to the capital city of Tyvol, materializing at the top of broad, gray marble steps leading to a stunningly graceful structure.

"What's this?" said McCoy.

"They call it the Cloistered Tower. It's the Publican's residence. It's also where they have official functions."

"Like the White House or Buckingham Palace."

Kirk nodded. The building was a collection of bold and elegant curves, with delicate spires and a domed center. Somehow, the Tower's architects had managed to construct an edifice that captured the sweep of waves and water that dominated their world, freezing the sea's restless power into a timeless tableau. Down the steps from where they stood, Kirk and McCoy saw a circular reflecting pool with three fountains spouting streams from abstract sculptures of native sea life.

The Tower was set on a high bluff, overlooking the sea itself. The starship officers walked to a stone wall at the edge of the plaza, gazing down at waves crashing on the shore hundreds of feet below. From this promontory, one of two that jutted out into the ocean to protect the harbor of Havensbay, they could see the entire city, a place of curves, crescents, and spirals—all the sinuous contours of water in motion. The winding streets, the walls, the homes and larger buildings—all seemed an extension of the element that reigned supreme on Akkalla and shaped the world in its image.

Even Tyvol's geography was determined by water. Although a major river cut the city almost exactly in half, each half was further subdivided by interlaced streams and channels cut by nature, and canals dug by human hands. The system of waterways sliced Tyvol into a hundred tiny islands, with small ferries and thousands of bridges connecting them.

Across the harbor entrance from the Publican's Tower, on a matching neck of rocky land, stood a sturdy fortress with stout walls and parapets manifesting might more than beauty, unlike the rest of the city.

McCoy nodded toward it. "What's that?"

"I guess that's the Paladins' Citadel, headquarters for the continent's defense forces."

They took a last panoramic look around at Tyvol's dignified elegance. If anything, the city exceeded its reputation, but something bothered McCoy. After a moment, he knew what it was. The slate-toned buildings, the ashen sky, the gray sea with its clockwork waves—Akkalla seemed a monochrome world, a place of haunted, doleful spirit, and it gave him a chill in spite of the muggy air.

"What is it, Bones?" asked Kirk, trying to fathom his friend's melancholy turn of mood.

McCoy didn't reply immediately. "I don't know," he finally said. "There's just something about this place. I hope we don't have to stay here very long. It'd be nice if they had Spock and Chekov waiting in there for us."

They walked to the glass front of the Cloistered Tower and found a pair of doors the height of four men. Silver-uniformed Grolian Guards opened them and stopped Kirk and McCoy in the vaulted foyer.

"State your business, please," said a guard with ornate medals and braid on his chest. He held a palm-sized recording device up to Kirk's lips.

"Admiral James Kirk and Dr. Leonard McCoy of the U.S.S. *Enterprise,* here to see the Publican. We're expect-ed."

The small recording device emitted a pair of beeps; it was evidently a two-way communicator. Kirk wondered idly who'd given the signal of approval.

"Follow me," said the ranking guard.

Boot heels on parquet floors sent sharp sounds echoing off the high stone ceilings as they made their way directly toward a reception chamber at the back of the palace. The rear wall was nearly all glass, offering an airy vista of the sea. Handwoven rugs with stylized seascapes lay scattered on the floor between velvet-covered chairs and couches, and tapestries hung on the other walls, depicting images Kirk guessed to be from Akkallan history and religion—battles at sea, both with other people and with monsters from the deep; ceremonies with heavenly rays of light piercing through a cloud cover that was evidently a fact of life here; great processionals winding through a city that looked much like the views of Tyvol Kirk had seen from the Tower plaza.

"Please wait here," the guard said, then left them alone.

McCoy stood with hands clasped tensely behind his back. "So how do we greet this Publican? Is he royalty or something?"

Kirk shook his head. "They've got an elective system here. The Publican is the head of the majority party of the Continental Synod—that's what they call their parliament. The continent is divided into twelve provinces, and they elect three representatives from each province. I think they're called overlords."

"So the Publican is one of these overlords?"

"Mm-hmm. So we just treat him with the same respect we'd show to any head of state."

"Good. I hate it when we have to bow and scrape."

Kirk grinned. "Bowing and scraping were never your strong points, Bones."

They turned at the sound of large wooden doors creaking open, and two Akkallans entered the reception chamber. One Kirk recognized as the Publican himself, Abben Ffaridor, an older man with a short, portly build, salt-and-pepper hair, and a jowly face. He wore civilian clothing, a simply cut black suit with a startling blue gemstone pendant on a silver chain. His companion was a woman, quite a bit younger but not youthful. She wore an embellished variation of the silver military tunic worn by the Tower guards, with fine black filigree around the collar, black braid across the shoulders, and red and blue medals on the right side of her chest. Her hair was lustrous and dark, swept low across one side of her forehead and pinned up at the back, framing a face that was aristocratic and striking, yet severe in the most martial sense.

McCoy came up behind Kirk as the Publican greeted them warmly, first clasping Kirk's hands, then McCoy's. "Welcome, welcome, Admiral Kirk, Dr. McCoy. I'm Abben Ffaridor. This is Jjenna Vvox, prime brigadier of all our defense forces. Come, come, please sit." He guided them to a grouping of seats in a corner of the room, facing the seaview. Kirk and McCoy sat on a couch, while the Publican stepped up onto a thronelike chair on a slightly raised platform. His adjutant pulled up a regular seat next to him.

"On behalf of all Akkallans," Ffaridor said cheerily, "I offer welcome to you and Starfleet. Now, as I understand it, your starship is visiting our world for, uh—"

"Servicing the Federation science outpost, Peer Ffaridor," Vvox prompted.

He blinked quickly, as if hearing that information for the first time. "Ah, yes, yes, of course. I hope their work here proves stimulating and useful to both the Science Council and Akkalla. I studied science myself when I was a boy. I'll never forget hours spent exploring the wonders—"

"Sir," Vvox interrupted, "your guests might be thirsty?"

"Yes, yes, of course, of course. How forgetful I can be. Can we offer you gentlemen some refreshment? The Tower confectioners make the finest pastries"—he patted his ample midsection as proof—"and we brew sweet tea from seaweeds, hmm?"

Kirk found himself momentarily distracted, wondering who was really in charge here. The ostensible leader of the entire planet seemed directed by his distinctly nonsubservient subordinate. He made a mental note to get McCoy's impressions later. "Thank you, sir, but I'm afraid our meeting has become more than just a simple courtesy call. We have an urgent matter to discuss with you."

The Publican leaned forward. "I'm sorry, Admiral. Why not get right to it then?"

"Well, my ship was delayed on our voyage to Akkalla. We had to divert to deliver humanitarian aid to a drought-stricken planet. Two of my officers were sent ahead in a science scout ship. They were supposed to begin evaluating the science outpost's work, and we were to rendezvous with them as soon as we were able."

"Was there some sort of problem?"

"I'm afraid so. It seems they never arrived."

"Oh." Ffaridor seemed befuddled by the news, and the brigadier spoke quickly.

"I can understand why you're troubled. But isn't it possible they met with difficulty out in space and never got anywhere near Akkalla?"

"Well, it's possible," Kirk said cautiously, "but not likely. We traveled to Akkalla by a similar course and encountered no evidence that they'd had any problems en route. If they had, we would've got some sort of distress call."

"What if their radio wasn't working?" she said, eyes flashing as if she considered it a challenge to come up with irrefutable possibilities.

"Their ship was also equipped with emergency message capsules."

"What if the ship were destroyed before they had a chance to launch a message capsule?"

Kirk spotted McCoy's growing annoyance with Vvox's negative attitude. "Then, in a worst-case scenario, we would at least have found debris or radiation. No, it's more likely that they reached Akkalla and then ran into trouble here, something that prevented them from landing in Tyvol and getting in touch with Dr. McPhillips at the science station."

The Publican had been silent during the exchange with Vvox, and Kirk was no longer sure whom to address.

By the look on his face, Ffaridor was no more certain who should reply.

Kirk saw the Akkallan leader glance at his military aide, and her eyes gave him a look of warning in reply. Ffaridor cleared his throat.

"This is distressing. I'm sure you'd like to find out the fate of your crew members as quickly as possible."

"We're glad to hear you say that, sir," McCoy cut in, prompting a sharp glare from Kirk. But the doctor pushed on. "Because what we'd like to do is start a search for them right away, with your permission, of course. As a physician, I'm most concerned about the condition of these two missing men—possible injuries and so forth. I'm sure you can understand that."

"Oh, I do, I do, Dr. McCoy. As for your request, a search would be—"

"Impossible," Vvox said firmly, never once looking to her leader for permission to speak. "Isn't that right, Peer Ffaridor." Her last words were a statement, not a question.

"Yes, yes, I'm afraid that's true, gentlemen. Our laws are quite strict in regard to foreign access to the planet. Off-worlders are permitted to set foot here only on a carefully restricted basis, like your science team."

"If there's to be a search," said Brigadier Vvox, "we'll take care of it."

McCoy raised a finger in protest. "But, sir, we are already—"

"What the doctor means," Kirk said, interrupting hurriedly, "is that we're all ready to start the search. It may take you some time to mobilize the personnel to—"

"The Paladins are always mobilized, Admiral," Vvox answered in a prickly tone.

"But with our starship technology—" McCoy began before Kirk could stop him.

"We're quite able to search our own planet, doctor," Ffaridor said, sitting up stiffly.

Kirk wanted to throttle McCoy on the spot, but it wouldn't have been a dignified means of public discipline. And besides, it was too late to do any good. However

50

unintentional, offense had already been given, and taken. The conference ended on a lingering note of tension, although Vvox and Ffaridor gave assurances that Akkalla's Paladin force would do everything possible to find the *Cousteau* if it had indeed landed somewhere on the planet.

McCoy managed to keep his mouth shut until he and Kirk had been escorted out of the Cloistered Tower. Once outside, Kirk had the first word.

"Trying for the Nobel and Z-Magnees peace prizes all at once, Bones?"

"Dammit, Jim, I just didn't like their attitudes."

"Well, the score's even then. I don't think they liked ours either." They started down the wide marble steps to the avenue snaking past the Tower compound fence. "You weren't really going to say 'We're already using ship's sensors to scan your entire planet,' were you, McCoy?"

McCoy's eyes crinkled, and he half-grinned. "Guess that would've been pretty stupid, now wouldn't it?"

"Yeah."

"Then I certainly wasn't about to say *that,* Jim. I'm highly insulted that you could even think it."

"Forgive me," Kirk said dryly.

They reached the street, then looked back up at the Tower. A pair of Grolian Guards halfway up the staircase looked back. "I guess they really are paranoid about off-worlders," McCoy said.

"Well, how can you blame them when people come along and insult their technical capabilities?" Kirk said. He flipped open his communicator. "Kirk to *Enterprise.* Two to beam up. Energize."

Kirk heard McCoy's voice just as the familiar humming began. "For once, I don't mind—"

"—having my molecules scrambled," McCoy finished as they sparkled back into existence on the starship's transporter platform. "I hope this first trip down there is our last."

"Me too—but I wouldn't bet on it." Kirk nodded an acknowledgment to the transporter technician as he and McCoy exited. "Y'know, I wanted you with me for reasons other than your renowned diplomatic expertise."

"Flattery. . . ."

"As you're so fond of claiming, you *are* a doctor, Doctor."

"Nobody was sick."

"Psychological evaluation—what did you think of the Publican and the brigadier?"

McCoy's brows jiggled. "Well, it was tough to tell who was in charge."

"You got that impression too."

"Didn't take a genius to notice."

"Can you give me thumbnail profiles on both of them?"

"I s'pose. Ffaridor seemed like he was being pushed against his nature. He seemed like a fairly open, friendly sort—but the kind who might not think twice about breaking his own rules if it'll please someone important."

"What about that little throne he sat on?"

"I wondered about that myself. It's a pretty standard symbol of power to have a ruler sit up where everybody else's gotta look up at him. But it seemed out of place on a planet you described as governed by elected representatives. 'Course, we don't know the history of the place . . . it might be perfectly normal for them."

"But he went right for it, looked comfortable sitting up there."

McCoy nodded. "Yeah. If a throne *is* an idea somebody forced on him, the fact that he seems to have adjusted might prove meaningful."

"In what way?"

"Just that he's willing to accept the trappings of power, probably even like 'em, if they enhance his own position—and even if they run counter to tradition."

"Okay. What about Vvox?"

McCoy snorted pensively. "Dangerous."

Kirk nodded, then started to turn away. "Thanks, Bones."

McCoy held Kirk's shoulder. "Jim, what about Spock and Chekov? We don't find them, they may not survive. If they *are* still alive, we don't know what kind of conditions they're in."

"Even if the Akkallans don't give a damn, we're already looking—as you were so ready to announce." They traded small, rueful smiles. Then Kirk shrugged. "There's not much we could do on the surface that sensors can't do from orbit."

"What if we find something and have to go down for a closer look?"

"We'll cross that bridge when we come to it."

"Let's hope we won't have to first start *building* the bridge."

Between the cave's natural dampness and the wood-slat cots they slept on, Chekov awoke stiff and chilled when he felt a hand poke his shoulder. He sat up and saw Ttrina standing over him and Spock, who was already awake. Her blond hair was matted and dirty, and Chekov felt in serious need of a shower or bath himself. However, the gun muzzle she had pointed at his nose convinced him there were things that took precedence over cleanliness.

"You, Chekov. Zzev wants to see you."

As Chekov got to his feet, Spock stood to go with him. Ttrina's weapon swung in his direction. "Not you. You'll get your turn."

Chekov winced as he took a step. Their hands remained bound behind their backs, and his shoulders ached. He meekly allowed the young woman to push him ahead as they crossed the main chamber to a branch passage. Then he stopped short, feeling acutely claustrophobic. He'd actually grown accustomed to the large cavern, but the prospect of entering a space that looked distinctly cramped made him dig his heels in.

"Keep going," Ttrina ordered, pressing her weapon into the small of his back.

"If it's all the same to you, I'd rather stay out here."

"It's not all the same to me. Zzev wants you in there—so in you go."

She planted a muddy boot on his rump and shoved him through the portal.

He stumbled and pitched onto his knees, sucking in a sharp breath of pain as a jagged outcropping of rock stabbed his leg. By reflex, he rebounded in the opposite direction but seized his panic and lowered himself gingerly to the floor. Ttrina placed a lantern by the opening, then pulled a blanket across like a heavy curtain, sealing Chekov inside.

"If you try to come out before I come get you, you'll be shot on the spot," she called through the blanket.

He settled back and sat cross-legged in a tiny cell that would have seemed crowded for two. "Damn," he muttered. "As long as there're no bats . . ."

Zzev looked up from his cot in a private corner of the grotto and motioned for Spock to sit on a supply container. "Drink?"

"Unnecessary," Spock replied evenly.

The Akkallan twisted off the cap of a plastic bottle and poured some amber liquid into a battered metal cup. He took a swig and smacked his lips. "Good stuff. You sure?"

"Quite sure."

"You haven't had anything to drink all day. I don't want to be accused of torturing you."

"Vulcans are capable of going without food and drink for extended periods. And sensory deprivation could be construed as torture."

"Hmm?"

"How long do you intend to keep Lieutenant Chekov in your isolation cell?"

"Oh, that. You misunderstand, Mr. Spock. That's not for sensory deprivation or any such diabolical purpose. He's been questioned several times today. And I must tell you, he's confessed to a series of crimes against the people of Akkalla."

Spock betrayed not even a glimmer of concern. "I don't believe you."

"Oh, I have the signed confession to prove it." He reached under his cot and held out a piece of paper printed out by a small hand-held computer. At the bottom were words penned in a shaky scrawl: *Pavel Illyich Chekov.*

Spock knew Chekov's middle name was Andreivich. The handwriting appeared to be Chekov's, but the science officer assumed the incorrect middle name to be a signal. He decided to keep the code private, rather than risk reprisals against Chekov. "The fact remains, I do not believe this to be an authentic confession—especially since we have committed no crimes against your people or planet."

"Very well. We'll have Chekov tell you himself later."

"You will fare no better questioning me."

"Oh, I know that. Never met a Vulcan, but I know enough about them. We're not even going to bother questioning you. But maybe you'd like to ask me some questions."

"As a matter of fact, I would. What does the Cape Alliance stand for?"

"A broad question, Spock. Let's see . . . where to begin. One of our great statesmen once said, 'What good is order without freedom, freedom without truth?' That's what we stand for—truth, above all else, then freedom, and finally order, in that order."

"A worthy credo, Zzev, but do worthy ends justify all means to reach them?"

"Since you're asking me that question, I take it you don't believe they do."

"No, I do not. Vulcan society is based on beliefs which are logical and therefore beneficial to the greatest number of a collective group. Standards of order must be upheld, since standards give a society the structural framework it needs to function."

"Oh, I agree," said Zzev, waving his hands in earnest arcs. "But what do you do when the structure is rotten to its core? Do you observe standards just to be polite"—he affected upper-crust airs—"Oh, *do* excuse me. *So* sorry we had to cancel civil liberties. *Do* join us for lunch, though." He puckered his lips and made a rude noise. "Or do you shatter those standards when they threaten to crush truth and freedom?"

Spock raised an eyebrow in thought. "Destruction may be beneficial if its purpose is to clear the path for a new and better social order. But history offers exhaustive evidence that revolutionaries often fail because they have no effective strategies for constructing a viable replacement for that which they have destroyed. Should you succeed, Zzev, how will history judge you?"

Their intellectual duel was interrupted by shouts echoing down from the cave's main entry. Ttrina ran in from outside, sweat pouring off her face, chest heaving as she tried to catch her breath. The other guerrillas gathered around her.

"What's wrong?" Zzev said.

"Paladins," Ttrina gasped.

"Where?"

"Went up . . . to the observation ledge . . ." She threw her head back and panted for a few seconds. "Saw them land on the north beach."

"That's it," Zzev called. "Let's break. Travel light."

"What would they do if they caught you?" Spock asked.

"Best case," Zzev said, "throw us in prison without a trial."

"Worst case?"

"Kill us on the spot."

The *Enterprise* had been in orbit around Akkalla for twelve hours, with no word yet forthcoming from the planetary government on the fate of the *Cousteau* and its missing crew. But Kirk withheld any judgments on how cooperative the Akkallans were being, since the starship's own scans hadn't turned up anything either. Prickly and xenophobic though they might be, the Akkallans had promised a thorough search, and it wasn't unreasonable that a half-day's efforts might fail to yield results worth reporting. Besides, protocol required that he give the Publican a chance to display his good will.

But, as far as James Kirk was concerned, protocol would only stretch so far. Twelve hours, frankly, wasn't that long for his men to be missing. If they'd been able to survive a crash landing, then they were probably all right. That being the case, Kirk was confident they'd find their way out or be found long before their situation became critical. After all, Akkalla wasn't an inhospitable planet.

But the moment he surmised the local government wasn't doing its damnedest to find his men—or if the time they were missing stretched much past a day—he'd find a way to kiss protocol good-bye.

"Readily Red" is what Sulu had playfully called Seena Maybri in the days since Admiral Kirk had been forced to alter the Akkallan assignment. The young Erithian lieutenant had spent all her subsequent waking hours in self-imposed scholarly seclusion, and when Sulu had gently suggested she was overdoing it, she'd parried his concern with defensive mutterings about the need to know everything ever written on marine ecology. And her heat-sensitive skin had darkened to its most stressed hue.

Still later, when the ache in her eyeballs cried out for a break, she found herself wishing Sulu would appear at her door. He didn't. And when her message on his computer channel also went unanswered, she was certain she must have offended him. So she painted her natural shyness with a heavy coat of sociable resolve and went looking for him.

She found him diving off the three-meter board into the ship's swimming pool, and she laughed at his ungainly form. She tried to stifle herself, but by the time he surfaced and saw her, she was still in the final stage of a resigned snicker.

"What's so funny?" he called above the splashing of a small gang of crew members horsing around at the shallow end. He paddled over to the side where Maybri stood.

"Just that I never pictured you being clumsy, Sulu. It's so refreshing."

"So's this." And he sent a handful of water in her direction. She dodged, unsuccessfully. "I never said I swam for anything other than fun."

"Good thing!" She braced for another splash. He faked— she flinched—they both laughed.

"Even if it is at my expense, it's good to see you smiling about something, Seena." He hauled himself up on the deck and wrapped a towel around his shoulders.

"I thought you were mad at me," she said, shading just a bit. "When you didn't call me back—"

"Sorry about that, but I decided you needed to snap yourself out of it. And I knew I'd hear from you when you ran out of chocolate."

With a flare of mock anger, she poked him in the ribs. "Well, you were right. About both. Were you going to be swimming for a while?"

"Yeah."

"Good. Let me change, and I'll join you."

Sulu's wide grin was the only reply he could muster before the intercom whistled and Uhura's voice called Maybri's name. She hurried to the comm panel on the wall. "Maybri here."

"Report to the transporter room in twenty minutes, lieutenant. You're joining the party beaming down to the science outpost."

"It's done," Cynthia McPhillips announced. In her mitted hands, she held up a baking tray full of brownies, fresh from the oven in the science lab kitchen.

Enzo Piretti probed the crust with a tentative finger. "Too hot. This is weird, Cindy. Kirk and his people are coming down here any minute, and you're cooking."

She set the pan down and started slicing rows of perfect squares. "I get nervous, I cook. You get nervous, Enzo, you sleep. To each his own."

"And Naw never gets nervous," Piretti said as the placid blue-green Rannican sat on a stool, batting his amber eyes innocently.

"But Naw pleasures when companions grow nervous. Enzo sleeps, Naw pleasures in quiet. Cindy cooks, Naw pleasures in food. Superior to compu-cooking."

"Thanks," McPhillips said. "I think." She extracted three cake cubes and offered them to her co-workers.

Naw-Rocki popped one in his mouth. "Fortuitous that Rannicans do not metabolize cake. Pleasurable taste does not therefore lead to pot belly." He slid a downy hand across his slender midriff.

"To whose pot are you referring?" Piretti huffed.

McPhillips took the last square. "Hey, if the physique fits—"

Her jibe was cut short by the beckoning tone of the communications screen, and McPhillips answered with a mouthful of crumbs. "Dr. McPhillips here."

This is Enterprise. *We're ready to beam down and start the evaluation. Are you all set?"*

"Come on down, Admiral."

"On our way. Kirk out."

She turned to find, once again, that her colleagues had targeted her with imploring looks. Well, Naw-Rocki's was imploring; Enzo's was frankly challenging.

"What is *with* you two?"

"Oh, you know damn well," Piretti said.

"Damn well," Naw-Rocki echoed, eliciting double-takes from both his friends.

McPhillips made a disgusted face. "He didn't talk like that till he met *you*, Piretti."

"Answer the question."

"You didn't ask one."

Piretti glared. "Are you or are you not going to tell Kirk about the new life form?"

"Come on, Enzo," she protested. "We're not absolutely sure—"

"We *would* be if the damn Akkallan government let us do our jobs. Are you gonna tell Kirk *that?*"

"Yeah, yeah, we'll tell 'em everything," McPhillips yelled, giving in just as they heard the sound of a transporter beam in the main lab area.

Kirk's first sight as he re-formed in the Akkallan lab was Dr. Cynthia McPhillips, wearing a tattered apron and oven mitts and holding a baking pan. The scientist sensed his surprise and blushed slightly.

"We knew you were coming, so I baked a cake?" she offered. She held the pan out. Kirk, Maybri, and McCoy all helped themselves while murmuring thanks.

"You bake great bribery," McCoy said as he chewed.

Cindy McPhillips laughed, put the pan down, and took off her apron. "Not my intention."

"Leonard McCoy, ma'am. Chief surgeon."

McPhillips shook his outstretched hand. "Dr. McCoy."

"This is Lieutenant Seena Maybri, our ecology specialist," said Kirk. "She's here to help me ask the right questions."

Maybri shook hands with McPhillips. "I've read your journal reports, Dr. McPhillips. You do impressive work."

"Well, I don't do it alone. My co-researchers, Doctors Enzo Piretti and Naw-Rocki." With greetings out of the way, McPhillips ushered the group to a conference table near the bay window with its ocean view. The cake came with them, along with pots of coffee and tea.

"Dr. McPhillips is too modest to say it outright," Piretti said, "but we've done some pretty important work here."

"That's what we came to judge," Kirk said.

"Well," Piretti countered, "what we've got for you isn't exactly what *we* came here to study."

McPhillips snapped him a look of disapproval, but the white-haired man responded with a blithe smile.

"I think we've piqued the admiral's curiosity, boss."

"Would anybody care to elaborate?" McCoy pitched in.

"I guess that would be me," McPhillips said. Her tone made it clear she would have chosen another method of introducing the subject. "Well, as you know, we came here to study the interrelationships of life and the environment. Akkalla's an unusual world in its ratio of land to water. And it's no easy task to study the deepest regions of major oceans. Even on Earth, we explored space regularly before we explored our own seas from top to bottom."

"I get the feeling," said Kirk, "that you're beating around the bush."

"You're right. The point is, it's not unusual for marine environments to be relatively unexplored, even on worlds with advanced technology. So oceans sometimes contain secrets and surprises long after the rest of a planet's become as boring as your backyard."

"What secret have you stumbled on?"

Piretti picked his teeth with a fingernail. "New life."

"Enzo." McPhillips banged her fist on the table.

"New life?" Maybri asked. "You found a new life form? *Totally new?"*

McPhillips nodded solemnly. "We're pretty sure, yeah."

Kirk opened his hands, appealing for clarification. "Could you be a little more specific?"

"Okay," McPhillips said. "We've got good evidence of a creature now living in Akkallan seas—a creature that was unknown before, according to local scientific records."

"Evidence?" McCoy echoed. "Like a specimen?"

McPhillips shook her head. "Not that good. Some sightings in murky water—"

"And bones also do we have," Naw-Rocki added helpfully.

Kirk glanced back to the science team leader. "Fossils?"

"They're not old enough to be fossils," she said.

"How old are they?" said McCoy.

"From an animal dead within the last ten years."

"Not to denigrate your work," Kirk said carefully, "but part of our mission—and yours, I'd imagine—is to seek out new life forms."

"I'm aware of that," McPhillips said.

60

"Then why is this particular life form such a big deal?" asked McCoy.

"What might've been merely interesting became a lot more than that when we took our findings to the Akkallans."

"What happened?" asked Kirk.

"Well, the Akkallan government reacted to our revelation by—get this—rescinding our permit to search the area where we found the bones."

The starship officers reacted with genuine surprise and concern. Maybri spoke up first. "What about the native scientists? They must've been interested—"

McPhillips shrugged. "Never got a chance to find out. As you already know, the Akkallans don't run the most open society in the galaxy. We were aware of that before we came. But we didn't know they could turn positively paranoid about offworlders—even Federation reps."

"When we first got here," Piretti said, "we were allowed to meet with local scientists, but only if we gave the Science Magister's office a detailed discussion agenda first. And there was a government guy at every meeting."

"Every meeting," McPhillips said in disgust. "All three of 'em. But even with those restrictions, I really felt like we were building a professional rapport with Llissa Kkayn. She's the head of the Akkallan Collegium."

"What's that?" asked McCoy.

"The planet's major university and science and research center, here in Tyvol."

Kirk tapped a finger on the tabletop. "When was the last meeting?"

"Eight months ago," McPhillips said.

"Eight months? What happened?"

"Right after we found the bones, we made that the A number one topic on our next agenda—and all of a sudden we couldn't get another meeting okayed."

Kirk rolled his chair back and paced to the window. "I don't get it. How come you never told the Federation science office?"

"Not permission," Naw-Rocki said softly.

Piretti expanded on that for the benefit of their visitors who might not be familiar with Rannican syntax. "All our messages had to be submitted in writing to the government, and they transmitted what they felt like approving. They didn't like it"——he made a slashing motion with his hand——"out it went. It got to be pretty obvious we'd have to wait for our evaluation visit to let anybody know what's been going on."

Suddenly, the bay window shattered as a small object crashed through it. Kirk reflexively spun away, his hands coming up to protect his face. As he fell, the object hit the floor and burst into flame, spewing a burning stream of liquid across the lab. Everyone scattered. The three scientists attacked the flames with chemical extinguishers and an area rug to smother the main fire. McCoy and Maybri got out of the way and went to help Kirk. Within a minute, the chemical spray had doused the flames, leaving an eye-burning mist in the air, mixing with the acrid smell of smoke. Piretti turned the ventilation fans to their emergency setting, and the fumes were visibly vacuumed from the room.

McCoy helped Kirk to a chair. "You all right, Jim?"

Kirk brushed shards of window out of his hair and clothing. The safety glass material had splintered into harmless, round-edged pieces. "Yeah, Bones. Fine. You and Maybri?"

"We're okay."

"Anyone hurt?" asked McPhillips.

"No," said Kirk. "What the hell was that all about?"

"That's the next part of the story," McPhillips said. "We're not very popular around here. For some reason, the Akkallan scientists and students at the Collegium all think we're part of some government conspiracy working against them."

"That's ridiculous," McCoy snapped. "You just got through telling us the government's been harassing you almost since the day you got here. Don't the scientists at the Collegium know that?"

McPhillips's fingers balled into fists of frustration, and she shook them in the air. "They don't trust their own government, but it's their only source of information. They only know what the Cloistered Tower *wants* them to know. The scientists and students didn't like their government to begin with."

"Which should've made you and the Collegium natural allies," Kirk said as they returned to the table.

"Right. But the government couldn't allow that, so they planted the seeds that sprouted into this." McPhillips gestured at the broken window and fire damage.

"The scientists did this?" said Maybri.

McPhillips nodded, her anger draining to sadness. "The government's done a great job convincing Akkalla's scientists and students that we're real bad guys."

Maybri shook her head. "Why would they believe anything coming from the government?"

"That's the beauty of it," McPhillips continued. "They control every avenue of information. They've got all sorts of subtle ways of manipulating what goes on here. And what're we going to do about it, three little scientists?"

"But what about direct contacts with the people at the Collegium?" asked Maybri. "Skirting the censorship and the government-controlled media."

"We tried that," Piretti said. "Once. We arranged a secret meeting with a couple of professors from the Collegium. Somehow, the Grolian Guards found out and arrested the Akkallans. Naturally, the scientists were told we tipped off the Guard, and they blamed us for the whole fiasco. They never trusted us again, and we've been under surveillance ever since."

McPhillips managed a short ironic laugh. "Yeah, Hhayd tells us it's for our own protection. Obviously, as you've seen for yourself, protection can be a selective thing."

"Who's Hhayd?" Kirk asked.

Piretti made a rude noise. "Vice Brigadier Rrelin Hhayd, commandant of the Grolian Guard."

"What's the Grolian Guard?" said McCoy.

"The elite batallion of the Akkallan defense forces. They police the capital city, they guard the Cloistered Tower and the Publican, and they handle special missions anywhere on the planet. The Paladins are the guys who do the dirty work. What was the old term? The G.I. Joe's."

"We didn't meet this Commandant Hhayd," Kirk said. "We thought Brigadier Vvox was in charge of the defense forces."

"She is," McPhillips said. "She's the highest-ranking military officer, and Hhayd is next in line. She's his superior, but they're pretty close from what we were able to figure out."

Piretti shook his head. "For my money, Hhayd's the real viper. Vvox has to mix with the politicians. She strikes me as a bit of a politician herself."

"And Hhayd?" Kirk asked.

"Military all the way," said Piretti. "We've seen them both at receptions at the Tower. He scares me, Admiral Kirk. I hope you don't have to do any business with him while you're here."

"Admiral," Lieutenant Maybri said softly, "I'm very curious about something."

"What part of this convoluted mess?"

"The original part, sir. The new life form. May I ask a question?"

"You're the ecology expert. Go ahead."

She turned to the scientists. "Do you have any idea why the government reacted so negatively when you presented your findings?"

McPhillips let out a frustrated breath. "Y'know, that's a tough question to answer. They clamped down so completely, once we brought it up, we could hardly make inquiries, much less get information. Something about this mysterious life form *scared* them."

Maybri wrinkled her nose quizzically. "Scared? I don't understand. Were they stunned or surprised?"

"As a matter of fact, no. I can't pin this down for sure, but I'd say what we were telling them wasn't news. Not to them, anyway. But it sure as hell made them nervous. And that's when we found ourselves locked in a box."

Kirk stroked his chin. "I wonder why?"

"So do we," said McPhillips. "We want to find out, but we need your help, Admiral."

"I'm not sure what I can do."

"We're just three inconsequential civilian scientists. You're a military representative of Starfleet. You've got the *Enterprise* to back you up—"

Kirk waved a cautionary hand. "Hold on, Dr. McPhillips. The *Enterprise* isn't a big stick to persuade authoritarian governments to see things our way. Maybe you didn't have the free hand you would've liked here, but this *is* their planet. And they can run it any way they choose. Sounds to me like they could've done away with you if they'd really wanted to. But you're all still in one piece—"

"Admiral, please," McPhillips said. "You have to help us. We've *got* to know what they don't *want* us to know. They're keeping a secret—and the *way* they're keeping it, I'm convinced it's a dirty one."

"Doctor, I'm as curious as you are, but I've got two missing officers to worry about. Until I know what happened to them, I have to rely on the good will of the Akkallan government. I'm not about to offend them."

"Admiral Kirk—" McPhillips's tone skidded toward desperation, Kirk's toward impatience.

"I'm sorry, doctor. Once my officers are accounted for, I'll consider your request—"

"Consider it?"

"—but I don't want to mislead you. My inclination is to pack you up and get the hell off Akkalla. My orders preclude meddling in the governmental affairs of Federation planets." He stood, making it clear he considered the argument near its end.

But McPhillips wasn't ready to surrender. She stalked around the table and planted herself toe-to-toe with Kirk. "Even if one of those planets is hiding some deep dark secret and interfering with an accredited scientific mission?"

Kirk couldn't avoid looking into her flashing eyes. He almost yelled but caught himself. Instead, his voice was deliberately soft. "If we had more proof, maybe I could do something. But we don't, and the Akkallan government isn't likely to let us get it. For now, would you please give Lieutenant Maybri your records so she can start the evaluation?"

McPhillips swallowed her anger. "Of course," she said curtly.

"You know the procedure, doctor," Kirk said. "First she'll review your data, then follow up with interviews of staff."

The scientist nodded. "Enzo, do you have the records?"

Piretti handed a box of computer cassettes to Maybri. Kirk took out his communicator and flipped it open as McCoy and Maybri took their places next to him. McPhillips and her people backed out of beaming range.

"Kirk to *Enterprise*. Transporter room, stand by. Dr. McPhillips, please try to stay out of trouble just a little longer."

"We'll do our best," she replied in an icy monotone.

As soon as they solidified in the transporter chamber, McCoy started in. "Jim, don't you think you were a little rough on McPhillips? Since when do you quote orders from on high?"

Kirk whirled on his chief surgeon. "Since Spock and Chekov are missing on a planet run by a government that gets more distasteful by the minute—*that's* since when. We've got enough to worry about without provoking the Akkallans into being even less cooperative than they already are." Then he gave Maybri a sharp glance. "And don't you start, lieutenant. I have my orders, and you've got yours. Get to work on that evaluation. I don't want to stay here a minute longer than is absolutely necessary."

"Yes, sir," she said in a tiny voice, then scuttled out of the transporter room. McCoy and Kirk followed. The doctor's mouth opened to continue their verbal jousting—and the whoop of the red-alert klaxon cut him off. Sulu's voice echoed from speakers all over the ship as alarm beacons flashed.

"Red alert—this is not a drill. Admiral to the bridge—all hands to battle stations. Repeat—this is not a drill!"

Kirk raced for the nearest turbolift. Fortunately for McCoy, it wasn't far. He was already two paces behind and managed to leap through the doors just as they hissed shut. "Bridge," Kirk said.

As he tried to catch his breath, McCoy noticed Kirk's heel bouncing with nervous energy, like a catapult winding up, and it propelled the admiral onto the bridge the instant the lift snapped open. But not a stride later, Kirk stopped short and McCoy plowed into him. Their eyes were drawn right to the main viewscreen, where the cause of the red alert was obvious: a massive space vessel surrounded by a swarm of tiny fighters, bearing directly at the *Enterprise*.

Sulu vacated the center seat and moved back to the helm console as Kirk stepped onto the bridge. "Mr. Sulu, report."

"The ships are from Chorym—"

"That's the second planet in the system."

"Aye, sir. As soon as we spotted them making orbital approach, we identified ourselves and requested their I.D. and purpose. They ignored our hails. I decided to go to red alert, just in case."

"You made the right decision, Sulu."

"Deflectors up, phasers armed and ready, sir."

Kirk sat back and crossed his legs. "Have they made any threatening moves?"

"No, sir, except that they're on a collision course."

"All right. Stand by for evasive maneuvers. Anything, Uhura?"

"Negative. Still hailing."

Sulu peered at his computer screen as the seconds ticked by. "Impact in thirty seconds . . . twenty-five . . . twenty . . ." His voice tightened.

"Stand by," Kirk said.

The helmsman's shoulders abruptly relaxed. "They've altered course, sir."

The giant Chorymi craft grew larger until it filled the entire viewscreen, crossing the starship's path and passing just below the *Enterprise*'s belly. "I believe they used to call it playing chicken," Kirk said evenly. "Bring us around, Mr. Sulu. Follow them." Kirk turned to Spock's science station, where a fresh-faced, willowy ensign sat on this shift. "Science Officer Greenbriar, sensor readout on those ships."

"That's Greenberger, sir." The young ensign brushed a blond strand of hair out of her eyes and punched up the data Kirk wanted. "The big ship is almost our size—two hundred seventy meters long—but a lot lighter, only thirty thousand tons. Impulse power only, capable of sublight speeds. Most of the inside was empty."

"Empty?"

"Yes, sir—cargo hold of some kind, I'd say."

"Weapons?"

"None that our sensors could detect. But the escort ships appear to be fighters, armed with photon cannons. By their size, I don't think they could do any damage to us, Admiral."

Kirk thumbed the intraship communications button on

his armrest. "Cancel red alert—secure from general quarters." He closed the channel, then leaned toward Sulu. "Keep our deflectors up, Mr. Sulu. And keep phasers ready just in case."

Apparently oblivious to the starship trailing behind, the Chorymi convoy continued descending. "They're entering the atmosphere, sir," Greenberger said as she tracked the mysterious ships on her viewer.

"Level off our orbit, Sulu. Greenberger, send a survey probe out. Let's see what they're doing here."

"Aye, sir." She punched in the proper firing code, and a dart launched from a hatch on the support pylon connecting the starship's engineering hull and primary saucer section. As it penetrated the fringes of Akkalla's stratosphere, the probe's protective casing heated from pink to fiery red, tracing a contrail across the sky. Tiny retro-thrusters fired to slow it down, and the heat shielding split lengthwise, separating and falling away. Like a butterfly out of its cocoon, the probe blossomed into operational configuration —a small dish antenna unfurled from the rear, and a sensing grid poked out of the front.

On the science station viewscreen, a scrambled image took shape. Ensign Greenberger prodded her computer; the wavy interference lines cleared, and the probe presented a crisp view of the Chorymi ships as they spiraled ever lower, seemingly intent on diving into the Akkallan sea.

"Maximum magnification, ensign—on main screen."

The whole bridge crew could see what was happening now. At very nearly the last minute, the giant Chorymi vessel flattened its flight path and skimmed barely above the waves.

"Sir." Greenberger turned to draw Kirk's attention. "I've been trying to find some more data on that Chorymi ship, what it might be doing here. It's classified as a harvest ship."

"What does it harvest?"

"Akkalla's oceans. There's a treaty on record between Chorym and Akkalla. It's a hundred years old. Chorym had the technology; Akkalla had the food just swimming around in the water. So they signed a deal that let Chorymi ships do the harvest, and then they split the take with Akkalla."

"Good work, ensign. But if there's a treaty, why the fighter escort?"

Before Greenberger could attempt an answer, Uhura pointed at the viewscreen. "Would you look at *that!*"

The little tracking probe relayed perfect pictures of the harvest ship hovering over an ocean beginning to churn with stormy violence. Greenberger's eyes were locked onto her sensor scope, and her fingers skipped across her computer panel in a frenzy of data measurement and recall.

"This is amazing," she said. "That harvest ship is creating a hurricane—right underneath it!"

The viewscreen displayed the results—a swirling wall of seawater surged up from the ocean as the harvest ship rocked above it, then tipped forward, opening its gaping jaws and swallowing great gulps of frothing white water.

Kirk and his crew watched with grim fascination until Greenberger's voice pierced the silence. "Admiral . . . I'm reading surface vessels coming into the area."

On the viewscreen, the broadened image revealed a motley fleet of four vessels charging toward danger beneath the voracious intruder. The boats were of different shapes and sizes, but none were large, and none were Akkallan military. The only identification was a banner flying from the stern of each. Greenberger manipulated the probe's camera to zoom in on one boat and keep it in sight long enough to get a good look at the flapping banner. The science officer snapped a still frame, then swiftly projected an enhanced and enlarged version on her console screen. Kirk twisted in his chair and peered at the picture. It featured a symbol and some Akkallan writing.

"Can you get a translation of that, Greenberger?"

She entered the inquiry, and a second later the information rolled across the bottom of her readout screen. "Cape Alliance, sir. But there's no information on what Cape Alliance is."

Back on the main viewer, a pair of the diamond-shaped Chorymi escort fighters broke formation and banked steeply, as if to strafe the small boats. There was no longer any doubt that those boats were trying to disrupt the giant spacecraft's harvest run, darting perilously close to the cyclonic waterspout being sucked up into the ship's mouth. But the diving fighters made only a mock attack, roaring directly over the struggling surface vessels without firing a shot. As for the boats, they appeared to be unarmed.

"What the hell is going on down there?" McCoy muttered. "Group suicide?"

Kirk shook his head but kept watching the dance of death being played out far below the starship's orbit. "I don't think so, Bones."

After more chaotic zigzags, one of the boats reeled to port and made straight for the vortex.

"If that's not suicide, Jim, what do you call it?"

Kirk held his breath—and the harvest ship's maw suddenly closed. The lumbering vessel lurched from its course and gained altitude as quickly as its bulk would allow. As soon as it began climbing, the surging storm abated, and the wall of water collapsed as if an internal support had been yanked away. The escort fighters joined their mother ship as it departed, and the four Akkallan boats circled like cautious beasts until they were certain they'd chased the interlopers away. Finally, the boat crews could be seen waving their arms and hugging each other in apparent victory celebration.

Though the starship's bridge crew had no rooting interest in the blood sport they'd just witnessed, the aversion of what had seemed certain horrible destruction of the surface boats brought sighs of relief around the command deck.

"I don't get it," Ensign Greenberger said, sitting limply in her seat. "Why didn't those Chorymi fighters shoot when they had the chance?"

"And if there's a treaty," said McCoy, "what was all the ruckus about to begin with?"

"Uhura," Kirk said, "any communications at all between the spacecraft and the surface boats?"

She shook her head. "Negative, sir."

"Mr. Sulu, what's the status of our search for the *Cousteau?*"

"Sorry, sir—negative."

Kirk stood and headed for the turbolift. "You have the conn, Sulu. Keep scanning for Spock and Chekov. If you spot anything, I'll be in my cabin."

For the next hour, Kirk pored over sensor data on their brush with the Chorymi fleet, reviewing technical specifics with Engineer Scott. He kept hoping for an interruption from the bridge with some bit of good news. But nothing came. When he and Scotty were done, he went back up to the command deck.

"Sir." Uhura turned as Kirk stepped out of the turbolift. Her voice was businesslike, as usual, but with an urgent undertone. "I'm picking up an Akkallan government broadcast, on one of their planetwide channels."

"Let's see it, commander—main screen."

Uhura locked onto the transmission: Publican Abben Ffaridor seated at a desk with the planet's stylized wave symbol mounted on the wall behind him. Ffaridor was already in midsentence, speaking angrily: "—continuing incidents of Chorymi treachery in total and arrogant violation of sworn treaties. No, there's no salt-washing the ugly face of deceit displayed so vividly by our neighboring planet. We accuse them, and they *will* be held accountable. But today, I'm forced to reveal the face of another enemy, one even uglier because it comes from our midst. Until now, we have been unable to unmask this sinister force, the true instigators of the state of near war between your world and Chorym. But today, we *will* unmask this secret foe. They claim to be learned people, people of science and goodwill —yet they disrupt accords that have enriched your world, made your lives better, and helped us acquire knowledge that can make us even more advanced than we are now. They would rob you of your future, if you give them the chance. They've already injected their poison into the Akkallan sea of life. With your help, we can stop it before it reaches the heart. What do these demons call themselves? The Cape Alliance—"

The Publican paused for just a moment, long enough for the name to draw looks of recognition from Kirk and his bridge crew. Then the Akkallan leader continued.

"—they steal the sacred name of the Cape of Judgment, where our legends tell us our ancestors purged themselves of life's hardships and their own sins and returned to the soul of Mother Sea, to live in eternal peace. But this Cape Alliance promises to bring you only eternal war. Your Publican and your Continental Synod will be working around the clock to solve this crisis that threatens our very existence. We ask for your trust—your vigilance—and your prayers. May the waves of Mother Sea be with you. Thank you, my fellow Akkallans."

The Publican's face, fiercely sincere, faded out, replaced by the government wave logo. Uhura cut the signal, and the deceptively placid blue-gray globe appeared onscreen again.

"Well," McCoy said, "we know more about the Cape Alliance than we did two minutes ago. Maybe we're finally getting somewhere."

"But we still don't know exactly who they are," Kirk pointed out. "And something tells me there's another side to this story—maybe a lot more sides. Greenberger, where's the Chorymi convoy now?"

"Continuing on a departure course, sir—bound for home, I'd say."

Kirk stood. "Uhura, contact the Publican. Ask for permission—no, *tell* them to expect me within the hour." He stepped up to the bridge's outer ring, and McCoy sidled over to join him at the turbolift. "Going somewhere, Bones?"

"Can't let you get in the middle of an interplanetary war all by yourself."

They entered the lift, and the doors snapped shut behind them.

Chapter Four

"LLISSA, WE CAN'T wait forever. You're the preceptor—
you're the one who has to make the decision."

Llissa Kkayn let the warm wavelets of Havensbay wash
over her toes as she stood barefoot on the beach. She caught
the imploring tone in Nniko's cadenced voice and turned to
the old man, more as a courtesy than out of any real need
for him to see her face. He was nearly blind now but never
needed any assistance getting around on Freeland Island;
after seventy years here, he knew every path and step. Llissa
did it more for herself, to see his calm eyes and the kindly
curl of his lips under a mustache that had somehow maintained the reddish hue of his youth, even as his wispy hair
had gone almost entirely to white.

Nniko leaned on his walking stick, its tan wood as gnarled
and knobby as his fingers. "Don't worry—you always make
the right decision."

She managed a tiny smile. "Is that what you always told
Grandma?"

"Mm-hmm. Eventually, she believed me. Too bad she
wasted twenty years to decide that. If you accept this fact of
life today, it'll only have taken you ten. You'll prove that
your family's improved from one generation to the next."

"You're a wonderful liar, Nniko."

"And you're a wonderful preceptor. Not as good as your
grandmother, but there's hope. If you can overcome this
hereditary predisposition toward doubting my word . . ."

"Was she the best preceptor?"

"She may very well have been. Kkirin Kkayn is a name
that won't be forgotten as long as there's a Collegium."

Llissa's next question came out in a small, forlorn voice. "How can I follow that?"

"Llissa Kkayn's a name that's sure to be remembered, too."

"For what?"

Nniko glared at her. "For *what?*" he sputtered. "For being just a young girl and practically running the place while her grandmother was sick and dying. For being voted in as the youngest preceptor, with just a couple of dissenting votes. For going on to do a damn good job for many long years."

"It's only been ten years, Nniko. How do you know how long it'll be?"

"I know. Remember?"

"Tell me the truth. Are there still Guides who wish my father hadn't left Collegium?"

Nniko made a distasteful face. "You know your father and I never liked each other."

"Mm-hmm, but I never knew why. Do you still remember?" she asked with a sly smile.

The old man arched his brows. "Everything I ever knew I still remember—including every mischievous thing you ever did as a child. So watch your step, young lady. Your father could never accept rules. He had to do everything his own way, even if it meant trouble for everyone else. He never learned that great things can be accomplished by teamwork."

"He teamed up with my mother to produce me. There must've been *some* good things about him," Llissa teased.

"Oh, sure. He was a brilliant theoretician. He had an incredibly annoying way of making intuitive leaps that turned out to be right."

"So what was so terrible about that?"

"He never wanted to do the dirty work to prove the theories. He disdainfully left that to the rest of us. And he couldn't teach. His way of doing things was his own peculiar brilliance, not something that could be passed along to bumpkin novi from the farming provinces. He had no patience for them—not for you, either."

Llissa nodded, a little sadly. "I remember that. We weren't very close."

"That wasn't your fault. You worshipped him, like any

74

good daughter. And all he did was treat you like a rather slow novus who—"

"That was his nature, Nniko. You can't blame him for that."

"No, maybe not. But I *can* blame him for deciding to leave so soon after your mother died. We lost so many to winter fever that year—we needed him. But Llaina was his only link to this place. Once she died, he had a huge fight with your grandmother, and that was it."

"I remember that, too," said Llissa. "I was fifteen then, old enough to understand what was going on. Y'know, I don't even know if my father's still alive. Nobody's seen him in years. He didn't keep in touch with anyone from those days."

"So, my dear," Nniko said, "you can be damn sure nobody wishes he was preceptor instead of you. You shouldn't be so hard on yourself. Tell yourself you're doing a damn good job."

Llissa crouched to address her reflection in a puddle left by the morning's ebbing tide. "You're doing a damn good job, Llissa Kkayn. That crazy old Guide Nniko said so, and you know he's always right." She looked up for playful approval. "How was that?"

"Getting there. But you can excise the 'crazy old Guide' part. Now, I'm going back up to the library—"

"Is Eddran still there?" she asked, suddenly chilled by acute anxiety.

"Of course he's still there. Eddran hasn't budged since you went off to contemplate. He's been pontificating to anyone who'll listen on why we should sever our ties to the government, throw their funds back in the face of the Synod, and join with the Cape Alliance."

Llissa rolled her eyes. "Oh great. By the time I get back up there, he'll probably have convinced the Guide Council to impeach me and toss me to the waves."

"Relax, Llissa. Nobody's listening to Eddran . . . as usual."

"Don't underestimate him," she said seriously. "He really believes what he's been spouting these last few weeks. And there's nothing more dangerous than a true believer."

"Spoken like your grandmother. And as we both know,

she was never wrong," Nniko joked. "I'm not worried about you being able to handle Eddran."

Llissa stood on tiptoes to plant a peck on the old man's cheek. "Thanks for the vote of confidence."

"You hurry back up now, Llissa. I'll hold the fort till you do."

She hugged him impulsively. "Thank you, Nniko."

"For what?"

"For being my father after my own father left. I don't know if I could've stayed if not for you."

"Oh, nonsense, Llissa. Your grandmother made you what you are. I just polished a bit around the edges. Now stop hugging me. People will think there's something going on between us. They'll say I waited until you started to look like your grandmother. You do, but you're much too young for me."

"You really loved her, didn't you?" She paused, then added, "Do you remember?"

"Of course I remember," he huffed, "and of course I did."

"How come you and Grandma never married?"

"Because she didn't want to get married again after your grandfather died. They'd only been together a few years when he drowned in that storm. And *I* never wanted to marry at all. My students were more than enough to keep me busy. Didn't need any offspring that came by my bad traits genetically. It was much more of a challenge spreading them through behavior modification."

"Did my mother and father love each other?"

"Yes, yes, I suppose they did. He had quirky ways of showing it, but he genuinely missed her when she was gone. I think that's part of why he left Collegium—too many painful reminders."

Llissa's brow furrowed. "Do you think I was a painful reminder?"

Nniko mulled over the suggestion for a moment. "Very possibly. Don't think I don't know what you're doing, asking all these imponderable questions. You're avoiding the issue at hand—you've done it since you were a child. Now I'm off, and you better hurry up. And don't worry so much about confronting Eddran and his allies. Your father loved confrontations too much, and you love them too little. In that one way, it wouldn't hurt you to be a little more like him."

Llissa watched as he hobbled up the path. He moved reasonably well for a man approaching his century mark, and the cane gave him an oddly rhythmic three-legged gait.

She bent to view her reflection in the tidal pool again. The face looking back had plain, pale features, stately at best, but not beautiful. Except for her dusky eyes. They'd always been the feature she was most proud of, just ahead of the brown hair cascading halfway down her back. She reached over her shoulder, and with a few deft motions banded the hair into a ponytail, considering briefly the notion of having it cut into some fashionable style. Then she and the reflection traded a smile—trendiness was a pursuit for the young. If she hadn't bothered with it in her own youth, approaching middle age was no time to change.

The preceptor of the Collegium has more urgent matters demanding her attention, she thought mockingly.

But mocking or not, the statement was true enough. As she walked along the shore, the sun peeked through a crack in the clouds. The warmth felt good, and she let her shawl slip off her shoulders. But she still felt the weight of history and tradition that rested on those shoulders, a weight grown heavier than she'd ever felt it before.

Llissa sat on dry sand just beyond the tide's reach, in the spot that had been her favorite since childhood. Across the bay, to the west, she could see the mouth of the Bboun, the great river that traversed nearly the entire width of the continent, starting in the Ppaidian Mountains as a streamlet suckled by runoff of winter snows, meandering down gentle valley slopes, nourished by tiny tributaries that gave it the power to carve the Central Gorge over millions of years, then broadening into a wide waterway splitting the capital city of Tyvol before pouring its water and silt into Havensbay and the sea.

Tyvol itself had been founded as a trading port over two thousand years ago, the heart of Havencoast, the continent's most powerful political entity during the thousand-year stretch when the Akkallan mainland was a jumble of warring provinces. But the unnamed isle in the bay, with its lush shroud of forest and pristine sandy rim, had remained

77

uninhabited—until Collegium's founding five hundred years ago. Llissa marveled at the courage of the first settlers; somehow, in a world where weapons and warriors ruled, the Twenty Guides believed with religious fervor that knowledge was the key to pulling their world out of its dark age of perpetual battle. It must have taken incredible audacity for that band of teachers to paddle out to the wilderness in the bay and build the first wooden school with their own hands.

The mainland warlords, if they'd even taken notice, probably reacted with derisive laughter. As far as the warlord of Havencoast had been concerned, the isle in the bay had never been of any strategic importance—he hadn't needed it for defense, and its location within his heavily fortified harbor meant no attacking force could ever take it and use it as a base—so no arguments were raised when the Twenty declared the tablet of dirt and trees neutral land, Freeland.

In essence, the teachers had stolen an entire island out from under the warlord's nose. True, it was an island to which he'd never paid much attention. But to have accomplished that much was quite nearly a miracle. The founders, however, didn't quit there. Was their next action part of a preordained plan, or did the Twenty simply improvise as they blundered blithely down their chosen path? To this day, Llissa had never been able to find out the truth. Scholars had argued for years about the motivation of the Twenty. But the simple facts were inarguable.

Within months after chopping the first trees on their newly acquired island, the Guides presented a pact to all the warlords, not only the lord of Havencoast. The Collegium Charter Compact stated that the isle of Freeland would maintain its neutrality in perpetuity, that the Collegium would be open to students from any province, that all warlords would forswear any attempts to annex the educational institution and its land, and that scholars on their way to Collegium would be guaranteed safe passage through hostile territories.

The astounding agreement approving Freeland's special status had been the first accord ever reached among all the quarrelsome chieftains on the mainland. Not that the fighting stopped. But the existence of the Collegium gave the provinces their first tangible, peaceful link, fortified as the center of learning was permitted to survive and grow. At first, new buildings of wood were added, then sturdier structures made of stone ferried over from mainland quarries. Citizens of warring provinces came together in common pursuits on Freeland, and when scholars returned to homelands they carried their new cosmopolitan outlooks with them.

Gradually, contacts between provinces shifted in nature. War gave way to trade, and battlefields turned to farm fields. Within a century and a half after the establishment of the Collegium, the warlords had signed the Declaration of Convergence and created the Continental Synod. A revolution started by an idealistic band who worshipped knowledge had finally been completed.

And the Collegium itself continued to grow, spreading across the original island and over to a pair of smaller patches of land off Freeland's northern shore. Other schools were founded on the continent, most by scholars who'd graduated from the Collegium to become Mission Guides devoted to serving people who couldn't come to Freeland. But everyone knew Collegium was the jewel, accepting only the brightest students of all ages.

Llissa had been born and raised here, wandering the stone halls first as a child at play. And right from the start, she'd been told about the heroes who built Collegium with strength of hands, dreams of hearts, and ideas of minds. Those pioneering Guides had been bold men and women. No matter what Nniko might say to her, Llissa had a hard time thinking of herself as bold or courageous.

Father always chided me for being a hothouse flower, absorbing knowledge from books, never facing the bruises that the real world had a way of inflicting—the world outside the Collegium campus.

"Books are just lifeless theories," he'd scold. "No bone to break, no blood to spill. No teeth to bite, no taste or smell to truly savor."

Maybe he was right. Maybe I'm about to be tested—really tested—for the first time in my life . . . the first time I've got to make survival decisions . . . and maybe I'm going to fail like a scared novus.

She felt the short-lived sunshine fade as charcoal-bottomed clouds scudded across the sky. Raindrops began falling, slowly enough to count each one as they touched her face like kisses. The rain was her signal: time to face the Council. Llissa tugged her shawl up over her hair and turned away from the beach.

The path led up a hillside and through the woods. By the time she reached the other side of the forest, the random droplets had resolved into a steady but fine drizzle. Pausing at the edge of the woods, Llissa closed her eyes and held her breath. Then she looked up at the weathered gray stone walls of the Collegium's main building looming before her at the crest of the hill. Lights glowed in almost every window, like eyes illuminated by the energy of creation. In every classroom, lecture hall, and laboratory, the give and take of learning went on. Llissa wanted to go into all those rooms, one by one, and bask in the warm, flowing tides of knowledge. But she couldn't—not now. There was only one chamber to which she could go. They were waiting for her.

The library stretched up four flights through the core of the building, but the conference room was on the ground floor, directly opposite the arched entry doors. Llissa walked briskly from the woods to the building, shook the rain off her shawl, and stepped inside. Mmaddi, a shyly pretty teen with wild amber hair, took the preceptor's damp outer clothing and held out her ceremonial red velvet cloak, trimmed with leather.

Llissa shrugged into it, then managed an ironic half-smile. "I don't suppose they all got tired of waiting for me and left, did they?"

Mmaddi shook her head. "No."

"I didn't think so." Llissa strode across the library rotunda, through patterns cast on the blue carpet by the skylight high above. After hesitating a moment, her young attendant hurried to catch the preceptor's sleeve. Llissa stopped. "What—" she snapped.

Mmaddi's fingers recoiled as if the garment was aflame, and her eyelashes batted fearfully. Llissa took the girl's hand in a reassuring gesture.

"Sorry, Mmaddi. I didn't mean to bite your head off. Something on your mind?"

"I know this isn't a good time to . . . to talk to you about this."

"About what?"

"I found out . . . found out that you want me to be a Mission Guide," Mmaddi whispered.

"That's right. You'll be a good one."

"But I don't want to go to some province on the other side of the world. I want to . . . to stay here and help you."

Llissa brushed the girl's cheek. "You've been helping me for a long time now, almost since the day you came here. You were such a little girl then, and you could barely say two words in a row, you were so scared."

"I've spent most of my life here. Please don't send me away."

"It's *because* you've spent most of your life here that you *should* go away, Mmaddi. You've got to experience other places, other ways of life. Believe me—I know what I'm talking about." She tilted Mmaddi's chin up and wiped a tear off the tip of the girl's nose. "We'll talk about it later. I have to go face the beasts now."

"About time," Eddran sniffed from the far end of the oval blond-wood table, where he perched with feet dangling and arms folded. He was a tiny man, barely up to chest level on an average person. His chin and nose both came to points, and Llissa was certain his teeth did, too, an opinion shared by others on the staff. But Eddran's mouth never opened wide enough to test the hypothesis. He never smiled, and when he spoke—which was often—his lips barely parted, as if he feared having the words tumble out before he could say them. As the other five Council members took their seats, Eddran remained balanced on the table's edge.

"The world's unraveling, and you're communing with nature," he droned.

"Eddran," said Nniko, not bothering to hide his annoyance, "stop playing gargoyle and sit in your chair like normal people."

The little man dropped to the floor and whirled on Nniko. "Like normal people? And what is that supposed to signify? Stooping to insults about my deformity, old man?"

"If you're referring to deformity of body, no. If you're referring to deformity of mind, affirmative," Nniko replied, suddenly swinging his walking stick up and smacking the table less than an inch from Eddran's whitened knuckles.

Eddran yanked his hands back with an involuntary yelp

81

and fell into his seat. There were snickers around the table, which Eddran answered with only a circuitous glare.

Llissa idly wondered if Nniko's aim was accidental or intentional. Maybe the old man could see better than anyone thought he could. She'd have to ask him later. She slipped into her own high-backed leather chair and glanced at the faces of her advisers. Each Guide wore a different color cloak, signifying their various departments. Ossage sat to her immediate right, a man a few years her senior with mottled skin and puffy eyelids that gave him the look of someone about to doze; Rraitine, a white-haired woman with bewitching green eyes and several chins; Nniko; Eddran; Ssuramaya, the only Council member younger than Llissa herself, with the swarthy skin common to Akkallans from the southern desert province; and Ttindel, a corpulent man with curly gray hair framing his fleshy face.

Whatever their outward appearances, all had several things in common. They'd been Guides at the Collegium for at least a decade, during which time they'd proven to be superior teachers. And they'd all volunteered the considerable time and energy needed to help the preceptor run the institution. They were among the finest minds on the planet. Even Eddran.

"I wasn't communing with nature, Eddran," Llissa said icily. "I was doing the same thing you were all doing—thinking about our situation. We have to reach a policy decision quickly." She gestured with an open hand. "What are your opinions?"

"The broadcast didn't accuse us of any collusion with the Cape Alliance," Rraitine said, her chins quivering.

Ossage roused himself. "Implied," he drawled.

Ssuramaya jumped to her feet, dark eyes flashing. Her clipped accent made her words sound even more urgent. "That's not so. We maintain our distance from the Alliance, and we maintain our integrity. The people will know what we stand for."

"We don't *stand* for anything." Eddran's voice dripped with carefully sculpted contempt. "We sit and debate—and the Publican tightens the rope around our necks."

Ttindel ran stubby fingers through his curls. "Hate to agree with Eddran . . . worst attack yet in today's speech. His 'learned people of science'—damned close to adding,

'Don't forget the folks at the Collegium'—only a matter of time until we're named."

Nniko clenched his fists and bounced them on the table. "Do we have so little faith in the Akkallan people?" he rumbled. "We don't agree with anything the Cape Alliance does. We keep saying so. Ttindel, Ossage—do you really believe they're not listening to us?"

"Put it this way," Ttindel replied. "One message from us, maybe a few people hear it. A deluge of propaganda from the government, everybody hears. Which do they remember?"

"And what about the starship?" Eddran interjected, sharp chin jutting forward. "Could it be mere coincidence that a Starfleet warship arrives just as the Publican starts the most blatant crackdown in recent times? We're on the edge of totalitarianism, and that starship is here to enforce it."

Llissa jabbed the air in protest. "We don't know that."

"We can guess. Don't be so naive."

"I'm not naive. I just don't happen to share every conspiracy theory you cook up, Eddran."

"Not all conspiracies are theories," Ossage said in his drowsy voice.

Ssuramaya leaned forward again. "I propose that Llissa go to the Tower to meet with Ffaridor and explain our positions and our concerns. Then, if this keeps up, we'll know that this is one conspiracy that's real."

"What a bold proposal," Eddran said sarcastically. "And I'll hand out sharp implements so we can prepare to take our lives when they come to arrest us for being part of the Cape Alliance."

Lips tightened into an angry line, Llissa spoke in a low voice. "Let's vote on Ssuramaya's proposal. All in favor—"

Four hands were raised: Llissa, Ssuramaya, Rraitine, and Nniko.

"Approved," Llissa said, without much satisfaction. "I'll go now and report as soon as I get back."

Eddran snorted. "If we haven't been thrown into prison by then. Or carried off by the political police from that starship."

Ssuramaya whirled on the short man. "We've handled our own Grolian Guards this long. We can handle a Starfleet starship, too."

The gauzy curtains were fully drawn back from the floor-to-ceiling windows, but thickening overcast outside dimmed the daylight, and Llissa felt an oppressive gloom pervading the room. By the slimmest of margins, she'd been handed a mandate for action. By nature, she was a conciliator—but what if her audience with Publican Ffaridor became a confrontation? And what if the *Enterprise* really had been summoned as a tool of enforcement? The Collegium already had sufficient enemies here on the ground.

As her council of advisers gathered their papers in silence, Llissa hurried out of the chamber. In the solitude of the rotunda, she stopped. *What in the name of sanity is going on here? And what makes me think I have any power to right it?*

Somehow, she had to believe in faith. But these days, faith was, at best, a life rope in the middle of storm-tossed seas. And it was fraying rapidly.

Two columns of transporter energy took sparkling shape on the plaza outside the Cloistered Tower, forming into Admiral Kirk and Dr. McCoy. McCoy stepped toward the Publican's palace, but Kirk took a deep breath of salt-tanged sea air and drifted instead to the wall at the edge of the overlook. From this perch, he could see the bay spreading below, with fishing and cargo boats clustered around Tyvol's busy wharfs, while other vessels lay at anchor offshore or sailed in and out between craggy cliffs standing like sentinels on both sides of the harbor's narrow entry.

"Doesn't this remind you of San Francisco?" Kirk said, glancing up at the cloud-streaked sky and feeling the damp breeze on his face. "The weather's even a little like the Bay area."

McCoy's eyes narrowed. "You sound homesick. Since when did you prefer the confines of Starfleet headquarters to being out in space with the *Enterprise?*"

Kirk's brows arched defensively. "Who said anything about being homesick? Can't a place remind you of home without you actually wanting to *be* home?"

"In certain circumstances, yeah. But I know you too well, Jim. And you've been mooning around for weeks."

Indignant, Kirk stiffened. "I have not been mooning around, doctor. Let's go." With an impatient stride, Kirk led the way up the steps to the Tower's glass doors. The guards swung them open from inside.

"State your business, please," said the senior guard, again holding the small recording/communications device up for Kirk to speak into.

"Admiral Kirk and Dr. McCoy from the starship *Enterprise* to see the Publican."

A single extended buzz came out of the hand-held intercom, prompting a frown from the guard. He raised the communicator to his own lips and pressed a button on its side. "Instructions, commandant?"

The guard cocked his head, and Kirk noticed the Akkallan wore a tiny receiver in one ear. Whatever his commandant was telling him made the guard squirm for a fleeting second. "Yes, sir. Yes, sir. In the North Wing. Right away, sir."

The guard slipped the intercom into a pocket in his uniform jacket and turned to Kirk and McCoy. "The Publican is very busy. If you wish to see him, you'll have to wait."

"Fine, we'll wait," Kirk answered. "But please make sure he and Brigadier Vvox know that we've got extremely urgent matters to discuss with them."

"I'll relay that message, sir." The senior guard waved his partner over. Kirk didn't know the specifics of Akkallan uniform markings, but it was clear the senior guard far outranked the other man. "North Terrace."

The younger guard clicked his heels together, looked at McCoy and Kirk, and began walking without a word. The senior officer noticed that the men from the starship hadn't yet budged. "You'll please accompany trooper second."

After a moment of grudging and calculated hesitation, Kirk and McCoy followed the guard down the broad hallway. Kirk noticed they were headed in the opposite direction from that taken on their first beam-down to the Tower, climbing a short flight of curved marble stairs with polished brass banisters.

At the top of the staircase, the passageway broadened into a window-enclosed veranda, with wicker seats scattered randomly.

"You'll be summoned," the guard said. Then he spun with parade precision and went back down the steps.

Kirk stood at the windows. The veranda jutted out past the edge of the cliff, offering a spectacular view of Havensbay hundreds of feet below. McCoy came over and peered out cautiously.

"I wouldn't recommend it for anybody with vertigo."

Kirk ignored the quip. His attention was focused on a small boat making its way directly for the cliffs supporting the Cloistered Tower. McCoy followed his line of sight; they could see a figure in scarlet standing at the bow rail, almost like a figurehead on an ancient sailing vessel.

"Another uninvited dinner guest?" McCoy muttered.

Kirk shrugged. "Looks like they're headed here."

The figure in scarlet gazed up at the lofty bluff as her pilot cut back on the engines and slowed the boat, aiming for the narrow docking slip. Llissa Kkayn felt extraordinarily insignificant arriving at the Cloistered Tower from sea level, a psychological detriment she definitely didn't need. Her unbidden appearance at the Publican's doorstep was already more than sufficient to make her stomach flutter and her nerves jangle. At times like this, she wished someone else was preceptor, leaving her to be a simple Guide responsible for her students and her classroom, and nothing more. To Llissa, the lure of Collegium life was the chance to charge over the horizons of knowledge, to learn what lay beyond and teach all of it to others. Political jousting had never been among the things she enjoyed, neither with members of the Akkallan government nor with her fellow Guides.

The ferry sidled up to the wharf as the pilot shut off the magnetic field generators powering the boat and tossed a mooring line around a piling. He cranked the line tighter, and the boat's flank bumped gently against the dockside padding. Llissa poised with one foot on the ferry's gunwale.

"I don't think I'll be too long."

The pilot nodded, and Llissa stepped off the boat. She paused, listening to the rhythmic lapping of tide against hull. No matter what got in its way, the sea kept rolling on. Water seemed such an insubstantial thing. How foolish for waves to keep battering against rock. Yet, eventually, the sea would always win. Llissa would have to be like the sea.

With a gradual tilt of her head, she surveyed the sheer

wall of rock rising three hundred feet above her. The switch-back path that had been used for centuries was still visible, like an implausibly long snake clinging to the cliffside. Fortunately, there was a power lift now, creeping up the bluff inside its skeletal steel scaffold. But first Llissa had to get past the guardhouse at the elevator's base, where a trio of troopers lounged in distinctly cavalier poses. They snapped back to military bearing as they saw her approach. Of all the Tower duty stations, this one was among the least demanding. Also the least supervised. And, Llissa figured, least likely to lead to promotion.

The ranking guard, a broad man with a cropped mustache and a savage scar across his cheek, blocked her way. "Who are you, and what's your business at the Tower?" He held his communications intercom up, and she spoke into it.

"Llissa Kkayn, preceptor of the Collegium. I'm here to request an audience with Publican Ffaridor."

"How long's it been?" McCoy asked, slouched deep in the pillows of a wicker loveseat.

Kirk shrugged. "Maybe an hour."

"And they say doctors keep people waiting." At the sound of footsteps coming up the stairs, McCoy straightened. "About time."

But instead of escorting them to see the Publican, the young guard deposited another supplicant—the figure in scarlet they'd seen on the bay ferry, who turned out to be a woman. She swept the room with one quick look, then turned a withering stare at the trooper.

"I thought you were taking me to see the Publican."

"No, ma'am. Waiting area."

"But they already *had* me in a waiting area."

"At least this one's inside the Tower, ma'am."

"Thank Mother Sea for small progress, is that it, trooper?" she snapped.

"I guess so, ma'am. You'll be summoned." With that, he made a hasty exit.

"It looks like a seller's market," McCoy said from behind her.

The woman spun, dusky eyes flashing with surplus anger. In her leather-trimmed velvet cloak, she presented a regal image. "What is *that* supposed to mean?"

McCoy warmed up his easiest Georgia-gentleman smile. "Only one Publican to go around, and lots of folks who want to see 'im, it would seem. I thought Akkalla didn't have any royalty."

"Hmm?" The comment, out of the blue, completely confused her.

"Where I come from, people dressed in red velvet cloaks usually have some sort of inherited title, and lots of money."

Her ire disarmed, she brushed the material with her finger, then released the throat clasp, slipped the cloak off, and draped it over one arm. Her clothing underneath was simple and subdued, with just a splash of color added by a scarf tied at her neck.

"Sorry to disappoint you," she said. "Actually, I do have an inherited title of sorts, but I'm afraid it's not at all royal."

"Doesn't really matter. What *is* your title?"

"Preceptor of the Collegium of Akkalla. My name is Llissa Kkayn."

Kirk had been hanging back, content to watch the McCoy charm work its magic. But the moment Llissa identified herself, he stepped forward. "The leader of the Collegium? We're very glad to meet you. We've got some important things to discuss with you."

Kirk's urgent tone drew a veil of caution across her eyes. "And who are you?"

Trying to reestablish the gentility Kirk had just shattered, McCoy answered first. "Leonard McCoy, chief surgeon, and this is Admiral James T. Kirk. We're from the starship *Enterprise.*"

Llissa nodded. "Ahh, you're absolutely right. We *do* have important things to discuss." She'd steeled herself for an expected confrontation with Ffaridor. Now that she was in the mood, why not test her mettle with these starship officers? "Why are you here to intimidate us?" Her voice was sharp and accusing.

Kirk blinked in surprise. "Intimidate you? What gave you that idea?"

"Then why else would a starship be visiting Akkalla just when the government is cracking down on scientists and teachers and students?"

"People who've committed their own sins should be

careful before they throw baseless accusations at anyone else."

"*Sins?* I don't know where you get your information, Admiral, but if you want to talk about baseless—"

"There's nothing baseless about it, preceptor. We were just witnesses to a completely unprovoked, violent attack by people from your Collegium—"

"We're students and teachers, not terrorists. We're not violent, and there's been plenty of provocation when it comes to—"

"Hold on just a minute, both of you," McCoy barked, loudly enough to stun the other two into silence.

"You're with *him*," Llissa said. "Why should I listen to you?"

"Because, my dear, *we* were gettin' along just fine before *he* got into the conversation. And," he continued with a side glance at Kirk, "speaking of renowned diplomatic expertise, Jim—"

"Bones," Kirk began warningly.

"Begging the Admiral's pardon, Admiral, sir."

Kirk opened his hands in surrender for the time being.

"Thank you," McCoy said. "Now, we've obviously got a misunderstanding here. Also obviously, we both have grievances to take up with the Publican and his government. Anybody got any objections so far?" He looked from face to face, getting only grim scowls in reply. But that was better than open hostility, so he went on. "Good. Now—and, Jim, don't you ever tell Spock I said this—but *logically*, this means we've probably got a common cause somewhere in all the name calling. As long as the Publican's got us cooling our heels, let's take advantage of the time. Hmm?"

Llissa blew out a long breath to release stress, while Kirk tugged at the bottom hem of his tunic, straightening it. McCoy knew that to be among the ways his friend dissipated nervous tension.

"That's more like it," McCoy said as he took each one by an arm and steered them to seats near the windows. "Preceptor Kkayn, why don't you go first. Why do you think the *Enterprise* is here to intimidate you?"

Now that she had to form a reasonable statement backed with supportive facts, Llissa was noticeably slow on the draw. She silently cursed herself for not having an inarguable case at the tip of her tongue. *Never mind the tip of my tongue—how about anywhere in my stupid brain?*

"Well . . ." she began numbly, "it's circumstantial, of course—"

Kirk barely raised his finger in debate, his mouth open as if to interrupt. McCoy cut him off with a sharp stare. Llissa continued, slowly.

"I don't know how much you know about us, but the Collegium is the finest educational institute on the planet. We don't take sides in political disputes. The Collegium's been carefully neutral since it was founded five hundred years ago. When this continent was a collection of tiny principalities constantly at war with each other, Collegium was a bastion of peaceful learning and research. We're not rabble, but lately we're being lumped in with rabble by the government. We're afraid the last vestiges of free thought on Akkalla are about to be snuffed out."

Kirk lifted a tentative hand. "Can I ask a question?"

"Sure, Jim, as long as it's not makin' accusations."

Kirk nodded. "Does this have anything to do with the Publican's speech today?"

"You heard it?"

"Yes, we picked up the signal aboard my ship."

"Then you have some idea of what we're worried about."

"Not exactly," McCoy said. "Are you part of the Cape Alliance?"

Llissa flared. "No—absolutely not! Why does everyone think we're part of—"

"Whoa, sorry. I didn't mean to imply you were part of anything. We don't even know what the Cape Alliance is."

"Although we did see them in action," Kirk added.

"What do you mean?"

"We watched them disrupt a Chorymi harvest fleet—"

"And almost get their damn fool heads blown off," McCoy said.

"Why didn't you do something to stop the Chorymi?" Llissa demanded.

"That's not what we're here for," said Kirk. "We don't interfere in local disputes."

"Then what are you here for?"

Kirk's jaw tightened. "For what I thought was a simple mission—which has gotten very complicated. I've got two officers missing somewhere on your planet. I can't get a straight answer out of anybody in charge—"

"Speaking of straight answers, you didn't give me one. What was that simple mission?"

"Evaluating the Federation science station set up on Akkalla to decide if it should get further funding or close down."

Llissa jumped to her feet. "And you claim you don't interfere in local disputes? That's the biggest lie I've ever heard."

McCoy rolled his eyes as Kirk rose up out of his seat. He and Llissa were back to pretruce positions.

"Preceptor, that outpost was a proper and approved science project—"

"Approved by who—the Publican? That explains why those so-called Federation scientists have fought us and sided with the government every step of the way. They refused to have meetings with us without preordained agendas, and then they canceled the meetings altogether. When we tried to meet secretly with them, they informed the Grolian Guard and had our people arrested."

"Your people have surrounded their facilities, thrown fire bombs, harassed them to the point where they're practically prisoners—they can't go outside without armed protection," Kirk shot back.

The sparring match was interrupted by the young guard. "The Publican is ready to see you now."

Kirk whirled on the Akkallan trooper. "Ready to see *who* now?"

"All of you. If you'll come with me, please?"

"Well," Kirk grumbled, loudly enough for only McCoy to hear, "isn't this just wonderful . . ."

His mood got no better when the guard led them into the audience chamber where they'd previously conferred with Publican Ffaridor and Brigadier Vvox. Ffaridor was nowhere to be seen. Vvox was there, accompanied by another Akkallan officer, a man of arrogant bearing. He had wavy hair and chiseled cheekbones framing stone-cold eyes, and Kirk noticed immediately that his uniform seemed more ornate than Vvox's, with fringed braid at both shoulders, a wide belt with black leather gloves tucked over it, and a jewel-handled dagger on his hip. On every finger he wore a ring, and he held a swagger stick under one arm.

From appearances, this other officer might have outranked Vvox. But she sat on the Publican's throne while he stood attentively at her side, as she had done for the Publican. With an imperious wave, she directed them to sit in three chairs clustered facing her.

"Brigadier Vvox," Kirk said, "we made a request to see the Publican."

"And that request was turned down, Admiral. The Publican's a very busy head of state—and he's dealing with a number of critical situations—"

"I'm well aware of that, but Akkalla *is* a member of the Federation, and my ship *is* here on Federation business. Your government has certain responsibilities—"

"And they've been delegated to me. I'm sure you don't handle every chore aboard your starship. This is my top aide, Vice Brigadier Rrelin Hhayd. He is supreme commandant of the Grolian Guard. Between us, we're in charge of all military and security forces on Akkalla, and I believe your difficulties are related to security matters. Correct, Admiral Kirk?"

"Correct, but—"

Vvox didn't allow him the luxury of qualifying his reply as she turned her attention to Llissa Kkayn. "As for you, preceptor, Publican Ffaridor asked me to pass along his assurances of support for the work you and your colleagues are doing at the Collegium."

"Then why did he try to put us in the same basket as the Cape Alliance terrorists?"

The brigadier leaned forward, her eyes radiating sincerity. "I was with him as he made his speech today. I followed every word. And I can assure you there was no such statement."

Llissa clenched her teeth, trying to hold on to the edge of anger she'd honed while arguing with Kirk. But she felt it melting in the harsh light of reality. Vvox's stolid adherence to the party line wasn't going to shred, not even unravel at one corner.

"He used the phrase 'people of science.' Do you expect me to believe he wasn't trying to imply that the Collegium is somehow involved?"

"If that's your interpretation, preceptor, he can't be held to it. I know his intentions."

Inside, Llissa sensed a whimper of defeat trying to climb up her throat. She swallowed it. "If we got that meaning out of his speech, other Akkallans did too. We have nothing to do with the Cape Alliance, and we condemn their methods—"

"But not their goals?" Commandant Hhayd interjected, his voice calm and barely audible. His choice of words carried the barbs he'd intended to embed in Llissa's plea.

For a moment, Kirk felt sorry for her.

"That's not fair! We don't agree with anything they say or do. If you insist the Publican didn't mean to link us with the terrorists, well, all I can ask is that he and his speechwriters be more careful with their choice of words."

Llissa swirled her cloak over her shoulders and stalked out of the room.

"Admiral Kirk," Vvox prompted, "do you have anything else you wanted to discuss?"

"As a matter of fact, yes—my two missing officers. We've given you a chance to conduct the search you promised, and we haven't gotten any word at all."

Hhayd took a half-step forward. "That's because we had nothing to report to you."

"You haven't found anything?"

"Not a trace of your men or their ship, which adds evidence to support the conclusion that they never reached Akkalla. They died in space."

"We'd have found something if that's what happened," McCoy hissed. "Are you saying you've called off your search?"

"Not at all," Vvox said. "As the admiral has pointed out, Akkalla is a Federation member. We'll do everything possible to fulfill our responsibilities to Starfleet. You'll just have to accept my assurances."

"What about protection for the science outpost?" Kirk said.

"The Grolian Guard is quite capable of protecting the outpost," Hhayd said, completely unruffled.

Kirk *wanted* to ruffle him—the Akkallan's smugness infuriated him. "Then how do you explain the fire-bomb attack earlier today, in broad daylight?"

"Determined terrorists are difficult to stop."

"I respectfully request additional security measures be put in place, Commandant Hhayd, or I'll—"

"We'll do what we can, Kirk. Our resources do have limits, and, frankly, the Akkallan defense forces have other pressing concerns."

"—or I'll be forced to report your failure to abide by treaty to the Federation Science Ministry and the Council itself," Kirk said, completing his threat without missing a beat. "I hope you'll relay my position to the Publican."

Vvox nodded. "Is there anything else?"

"Not at the moment, brigadier." Kirk flipped his communicator open. "Kirk to *Enterprise*—two to beam up."

The transporter beam caught Kirk and McCoy, and they sparkled and faded. When they were gone, Vvox crossed her arms and slouched back in the throne's deep cushions.

"They're not happy, Rrelin."

Hhayd smiled sardonically. "Can't say as I blame them. We weren't very cooperative. How long do you plan to keep this up?"

"What makes you think I *plan*—"

"Because you *plan* everything," he said, caressing her cheek with his powerful hand. He wasn't a brawny man, but his tailored uniform emphasized his narrow waist and broad shoulders. His physique and movements hinted at sinewy strength.

Jjenna Vvox placed her hand over his and kissed his fingertips lightly. "Then let's do something spontaneous—if you don't have any pressing appointments."

"Even if I did, you could . . . order me to your office. You are my commanding officer . . ."

She nodded. "That's true. I'm glad you still remember that, Commandant. All right—I'm ordering you to report to my office."

He snapped to attention. "Here in the Tower, or at the Citadel, Brigadier Vvox?"

She licked her lips seductively. "Here in the Tower. I don't want to wait through a boat ride across the strait."

Hhayd batted his eyelashes. "When, Brigadier?" he teased.

She rubbed her hand on his chest. "Now."

He stepped back and saluted. "I'll report to your office immediately."

"Very good, Commandant. I'll be waiting."

By the time Hhayd arrived, she'd changed into a robe held closed only by a sash at her waist. She met him at the door and led him to the sleeping cubicle just off the office chamber, an alcove with a bed, a small glass-top table and a pair of chairs. A bottle of aqua-tinted wine stood on the table and Vvox filled two goblets, handing one to Hhayd and sipping from her own.

But he wasn't interested in the wine and closed her in a rough embrace. After a lengthy kiss, they sat on the edge of the bed. "I wonder how long we can juggle things," she said.

"What about Ffaridor? You're not losing control of him, are you?"

Vvox slid back against a mountain of pillows, tucking her feet under her with a disdainful laugh. "He doesn't get a scrap of information without my approval. He sees the world the way I paint it." Then she paused. "Besides, if he gets cranky, I just take him to bed."

Hhayd stood up abruptly and paced by the bedside.

"Rrelin," she scolded, "you're such a jealous little boy. Although, now that I think of it, Abben *is* quite an accomplished lover. There's something to be said for experience."

Her current partner lunged across the bed and clamped his fingers around her wrist with a grip painful enough to make her wince. "I don't want to hear about it," he said angrily.

Vvox wrenched free of his grasp. She sat up on her haunches and poked him with a threatening finger. "Let's get one thing straight—I do what I have to do to maintain our position of authority."

"Certain things *I* don't want to know about."

Her lips curled into a cruel half-smile. "Yes, but I enjoy seeing you squirm."

"You're playing a dangerous game with me, Jjenna," he snarled. "If I were you, I'd be careful."

She launched herself at him before he could react, pinning him to the bed. She sat on his stomach, pressing her full weight down on his shoulders. "Don't threaten me." Her tone was anything but playful.

"I'm not. But you never know when the rules might change, in spite of all your careful planning. That happens, you might not be on top anymore."

"I'll be on top whenever I want to be, Rrelin. For the good of your career, I'd suggest you remember that."

Summoning all his strength, he managed to shove her off and he rolled to his feet, retreating to one of the chairs and his wine goblet. "I never should've let you seduce him," he said petulantly.

"I didn't need your permission," she shot back, settling on her pillows again. "Your *acceptance* of my decision simply made things easier for both of us."

"It was supposed to be temporary—just until we could pick our spot to overthrow him and declare ourselves military rulers. That's the only reason I agreed—"

"You agreed because I gave you no choice. Your main failing is that you're a slave to your impulses. And I know how to manipulate those impulses."

"*Your* main failing is, you're a prisoner of your schemes and rules."

"I *make* the rules," she said sharply. "And those schemes you like to ridicule have brought us to the brink of absolute power. Within two weeks, we'll make our move."

"Not while the *Enterprise* is here."

"I'll think of a way to eliminate that unforeseen complication. Don't you worry about it, my love . . ."

Poised over the sunken tub in his bathroom, Abben Ffaridor dipped a toe through the bubbles and down to the water, testing its temperature. "Perfect." As he stood in his velvety robe, he caught a side view of his reflection in the opposite mirrored wall. He turned and faced himself, eyes narrowed in studied silence. He lifted his shoulders and straightened his posture, pleased to see that such a simple adjustment flattened the bulges and folds at his waist. The upper torso that had once been muscular and firm from youthful summers spent working at the docks of Tyvol had rounded into flabby bulk—or had it?

Maybe it was only the slouch brought on by desk work that made it appear that way. So he was a little thicker through the middle; who wasn't at his age? He decided happily he'd held up remarkably well.

"Room for one more, Abben?"

At the sound of the silken voice, he opened his eyes to see Jjenna Vvox wearing a robe that matched his own. "Of course—you know there's always room for you, Jjenna."

She came over to him and they sat on a bench adjacent to the tub. "You look worried, my love."

"Well, I was just looking at myself in the mirror, and I wasn't sure I liked what I saw."

She began massaging his shoulders. "What was that?"

"An old man."

"You're not old, Abben."

"Well, then, a man to the far side of middle age. Do you think I'm still in good shape? Be honest."

In answer, she held his face with both hands and gave him a soul-probing kiss. "Need I say more?"

"No, no, that was just fine."

"Not that I ever talk about what we do, but if I did, I'd say you were the best lover I ever had."

"Well . . . what a nice way to end a long day. You look tired yourself, my dear brigadier."

"I am. I just had a lengthy meeting about security matters with Commandant Hhayd. That man could tire anyone out, once he gets going."

"I'm still not sure about him. Maybe we promoted him too quickly."

"Not at all, Abben. He serves me quite well."

"How did your meeting with Admiral Kirk go?"

"As well as can be expected. We had an additional complication—Preceptor Kkayn came over to plead for the Collegium. I saw them both at once."

"Anything I need to know about?"

"No. You're much too busy to worry about these little nuisances. I don't know how you managed before you had me running interference for you."

"I wonder the same thing, Jjenna. Sometimes I don't think I tell you often enough how much I appreciate everything you do. And why won't you let me tell the Synod? I think you deserve public recognition. No other brigadier has ever handled as much as you."

"Knowing I'm helping you is all the recognition I need, my love. Good work is its own reward." She stood and started to shrug out of her robe. "Enough talk about business. You said it yourself—the end of a long day. Let's just play . . ."

"Jjenna . . . one more question." He faced her. "You know more about what goes on in this government than anyone. Am I a good Publican?"

"The best." She kissed him again. "Now let's get into that tub before the water gets cold."

Jjenna Vvox turned her fur collar up around her ears and under her chin as she watched the waves roll in. She sat alone on the balcony of her quarters in the Citadel. Across the harbor, lights still burned in the windows of the Cloistered Tower. To the west, streetlamps wound up and down the hills and bridges of Tyvol like gleaming necklaces carefully arranged on midnight velvet. Down below the Citadel's cliff, sea birds called in haunting harmony as they settled in their nests for the night.

She was tired. It wasn't easy constantly grooming the egos of two preening men. Was it worth the time and effort? She had a planet to run, and exercising her expanding powers while maintaining the facade of Ffaridor's leadership was becoming increasingly difficult. It was time to end the charade. As the wind fluttered her hair, now released from its daytime confinement and flowing over her shoulders, she allowed herself a widening smile. She now knew her next step on the march to consolidating power over Akkalla. She would share it with Vice Brigadier Hhayd first thing in the morning, and he would support it fully.

As usual, she would offer him no choice.

Chapter Five

SULU TAPPED THE code keys and the food synthesizer obliged by delivering his breakfast order within seconds. He glanced around the mess lounge, trying to decide where to sit.

Seena Maybri waved from a table in a cool grove of miniature evergreen trees and Sulu ambled over to join her.

"Good morning," he said, looking at her tray. "You're almost done. You must've been the first person up this morning."

"I'm having so much fun doing this evaluation," she said, beaming. "I just can't wait to get back to it once each shift is over."

"I'll bet you've been working on your time off, too."

"I have not!" she protested—then shrugged meekly. "Well, maybe a little. I just want to impress the admiral."

"And what's that you're drinking—?"

"Oh, nothing special," she said, cupping a protective hand over her mug.

He leaned closer to her tray and sniffed.

She knew her face was darkening to a medium red and she confessed. "Oh, all right—it's chocolate milk. This is your fault, Sulu—you got me addicted!"

"Ahhh, but what a wonderful addiction," he chuckled.

She sipped the drink with a vaguely guilty expression in her eyes. Then she brightened. "I have to beam back down to the science outpost today. Some more data I need."

"By yourself?"

"Mm-hmm."

"Well, Admiral Kirk must be impressed *already*. He

usually doesn't give people on their first assignments so much independence. When do you expect to be finished with the evaluation?"

"Tomorrow. Then I hope I'll have a chance to do some research of my own. Akkalla's such an interesting planet."

"'Interesting' is one way to describe it," Sulu said, a dubious scowl creasing his forehead.

Maybri bit her lower lip and her hair tufts quivered. "Oh, Sulu, I'm sorry. I feel so dumb sometimes. I'm so wrapped up in my first big assignment, I almost forgot about Mr. Spock and Chekov."

"That's okay. You've got your job to do, and that's what you should be thinking about."

"But it was supposed to be their job. Any signs of them at all?"

He shook his head and sighed. "But if they didn't break up in space, if they made it to Akkalla, I'm sure they're alive. And if they're alive, we'll find 'em. Admiral Kirk won't leave here until we do. I *know* that."

Elbows propped on the dark wood table, Brigadier Vvox peered past her steepled fingers at the topmost of the Yome game stand's seven circular platforms. On each level, multiple geometric playing pieces stood in adjacent triangles marked on the platforms, which in turn pivoted off a central support post.

"Sometimes I think you like playing that damn Yome game more than you like making love to me," Rrelin Hhayd huffed as he entered Vvox's office.

"Sometimes I do," she said, without shifting her gaze from the seventh level. Her hand snatched a piece like a hunting animal pouncing on its prey and moved it to the next platform down. "Your move," she said with a satisfied smile.

"Considering." The metallic-voiced reply came from a computer console the size of a fat book, resting on the table next to the game pedestal.

"It's a shame computers don't have facial expressions. I'd love to see how annoyed this one is right now," she said to her adjutant as he sat in the chair next to her.

"Was that a good move?"

"If you knew anything about Yome, you'd know it was an excellent move."

Hhayd shrugged. "Too many rules to remember. Just don't have the patience for it."

"I know. Sometimes I wonder about that. Patience is more than a virtue for a military leader. It's a necessity."

"That's debatable. But you've got enough for both of us."

Vvox shook her head. "No, it's not debatable, Rrelin. Patience is what gives you the strength to pause before striking at an enemy—to weigh the advantages and the dangers, to foresee the consequences and be prepared so you're never surprised. This morning's little action, for instance. Is it done?"

He nodded. "Kirk will have a little trouble locating his Federation scientists today."

"Good."

"Now," he said, "we get to see just how good you are at predicting consequences."

The *Enterprise* looped around Akkalla in a lazy elliptical orbit, and Uhura had come to the decision that planets without much surface land mass got boring to the eye pretty quickly. She'd seen quite a few worlds over the years from her post at the starship's communications console, and her artful sensibilities hadn't dulled in that time. She was still able to appreciate nature's handiwork in the intricate sculpture of a coastline, or chains of islands, or the endlessly swirling kaleidoscopic clouds shrouding the gas giants. But Akkalla was an unremarkable blue-gray ball, and she'd begun to ignore its presence on main viewer. In idle moments, she wondered if she'd even notice if the planet suddenly disappeared from the screen.

This, however, was not an idle moment as the turbolift doors whooshed open and Kirk strode onto the bridge. "Uhura, has Lieutenant Maybri checked in?"

"Yes, sir. She's ready to beam down when you give the order."

"Good. At least we can get this evaluation over with today." He pressed a comm button on the command chair armrest to activate shipwide page. "Lieutenant Maybri, report to the transporter room, please." He turned back to

Uhura. "Commander, get me Dr. McPhillips down at the science station, please."

"Aye, sir." Her graceful fingers skipped across the console. *"Enterprise to Dr. McPhillips—"*

Kirk waited expectantly as Uhura tried several frequencies. "Problem?"

"No response, sir."

Kirk leaned one foot on the step up to the outer bridge level. "Can you tell if it's an equipment problem?"

"Everything's working at our end, and the transmission is being received at their end. It's a clean signal, too, no interference or jamming."

"Then there's nobody there to receive it."

Sulu half turned from the helm console. "Admiral, do you still want Maybri beaming down there?"

"Good point. But none of your business, Mr. Sulu. Mind your station."

"Sorry, sir. I just meant—"

"I know—friendly concern's not a court-martial offense." Kirk hit his intercom switch again. "Security. Have two guards report to the transporter room and accompany Lieutenant Maybri to the planet." He changed channels. "Transporter room, is Maybri there yet?"

The transporter officer, a felinoid ensign, flattened her whiskers as she extended a clawed finger toward the intercom button. "Yesss, she's here, sirrr."

"Lieutenant—"

Before Kirk could continue, the transporter room doors snapped open and two security officers entered, a man and a woman. Maybri had seen them around the ship but didn't know either one by name. The man was a baby-faced ensign with shoulders broad enough to fill the doorway.

"Are you Maybri?" the woman asked, her voice a musical lilt. She had mahogany skin, elegant cheekbones, and short frizzy hair. "I'm Lieutenant Santana. Admiral Kirk's ordered us down to Akkalla with you."

Maybri's tall ears perked to full height. "Admiral!"

"Yes, lieutenant, are you still there?"

"Why are you sending two security people to nursemaid me? I think I've proven that—"

"Lieutenant, we can't—"

"I've proven that I'm—"

"*Lieutenant, I'm trying to—*"

"—completely capable of doing my—"

"*Lieutenant Maybri,*" Kirk roared, "*shut up and listen. That's an order.*"

Stunned, the young Erithian fell back an involuntary step. "Yes, sir," she peeped.

"*Now, then—except for this regrettable tendency to not let your commanding officer get a word in edgewise, you have done a capable job. But that's not the issue. We haven't been able to establish contact with the science outpost. Considering the unstable political situation down there, it's very possible something serious has taken place.*"

"Like what, sir?" asked Maybri, her voice barely audible.

"*Well, Maybri, I don't know. Which is why I'm going against my first inclination to keep you aboard ship and send just a security team. I've decided I want your assessment of the situation down there, whatever you find.*"

Maybri bounced excitedly on her toes. "Thank you, sir. I'll do my best."

"*You're in charge of the landing party, lieutenant. That means you're responsible for your safety and theirs.*"

The security ensign leaned over to Santana's ear. "That means we could be in trouble," he murmured with a rough Slavic accent.

"*You're not to leave the outpost compound without my express orders. Check out the lab first—unless there's immediate danger. In that case, beam back up instantly. Do I make myself clear?*"

Maybri and the two guards materialized in a courtyard about fifty meters from the lab building, on the side away from the waterfront where previous anti-Federation demonstrations had taken place. Misty raindrops danced on the breeze as if uncertain whether to fall or simply fly. There was no activity around the outpost, at least none that could be seen from their beam-down position.

"Let's check around this way," Maybri suggested, leading Lieutenant Santana and Ensign Vlastikovich down the path that led to the docking area and the seawall. The security officers took phaser pistols out and held them at the ready.

But no arms were needed. They poked their heads around

the corner of the building to survey the waterfront and found no one there. No boats either. Nothing.

"Hey, Maybri," Santana prompted, "aren't you forgetting something?"

The Erithian's saucer eyes darted in sudden panic. "I am?"

Vlastikovich raised his gravelly voice an octave. "'I'll check in as soon as—'"

"—as we beam down," Maybri finished. "Oh, lords!" She snapped open her communicator. "Maybri to *Enterprise.*"

"Kirk here. Report."

"Well, there's nothing suspicious outside, sir. No activity at all. Doesn't look like anybody's here. No boats docked. Should we check inside now?"

"At your discretion, lieutenant. Be careful."

Suddenly feeling like a commander, Maybri straightened confidently. "Aye, sir. Landing party out." She glanced at the guards flanking her. "You heard him. Let's get to it."

They approached the lab entrance at a front corner of the sturdy stone outpost building and found the door hanging off its hinges. The warning sign gave Maybri's skin a tinge of shading, but she forced down her own sense of foreboding.

"Somebody obviously didn't believe in knocking," Vlastikovich said. The door was jammed, and he shouldered it open with a grunt, revealing a dark staircase spiraling up.

Santana swung her flashlight toward the top and took the lead, making her way slowly. Their boot heels clanged on the metal step plates, so sneaking up was out of the question. When they reached the top, Santana was the first to peer around the corner, into the lab area. She let out a low whistle as she pocketed her light.

"Wow. Whoever didn't believe in knocking didn't believe in cleaning up, either."

"Let me see," Maybri said, stumbling at the top step and bumping into the guards. When she'd steadied herself, they parted shoulders and she squeezed through. "Oh—"

The main lab looked like a Chorymi harvest ship had blasted through it. Furniture was upended, expensive equipment dismembered, computer data cassettes tossed everywhere. Maybri wasn't prepared for anything like this, and she fumbled for her communicator. "Landing party to *Enterprise,*" she said, voice and ear tips quivering in unison.

"Kirk here. Report, lieutenant."

She swallowed to moisten her mouth. "It's a mess, Admiral. Somebody ripped the place apart."

"Are you all right?"

"Yes, sir, we're fine." She realized what he might really have meant, and took a chance at second-guessing him. "If you meant me, I'm okay, sir."

"I had a hunch you would be, Maybri. Is the situation immediately dangerous?"

"I don't think so, sir." She looked at her escorts for concurrence. Vlastikovich gave her a thumb's-up signal as he and Santana searched the lab and adjoining rooms. "I'll put one guard on lookout while we dig through for anything useful."

"Make it fast, lieutenant. I don't want to lose any more people."

Dammit all! Kirk thought as he hunkered down in the command chair, arms folded and legs crossed. The turbolift doors hissed open, and McCoy stepped out, taking up his accustomed position behind the center seat.

"Maybri just called," Kirk said. "The lab's been trashed."

"You think Preceptor Kkayn lied to us about the Collegium's people being responsible for harassing McPhillips's team?"

"Got any other strong suspects? I'm open for suggestions, Bones."

"Well, I don't trust anybody we've met from the government."

"You're a perceptive man, McCoy." Kirk unfolded himself and vaulted up to the turbolift. As the doors whooshed open, he paused only long enough to tell Uhura, "Call Maybri and tell her I'm beaming down for a look at the damage."

Uhura started to reply, then frowned and raised a hand to her earpiece. "Admiral, I'm picking up—" Her voice trailed off.

He came over to her station. "What is it?"

"It's over. I was monitoring planetary channels, and someone broke into the government broadcast and commandeered the frequency."

"Play it back."

The communications officer recalled the recording from her computer file, and the blank viewscreen above her station came to life with still images of Dr. McPhillips and her two staff members, followed by the emblem of the Collegium. An angry male voice spoke with purposeful intensity: "These are the offworld contaminants posing as scientists. They are enemies of Akkalla, and they've been placed under people's arrest by the concerned scientists of Akkalla. They will be held for people's trial. We will strike more blows for freedom." The picture was replaced by slashes of electronic interference, then a government signal declaring that control of the airwaves had been reestablished.

"Certainly points a finger at the Collegium," McCoy said. "Maybe even a whole hand."

"I'm not so sure." Uhura thoughtfully tapped a fingernail on her console. "Why would they want to reveal their identity?"

"Aye," Scotty added. "Wouldn't that make 'em subject t'immediate arrest?"

"Not if they've already gone into hiding," said McCoy. "Easy enough to check on that, Jim."

"I plan to, Bones. If they *have* gone into hiding, we know who's got our people. Maybe Spock and Chekov, too. And if they're not hiding, then the Collegium may not be responsible for what we just saw, and somebody transmitted that as a hoax."

"Which leaves us where?" McCoy said. "Up the proverbial creek."

"We've still got a paddle or two," Kirk cut in. He turned to the blond ensign subbing at Spock's science post. "Greenbriar—"

"Greenberger, sir."

"Right. How are you at detective work, ensign?"

"Like a terrier, sir. I don't give up."

"Good. Take Uhura's recording and run every kind of analysis you and the computer can think of. I want to know everything possible about that transmission. Rip it apart, and maybe we can get some hints as to where it came from."

"Yes, *sir.*"

Uhura keyed a series of switches on her panel to patch her station into the science post. "Data transferred, sir."

"Contact the landing party. Tell them we're beaming them up now."

In the Collegium's conference chamber, Llissa Kkayn and her Council of Senior Guides sat around the oval table—except for Eddran, whose short legs propelled him from one end of the room to the other like a manic wind-up toy.

"We didn't do it," he railed, "but everyone will think we did, so what's the difference? Maybe we *should* join the damn Cape Alliance! As long as we're going to be executed for high treason, it might as well be for acts we've actually committed! It's a plot—a plot hatched by our scummy Publican and his military monsters. I warned and warned and warned, and did any of you listen to me? No!" He halted and struck a challenging pose, his beak of a nose stuck up in the air. "What are we going to do?"

Ssuramaya's dark skin glistened. "You can't be serious about us joining the rebels, Eddran."

"Why not?" asked Ossage, eyelids drooping enough to make him appear ready to nap. "We're running short of alternatives. Eddran's right about this much—our survival may be on the line any time now."

The old man, Nniko, thumped his walking stick impatiently on the floor. "We're in trouble—there's no doubt of that. But how we react may decide the future of the Collegium for all time to come."

"Nniko is correct," Rraitine said softly, smoothing her silvered curls. "Our own survival may very well be called into question, but the survival of this institution is also our responsibility."

"Yes, yes," Ssuramaya agreed with a vigorous nod. "We mustn't do anything to tarnish Collegium. Political crises come and go. But this place must last forever. It is a jewel, and we are its guardians."

"That's very picturesque," Eddran sneered. "But high-flown words won't save our behinds. And if we're dead, then nobody's going to be left to protect this so-called jewel. The time's come to fight. Others have already paved the way. If we join them, we might have the strength to save Akkalla from the madmen in the Tower."

Ttindel pointed a pudgy hand at Preceptor Kkayn. "Llissa, nothing to say?"

She stood. "I'll be in my apartment, reaching a decision. We'll reconvene here in three hexos—and vote then on my recommendation."

Eddran pounded on the table. "What if we disagree with your recommendation?"

"Then I'll resign, and you can pick a new preceptor."

Stunned silence for a moment, then chaotic argument, with her allies pleading for Llissa to stay no matter what and her opponents protesting her timing. Eddran's voice sliced the din: "You should resign *now!*"

It was the last thing Llissa heard as she marched out of the conference chamber.

Walking briskly, she went directly to her suite in a wing of the main building, passing through dark-paneled corridors decorated with paintings of past Collegium leaders and the school as it grew over the years. She reached her hand-carved door, burst through, and slammed it shut behind her. With a strangled snarl of frustration, she threw her ceremonial cloak in a heap on the patterned rug and slumped into the cushions of her couch. Then she heard a tentative rap on the door.

"Go away."

"I can't," came the muffled reply. It was Mmaddi, her young attendant. "It's . . . it's very important, Llissa."

The door creaked, and a fringe of frizzy amber hair edged in. Then came the pale face, eyes wide with worry. Mmaddi stopped there, poised in the tiny crack of an opening.

"The *Enterprise* is calling you."

For an uncomprehending moment Llissa remained anchored. Then she bolted from the couch to an ornate cabinet and slid aside the front panel, revealing a communications unit, incongruously modern in a room decorated with antiques and dominated by bookcases filled with ancient volumes. "Come in. Close the door."

Mmaddi did as she was told, darting over to watch as Llissa pressed a power button and the viewscreen glowed ghostly blue. Then James Kirk appeared. Llissa was relieved to find no fury in his expression, just a terse glare.

"Admiral Kirk."

"Preceptor Kkayn." He dipped his head for an instant of minimal politeness.

108

She decided to take the offensive and felt an astonishing sang-froid considering the circumstances. *The peace of the innocent?* she wondered. *Or of the lamb resigned to slaughter?* "You saw the phony broadcast?"

"Phony? So you deny your people had anything to do with it, or with kidnapping our scientists?" His tone was flat and careworn.

"I told you before—we're not terrorists. We're teachers and researchers and students. We don't study abduction and explosives here." Llissa took a deep breath. Mmaddi drew closer, and Llissa glanced her way long enough to offer a reassuring nod. "Look, Admiral, we can claw each other for hours, but it's not going to get us anywhere. You don't believe me when I say the Collegium had nothing to do with the disappearance of your scientists, and I don't know whether to believe you when you tell us you're not here for purposes of military intimidation. Meanwhile, since the moment we met, things have gotten much worse for both of us. Can we agree on that much?"

Kirk managed a gallows smile. *"I suppose."*

Mmaddi was at Llissa's ear now. "What're you going to do?" she whispered.

"Don't worry," Llissa murmured, then addressed Kirk again. "As your Dr. McCoy would say, the logical thing for us to do is find some common ground."

"It would . . . thrill McCoy to know you prize his devotion to logic," said Kirk. *"How do you propose we find this common ground?"*

"A meeting, just the two of us. I trust my own instincts, Admiral."

"All right. It's your idea, preceptor. There's no neutral turf to meet on—your Collegium or my ship?"

"I don't think it's safe for you to come here."

"You're willing to come aboard the Enterprise?"

"I trust you that much. And I've never been on a starship. I'm an educator—this should be educational."

"Llissa!" Mmaddi hissed in alarm. "How can you—"

Llissa silenced her with a sharp look. "If anyone asks where I am, *don't tell them.*" She held Mmaddi by her shoulders and gazed into the girl's fearful eyes. "Sometimes you have to go where you'd never dream of going to *save* your dreams. Do you understand that, Mmaddi?"

"Not . . . not really."

"Well, I'm not sure I do, either. If this all works out, maybe we both will." Llissa turned back to the viewer. "I'm ready, Admiral Kirk. Uh, how does this work now? What do I have to do?"

"Nothing. Just stand close to your comm unit. We've already locked onto your coordinates. You've never traveled by transporter before?"

"No."

Kirk smiled. *"Well, you're in for another educational experience, then."*

For the moment, Llissa forgot about their dispute and felt herself enveloped in the anticipation of a new adventure. "What does it feel like?"

"A tingling sensation. Rather pleasant, actually . . . Ready?"

Llissa Kkayn nodded. "Ready."

Too amazed to be frightened, Mmaddi watched as her mentor turned to glittering bits that danced and shimmered with a brilliance that first made her blink, then faded to a glowing outline . . . then were gone! Llissa didn't have to worry—Mmaddi wouldn't tell anyone where the preceptor had gone. She wouldn't know where to begin.

—and in a subjective instant Llissa found herself in the transporter chamber of the *Enterprise.* Kirk stepped around the control console to greet her with an outstretched hand that also served to help her down to the deck. The assistance was welcome, since she felt a flush of disorientation and nearly missed the step.

"Happens to everybody." He smiled. "Welcome to the *Enterprise.*"

"Thank you, Admiral Kirk."

He turned to the transporter technician. "Ensign, no one is to know Preceptor Kkayn's come aboard."

The technician purred and flicked her whiskers. "Yesss, sirrr."

"This way, preceptor." He led her out, and they followed the curving corridor to a small briefing room. The doors slid shut behind them, and they sat at opposite sides of the table. "I thought you might want to keep this a secret visit."

110

"I appreciate that. Although, frankly, who knows if I'll ever see the inside of a starship again? Unless we end up at each other's throats, I'm probably going to want a more extensive tour before you transport me home."

"My pleasure. Can I offer you something to eat or drink?"

"Yes. Thank you."

Kirk moved to the food synthesizer outlet and punched in. The lid retracted, revealing a tray that held a pot with steam venting from its spout, a pair of cups, and a platter with assorted pastries and fruit sections. "This is tea. We've always considered it to be a civilized drink, so I thought it would set the proper tone," he said, carrying the tray to their table.

He poured and sat down again, this time next to her. She lifted her cup for a toast. "Then here's to civilized discourse, Admiral Kirk."

"Civilized discourse." They clinked their cups together, and she started to sip. "Wait," he blurted. "Better let it cool off—"

Her eyes widened as the boiling liquid burned her mouth.

"Sorry," Kirk said. "I should've told you tea is served very hot."

With arched brows, she bit off a small chunk of danish. "'Starfleet Admiral Scalds Educator,'" she quoted, as if reciting a headline. Kirk smiled sheepishly. "Well. 'Starfleet Admiral'—how do we stop arguing?" Llissa asked.

"I suppose we both have to offer some proof of our positions."

She spread her hands in supplication. "I don't have any tangible proof to show you. All I can do is let you read the history of the Collegium, if you want to see what we've been standing for these past five hundred years."

"I'd like to see that history—but just out of curiosity," Kirk said. "You weren't in hiding when I contacted you, and you were willing to come up to my ship. That's proof enough for me."

"Well, that's a relief—but don't expect me to let *you* off that easily."

"What would make you believe that the Federation science team wasn't in collusion with the Publican and the government?"

"I'm not sure. I mean, this isn't a court of law. Maybe if I had some idea what they were working on."

"Well—" He snapped his fingers and reached for the tabletop intercom. "Lieutenant Maybri, report to the admiral in briefing room 6B." He clicked it off. "Whatever we know about their work, you'll know. I just hope that's enough."

"So do I. You and the *Enterprise* can leave Akkalla any time you want. But I can't, Admiral Kirk. This is my home, and the Collegium's been my whole life. Whatever's going on there, we have to beat it—or it's going to beat us."

"You're right about one thing—this ship *can* leave Akkalla whenever I give the order. But I won't do it until I find out what's happened to my two officers and those three scientists."

"Maybe we've just stumbled onto that common cause."

The hatch swished open, and Lieutenant Maybri rushed in, skidding to a stop as she took in the unexpected scene—Admiral Kirk hosting some sort of tea party. "Sir?"

"Ah, Lieutenant Maybri, this is Llissa Kkayn, preceptor of the Akkallan Collegium."

"Preceptor."

"When my two officers turned up missing, she stepped in and took charge of evaluating the Federation science outpost." He noticed that the young officer was still standing stiffly, and he motioned to a chair. "Lieutenant, what's the status on that report?"

"The preliminary report's done, sir. I wanted to ask Dr. McPhillips and her staff a few more questions and get some fill-in data before going to the final. That's when, well, we found the outpost the way it is now."

"I'd like Preceptor Kkayn to see the report."

"Here?" Maybri nodded toward the computer console built into the end of the table.

"Here." Kirk pushed his chair back. "Preceptor, if you'll move down to the computer—"

The Akkallan sat in the end chair as Maybri and Kirk stood behind her.

"Computer on," Maybri said.

"Working," the terminal replied.

"This is Lieutenant Seena Maybri, requesting access to work file EVAL-one-double-A. Verify security voice lock."

Console lights blinked in code sequence. *"Verified. Access approved."*

"Display preliminary report draft." As the first words of the report flashed onto the screen, Kirk leaned forward.

"If you don't mind, I'm going to read with you," he said. "This is my first time seeing this report. And I'd like you to stick around, lieutenant, just in case we have any questions."

"Aye, sir."

They skimmed the dossier with hardly a comment—until they reached the paragraph headed *New Life Form*. After descending into a progressively deeper slouch, Kkayn sat upright as if she'd been jolted by an electrical charge and gaped at the screen. With suddenly intensified interest, she studied every word, backtracking and rereading sections like she was trying to commit them to memory, mumbling repetitively all the while: "This is amazing . . . I just don't believe it . . ."

Finally, she swiveled away from the computer. "How long have you known about this suspected new life form?"

Kirk nibbled on his lip. "McPhillips mentioned it when we first met with her a couple of days ago. But we didn't know any details. Maybri, where did you get all this extra background?"

"From their files, sir. At first, I wasn't sure how much bearing it had on the evaluation. But they kept shoving me in that direction, so I really dug into it. Even though they don't have hard proof, what they did have was enough to convince me it was important, maybe more important than anything else they've done since they came to Akkalla."

Llissa Kkayn turned somber. "We never discussed this with your scientists. It never came up in the three meetings we had."

"I know that," said Kirk.

"Then how did they find out?"

Maybri's ear tips curled inquisitively. "I don't understand. What do you mean, how did they find out? How did they find out *what?*"

"About our secret work."

"Your secret work?" said Kirk.

"It's a long story, but for quite some time Akkallan scientists have been exploring the possibility that there's a

113

mysterious life form in our oceans. Damn! Why didn't Dr. McPhillips and her people ever talk to us about this?"

"They wanted to, but they were led to believe you Collegium scientists resented their just being on your planet."

"What gave them that idea?"

"What else were they supposed to think, with all the obstacles you put in the way of building a strong cooperative relationship?"

"Obstacles—"

"Obstacles—requiring a detailed agenda in advance, then canceling outright—"

"*They* did that, not us—"

Kirk and Llissa fell silent as they belatedly realized what should have been evident before. Kirk gave himself a mental kick for losing his sense of perspective. "Who told you McPhillips wanted agendas?"

Her mouth set in a grim line, Llissa shook her head. "The government science office—the buffer between us and the Federation outpost."

Kirk nodded. "And unless I'm already senile, they're the same people who told McPhillips *you* were being obstinate."

"I think we've finally settled our differences, Admiral. The question is, is it too late to do anything about it?"

"As my science officer is fond of saying, there are always possibilities. Especially now that we can stop fighting each other and pool our resources."

"That may not be so easy." Llissa paced near the computer. "This fake government broadcast today has really split the Collegium Council. The only hope I have of pulling them back together is to prove that your outpost was working on the same suspicions we were."

Maybri tilted her head. "Isn't this report enough for that?"

"I wish I could say yes. But I'm just not sure. If we could get some harder data, some maps, some artifacts—"

"Maybe we can," Maybri said. "Sir, we didn't have enough time to search every corner of the lab. Let me go back."

"That suggestion doesn't thrill me, lieutenant."

114

"But," Llissa interjected, "as Dr. McCoy would say, it is logical."

Maybri blinked in confusion. "As . . . Dr. *McCoy* would say?"

"It's a long story, lieutenant." Kirk stood. "As for going back to the lab, we'll go with you."

The landing party beamed into the deserted science lab. Kirk sent Santana and Vlastikovich outside on patrol, while Uhura attempted to crack the lab's secure computer memory banks. Then he, Maybri, and Llissa split up to comb the place for more physical evidence. They searched everywhere, sought out secret caches, pried up floorboards, but their efforts proved futile.

Until Maybri's silky voice sang out: "Bones!"

Kirk and Kkayn found her wedged into a tiny space beneath a sink.

"Uh, I could use a little help getting out of here."

Only her boots stuck out, and Kirk grasped her ankles, maneuvering carefully, inching her out of a long storage cabinet under a work counter. Once freed, she proudly displayed her treasure: a pair of brown bones in a protective wrap.

Kirk helped her up. "Those must be the ones McPhillips told us about."

With care tender enough for saints' relics, Llissa pulled back a corner of the wrapping. "They look like the ones we have. We figured them to be about nine thousand years old."

Kirk frowned. "But McPhillips told us these were only *ten* years old."

"Then it should be interesting to get these back to Collegium and compare."

"At the risk of offending you, preceptor, we'll probably get a more accurate dating with the equipment aboard the *Enterprise.*"

"That may be true, but my researchers should have the first look. If they believe these are authentic, no matter how old, that'll give you the credibility we'll need for me to persuade my council to join forces with you."

They were interrupted by the insistent beep of Kirk's communicator. He flipped it open. "Kirk here."

"Santana, sir." The security guard's voice was low and urgent. *"A couple of boats just pulled in. They look like military boats—"*

"Take cover and beam up now. Kirk out." He dialed a new frequency. "Everybody pack up. Kirk to *Enterprise*—stand by to beam up landing party—"

McCoy cradled a bone in his long fingers as he hunched over the table in the main briefing room. Kirk, Maybri, and Preceptor Kkayn listened to his conclusions.

"They're from a creature dead about ten years, no sign of unusual disease or fractures, at least in these two bones. Can't very well speak for the rest of the skeleton, wherever it may be. I'd say the owner of these lived in the ocean and died there, too. As for what the owner was, well, I really couldn't even guess, beyond the probability that it was mammalian."

"Doctor," said Llissa, "how much do you think you could tell by comparing these bones with others that I think are similar?"

"Well, that's hard to say. I s'pose we could tell if they came from the same kind of animal, whether they were comparable in age, that sort of thing."

"What about comparing them to the physiology of a living Akkallan?"

"I don't have any data on Akkallans."

"But you *have* a living Akkallan—me. I'm a healthy, typical Akkallan female."

"Would that be worth doing, Bones?" asked Kirk.

"Well, sure it would, Jim. First stop in comparative anatomy is having something to compare to. I won't even charge you for the office visit, preceptor."

The physical didn't take long—McCoy's scanners saw to that. Once the computer had digested the results, Kirk and Maybri reconvened in the doctor's office, where McCoy displayed an assortment of charts, cross-sectional scans, and diagrams on the wall screen over his desk.

"The artwork's great, Bones, but what does it mean?" said Kirk.

The ship's surgeon hefted one of the sample bones. "Well, I could switch this with Llissa's tibia—"

Kirk raised an eyebrow. "First-name basis?"

"Well," Llissa said, "once a man's scanned your innards, you might as well dispense with formalities."

"Okay. What about her tibia?"

"I could replace it with this bone, and she'd never know the difference, except for this one being a little longer than hers. Joint structure's identical."

"Isn't that odd for a bone that's from an unidentified creature you say lived in the ocean?"

"In a word, yes. Can I explain it? No—not yet, anyway."

"Now that we're on the same side, it's time I filled you in on all the pertinent background," Llissa said.

Kirk rubbed his hands together. "Does it clear any of this up, or does it add to the confusion?"

"Both."

"I was afraid of that," McCoy said sourly.

"Some of our scientists believe this new life form is actually something very ancient, something we never knew for sure was real. Until the first evidence was collected, oh, maybe twenty years ago, the common belief was that these things were mythical. They were called Wwafida."

"And now?" Kirk asked.

"Now, a lot of us believe they once existed. We think our nine-thousand-year-old fossils prove that."

Kirk balanced the tibia in his palm. "But this isn't a fossil. This is a contemporary bone."

"Right," Llissa said, her voice rising in excitement. "And if we can match this to the fossils, that could be what we need to prove these creatures are still alive today."

Keeping the bone in his hand, Kirk began to pace. "This—is—getting more complicated by the minute . . . but it's not getting us any conclusive answers to anything! What is so controversial about this mysterious, possibly mythical creature that anybody who knows anything about it gets targeted for destruction?"

Llissa ran nervous hands through her hair, releasing a clasp and letting her dark tresses flow over her shoulders. "The debate over the existence of the Wwafida is the cause of the state of war between Akkalla and Chorym."

McCoy whistled in disbelief. *"Now* we're getting somewhere."

"Keep explaining," Kirk said.

"Some of us believed these creatures may be intelligent.

117

Those who did wanted the Chorymi harvest ships to stop working until we could figure out, one, did these creatures exist, and, two, were they sentient beings. Because if they were really out in the seas swimming free, then their lives were endangered by every harvest."

"Was the Collegium part of that group demanding a halt to the harvests?" Kirk asked.

"Some of our scientists were, along with some independent scientists and politicians."

McCoy took the bone back from Kirk and wrapped it with the other one. "I bet that's where the Cape Alliance came in."

"The Alliance has been around for years, but when the Collegium didn't support their stand against the harvests, that's when they turned really radical and started disrupting the harvests by actually going out in boats."

"What did the Chorymi do?" said Kirk.

"At first, they pulled up in a hurry whenever any surface vessels were in a harvest zone. After all, the harvests were part of a treaty with us, and the Chorymi appealed to our government to get the Alliance to stop interfering with legal harvest work. So the Alliance went underground, and the Publican got the Synod to vote for sweeping military powers to crush the Alliance."

"Obviously," McCoy said, "it hasn't worked."

Llissa shook her head sadly. "No, it hasn't. And everything's been unraveling for the past year or so. The Paladins and the Grolian Guard have more and more power, and under Vvox and Hhayd they abuse it. The Chorymi gave up on Akkalla ever abiding by the treaty, and they started raiding our seas whenever they felt like it. There's nothing the Paladins can do to stop them, and they don't share what they take with us anymore." There was a catch in her voice, and she took a deep breath, trying to hold on to her composure. "The Cape Alliance is crazier than ever, and now my Collegium's practically under siege, probably a step away from all of us being arrested . . . and I don't know what to do about any of this."

McCoy touched her arm, but she brushed the kindly gesture away, spinning to view her reflection off the viewscreen.

"I'm sorry," she said with a desolate sigh. "This is the

first time I've strung all those disastrous events together in one sentence."

Kirk shook his head. "There's something I don't get. Why is the harvest so important to Chorym that they're willing to risk interplanetary war?"

"Well, for one thing, there's not much risk. They're much more advanced than we are, technologically. If there's a war, Akkalla's the battlefield—and we'll lose it."

"Advanced or not," McCoy said, "it seems like an awful lot of trouble to satisfy a yen for seafood."

"Not if you've got no choice. More than a century ago, the Chorymi ignored the fact that their planet's climate was drying out. They just went blithely along, plundering their own resources, in spite of the fact that deserts were advancing all over Chorym. It reached a stage where they were desperate, and our oceans promised salvation. Oh, they'd had interplanetary travel for a long time, and we traded back and forth. But what they proposed went way beyond all that. They presented the idea of building fleets of flying harvest ships. Not only would they split the catch with us, they'd also pay us with the only resource they had left in any abundance."

"What was that?" asked Kirk.

"It happened to be something we needed—rhipileum. It's an energy ore. We have such a small land mass on Akkalla, we don't have a lot of mineral wealth that's readily accessible. So we stumbled along with lagging industrial development. But Chorym's rhipileum was the missing key to our future. Our standard of living jumped ahead at the speed of light, it seemed. We advanced more in the last hundred years than in the previous five hundred. So you can see that it wasn't the popular thing to do, raising difficult questions that might put an end to all that."

"But the questions have already been raised," Kirk said. "Akkalla's not going to be able to run away without answering them."

Llissa nodded, sad resignation in her eyes. "I suppose I've always known that. But it's only in the last few days that I've really accepted it. The answers might destroy Akkallan society as we know it, but that's happening already anyway. If we have to lose everything we've built, I'd rather know it was for the right reasons."

Llissa took a deep breath. "We have to know if these creatures are real and if they're intelligent. And if they are, we'll use the truth to appeal to the people of Akkalla and Chorym. We may have to take our case all the way to the Federation Council, and we'll need the weight of outside authority to win. Admiral Kirk, will you help us?"

Chapter Six

KIRK STOOD BEHIND the transporter console, fingers cupped over the control lever. "I'll give you an answer within the hour."

"And I'll work on softening resistance at my end," Llissa said, taking her position on the platform. She managed a wry half-smile. "I never thought I'd hear myself say this, but you may be our only hope. Now, what is that word?"

"Energize."

"Right. Energize."

His hand moved forward, and the unit hummed to maximum power. Preceptor Kkayn beamed home to face her own set of consequences.

Returning to his cabin, Kirk summoned McCoy, Scott, Uhura, Sulu, and Maybri, filling the office cubicle. The scent from a fresh pot of coffee successfully tempted everyone into taking a cup—except Maybri, who ordered hot chocolate from the food synthesizer, eliciting a smirk from Sulu.

"I wish Spock was here," Kirk said.

McCoy raised an indignant eyebrow. "What're we, chopped liver? And besides, we wouldn't have room for him."

"You're right, Bones. And you're not chopped liver."

"I wish he was here, too," McCoy relented. "That confounded logic does come in handy at certain times."

"Well, Preceptor Kkayn seems to have got the impression you're a logical man, McCoy. Analysis, please?"

"All right, but don't expect me to quote the odds. It comes down to this—we don't have any choice. We have to help Llissa."

"That's a statement," Kirk said. "I asked for analysis."

"Okay. Helping Llissa prove these Wwafida are real may be the only way to pressure the Akkallan government, and that may be the only way to spring the science team. On top of that, it's the right thing to do."

"What about Mr. Spock and Chekov?" Sulu said. "How does this affect our search?"

Kirk nodded. "Relevant question. Opinions?"

"Well, sir," Maybri began, "it may help the search. Cooperating with the Collegium may tie us into new sources of information."

"Besides," McCoy snapped, "I don't think offending the Akkallan government is going to make one damn bit of difference."

Kirk turned to his chief engineer. "Your analysis of the Chorymi vessels, Mr. Scott. Do they pose any military danger to us?"

"Not unless they ram us, sir."

"Uhura, what about the classified data you got from the science outpost?"

"Still descrambling it, Admiral. It's going on simultaneous feed to the science department computer. And it'll be ready to share with the Collegium, if you give the order."

"Good. What about the Prime Directive? Would we be violating it by helping the Collegium prove this life form exists?"

"How would that be interfering with the normal evolution of Akkallan life and society?" McCoy said. "If anything, the government's doing that by obstructing the normal course of scientific exploration."

"Aye, sir," Scott added. "Y'd just be settin' things t'rights."

In turn, each officer nodded as Kirk looked around the room. "Let the chips fall where they may," McCoy said.

"Then that's it. Thank you. Return to your posts."

Everyone left but Dr. McCoy. "Waste of time, Jim."

Kirk responded with a noncommittal shrug.

"You already had your mind made up."

"Nothing wrong with a consensus."

"You turning conservative in your old age?"

Kirk bristled. "Tricky situations require cautious approaches."

On his way to the door, McCoy paused for a glance over his shoulder. "Just so long as caution doesn't evolve into paralysis."

The door hissed shut behind him, leaving Kirk alone. He sat at his desk and swiveled the intercom screen toward him. "Kirk to bridge. Commander Uhura, get me a channel to the Publican. Pipe it down here to my quarters."

The communications officer nodded. *"Aye, sir."* Her face faded from the screen.

As he waited, he thought about McCoy's remark. *Am I getting old and cautious? Years ago, would I have done this any differently? Am I less bold—or more wily? I'd like to think I've learned a few more tricks over the years. Or have I just learned to sidestep confrontations? It's results that count, isn't it, McCoy? Damn you—where the hell are you when I want to argue with you? Or do I want to argue . . . had my chance before you walked out that door. Am I smart enough to know I don't have to fight every time someone throws down a gauntlet, or just too tired to be able to?*

"Bridge to Admiral Kirk." Uhura appeared on the viewer.

"Go ahead, commander."

"Uh, it's not the Publican, sir."

Kirk scowled. He wasn't surprised. "Vvox?"

"Aye, sir."

"All right." He squared his shoulders as the image onscreen changed to the Akkallan brigadier in what Kirk guessed to be her Citadel office. The wall behind her bore an impressive display of martial cutlery. "Brigadier Vvox, I asked to speak to the Publican."

"He's unable to talk to you, Admiral. He's occupied with the current crisis. I've been given full authority to represent Akkalla in diplomatic matters."

Kirk stifled the urge to cut the transmission right then and there. "Then I'll make this as brief as possible. Have you found our missing shuttlecraft?"

"No. No sign of it. I'm sorry to have to conclude that it's probably at the bottom of the ocean."

Out of reflex, Kirk felt his teeth gritting. "Are you continuing to look?"

"Our military resources are required for more pressing matters. Was there anything else?"

"We request permission to start our own search."

123

"Permission denied."

"On behalf of the Federation, I'm appealing to you to ease up on your crackdown on the scientists of the Collegium."

A flash of anger sparked in Vvox's eyes. *"Our internal affairs are no concern of yours."*

"They are when they endanger people I'm responsible for."

"What people?"

"The scientists from the outpost and my missing crew members."

"We searched for your crew members. A complete report on our efforts is being written up. I've certified it myself, and a copy will be waiting for you if you'd care to pick it up. As for the science outpost, those researchers were taken prisoner by the renegades from the Collegium. The only way we can hope to liberate them is to crush the movement to overthrow the Akkallan government. And that's what we're doing, Kirk. If we find any of your missing people, and they're still alive, they'll be returned to you as soon as we're satisfied they're not involved in crimes against the state."

"And what if you decide they *were* involved in alleged crimes?"

"They'll be tried—and if they're found guilty, it'll be up to the Synod to decide their sentence. They could be executed."

"Now just a minute, brigadier, that would be a serious breech of—"

Vvox interrupted. *"That wouldn't be a breech of anything, Admiral. You know as well as I do that it's standard practice for offworlders to be subject to the laws of whatever planet they happen to be on."*

"Is that your final position?"

"Yes, it is."

"Then you leave me no choice but to file an official diplomatic protest with your government and the Federation Council. You and your Publican better be prepared to take the brunt of Federation sanctions."

"Good-bye, Admiral Kirk."

And Vvox's image abruptly went to black, leaving Kirk sputtering, without even having had the satisfaction of terminating the argument from his end. Before he could turn down the flame under his simmering anger, an intense Sulu appeared on the desktop screen.

"Sir, we've found something."

"The *Cousteau?*"

"I think so. Greenberger's confirming now."

"On my way up. Kirk out."

By the time he reached the bridge, a schematic of the planet's surface was already displayed on the main viewscreen. Sulu and Ensign Greenberger huddled at Spock's science station, and Kirk joined them there.

Sulu pointed at the map on the viewer. "There, Admiral —that coastal island."

Kirk squinted at a flashing pinpoint on the ocean side of a fair-sized island off the continent's southwest shore. "What exactly have we found?" he asked carefully.

"The *Cousteau,*" Greenberger answered. "As far as I can tell from sensor readings, she's washed up on the beach, completely nonfunctional, no power readings at all."

"Any signs of life?"

"Just indigenous flora and fauna, sir," the young science officer said. "No humanoids nearby."

"What about on the rest of the island?"

"Still scanning, sir. There are some larger primates in the jungle that show up at first glance as very similar to humanoid. That slows the process down a bit."

Kirk sat in the command chair, hands clasped. "At least we've got a focus for the search. Direct all scanners to bear on that island."

"Already done that, sir."

"Good, Ensign Greenberger. You've earned your pay for the week. Mr. Sulu, are you familiar with the terrain?"

"As much as possible from sensor sweeps, sir."

"That'll have to do. Get a detailed topographical record from Greenberger and equip a landing party—you, two security guards, and Dr. Chapel, in case you find survivors in need of medical care."

The four starship officers materialized on the beach of Shiluzeya, about fifty meters from the shuttle wreck. Under threatening, iron-gray skies, Sulu led them toward the craft, taking out his communicator as he walked. "Landing party to *Enterprise*."

"Kirk here. Report, Sulu."

"She took quite a beating, Admiral." The landing party circled the hulk, with one of the security guards backing off to stand watch and the other forcing the side hatch open and climbing inside. Chapel followed him in.

Sulu ran a hand over a scorched scar on the rear quarter panel. "It looks like they were attacked."

"They must've run into a Chorymi harvest fleet that didn't want spectators."

"That'd be my guess, sir. We'll take careful tricorder readings and some samples of the ship's skin for analysis—see just what we're up against. From the looks of it, they must've been able to make a controlled emergency landing. The crash damage itself doesn't look that bad."

Christine Chapel and the security guard jumped down from the shuttle, and she flipped open her own communicator. "Admiral, Chapel here."

"Report, doctor."

"We searched the inside of the ship, and there's no sign of injury—no blood or used first-aid equipment."

"Does it look like they abandoned ship in an orderly fashion?"

"I'd say so, sir," Chapel replied. "One of the life rafts is missing, and medical and survival gear is gone, too."

"Admiral," Sulu interrupted, "it looks like she took on water, but never enough to sink. The tide must've pushed her here. Tell Greenberger to chart the speed and direction of all the currents that reach this island. In case the black box doesn't have complete data, then we'll at least be able to estimate where they originally landed. Anything else we should search while we're here?"

"Negative, commander. Greenberger hasn't turned up anything on concentrated sensor scans of your area. Just make complete tricorder readings, get the black box, and beam up as quickly as possible."

Kirk pivoted his seat to face McCoy leaning on the railing behind him. "If it's not bad news, then it's good news."

McCoy summoned an unconvincing half-smile. "At least

126

we know they were alive when they landed. Knowing Spock and Chekov, I'd say that's as good as a guarantee that they're still alive . . . somewhere."

"Admiral," Uhura said, "Preceptor Kkayn is contacting us."

"Onscreen, commander." Kirk and McCoy both faced the small viewer above the communications console as Llissa's face appeared.

"Good news," she said. *"My council has invited you here to meet with them. And this gives me a chance to return the favor to you and Leonard and show you around my territory."*

Shaded by dappled patterns from shafts of light flowing through the skylight, Llissa waited for Kirk and McCoy in the rotunda of the library wing. She scuffed a toe in the thick nap of the blue carpeting, then looked up as she heard the sound of transporter beams and saw two shimmering silhouettes take shape.

"Admiral—Leonard—welcome to Collegium."

"Thank you," said Kirk.

McCoy didn't reply; he was occupied craning his neck for a look around the high dome, following the beams of light from vaulted ceiling to floor. "Wow . . . this looks like some kind of cathedral."

"In a way, I guess it is," Llissa said. "A cathedral to learning and science, dedicated to the future. Come this way."

They followed her through the rotunda and down a short hallway leading to the conference chamber. Pushing open the heavy, carved-relief doors, she motioned them in ahead of her, to be greeted by faces with varied reactions: Ttindel and Ossage impassive; Eddran openly hostile; Nniko and Rraitine hopeful; and Ssuramaya radiant.

"My fellow Guides," Llissa announced, "I present Admiral James Kirk and Dr. Leonard McCoy from the starship *Enterprise,* two men who've proved to me that sometimes you really *can* trust offworlders."

Later, Llissa walked between Kirk and McCoy down the paneled gallery, with paintings arranged on both walls. "I hope that wasn't too painful," she said.

"Well," McCoy drawled, "it could've been worse. Nobody chucked any rotten fruit at us."

"Under the circumstances," Kirk offered, "I guess it balanced out. The positive group seemed warmer than the negative group was cold."

Kirk stopped and turned to view the paintings—serious faces staring down from the past and portraits of an island sanctuary growing to greatness with the passage of years.

"This is our rogues' gallery," Llissa said. "I spend a lot of quiet time alone here, sort of communing with the ghosts who founded this place and built it into something singular."

There were no young visages here, just faces worn and creased by work and trial, but seeing through the ages with eyes brightened by wisdom earned from the experiences of lives devoted to a cause. McCoy noticed that Llissa had paused before one painting of a woman with silver-blond hair, regal bearing, and dusky, deep-set eyes. The nameplate at the bottom of the frame said *Kkirin Kkayn*.

"Your mother, Llissa?"

She shook her head, her eyes wistful. "My mother died when I was a girl. This is my grandmother. She was preceptor before me. Of all the people I've known in my life, no one shaped me as much as she did."

McCoy rested his hand on Llissa's shoulder. "She looks like she was a great lady."

"Uh-huh. Probably the best preceptor in Collegium history. She presided over a golden age here, and I'm presiding over the demise of everything she worked to preserve."

With a gentle but insistent touch, McCoy turned her so they faced each other. "If she was the woman you just described, she'd know you were fighting to do just what she did. We haven't known you very long, but I'm a damn good judge of character—right, Jim?"

"Right, Bones."

"And I know you are one formidable lady, Llissa. You got *us* into this, and that was no easy task. And there's something you should know about me and Jim Kirk."

Llissa swallowed and spoke in a hoarse whisper. "What's that?"

"We don't let our friends down, and we don't like to lose. Now, if that's a window over there, and not a painting—"

"It's a window."

"—then we're witnessing something miraculous on this planet of yours—sunshine. Let's go out and enjoy it. You can show us the campus." McCoy linked arms with her and guided her toward the door at the end of the gallery, with Kirk tagging along behind.

Shadows frolicked on the forest floor as sunbeams danced through leaves sighing in the breeze. "Y'know, this place isn't so depressing when it's not rainin'," McCoy grinned, still arm in arm with Llissa, forcing Kirk to follow them on the grassy path.

"We don't think it's depressing when it rains," Llissa said. "Rain is part of the cycle of life on Akkalla. Without it we wouldn't be here."

"Don't get me wrong, Llissa—it's part of my planet's life-cycle too. But to us, rain conjures up songs of lost love and thoughts of dreams unfulfilled."

"Your people are a morbid lot."

"Sometimes."

The path routed them to a clearing where a low building of rough-hewn wood stood. It appeared both old and new at the same time, a dichotomy explained when Llissa told her guests this was the first Collegium building, constructed by hand five hundred years before, now restored to original condition and serving as a museum and study center, preserving the story of the founders along with their handiwork. She took them inside to view shelves of old books and display cases containing documents, tools, and articles from daily life. One special case held a single yellowing scroll, neatly hand-penned in old Akkallan, with a dozen signatures scrawled at the bottom.

"What's this?" McCoy asked, peering through the protective shield over it.

"That's the Charter Compact I told you about."

"Oh, right, the agreement signed by the warlords establishing this island as an educational sanctuary," McCoy said, reciting like a proud schoolboy.

"Funny," Llissa said bitterly, "how easy it is for people to ignore timeless principles when they don't serve their needs."

Kirk looked out a window with a clear view down to the bay, and Llissa joined him, her mood brightening.

"Come outside. I'll show you my favorite place on the entire island."

With Kirk and McCoy in tow, Llissa left the museum and descended the hill to the beach, facing the mainland and the mouth of a river emptying into the harbor.

"That's the Bboun River. When I was a little girl, if nobody could find me anywhere else, my grandmother knew to look for me here. She was the one who first showed me this spot and told me about the Bboun, how it begins in the Ppaidian Mountains all the way on the other side of the continent, just a tiny stream, barely a trickle. And by the time it reaches Havensbay it's a mighty river. She told me that's what Collegium was like—starting with a trickle of knowledge all those years ago, becoming broader and deeper as it flows toward the future. I just hope—"

She was interrupted by shouts from the top of the hill and turned to see Mmaddi running down from the museum.

"Llissa! Llissa! It's happened!" The girl stumbled into Llissa's arms, chest heaving as she tried to catch her breath. Judging by the brambles and leaves tangled in her hair and the scrapes on her face and hands, Mmaddi had rushed headlong directly through the most dense part of the woods.

"What is it, Mmaddi? *What's* happened?"

"Martial law," she gasped, clutching at a stab of pain in her side, nearly doubling over. She allowed McCoy to ease her down to the ground, and her breathing calmed a bit.

"First-stage martial law?" Llissa said.

Mmaddi nodded. "Message . . . message from Hhayd . . . to you. You have to go . . . go back. Need you now!"

"You two go up," McCoy said. "I'll help her back. We'll be right behind you. Jim, if you have to leave without me, don't worry. I've got my communicator."

Without another word or a moment to waste, Llissa and Kirk rushed up the hill and through the woods. When they reached the main library building, they found the members of the Guide Council in the conference chamber. Llissa did a mental count and came up one short.

"Where's Eddran?"

Ssuramaya spat a curse. "He fled like the little coward he is."

130

"Exactly what's going on? Where's Hhayd's message?"

Rraitine handed her a paper with the transcription: *First-stage martial law has been declared this day, by order of Publican Abben Ffaridor. Because of suspected complicity in terrorist actions endangering the duly elected government of Akkalla, Guides and students of the Collegium should consider themselves detained pending arrival of Paladin and Grolian Guard forces to begin questioning. At that time, official arrests may be made. No Collegium personnel are to leave Freeland . . .*

Llissa crushed the paper into a ball and hurled it across the room. "Those bastards. Does anyone else know?"

Leaning on his cane, Nniko shook his head. "We didn't want to cause a panic."

"We can start beaming your people up to the *Enterprise*," Kirk said.

"Admiral, we have two thousand teachers and students here. Hhayd's forces are probably already on their way. There's no way we can organize an evacuation," Llissa said, her fury darkened to sorrow.

"There's got to be a way to get some of you to safety."

"How would we choose? Ssuramaya, make the announcement—*calmly*. Please don't incite a riot. Tell everyone to report to their rooms and stay there until they hear from me."

Ssuramaya's anger smoldered in her eyes, but her voice was docile. "Yes, Llissa." As she left, McCoy and a limping Mmaddi entered.

"Llissa, we discussed this before you came in," Nniko rumbled. "You can't stay here. Go with Kirk."

She stared at the old man. "I have to stay. I'm responsible for this place. When it ends, I have to be here for that ending."

"But we don't know that this is an ending. They can take us all away, but I can't believe they would destroy Collegium itself. No government can last long if it neglects the physical realities of its world. Akkalla will always need science and education if it's to survive."

"Maybe this government doesn't believe that anymore, Nniko. You're counting on rationality. That's been a very rare commodity on Akkalla lately."

"All right," Nniko said, rapping his walking stick on the

table for emphasis. "Say the worst happens. Say they put a torch to this place and burn it to the ground. Nothing left but ashes. That's a sure signal that this tyranny can't last. Someone who remembers what went before has to survive to bring the past to life again, to save the world from having to retrace the whole laborious trail of history."

With fear filling her eyes, Llissa backed away and answered with a vigorous shake of her head. "I can't do that."

"Yes, you can," Rraitine said, her green eyes sparkling with a will to endure. "Some of us will escape this. Some will join the active resistance. Others will simply disappear, drifting to the corners of the continent, hiding in plain sight. And when the time is right, when the call comes, we'll answer it. We'll help you to rebuild."

"And that's only if events take us down the worst road, Llissa. Perhaps they won't—perhaps this is a horror that we can fight . . . overcome it," Nniko said, his tone serene.

Kirk and McCoy had been hovering on the fringe of the Collegium group, listening and observing. Now Kirk stepped forward. "We'll help you fight it. My ship, my crew, and the Federation. But they're right, Llissa, someone from your side has to stay free to coordinate the resistance and guide us. It's your world to save. There's never any guarantee, but you haven't lost yet."

Llissa turned uncertainly, looking at her colleagues. "How will you escape?"

"We have the research subs," Ossage said, his sleepy eyes widening, caught up in the crisis. "We can go up the Bboun, to the badlands."

"And Freeland has beaches to escape from by raft," Ttindel added, hands folded across his bulging belly.

"But rafts and subs—how many of you can get away? And how will you choose who stays and who goes?"

Nniko shrugged. "However many escape is better than none. And as to choosing who goes and who stays, we'll figure out how many spaces we have, and each of us will choose a share. We'll have no time for argument, and instant deadlines do wonders for simplifying a problem."

Rraitine put her arm around Llissa's shoulder. "But *you* have to leave *now*. Go to the starship."

Ssuramaya hurried back into the chamber. "Hhayd's

patrol cutters are coming. We can see them across the bay. Llissa, you've got to get away from here."

"We've already convinced her," Nniko said. "Haven't we?" His white-haired head lowered close to Llissa's face.

The preceptor's lips twitched. "I guess you have."

"It's got to be now, Llissa," McCoy said, his voice soft but insistent.

She nodded, and Kirk snapped his communicator open. "Kirk to *Enterprise*. Three to beam up."

Llissa looked at her old friends. "I don't know if we'll see each other again. There's so much I want to say to you—"

"No time to be verbose," Nniko scolded. "Go, and don't think you're the lucky one. You'll have lots of work to do, all by yourself. Down here, we'll have others around for help. We'll be together again."

As Kirk and McCoy had seen her do before, Llissa Kkayn assumed a regal stance. "Mother Sea protect you all."

"And you," the others replied in a murmured chorus.

Kirk raised his communicator. "Beam us up, Mr. Scott."

With flat prows butting through the receding tide, four Paladin landing craft beached on the sandy shore of Freeland. Vice Brigadier Hhayd shouted an order, and a hundred well-armed troopers in gray-blue fatigues and helmets clambered over the sides and down the front ramps. They formed into small patrol squads, standing at rest until their commandant waded ashore and faced them, a regimental dandy in polished jackboots and black leather gloves, ascot tied at his throat, a pearl-handled dagger on his hip.

"No weapons fired unless they look like they want a fight. My guess is they won't have the stomach for anything serious. When your leaders give the signal, fire over their heads first. They're not soldiers like we are. They're probably running all over in a panic right now. It's likely the only danger to us is in being run over by fleeing academics." He chuckled at his own joke, and a few of the troopers smirked. "We're here to subdue this island and secure it. The prisoners will be held here until the brigadier and the Publican decided what to do with them. Make this operation quick and neat. Now, go—"

In purposeful cadence, the squads marched up the beach

and through the woods. Hhayd took up a position in the middle, using his troopers as a protective buffer.

Once past the barrier forest, the Paladins fanned out to surround the campus buildings. And still no signs of Collegium's inhabitants, only unnerving stillness that made Hhayd wary. *Where are they?*

With a full squad primed for combat, Hhayd entered the main library, strutting through the rotunda to the conference chamber. He threw the doors open and found a group of Guides and students sitting calmly at the table and on the floor.

"Scared rodents in a burrow," he sneered. "Who's in charge here?"

Nniko raised a wizened hand in acknowledgment. "That's me, commandant."

"Name?"

"Nniko."

"Where's the preceptor?"

The old man shrugged with calculated innocence. "Must be here somewhere."

With a swift swing of his arm, Hhayd slammed the butt of his weapon on the table, causing more than a few other people to jump, including a couple of his own troopers.

The commandant spun on his heel and marched out of the chamber. "Keep them here," he barked over his shoulder. "I'll be back."

Mmaddi brushed her auburn hair out of her eyes and tilted her face up to Nniko's. "Ssuramaya and Ossage got away with twenty on the subs," she whispered. "Thirty took the rafts."

The painting had begun as a soothing seascape, rolling breakers caressing a peaceful beach in airy shades of blue. But the more Abben Ffaridor dipped brush to palette, the more he found himself choosing colors that turned the picture dark and melancholy. A few beams of sunlight were overpowered by thunderhead clouds, while the waves grew to malevolent proportions, pounding the beach without mercy.

Ffaridor had retreated to his studio to escape his blackening mood, hoping imagination would free him. Instead, the mood ruled, forcing his hand to translate inner turmoil into

134

tangible representation. He didn't notice Brigadier Vvox come into the studio.

"Cheerful," she said.

With a spasm of startlement, he spun around. "Oh, it's you."

"Who else knows where to find you when you need to get away from problems?" She massaged his neck.

"Have we done the right thing?"

"We did what we had to do to preserve Akkalla."

He shook his head dubiously. "The Synod doesn't agree with that assessment."

"They have no grip on reality the way we do. What're they so mad about? We only declared a first-stage alert. The Synod hasn't been dissolved. They're still part of the government. Let them try to come up with solutions instead of criticizing everything we do!"

Ffaridor held her hands. "Jjenna, I'm surprised at you. Where's the calm, controlled adviser? I don't need the hot-blooded soldier."

"I'm sorry, Abben. But those idiots make me furious."

Choosing one finger at a time, he kissed her hands. "Don't let them. I'll handle them."

After a few quiet moments, she muttered a curse. "Every time discussing the Synod makes me boil over, I forget what I really came to tell you. I have great news."

The Publican's sad eyes opened with anticipation. "What?"

"The interrogation of the terrorists we already have in custody paid off—interrogations *you* didn't want conducted, my love," she admonished.

"I had no objections to interrogation—I prefer the word *questioning*—I just didn't want there to be any torture. These are our own people, for sea's sake, not enemy soldiers."

"That's where you're wrong. They endanger our way of life, they endanger Akkalla itself, and that makes them the enemy. And the methods we use aren't torture. They're simply . . . persuasive."

"Then tell me what you found out."

"Enough to track down a renegade cadre on Shiluzeya. Our catch includes some very special prisoners. I thought you should meet them."

"Here? Now?"

Vvox nodded. "They're downstairs. Take off your smock." She reached around to untie the knot, and he slipped his painter's apron off. They hurried down from the parapet containing his studio and entered the reception room. There, in a corner, were six Grolian Guards circling a pair of bedraggled men in black pants and tattered shirts, not Akkallan dress. Then Ffaridor noticed the taller man had pointed ears. *A Vulcan.*

"These are the two officers from the starship. There names are Spock and Chekov." An arrogant smile danced on her lips. "They may prove to be very useful to us."

Ffaridor drew her aside. "I don't want them tortured," he said, his voice low but firm.

"They won't be hurt, but I have to be able to use all the tools we have to find out what we need to know. They're the commodities we'll need to deal with Kirk if he causes us any trouble. You know how desperate he is to have them back. There's nothing like having what someone else wants to give *you* the upper hand."

A young Tower guard strode into the reception hall, coming to parade stop with an echoing click of his heels. "Commandant Hhayd requests permission to enter."

The Publican opened his mouth to answer, but Vvox spoke first. "Permission granted."

Hhayd, who was waiting just out in the corridor, rushed in and snapped to respectful attention when he saw how many others were already there. With witnesses about, he'd have to abide by military protocol. "Commandant Hhayd reporting, Publican Ffaridor." He cradled a package protectively under one arm.

"Yes, yes, Hhayd. Tell us what happened."

"Mission accomplished at Collegium."

Vvox grinned, but Ffaridor's face reflected a churning mixture of relief and anxiety.

"Any resistance?" asked Brigadier Vvox.

"Some." Hhayd was glad he could lie without blushing. "But we managed to take the island without bloodshed."

"Very commendable, very commendable," said Ffaridor.

"Did you capture Preceptor Kkayn?"

Hhayd averted his gaze from hers for just an instant. "Uh, no. She was nowhere to be found. There's no way she could've escaped. She must not have been on the island when we landed. But she's separated from all the people and facilities at Collegium. Without it, she's got no power or influence. We won't have to worry about her, Publican Ffaridor." He placed his package on a lamp table and started to unwrap it.

"What's that?" Ffaridor asked.

"A special prize." He straightened and held out three fossil bones, turned brown with age. "These are the ones we needed to find. The ones they claim are from the Wwafida."

The Publican gave a snort of contempt. "Wwafida are legends, nothing more, nothing more. Those are obviously fakes."

"But they could still be used to undermine us. Scientific lies perpetrated by determined frauds are the hardest of all to refute," Vvox said. "Destroy them, and the frauds have nothing to base their lies on."

With an emphatic nod, Ffaridor waved Commandant Hhayd from the room. "Yes, yes, yes—destroy them. Do it now."

"Dismissed, commandant," Vvox said. "And I'll see you get a commendation for this mission."

Publican Ffaridor clapped a hand on Vvox's shoulder. "This is a great day for us, brigadier. We'll have to . . . properly note it later on."

"Yes, we will, sir. I'll see to it."

He rubbed his hands together as he strolled back toward the new prisoners. "Now, what to do with these two . . ."

"If I may speak," said Spock.

"Yes, yes, I suppose so. Your name again?"

"Commander Spock, first officer of the U.S.S. *Enterprise.* And, judging by your earlier comments, I deduce that the *Enterprise* is in fact orbiting Akkalla. I request that you return us to our vessel without delay, since we were on a sanctioned mission before being captured by your rebellious Cape Alliance. Your government is required by law to do so."

"Yes, yes, Commander Spock. We, uh, should like to accommodate your request, and we will at the earliest possible moment. But that moment is not yet at hand. You see, as you may have guessed, we are in the midst of a serious crisis on Akkalla—under attack from outside and inside. I'm afraid we're going to have to appeal to you and your colleague for a bit of cooperation. Anything you can tell us about the Chorymi fleet that attacked you and the renegades who took you prisoner would be extremely helpful. I ask you this as the leader of all Akkalla."

Spock's eyebrow lifted consideringly. "May we contact our ship and inform our commanding officer that we are alive?"

"We'll take care of that, commander. We've been in regular contact with Admiral Kirk since he first discovered that you were missing. I know how concerned he and your shipmates are. I'll advise him of your condition myself and ask his permission to debrief you regarding your, uh, unfortunate adventures. Meanwhile, I hope you'll accept my personal hospitality here at the Cloistered Tower. Brigadier Vvox, have these gentlemen shown to guest quarters where they can clean up. Once you're more comfortable, please allow me the honor of having you as my guests for dinner."

"Very well," Spock said. "As long as you inform Admiral Kirk of our status immedately, we accept your invitation."

Vvox pointed to the soldier in charge of the Grolian Guard detail with Spock and Chekov. "Trooper, escort the Publican's guests to the north wing rooms. See that they have whatever they need to freshen up, including some new clothing."

"Yes, brigadier." The guardsman glanced at the starship officers. "This way, please."

With an avuncular smile pasted to his face, Ffaridor watched them and the guards leave. Then he whirled on Vvox. "I know what to do with them," he said, his voice taut with the excitement of a man discovering a new route circumventing disaster.

Vvox's eyes narrowed suspiciously. "What do you mean?"

"I need a way to keep a restless Synod from boiling over and burning me badly. Martial law threatens their power, and you know they'll stand for *anything* but that. It's not enough for me to claim that the Alliance terrorists and the Chorymi bandits are set to destroy Akkalla. Now I can show them that the Federation is against us, too."

"How?"

"By presenting these two starship officers as offworld spies sent to work with the scientists and overthrow the government."

"But the Synod isn't just going to sit there. The over-lords'll want to ask questions. And I don't think Commander Spock is going to stand in front of the Synod and admit that he's a spy."

"Then we don't allow them to ask questions. From the moment we sent them the martial law declaration, the overlords've been demanding that I come down there and explain myself. So now I'll go, and we'll parade these two starship officers as mute evidence." The Publican began to pace, mumbling to himself. "Yes, yes, I see how to do it."

The guest rooms were spacious, with furnishings spare but tasteful. Thick, ornately patterned rugs and vivid tapestries on every wall were the only touches of opulence. Spock lay on the bed, head propped on a pillow and fingers interlaced above his chest, engrossed in contemplating the state of seemingly friendly yet insistent custody in which he and Chekov currently found themselves. They had fallen into the hands of two groups squared off in ever more bitter struggle. Yet, in spite of their distinctly adversarial stance, both sides appeared similarly anxious to utilize a pair of Starfleet personnel for strategic political gain.

On the surface, he and Chekov seemed better off under the protection of their latest benefactors. But logic dictated that such a surface could not be self-supporting. It was more likely a single facet of a polyhedral figure, the totality of which could not be viewed from any one side. He would have to explore it from many vantage points in order to maximize his chances of having sufficient familiarity with it to make informed choices. A knock on the door intruded on the process, and Spock sat up.

"Come in."

The door opened, and Chekov entered, dressed in simple but comfortable slacks and a pullover top. The Russian carried a tray with a decanter of lavender liquid and a pair of cut-crystal glasses. "They left this in my room, sir. I didn't feel like drinking alone."

"If you are asking me to join you in imbibing—?"

Spock motioned him toward a high-backed armchair adjacent to the bed. "Thank you, Mr. Chekov."

They each took a filled glass and Checkov raised his. "To freedom."

"A reasonable dedication," Spock nodded.

Chekov took a tentative sip of his drink, and grimaced. "This will never replace vodka." He swallowed a more robust swig. "Mr. Spock, are we guests or still prisoners?"

"That is exactly the question I was considering when you came in. Since we are not in fact free to go, I would have to conclude that we do indeed remain prisoners of a sort."

"Still, as prisons go, this one isn't bad," said Chekov, glancing around the room.

"To creatures accustomed to liberty, all confinements, no matter how outwardly comfortable, eventually take on the harsher qualities of the most barren penitentiary."

"Admiral Kirk would not let them hold us, especially since we have not committed any crime."

"None that we are aware of. But the admiral may not be in a position to facilitate our release. He may not even be aware of our presence here."

"You think the Publican was lying when he said he'd contact the ship?"

"It is a possibility, lieutenant, one we cannot discount until we have proof that word of our whereabouts has in fact been transmitted."

Chekov drained his glass and refilled it. "I guess we should know more about what's going to happen to us after they debrief us."

"We must be careful what we say, Mr. Chekov. We know very little about the factual background of contemporary events and conflicts here on Akkalla. We should avoid anything that might present the appearance of taking sides."

There was a sharp rap in the door.

"Come," Spock said as he and Chekov both stood and took a step forward. Brigadier Jjenna Vvox swung the door halfway open.

"The Publican asked me to see that you were comfortable and that you enjoyed dinner."

"Everything is satisfactory," Spock replied. "Except for

the uncertainty about the length of our stay in your custody."

"Ah, yes—that's the other thing I came up to tell you. The Publican would like you to appear before our Continental Synod tomorrow morning."

"For what purpose?"

"Just to answer a few questions, nothing extensive. Then you'll come back here for a little chat with me—and then you'll be on your way back to your starship. Will we have your cooperation?"

"Affirmative," Spock said.

"Excellent. Your escort will come get you in the morning. Rest well."

"It was really sweet of you to invite me here, Leonard." Llissa Kkayn bent over to sniff a cluster of pink and purple magnolia blossoms, petals blooming at their summer peak. Then she hugged herself and whirled like a delighted schoolgirl in an enchanted forest, reveling in the splash of fragrances and colors swirling around her. "I can't believe you've got something like this inside a starship!"

McCoy watched her and couldn't help grinning. "Technically, this is the botany conservation and observation lab, but I just call it the park. We've got it for two reasons: growing samples of plants we find on different planets, and giving the crew a place to sort of get back to nature, at least a little bit."

"And what are these called again?"

"Magnolias."

"What planet are they from?"

"Earth—as a matter of fact, they're from Dixieland, my home turf."

"Dixieland . . . what an interesting name for a city."

"Uh, it's just a nickname . . . I'm actually from a place called Georgia." He wondered how much of Terran geography she really cared to hear. "And magnolias are really from somewhere else—a place called Mississippi. But they're my favorites anyway."

Llissa ambled farther down the serpentine path. "This park seems so big. How do you have room for it?"

"Well, it's not as big as it looks. Creative layout and planting give the illusion of wide-open spaces. Old-time spaceships took along plants for some very sound scientific reasons—not just for effect. They used up carbon dioxide and produced oxygen, helped keep the air breathable."

"I'll have to keep that in mind if we ever develop spaceflight on Akkalla."

"Oh, I'm sure you will."

Doubt clouded Llissa's dusky eyes. "Right now, I wouldn't put a big wager on that."

"Hey, what happened to that smile?"

"Oh, Leonard, how can I smile knowing what's going on down there? I should *be* there, helping. What am I doing here, safe, while everyone else's life's in danger—"

"You're here because this is the only way you really can help. Now, there's nothing wrong with feelin' a little guilty. Just don't let it get the best of you, all right? I have to be getting back to sickbay. Got some work to do before I call it a night. C'mon, I'll bring you back to your quarters."

"I think I'd like to stay here a while. Am I allowed?"

"Sure—just don't get lost in the woods."

"'Night."

She watched him disappear around a bend in the path, then turned and just wandered. After a while, she found a wooden bench and sat, closing her eyes and letting her other senses play among the scents and sounds.

"Sleeping on park benches isn't allowed, preceptor."

She looked up and saw Kirk smiling at her. "Have a seat, Admiral Kirk."

"How did you find your way here? Let me guess— McCoy."

"How did you know?"

"Well, as he constantly reminds me, he's just an ol' country doctor," Kirk said, imitating his friend's drawl. "This is his favorite place on the ship. Sometimes I think he'd like to move sickbay down here."

Llissa laughed. "What brings you here so late?"

"Confession? It's my favorite place, too. Peaceful, quiet. I'm from the country myself, a farm in a place called Iowa. We've got a saying on earth—you can take the boy out of the country, but you can't take the country out of the boy. I guess it's true. Where is the good doctor, anyway?"

"He just left—said he had some work to finish up. I decided to stay and be by myself for a while."

142

"Oh, I'm sorry." He started to get up, but she caught his arm and tugged him back to the bench.

"No, please stay, Admiral. I don't mind the company."

"What're you thinking about?"

She gave a careworn shrug. "Just wondering if my pig-headedness when it came to trusting you might've caused this whole disaster."

"Preceptor, that's ridiculous."

"Call me Llissa, Admiral."

"Even though I haven't seen your insides?"

"Hey, I'm open-minded."

"Fine, and you call me Jim."

"Deal." They shook hands to seal it. "Now that we're on a first-name basis, why are you calling me ridiculous?"

"Because I was just as pig-headed as you were. If there's any blame, we have to share it. But I really don't think it made much difference. Events were already set into motion we just couldn't control."

Her shoulders slumped, and she sighed deeply. "I don't want to spend the rest of my life as an exile, Jim."

"That's not going to happen," he insisted. "You've got to have a positive outlook. Just like I've got to believe I'm going to get my men and the outpost science team back in one piece."

"I'm so sorry." She shook her head. "I'm so wrapped up in my own problems—at least I'm alive and I'm safe. I feel like an idiot for not thinking about your people in trouble. What are they like, your two officers?"

"Well, Pavel Chekov is bright, inquisitive, competent. I was his first commanding officer, and I've known him since he was an ensign barely old enough to shave. He's not that old now, and he's got a great future ahead of him. He could be anything he wants to be in Starfleet."

"What about Mr. Spock? He's a Vulcan, right?"

"That he is," Kirk chuckled. "Funny thing, though, he's only half-Vulcan. His mother is from earth—and we never get tired of reminding him of that fact. I've known him more than a dozen years. He's always been there, always ready with the answers when I need them."

"Is he your friend?"

Kirk remained quiet for a few seconds. "There was a time when I wouldn't have known how to answer that. Vulcans are not exactly . . . forthcoming about their feelings. But I've got no doubts that Spock's the most loyal friend a man could ever have. I've never met anyone with more integrity, intelligence, strength—oh, he's got his flaws, but we bring the human out in him every so often—kind of makes up for them." He grinned, then turned pensive again. "He'd give his life to save this ship and crew. I know that as surely as I've ever known anything. He wouldn't think twice about it, if it were the 'logical' thing to do. If I ever gave up command of the *Enterprise,* he's the only man I'd trust with her."

Kirk looked up at the ship around them.

"If command is what makes you happy, why would you give it up?" Llissa asked.

Jim Kirk shrugged. "Gotta go home sometime."

"I hope I get to go home," Llissa said in a small voice.

They shared a sad trace of a smile as artificial twilight shadows crept across the starship's park.

Chapter Seven

SPOCK AND CHEKOV waited in a private gallery perched high over the round amphitheater of the Synod chamber, watching as the overlords prepared for the session about to be convened. The chamber contained seats and individual desks in four concentric levels, each one nearly a complete circle, with a small wedge sliced out from floor to ceiling directly opposite the observation gallery. There, a simple pulpit rose perhaps three meters above floor level. On both sides of the pulpit, Akkallan flags hung down from gray walls ringed with geometric wave patterns limned in blue. Arched windows above the top ring of seats allowed daylight to stream in from all sides of the chamber.

The eighty overlords, both male and female and of widely ranging ages, were variously at their desks dozing or skimming papers, circulating, or knotted into small, animated discussion groups. Amid the general chaos, one member picked his way through the rows and mounted the steps to the pulpit. He was tall, rail-thin, with flowing white hair and a surprisingly youthful face, and he arrived at the top platform with a flourish, wielding a gavel.

"Overlords, overlords," he boomed, his voice resonating through the cavernous chamber without any electronic amplification, carrying in a cadence suggesting that his words had long since become traditional opening oratory. "This session of the Continental Synod is called to order to consider matters regarding maintenance of our lands blessed by Mother Sea. Come to order, come to order, I, Ddenazay Mmord presiding."

The din of members ending conversations and moving to

their places subsided quickly, and Mmord cleared his throat. "As you all know, my peers, we have a special session today. Publican Abben Ffaridor has seen fit to respond to our request by coming to speak directly to us this morning." The white-haired man turned and looked back down the steps leading to his rostrum. "Peer Ffaridor, the members will receive you now."

As Ffaridor climbed to the speaker's platform, Brigadier Vvox entered the gallery. "Commander Spock, Lieutenant Chekov, the Publican will be introducing you to the Synod any moment now. Come with me. When he calls for you, you'll go in and stand at the base of the pulpit."

The starship officers followed her down a set of switchback ramps to ground level, then around a hundred and eighty degrees of the circle until they reached a foyer behind the rostrum and listened to the Publican's extemporaneous speech.

"—understand your concern over the declaration of first-stage martial law. So I've come, on the one hand, to reassure you—but on the other, to warn you not to take this crisis lightly. Just a day or so ago, our forces captured a terrorist cadre on Shiluzeya, where they operated from several base camps, inciting war between Akkalla and Chorym and plotting to overthrow this government—including you, peers of the Synod—"

Keeping behind Vvox, Spock and Chekov edged forward to catch a glimpse of the Publican standing alone in the pulpit. He spoke easily, maintaining a calm sincerity of tone that gave added credibility to words that were nothing short of incendiary. "He has an effective rhetorical technique," the Vulcan murmured.

"—also liberated a pair of captives for whom we've been searching without success ever since they disappeared on an ill-fated scientific mission. They are officers of the Federation starship *Enterprise,* and I offer them to you as an exhibit. Gentlemen?"

Brigadier Vvox waved them out onto the Synod floor, and Ffaridor beckoned them up to the rostrum. "This is Commander Spock and Lieutenant Chekov," the Publican said when they'd reached his side. "Will you confirm your identities for the assembled overlords, please?"

Spock's slitted eyes scanned the chamber. "The Publican has correctly identified us."

"And you were sent here to work with the Federation science outpost in Tyvol?"

"Affirmative."

"Thank you. That'll be all. You can step down."

Spock's eyebrow elevated, betraying his surprise at the brevity of their appearance with Ffaridor. Chekov remained in place, waiting for a signal from his commander.

The white-haired man who'd opened the session strode out into the well of the chamber and squared his shoulders as he glared up at Publican Ffaridor. "By what right do you cut short debate?" he thundered. "We of the Synod have questions to ask these men."

"By rights established in the Declaration of Convergence and Articles of the Continental Synod, I can present exhibits without entertaining debate or inquiry from the overlords. The Lord Magister knows this as well as I do."

Chekov frowned, feeling insulted. "Exhibit!" he muttered. Only Spock heard.

Ddenazay Mmord crossed his arms in a belligerent stance. "The Lord Magister also knows the Publican has been abusing his declarant powers. In the interests of harmony between Synod and Tower, I . . . request that you relinquish the right of sole presentation and permit the peers to satisfy their own curiosity in these matters."

"Satisfy their curiosity? My word should be enough to quash all rumor and doubt."

"I'm afraid it's not, Peer Ffaridor. Will you yield?" Mmord's question carried the urgency of a demand.

"As I stand here, I am not simply one man who happens to be Publican of Akkalla. I have to protect the powers that all Publicans will need in the future—if we're to have a future. Brigadier Vvox, take them."

The Akkallan military leader beckoned Spock and Chekov down to the floor and hustled them out the back of the chamber. A dissonant tremor of voices rolled down from the overlords as they measured what they'd just witnessed, and Lord Magister Mmord seized the moment before reaction could rise like a tidal wave. He hammered his gavel on the nearest desk.

"Will you yield?" he repeated with a force that silenced everyone else.

Ffaridor leaned on the podium, jaw jutting in defiance. "No. And I'm not finished with my statement. I presented these men to you as proof that the starship was sent to help the so-called Federation science outpost undermine our government, to work with our own misguided scientists to upset the balance that has given Akkalla a rebirth and brought us progress never even dreamed of!"

The chamber erupted into a clamor of arguing voices. Quite pleased with himself, Ffaridor came down from the pulpit, and Mmord rushed over to confront him. "We had a right and responsibility to ask questions of your starship officers and you. You're not above the law, Abben."

"I *am* the law, Ddenazay."

"You leave us no choice but to bring a contempt action against you. You risk recall and trial."

All too aware that Mmord towered over him, the Publican drew himself up to full height and puffed out his chest like a fighting cock strutting its most menacing plumage. "Bring it to the floor, if you dare. See how easily your resolution goes down to defeat. See what happens to your influence when the other overlords see you trying to tie the hands of a Publican in time of war and civil strife." With imperial disdain, Ffaridor swept past Mmord and out of the chamber.

Mmord turned to see chaos, overlords on their feet and waving their hands, turning the house of government into a churning cauldron of anarchy. He saddled his own fury and climbed back up to the pulpit to face the daunting task of restoring order.

The dark facade of the Citadel loomed over a shadowed courtyard like a stern and glowering face. With none of the grace of the Cloistered Tower, it displayed no pretense to being anything other than a brutish garrison with bulging ramparts. As Vvox and a half-dozen Grolian Guards escorted Chekov and Spock toward the fortress, the Russian curled a disapproving lip. "I don't like the looks of this hotel, Mr. Spock," he murmured.

One of the guardsmen pulled open the armored door, using all his weight to swing it out on creaky hinges. Inside, the entry hall was dim and drafty, with a damp mustiness pervading the air. Brigadier Vvox suddenly halted and spun on the starship officers. "You'll go with these guards," she said, her tone even but commanding.

"I thought we were free to go," Chekov said.

"After completion of debriefing, Lieutenant Chekov. I'll be meeting with you shortly." She strode up a broad stone staircase and through a door, out of sight.

"If you'll come with us, please," said the chief of the escort squad.

Chekov tried to lock gazes with the guard, but the Akkallan's eyes were hidden beneath the shadow of his helmet visor; so, too, the other guards.

"I suspect we have little choice for the moment," Spock said.

The faceless guardsmen ringed them, as if to confirm Spock's statement, and led them through a windowless corridor, then down a narrow flight of steps to a stout metal door standing open. "In here, please," the squad leader said.

Chekov hesistated, considering a stroll in another direction, when he noticed the guards' fingers moving inconspicuously toward the triggers of their weapons. Suicide was not the most useful alternative, so he meekly followed Spock into a room that turned out to have a grate-screened window, some threadbare parlor furniture, and no other way out. The guards retreated, and the door swung closed with a disconcerting but distinct clattering of a lock engaging. Stark shafts of light filtered through the small window, falling across the wood-plank floor.

Chekov sighed. "I have a bad feeling about this."

Hhayd and Vvox faced each other across the combat pool, brightly lit in a stone-walled room in the Citadel. They each wore a gossamer gray suit covering their bodies from neck to toe, outlining every contour and curve and muscle like an impossibly taut skin. Each held a weapon shaped like a dagger, except that a translucent tube replaced the blade. They bowed toward each other, then activated small power packs worn on their belts. When switched on, the packs sent surges of energy along nearly invisible filaments woven into the tight garments, causing them to glow blue-white, with the exception of strategic portions of the body—chest and abdomen, groin, biceps, and thighs. Those sections had no filaments, just the stretch material of the suit itself.

Vvox twisted the handle of her weapon, and it too pulsed with a blue-white energy field. Then she touched it lightly to the glowing area of her suit, each contact sparking a strobelike flash. "Ready, Rrelin?" she called across the pool, slipping on a headband to hold her hair.

He nodded, and they both dove feet-first into the water, deep enough to be well over their heads. They maneuvered around each other in balletic slow motion, probing for weakness. After a few feints, they began using their hand weapons to thrust and parry in a weightless, three-dimensional match of wits and physical prowess, always aiming to hit those critical body parts unprotected by the energized filaments. Using feet and arms and buttocks to bounce off the walls and floor of the tank, they twisted and pirouetted through their mock battle, with Hhayd scoring the first touch, on her unshielded left upper arm. The magnetic jolt stung, but not enough to make her lose control. As she swam away, she kicked him playfully in the gut with a powerful stroke of her legs. But before she could marshal a counter-attack, he dove down from the surface, faking a blow to her chest, then going for her thigh—*a hit!* This time, a solid strike. She almost opened her mouth and gave up precious stored oxygen. The stun effect made her leg twitch uselessly—she couldn't escape. He poised for a lethal contact, his probe aimed right for her chest.

With a desperate swipe, her free hand jarred his attack arm and his weapon drifted free, sinking toward the bottom. Caught off guard, he hesitated—his fatal error. Her back to the pool wall, Vvox tucked her knees and pushed with all her muscle power, darting straight for him. Hhayd started a contortion of escape. Too late. Her probe jabbed him hard in the chest, channeling its full magnetic force through the gap in his deflective suit, and his mouth and eyes opened wide in pain and amazement. As air rushed out of his lungs, he paddled limply to the surface, his head bursting through, gulping and roaring in agony in the same instant.

Muscles straining, he flopped out onto the deck, chest

heaving as he lay on his side. Vvox bobbed up from the bottom and floated on her back, catching her own breath.

"I—had you on—the run," he panted. "You—can't hold your breath the way you used to . . . getting old."

"But I still won."

She got out of the pool and spread a fluffy towel, beckoning Hhayd to join her. Bodies nested together, they lay back and rested.

"What happened this morning in the Synod?" he asked.

Vvox rolled her eyes in disgust. "I knew I shouldn't have let him do it. I knew the overlords wouldn't take kindly to having their noses rubbed in their own impotence."

"What's happened since then? Are they going after him?"

"Oh, yes indeed, my love. He may be the first Publican ever thrown in prison during his term of office. My agents tell me Mmord was spitting fire after Ffaridor stomped out of there. And Mmord isn't one for idle threats."

"But how many overlords have the nerve to take on the Publican?"

"Until today, not too many. If Fearless Ffaridor hadn't gone into their place and personally offended the entire Synod, we probably could've gone on like this indefinitely."

"And now—?"

"Now—?" she repeated. "Time is running out."

"That means *our* time is running out."

"Very perceptive, Rrelin."

"Is that the best you can do? This isn't the time for witty rejoinders. We've got to *do* something. You're obviously losing control of him."

"I am not," she bristled.

"What do you call it?"

No longer feeling amorous, Jjenna Vvox wrapped herself in a towel and sat hunched and cross-legged. "This bickering isn't getting us anywhere."

"Neither is all your careful planning."

"Okay, you're so brilliant, Rrelin. What great ideas would you care to share?"

"Get rid of him," Hhayd said icily.

"What do you mean?"

"Assassination."

"No!"

"Why—will you miss crawling into bed and servicing the most powerful leader on the planet?" he mocked.

Her hand lashed out and she slapped him across the cheek with a stinging smack.

"That's no answer to our problem, Jjenna. Give me a good reason not to kill him."

"We still need him to give this government legitimacy before we take it over."

"That's what you call what he did this morning? Giving the government legitimacy—?"

"Even as a figurehead, we need him as a distraction. He and the Synod keep each other occupied while we make things happen."

"What happens when the Synod votes to recall him?"

"They won't have the chance."

Hhayd's eyes squinted in suspicion. "Why not?"

"Because we're going to arrest the overlords and put them in prison until we can take over."

He continued glaring out from under half-closed lids. Then he started to chuckle, a low, mirthless sound coming from his throat. "Arrest them?"

"Mm-hmm. Skip right to third-stage martial law. Brilliant?"

"Let me think about that for a bit. Will you get his authorization?"

"Of course. He is the planetary leader, after all. And with his signature, it'll all be perfectly legal, according to the Articles of the Synod."

"Are you sure he'll agree? How're you going to convince him? It's a big leap to go from yelling at Mmord to throwing the entire bunch into prison."

"When Mmord threatened to start a contempt action against him, the Synod became a danger to him. I really think he never believed they'd go through with it. But when I tell him they are—"

"—and he always believes you—"

"Yes," Vvox purred, "he does. When he hears it from me, he'll be willing to do almost anything to protect himself. I don't think this'll be any problem."

"Don't forget—anything that threatens his power threatens ours."

Her eyes flashed angrily. "I don't need you to tell me the

obvious—" She unfolded herself as if to stand, but he gripped her shoulder and pushed her roughly onto her back.

"But you do *need* me," he stated.

She struggled briefly, trying to get up, then relented with a seductive smile. "Of course I need you, love. Why would you even ask such a silly question."

"Oh, you misunderstand. It wasn't a question."

"I see," she said, with a short, hollow laugh.

"Good." They kissed. For the moment, their lust for power was subordinated to another kind of lust, one with more immediate rewards.

Lord Magister Ddenazay Mmord leaned wearily on his podium, peering down at the Synod Chamber floor where a woman overlord droned on about the Publican's trespasses against decency and good government. She stopped for a breath and Mmord quickly gaveled the members to attention. "Thank you, Peer Llutri. We've worked long and hard today, without even a mid-noon meal. I propose that we adjourn until fifty-four. It's so late already, this can be our dinner. Then we can debate into the evening—and, I devoutly hope, we can also vote on the resolution. Immediate action is imperative. If we wait, we may not be able to counteract the consequences. Objections? No objections," he said rapidly, not waiting for a dissenting voice. The gavel came down with an echoing crack. "Adjourned till fifty-four," he mumbled, wiping his brow in relief. He settled on his stool, unable to summon the energy to go down the staircase without falling. The other overlords gathered their papers and filed out, some by exits on each seating level, others passing the base of the pulpit and leaving via the foyer behind the Lord Magister's rostrum.

Shouts filtered into the chamber from the rear foyer and several overlords stumbled back inside, falling over others trying to make their way out for overdue meals. Mmord roused himself enough to lean down for a closer look, just as armed Paladins in gray-blue combat uniforms and helmets marched in. He heard panicky shuffling of feet across the chamber, too, and saw overlords being forced back by troopers on all four levels. Other than the punctuation of footsteps, the place was filled with an unaccustomed quiet, with no voices rising in parliamentary speech. Almost out of reflex, Mmord fumbled for his gavel, slammed it once on his podium, and heard his own voice demanding, "What is going on here?"

All motion stopped; all eyes turned his way. One trooper ambled down to the chamber well, tipped his helmet back, and squinted up at the Lord Magister. "By order of the Publican, third-stage martial law is hereby declared. You and all your colleagues are under arrest."

Ddenazay Mmord blinked in disbelief. For the first time in his life, he couldn't think of a thing to say.

The last rays of cloud-shrouded afternoon light banked steeply through the window grating of the cell, and Spock sat in straight-backed composure while Chekov paced.

"I do not believe this," the Russian grumbled. "They keep us in here all day, they never come to question us—not for even ten seconds!—they don't tell us a thing—I just do not *believe* this. Sometimes I think we were better off in the cave." He stopped suddenly, reconsidering. "Forget I said that."

"Mr. Chekov, your pacing is accomplishing nothing."

"Maybe, but I just can't sit there and meditate like you, sir."

"But rather than dissipating nervous tension, your activity seems to have the opposite effect—that of maintaining your anger or even increasing it."

"I wish to be angry, Mr. Spock. I wish to be *very* angry at these Cossacks! Keeping us locked up like common criminals."

A key turned in the lock. "Stand back," called a voice, and the cell door swung in. A guard stepped in, weapon up, located Spock and Chekov, then motioned another guard to bring in a new prisoner—a tall white-haired man with a lean build and stooped shoulders. He seemed disoriented, head twitching like a nervous bird. The guards left, and the door slammed shut.

Chekov looked at the newcomer. "You are the Lord Magister from the Synod!"

The man took a deep breath, weaving as if about to faint. "Yes, yes, I am."

Spock stood. "We are the officers from the starship *Enterprise*."

154

The man nodded. "I know." He steadied himself, regaining some of the presence he'd exhibited from his speaker's pulpit. "It seems we've been trapped in the same net."

"Why are you here?" Spock asked.

"Just let me sit down here, gentlemen." He eased himself onto the worn cushions of a battered armchair. "Our esteemed Publican has declared a full third-stage martial alert."

"What does that mean?" said Chekov.

"It means he's declared himself sovereign military ruler of Akkalla. He's disbanded the Synod. And he's had all the overlords arrested. Since I'm the Lord Magister, I've got privileged accommodations along with you. The rest are in considerably less stylish quarters down in the bowels of this Citadel, lacking amenities like cushions and windows."

Chekov swallowed. "Mr. Spock, I think we're in a lot more trouble than we thought."

The tall man extended his hand, palm up. "I'm Ddenazay Mmord, once and perhaps future Lord Magister of the Continental Synod."

"I am Lieutenant Pavel Chekov." He offered a tentative hand, unsure of proper protocol. Mmord took Chekov's hand and placed it palm down on top of his own.

"And I am Spock—first officer and science officer of the *Enterprise*." The Vulcan did not offer to participate in the greeting ritual.

"Sounds like you're an important man." He waved a hand around. "We're all important men. We're in the best cell."

"Why would the Publican place you all under arrest?" asked Spock.

"Because we were a threat to his power. Idiots that we are, we warned him before we did anything to stop him. That gave him the time he needed to protect himself. Although this bears the mark of Brigadier Vvox. Ffaridor never wielded power quite so—forcefully?—before getting involved with that one."

Spock pulled a chair over and sat close to Mmord. "To what sort of involvement do you refer?"

"Everything under the clouds. She's become the only adviser he listens to, she controls who he sees, what he hears . . . and from all the rumors drifting about, it's pretty certain they're also lovers. He may be the Publican, but Brigadier Vvox seems to be running the planet."

"It wasn't always that way?" Chekov asked.

"Oh, no, no, no. When we made Ffaridor Publican—"

Chekov frowned. "When *who* made him Publican? I thought your leaders were elected democratically."

"We are. Then the leader of the majority party becomes Publican. We chose Ffaridor for that as sort of a compromise. Our previous leader stepped down after a period of serious fighting within the party, so we looked for someone who had no enemies. That was Abben Ffaridor, mild-mannered, inoffensive, and moderately ineffectual. Frankly, we picked him because we thought he could be controlled." He snorted a bitter laugh. "We were right about that—and wrong about who'd be doing the controlling."

"Have you known Publican Ffaridor long?" Spock asked.

"Oh, yes. We were elected to the Synod at the same time. I took it very seriously all these years, and he was more a gentleman politician, almost as if he were dabbling until something more interesting came along."

"How did Brigadier Vvox manage to exert such strong influence over him?"

Mmord shrugged. "Proximity. And I guess she was shrewd enough to recognize an opportunity—and ruthless enough to grab it."

Chekov rested his elbows on the back of Spock's chair. "What are you going to do about this?"

"My opportunities appear to be limited at the moment. It's strange. I saw all this coming, saw the changes in Ffaridor. It didn't happen overnight, but I knew him well enough to see what was happening, to see him molded by her."

"Yet you did nothing?" Spock said.

Mmord rubbed his bloodshot eyes. "My mistake. You see other people make them, and think you never will. Then it turns out you're not immune. And there's a good chance this one will take me to my grave."

Abben Ffaridor stood at the window of the reception lounge, watching the setting sun stain the cloud bottoms with broad strokes of red and gold, trying to commit to memory the contours of the clouds and the casual way nature cross-stroked them with fleeting brilliance. At the sound of footsteps coming down the corridor, he turned to see Ddenazay Mmord escorted in by two Grolian Guards in formal Tower uniforms.

"Wait outside," he said to the guards. Then he motioned toward a pair of chairs, and he and the prisoner sat. "I'm sorry it had to come to this, Dden."

"No, you're not. Not unless Vvox told you to be."

"Is that how it looks to you? That I've become Vvox's puppet?"

"That's exactly how it looks."

Ffaridor shook his head sadly. "Can't you believe that she and I simply share the same visions of what this planet can be?"

"Her vision is a military dictatorship, with her in charge. Is that yours, too?"

"No, no. You're mistaken about that."

"Do you remember the motto of the Declaration of Convergence?"

"Of course I do. 'What good is order without freedom, freedom without truth?' Every Akkallan child has to memorize it."

"Memorizing and understanding are two different things, Abben."

"Can you understand this?" the Publican implored. "What good is freedom or truth without order, my friend? Order must come first. How can we have a world without a solid structure for society? Can't you see that's crumbling now? We're under assault from the Chorymi, from our own scientists, and now from the Federation itself."

Before Mmord could respond, the sharp clicks of military boots echoed through the hallway, and Brigadier Vvox strode in. "I'm sorry I was delayed, sir."

"Quite all right, quite all right. Ddenazay and I needed a few minutes alone. Now, what were you going to say, my friend?"

"Does it matter?" Mmord's eyes remained fixed on Vvox, who glared coolly back at him.

"Yes, yes, of course it matters! I want to resolve this and release the overlords as quickly as possible."

Mmord turned back to his old colleague. "I wish I could believe that."

"Isn't that our intention, Jjenna?"

"Of course, sir."

"Well, if it isn't, you're risking violent revolution, Abben. You may control the official news media, but there are other information channels, and you can't control every single one of them."

"Don't underestimate us," Vvox said tightly.

"Jjenna," Ffaridor scolded. "Ddenazay, I need the Synod out and functioning. We're a small world. We need everyone working together, especially now."

"Then why did you pull that high-handed stunt with the starship officers today? Why didn't you let us question them?"

"I—I didn't see the need."

"Well, then you didn't have your eyes open. If you want us to believe your accusation against the Federation and its science outpost, prove it. Have those officers make a public confession before the entire Synod, let us question them, and I can almost guarantee you our support."

"That demand is out of line," Vvox said.

"That's not yours to decide," Mmord flared. "He's the Publican, not you—brigadier."

"I'm his adviser."

"You're his *devil*. You're the most dangerous thing that ever happened to him or this government. And this planet's only hope is for him to recognize that before it's too late!" Mmord snarled, rising out of his chair.

"How dare you challenge the Publican's mandate!"

"How dare you arrest the entire Synod! As soon as we reconvene, you'll both be charged with high treason!"

Shouting voices brought the guards hustling back in, but they skidded to a halt as the Publican raised his hand. The verbal jousting continued.

"What makes you think you'll be reconvening any time soon, Lord Magister?"

Ffaridor stepped between them. "That's enough! This isn't solving anything!"

"There's nothing to be solved," Mmord said, suddenly hushed.

"I was hoping you'd feel differently," said Ffaridor in sorrow. "Guards, take him back to the Citadel. Jjenna, leave. I want to be alone now."

"Yes, sir." She followed the guards and the prisoner out into the hall. "Put him in the lower cells with the other overlords," she told the guards in a low voice.

They shoved Mmord toward the Tower's front doors, and he went along without struggle. Vvox watched them go. "We'll see who's tried for treason," she muttered.

The cell door creaked in, and Brigadier Vvox stood in the opening. "Commander Spock, Lieutenant Chekov. I just wanted to see if you were comfortable."

"We'd be more comfortable," said Chekov, "aboard the *Enterprise.*"

"I'm sure you would, but we just can't accommodate you quite yet. Would you care to take a walk with me?"

"Do we have a choice?"

"No, Mr. Chekov, you don't." She turned, and they got up to follow.

"No guards to accompany us?" Spock mused.

"Not needed. This is a rather heavily fortified place. Even if you got rid of me, you wouldn't get very far."

The hallway was barely wide enough for two to walk shoulder to shoulder, with stone-block walls that angled in as they reached the ceiling. There was little doubt the Citadel was quite old, but plenty of bright lighting made this section seem somewhat less dungeonlike. Vvox led the way down a short flight of steps to a vaulted room with museum-piece torture racks and shackles around the perimeter. But the dominant features were a pair of clear, modern tanks, three meters high by two across and filled with water. Each one had a winch over the open top, and Chekov's jaw dropped in horror when he realized that one of the tanks was occupied by a naked man, hanging upside down from the winch, flailing and writhing, trying vainly to right himself and rise to the top. Every time he seemed about to succeed, the guard operating the winch would yank the prisoner up, dangle him by his feet in the air for a second, then dunk him back into the water.

The corners of Spock's mouth tightened, and Chekov noticed. It was as close as he'd ever seen the Vulcan come to betraying anger. "I had been led to believe that Akkallans were too civilized to resort to torture, brigadier."

"Oh, this isn't torture, commander. It's just an interrogation enhancement technique, useful for softening resistance."

"That's what he said," Chekov sneered. "Torture."

She ignored the comment. "Every air-breathing being has a fear of drowning. The tank stimulates that fear, without actually damaging the subject. It's quite effective, and it's never fatal—unless we want it to be."

Spock crossed his arms, deliberately shifting away from the torture tank. "Presumably, you have a purpose in demonstrating this."

"Yes, I do," Vvox said. "We would like you and the lieutenant to appear on our broadcast to confess your collusion with the Federation science team and the Cape Alliance."

"Indeed. Could you endeavor to be more specific?"

"Mr. Spock!" Chekov blurted.

The Vulcan silenced him with a look.

"Well, you would be asked to tell how the Federation scientists had collaborated with the Alliance to spread false information and disrupt the long-standing harvest treaty with Chorym, leading to war and the overthrow of the Akkallan government."

"And when would you like us to do this?"

Chekov stared dumbfounded at Spock.

"Tomorrow would be perfect," Vvox said. "We could work on your exact text tonight, do the broadcast first thing in the morning, and probably have you freed by midnoon. Your confession would also help the Publican convince the members of the Synod and settle that dispute, too. You'd be doing Akkalla a great service, uniting us behind the Publican and his leadership."

At the brigadier's words, Chekov could no longer contain himself. "Sir, how can you think of—"

"Mr. Chekov, allow me to respond. Brigadier Vvox, you are asking us to lie. That, quite simply, is impossible. We will not cooperate."

Vvox shook her head. "But reasonable cooperation is so much more pleasant for both of us than the tank."

"Vulcans have the ability to place the body in a sort of trance or stasis, during which respiration is reduced to almost imperceptible levels. We require no intake of additional oxygen for a period of some days. Should deprivation by immersion exceed that, I would die, and that would certainly preclude the confession you seek."

"Then there's always Lieutenant Chekov."

The younger officer's lip curled scornfully. "Russians have the same ability as Vulcans. You won't get anything out of me."

"That may be true, but I will have to try. I'll give you some time to think about the proposition in your cell."

At the sound of the door buzzer, Kirk looked up from his desktop computer. "Come." The door slid aside, and Lieutenant Maybri and Ensign Greenberger entered, arms laden with printouts, computer data cassettes, and hard copies of photographs, maps, and charts. Kirk couldn't help chuckling as he waved them over to an empty table.

"It's all here, sir," Maybri said, flexing her elbows after she and Greenberger had dumped their loads.

Greenberger puffed a breath past her nose, aimed at clearing away the blond locks fallen across her cheek. "We've organized everything so you'll have no trouble getting the Akkallans to understand. You've got data on the shuttle, where it went down, the path it took—"

"—and," Maybri chimed in, "everything on the new life form, enough evidence to warrant further investigation and to prove the science outpost was doing legitimate research."

Kirk suppressed a smile. "Good work, Maybri, Greenberger. You two should be running the science department on some starship one of these days."

"Thank you, sir," they both said at once. They turned and left Kirk's cabin.

With a grin, Kirk sifted through the material they'd brought him. The two young science officers certainly were thorough. They might indeed be ready to give Spock a fight for that bridge science console. For the moment, it made Kirk feel a bit better to know he had two young officers he could rely on.

He pressed the intercom button. "Kirk to bridge. Communications—get me a channel to Publican Ffaridor or Brigadier Vvox."

"Lieutenant Lin here, sir." The face of a young Chinese

officer appeared on Kirk's viewer. Lin's straight black hair fell across his forehead as he touched the transceiver in his ear. *"I'll get right on it and pipe it down to you, sir."*

"Fine. Kirk out." He shut the intercom off, and the screen blanked out.

Bending low, he opened a cabinet under the computer and pulled out a slim leather briefcase, holding it up against the pile of paper and cassettes left by Maybri and Greenberger. "All of that is not going to fit in this."

"Lin to Admiral Kirk."

Kirk turned to find the swing-shift comm officer on the viewer, looking perplexed. *"I'm sorry, sir, but I couldn't reach the Publican or Vvox."*

Kirk's face flushed. "Couldn't—reach—them?" he sputtered through clenched teeth.

"I got one of the guards . . . said they were both too busy and couldn't be disturbed. Should I try again la—"

"No," he snapped. "Kirk out." He pounded the button with his fist, then stuffed as much as he could into the briefcase, fastened it, and headed for the door. As it snapped open, he ran directly into McCoy. The doctor staggered to the opposite wall.

"Sorry, Bones." Kirk steadied him, then strode off. "No time to chat."

"What's your hurry, and where're you going?" McCoy rushed to catch up.

"The hurry is, I've had it with Vvox and Ffaridor avoiding me—"

"They're *both* doing it now?"

"Yep. And where I'm going is the Cloistered Tower to give them a piece of my mind and a lot of data from our computer."

"Well, I didn't have anything exciting planned for the evening," McCoy said.

"I didn't ask you to come along."

McCoy clapped him on the shoulder. "That's the great thing about old friends, Jim. They can read your mind."

They materialized on the steps of the Publican's residence, with floodlights casting pools of white on the plaza and tall beams up the front of the building. Kirk opened the glass doors and found the lobby empty. No guards in sight.

"Strange."

"Do we go in? Or is this a trap—they convict us of trespassing on the spot and toss us off the cliffs."

"Let's go," Kirk decided.

"Fine—go where? How do we find anybody?"

"I don't know. Let's try this way. At least it's familiar." He pointed down the hallway that led to the reception area where they'd met the Akkallan leaders before. With a fatalistic shrug, McCoy fell into step behind him.

The Akkallan sky was black now, with just the faintest tendrils of orange fire fading at the horizon. Still in the reception hall, Ffaridor stood at the windows, transfixed by the view. He'd wanted his meeting with Mmord to be conciliatory, not a continuation of the battle. Never mind the liberties he'd taken with the truth in trying to pass off the Starfleet prisoners as dangerous conspirators. Small lies were sometimes necessary when the risks ran high. In the end, if he saved Akkalla from the Chorymi threat, who would care? Who would even know? He felt a pang of guilt over his willingness to sacrifice these two offworlders on the altar of desperation, but this was war. People died in wars. Ffaridor felt events getting away from him, sifting through his fingers like grains of sand. The more he tried to staunch the flow, the more fell from his grasp.

In the window, he saw a reflection of movement behind him, and he turned to find a figure emerging from shadows, a figure dressed in unmarked gray fatigues, with a hood over its head and a mask across its mouth. Only the eyes were visible—light, deep-set eyes, eyes quietly burning with a deadly fire. The hands were gloved in black leather, and a dagger gleamed in one, held carefully by determined fingers. The figure moved quickly, noiselessly, crossing the space in the center of the room in effortless sliding strides.

Ffaridor froze. He did not run—or could not. He felt dampness under his arms and down his back. His mouth turned dry and gluey. "What are you doing here?" he croaked.

The only answer was the flash of a dagger's blade.

* * *

"Are you sure it's this way?" McCoy whispered.

"Yes, I'm sure."

Kirk tiptoed around a corner. A clash of ceramic on stone screamed down the corridor, and they skidded to a stop. Then a second crash and the shrill scraping of heavy furniture being dragged in a panic made them sprint toward the location of the scuffle—the reception parlor. The doors were ajar, and Kirk burst through.

The Publican was scrabbling along the floor like a crab, trying to escape from a masked assailant. The attacker's dagger flashed down once, twice, three times, with Ffaridor fending off the blows with a shredded seat cushion. Blood streaked the crumpled rug and the floor, chairs and tables were upended, and the Akkallan leader shrieked as the blade found its mark. But the blow wasn't a fatal one, and he skittered behind a broken lamp table, shoving it into the assassin's path. The hooded figure tripped over it, tumbled, and slid face-first on the bare floor.

Kirk pulled his small hand phaser from his belt and dove over a couch, just as the attacker scrambled to get away. His raised knee caught Kirk in the stomach, knocking the wind out of him. But the missed tackle still sent the hooded man tumbling, and Kirk rolled, raised his phaser, and aimed.

The assassin's foot lashed out, and the phaser went flying. He lunged after it, and Kirk managed to grab his ankle, sending the man sprawling. McCoy, tending to the dazed Publican, sprang from his crouch, scooped up the phaser, aimed, and fired in one smooth motion, dropping the would-be assassin two paces away. The surgeon maintained a combat stance, weapon pointed at the unconscious figure, as Kirk sat up and hobbled to his feet.

"Thanks, Bones."

"I *told* you you needed me to come along."

Kirk held his palm out for the phaser, and McCoy started to pass it over, then withdrew it. "On second thought, maybe I should hold on to this."

Kirk wiggled his fingers impatiently, and McCoy surrendered it. Then they moved to help the Publican, who was crumpled against the fireplace. McCoy kneeled for a quick examination. Ffaridor was conscious, and as they propped him in a more comfortable position, his breathing eased. Blood oozed through a gash on his right arm.

"Well?" Kirk hovered over his medical officer's shoulder.

"The wound appears superficial. If I had my medical kit—"

"Why don't you have your medical kit?"

"I didn't think I'd need it. I thought this was a diplomatic visit."

Ffaridor licked his lips. "Call for help," he whispered, looking up at the wall behind him, toward a flush-mounted intercom panel with a black button and a red one. "The red one, Admiral."

Kirk pressed it, setting off a whooping alarm siren. Within seconds, Grolian Guards charged in from both ends of the room, a half-dozen in all, sidearms drawn, cocked, and pointed at Kirk and McCoy.

"Not them," Ffaridor said, trying to stand.

"You rest right where you are," McCoy snapped.

Hands spread in a nonthreatening pose, Kirk stepped over to the hooded figure. "Here's your man."

"What's going on here?" It was Brigadier Vvox, swaggering into the reception chamber, eyes darting across the room.

Her arrogant facade slipped for an instant as she saw the blood on Ffaridor and gasped. McCoy was already ripping the Publican's sleeve with a red-handled pocket knife and fashioning a tourniquet. "Someone tried to kill your Publican."

"What are you two doing here?" she demanded.

"As it turned out, saving his life," Kirk said. "At least you could thank us."

She stamped her foot. "You break into the Tower illegally—"

"We interrupt a murder in progress," Kirk cut in, "risk our lives, and catch the assassin—"

"This man needs medical assistance," McCoy said, helping the Publican to a chair. "I'd be glad to—"

"Our doctors can take care of him." She jerked her thumb toward the door and addressed one of the guards. "Get the Publican's doctor—*now.*" The guard saluted and trotted out. Hands on hips, Vvox turned back to the trespassers. "You've committed a serious offense, Admiral—"

"Forget it, Jjenna." Ffaridor said. "And thank you both."

Vvox wheeled to face the guards standing over the assailant's body. "Get him out of here."

"Wait," Ffaridor said. "I want to see his face first. He got in without tripping any alarms or attracting the attention of the guards."

"There were no guards," Kirk said. "Not in front anyway. That's how we got in."

Ffaridor's eyes widened. "He *must* be an insider, then. Unmask him."

Uncharacteristically flustered, Vvox blanched, frozen in place. Ffaridor nodded to one of the guards, who rolled the attacker over and tugged off the hood and mask—revealing the face of Commandant Rrelin Hhayd.

"Well, I'll be a sonofagun," McCoy murmured.

Vvox bent to one knee next to him. "Is—is he dead?"

"No, just stunned," said Kirk. "He'll be coming around in an hour or so."

"Then that's when he'll be executed," Vvox growled, straightening.

"He has to be questioned first," Ffaridor said. "This had to be a conspiracy."

"It may not have been," Vvox said. "He is the commandant of the Grolian Guard. It wouldn't have been hard for him to arrange for the guards to be called away from the front on some false order."

"I want him questioned," Ffaridor repeated. "You do it, Jjenna."

A breath caught in her throat. "Yes, sir. I'll take care of it. And I'll find out the truth. Take him to the Citadel."

A pair of guards grabbed Hhayd's limp form by the arms and hauled him out. Vvox faced another pair. "Escort the Publican to his quarters."

"No, no, Jjenna, I can wait here for the doctor."

She held his uninjured arm and gently coaxed him toward the door. "You're hurt, you're in shock, you need to get off your feet, and you need to be kept warm. Isn't that right, Dr. McCoy?"

McCoy knew she was trying to rush Ffaridor out and away from Kirk, but his medical ethics compelled him to be honest. "Yes, he should be—"

"Thank you for your help, Dr. McCoy," she interrupted, making certain Ffaridor left without another word to the

166

starship officers. When he was gone, her concerned expression hardened. "If I had my choice, you'd be prosecuted for coming down here without authorization. But the Publican has generously waived the law in this case. But let this be a warning to you, Kirk. This building will be sealed. No one will be allowed in without my permission. Now, it's true, I can't keep you from using your transporter to breach our security shield. But if I find you or any of your officers here again, you'll be imprisoned without a hearing. Go back to your ship—*now.*"

Briefcase clutched under one arm, Kirk flipped open his communicator and spoke through clenched teeth. "Kirk to *Enterprise.* Two to beam up. Lock in and energize."

The shimmering began, and he and McCoy faded and dissolved.

Her face taut, Vvox turned to the remaining guardsmen. "If anyone from the starship transports back here, grab them. If they resist, do whatever has to be done to place them in custody. If you have to, kill them."

Chapter Eight

OUTSIDE THE CITADEL, the pearl-gray light of early morning cast faint shadows in the courtyard. But down where Rrelin Hhayd was imprisoned, there were no windows to tell him it was dawn. He lay on a slab-hard bunk, curled on his side. The bare bulb overhead flickered on, painting the tiny cell in harsh white light. At the sound of a key in the door, he shook himself awake and swung his feet to the floor, still wearing his combat fatigues as the door opened enough to allow Brigadier Vvox to enter.

Hooking her toe on the leg of a tripod stool, she slid it across the uneven stone floor with a grating sound. Then she sat. The cell door remained open, enough for Hhayd to see two armed guardsmen outside—troopers who used to jump to the cadence of his orders.

"So," he said, "you're my inquisitor. How ironic."

Vvox shook her head scornfully. "I only have one burning question." Her voice was flat. "How could you be so stupid?"

Hhayd chuckled. "Stupid? For taking a positive step toward what we both wanted?" His forced smile disappeared. "I did what had to be done."

"First of all, it didn't *have* to be done. Second, even if it did, this wasn't the time. And finally, you failed."

"At least I tried. Better than planning and planning and planning again, twisting with every breeze that blows, and waiting to navigate a course that never hits a wave or a storm. Well, there's no such course, and the fool who thinks there is never leaves the harbor."

"Very sure of yourself, Rrelin."

"You know me—never look back. So, interrogate me."

"I did. I found out nothing useful. I had you executed."

"Just like that?"

"Just like that." She stood, kicked the stool against the wall, and left the cell. But the door didn't clang shut. Instead, Vvox came back in with a powerful Grolian sidearm in her hand. She slipped a muffler over the muzzle, raised it, and fired. With a deadened thud, the projectile exploded in the center of Hhayd's chest, throwing his body against the wall, draping him grotesquely off the end of the bunk, arms dangling and legs askew like a discarded rag doll.

"Screen on, please," Kirk said. The wall-size viewer in the main briefing room glowed, and the room lights dimmed slightly. "Okay, Llissa. It's all yours."

Llissa Kkayn prowled around the table, where the admiral now sat with Scott, Sulu, McCoy, Maybri, and Greenberger. "Thanks, Jim. I wish I'd had more time to grab things or have them beamed up before Collegium was occupied, but these'll have to do." She thumbed a remote control in her hand, and the computer obliged by flashing a florid painting of a sea creature with some strikingly humanoid features, ornately rendered. "This is an illustration from an ancient religious text, dating back, oh, maybe eight hundred years. Not many books survive from before that era, so this is one of the earlier paintings with lots of detail."

"Details of what, Llissa?" McCoy asked.

"Of a creature called a Wwafida. Akkallan legends devote a great deal of time to a civilization of humanlike beings that lived in the sea."

Maybri's ear tips twitched curiously. "A civilization? Not just creatures swimming around in the ocean?"

"That's right. A civilization, with everything that implies —communication, culture, highly evolved social order. At least that's what the legends say. We Akkallans believe life began in the sea here. Maybri was telling me that's probably true on many if not most worlds that have advanced forms of life. And here, as you've seen, even modern life revolves around the sea. That's no great surprise on a planet where we don't have very much dry land. The Wwafida were supposed to be people who'd been born on land, and after they lived good lives, their reward was to turn into these sea creatures for the final stage of their lives and then die in peace in Mother Sea. The change was called senescence, or sanctification."

"How far back do these legends go?" Kirk asked.

"Well, we have some forms of recorded history—carvings, engravings, stone tablets, cave paintings—dating back about ten thousand years. Before that, it was just oral history. For all of those ten thousand years, Akkallans have lived and died on land, as far as anybody can figure out, just like we do today."

Greenberger raised her hand. "Did anybody ever investigate to see if these Wwafida ever actually existed?"

Llissa nodded. "Some people wondered. Some people did more than wonder. My father was one of them. He worked at Collegium when I was growing up, and he was something of a genius, spread over a whole batch of fields. He was a biologist, an archeologist, a paleontologist, and a historian. One of the things I remember most vividly about him was how he was always trying to make things fit together. To him, science was a puzzle with mismatched pieces. But he believed the pieces might match if you arranged them exactly right, or found some that were missing."

McCoy sipped a cup of coffee and reached for a donut on a platter. "Where is your father?"

"I don't know. He left Collegium after my mother died—I was a child—because he didn't like the way things were done. He always was a bit of a maverick, didn't get along too well with colleagues. We were never close anyway, so we didn't keep in touch. But he was still working, on his own, trying to shove those puzzle pieces together. I heard about him from other people, read things he wrote—"

She stood in silence for a moment. "Anyway, he suddenly disappeared about five years ago."

Kirk cocked his head. "Disappeared?"

"That's the way it seemed. Nobody knew where he was. He stopped publishing." She shrugged. "Some people said he drowned in a storm while he was out in a small boat by himself. But no wreckage or body was ever found. So, he might be dead, or he might be alive. Nobody knows. But before he dropped out of sight, I *know* he was working on trying to prove the Wwafida were real—and still existed."

170

McCoy's eyes narrowed reflectively. "That's how all this started, isn't it, all this questioning of the harvest treaty."

"Yeah. He managed to discover a previously unknown underwater mountain range. He didn't have the resources or equipment to really explore the way he wanted to. So he came to us at the Collegium and made peace with us long enough for a cooperative venture. That's when we retrieved those fossil bones, the ones that looked an awful lot like the contemporary ones your Dr. McPhillips found."

"Did you ever prove they were Wwafida fossils?" asked Maybri, hunched anxiously over the table.

Llissa shook her head. "Well, I shouldn't say definitively no—my father thought they were. Our scientists didn't agree. That led to a huge fight. He demanded the bones back, and we refused to let him have them. And that was the last time he ever spoke a civil word to anyone connected with Collegium."

"I wish I could get those fossils into our lab," McCoy said.

"So do I. But Hhayd's Paladins probably tore Collegium apart, and if they found the fossils, I'm sure they're ground to dust by now."

Maybri bounced her balled fists on the table. "Then we'll just have to find some more."

"That," said Kirk, "sounds like an excellent idea."

Llissa's squared shoulders relaxed for the first time since she'd started her presentation. "I was hoping someone would say that." She grinned.

"What would our next step be?" Kirk asked. "Can you locate that mountain range?"

"I could if I had all our charts, but I don't."

"Charts," Kirk mused. "Particular charts, or just complete charts of the planet's underwater geography?"

"Any charts, as long as it's all there."

"Greenberger, that's your next assignment," Kirk ordered. "Work with cartography and geology to do a full scan of Akkalla."

Llissa slumped into her seat, her face dour. "There's a big problem, even after we locate the mountains."

"What's that?" Kirk asked.

"We have no way of getting down there. My research subs aren't on the *Enterprise*. Do you have anything that can dive six thousand meters under an ocean and protect people from the pressure?"

Maybri spoke first. "We did—the *Cousteau.*"

"Scotty," Kirk said, "you've looked over the damage reports on the *Cousteau*—"

"Aye, sir."

"Do you have what it takes to fix her?"

The chief engineer stiffened as if insulted. "Capt'n, I've got what it takes t'fix anythin'."

Kirk suppressed a smile. "We're counting on you, Scotty. Let's get to work. Proving these Wwafida are real may be the only way we'll get Spock and Chekov—and the science team—back alive."

Chekov stood on his toes to peek out through the peephole in their cell door. "They're coming."

He skipped back as the lock clicked and the door creaked open. Four burly guards stepped in, with chains and manacles obviously meant for Chekov and Spock.

"Akkallan jewelry," Chekov muttered. With one guard pointing a weapon at them, Chekov and Spock submitted, and their legs and hands were soon in irons. A single sturdy chain linked them together as they were led from their cell, but the guards refused to tell them where they were going.

They negotiated several levels of descending steps, a walk made considerably more difficult by the leg shackles. Finally, they exited into open air and a damp drizzle as they stood on a shelf of rock cut out of the cliff wall. Spock guessed the Citadel to be directly above them at the top of the crag. The guards motioned them to continue down metal stairs hanging onto the sheer rock as it inclined steeply down to the bay. At the bottom, they reached a spindly pier where they were added to a score of milling prisoners, also bound in chains.

"I see they're treating you like real Akkallans," boomed a familiar voice.

Spock and Chekov turned to see the weathered-granite face of Zzev, the leader of the Cape Alliance band that had first welcomed them to the planet. He shuffled a little closer to them. "Didn't expect to see you two again."

Spock's voice was neutral. "Our presence here should be ample proof of our contention that neither we nor the science outpost were working in concert with the government."

Zzev's head angled in a conciliatory gesture. "I guess we were wrong about you after all."

"A little late for regrets," Chekov hissed. "If you'd trusted us before, we could've worked together and wouldn't be in these." He shook the heavy metal cuffs on his wrists.

"What's passed is past, Chekov. Knowing what I know now, maybe we'd have done it differently. With a little luck, maybe we'll get a second chance."

"Indeed?" Spock asked. "Should we be extricated from this, might we consider that a firm proposal?"

"Maybe. Why don't we worry about it when it happens."

"If it happens," Chekov said glumly.

"We were not informed as to our destination," Spock said.

"We're being taken to an offshore prison," Zzev said. "They need more room in the Citadel. I guess they're planning plenty of arrests. Akkalla is now under third-stage martial law. You're going to see people arrested for having the wrong color hair."

A cutter with military markings glided up to the pier, and two helmeted guards secured its mooring lines to the pilings.

"Where is this prison?" asked Spock.

Zzev didn't answer immediately. His attention was momentarily distracted by a pair of late-arriving guardsmen who trotted down to exchange places with two troopers about to board the cutter with the prisoners. The two who'd been replaced seemed not to mind missing this trip, and they climbed back up toward the Citadel, disappearing inside the mountain's tunnels and passageways.

"Uh, on a very small, inhospitable island. So small, it doesn't even have a name."

"Who are the rest of these people?" Chekov asked as they were herded onto the boat rocking on gentle swells at dockside.

"Some are Cape Alliance, others just unlucky enough to be falsely accused."

Five armed guards joined the two crewmen piloting the cutter, while the prisoners sat on short benches in a rear compartment arranged like a Roman slave-galley without the oars. The two newcomers to the guard detail circulated among the prisoners, locking chains to floor anchors and securing shackles. Up in the cockpit, the pilots belted themselves into their seats and called for the moorings to be detached. Deep inside the boat, engines hummed to life with a turbinelike whistle but produced no vibration at all.

"What motive power source does this vessel use?" said Spock.

Zzev shrugged. "Electromagnetic field produced by the craft exerts force against conductor molecules in the water. No moving parts. Very efficient."

"Indeed."

The cutter accelerated smoothly away from shore, navigating around shoals and passing through the strait between the two towering cliffs protecting Havensbay. Once clear of hazards, the pilots throttled up, and the craft surged ahead but lurched over each wave it was forced to traverse. That stumbling didn't last long, as hydrofoils unfurled from housings on both sides of the hull. They lifted the boat above the whitecaps, and it skimmed toward open water.

The rhythmic splash of waves brushing beneath the boat, the hum of the field generators below deck, and the warmth of the cabin all conspired to make Chekov doze. As he flopped forward, a chain dug into his side and he jerked upright, reorienting himself. Unfortunately, he was still on a prison transport, and a glance around told him there was no land in sight. He wondered how far offshore this island was.

Next to Spock, Zzev leaned over and whispered out the side of his mouth. "Whatever happens, don't interfere, and stay low."

One of Zzev's hands slipped out of an unlatched restraining cuff, and he slowly bent down to reach under a blanket beneath the bench. When he sat up, he cradled a palm-sized hand-weapon, then held it out of sight between his legs, pretending he was still firmly chained. Spock scanned the cabin and perceived that three other prisoners appeared to be free and armed. Had he not seen what Zzev did, he never would have noticed anything unusual. Apparently, the five guards hadn't noticed either. They stood at their posts,

174

three at the front of the cabin, two aft, watching but not seeing.

The guard in the right front corner made a half-turn toward his two troopmates, and he subtly pointed his weapon away from the prisoners. "Now!" he shouted, and he gunned down one of the other guards at point-blank range. All in a single instant, Zzev and the other three armed prisoners wheeled to target the unsuspecting guards and pilots. As Spock, Chekov, and some of the others still shackled dropped to the floor, a flurry of shots volleyed around the cabin for no more than five seconds. Then, as suddenly as the shooting started, it was over. Spock and Chekov sat up and took stock. One guard was wounded and out of commission, two other troopers and two bystanding prisoners lay dead, and the fifth guard and the pilots were under the gun and disarmed. The lightning-quick revolt was a success.

"How did you infiltrate one of your own agents into the Grolian Guard?" Chekov asked as Zzev unlocked their chains with a pick. All around them, prisoners and jailers traded places.

"Not everybody agrees with what the government's been doing. We have a small fifth column, but it's growing. And there was plenty of confusion at the Citadel this morning. I understand Commandant Hhayd tried to assassinate Ffaridor last night, and this morning he was executed by the brigadier herself."

Chekov flexed his wrists. "What happens now?"

"Well, we've got some prisoners and a powerful new cutter for the Alliance."

"I am still interested in pursuing our proposal to cooperate with each other. We have the resources of a starship to help you," Spock said.

The Akkallan rebel pointed a thumb at the glowering sky. "But your starship's up there. We need help down here."

"We may be able to afford such assistance, once we ascertain together what it is you require."

"Weapons. Top of the list."

Spock shook his head. "We cannot get involved in the fighting."

"Then what can you do?" His voice was bitter.

"We would like to help settle your disputes," Spock said. "If you will allow us—"

"Zzev! Come up here—hurry!"

The shout came from one of the rebels in the cockpit, and Spock and Chekov followed Zzev as he stepped around the new prisoners huddled in irons in midcabin.

"What is it, Ppeder?"

Ppeder sat in the primary pilot's seat, one hand lightly gripping the steering bar, the other resting on the throttle. He was a stocky man with a short muscular neck and a stubbly black beard. "Incoming message—listen—" He turned up the volume on the cutter's radio.

"—sighted harvest fleet heading for your immediate vicinity. You are ordered to abort your transport mission and return to coastal waters until harvest area is declared clear. Do not engage—repeat—do not engage! Estimated harvest danger zone coordinates—seventy-five slash one-forty-nine. Acknowledge—"

"Do it," Zzev ordered.

Ppeder touched the transmit toggle and spoke into the unit. "Acknowledged."

"It's a good thing we heard that," Chekov said with a relieved grin. "We could've sailed right into the mouth of—"

"Full ahead," Zzev said. "Intercept."

Chekov stared at him. "Are you insane?"

Zzev shook his head. "No. Alliance members have sworn a pledge to do whatever we can to stop the harvests, even if it costs us our lives."

"I can understand your devotion to principle," Spock said, "but I submit that such devotion may be counterproductive. You are a leader in your movement. Your presence is necessary to—"

Zzev cut him off. "Nobody's more important in the Alliance."

"Theoretical egalitarianism is rarely logical when applied to practical situations. Should you die in this action, there would be no opportunity to make use of the capabilities of the *Enterprise*. I urge you to consider that."

"This comes first, Spock. There's no other way. It's not our intention to commit suicide, believe me. We've developed techniques and strategies for this. We haven't lost any lives yet, not at this."

"There's always a first time," Chekov mumbled.

"We're not going to be alone," Ppeder said from the pilot's seat. "We've got two boats headed for the zone. We've been in contact."

Zzev pumped a clenched fist. "Good!"

Something raised the hackles on Chekov's neck—a prickly rumbling suddenly surrounding the cutter, permeating the air itself, mixing with the salt spray swirling around the speeding craft. The vibration picked up in intensity.

"There—! Out there!" One of the rebels, a curly-haired woman, pointed skyward off the port bow. They all looked and they all saw it—the Chorymi harvest fleet, a lumbering mother ship with a half-dozen fighters flitting like gnats off its mighty flanks.

Off in the distance, the other two Alliance boats skipped across the waves toward the same imaginary point of intersection as the liberated military vessel. Although the harvest ship hadn't even begun its final approach, the seas were already churning with high waves buffeting the cutter and breaking across the bow, spewing foam and spray through the cockpit windows.

Chekov eyed the Akkallan rebels. Suicidal or not, they were committed to this course. Shielding his face from glare, he looked up at the space fleet and his stomach heaved—it wasn't seasickness, in spite of the roughening water. It was the sight of the mother ship tipping forward, its maw opening, beginning its inexorable descent to the ocean's surface. *"Nyeba shchaditye nashi byedni gluppi dushi,"* he said prayerfully.

"What was that, Chekov?" Spock asked.

"Heaven have mercy on our poor stupid souls. . . ."

Viewed from behind, the light spilling from the *Enterprise*'s open hangar bay glowed like a warm hearth in a frigid and endless night. In an auxiliary control room suspended high over the cavernous hangar deck, Engineer Scott nudged the tractor beam directional stick and eased the crippled marine shuttle *Cousteau* toward a comfortable and dry berth for repairs. Scott followed his progress on a pair of screens above the console, one displaying a green-line schematic while the other showed actual pictures from cameras mounted at the starship's stern.

"Just a wee bit further," he coaxed as the powerless little craft inched forward. With his free hand, he punched up a closer angle on the video image viewer, revealing more details of the damage. "Y're bent and bruised and water-logged, lassie, but we'll have y' goin' again."

Scott thumbed the intercom. "Engineer t'bridge."

"Kirk here."

"She's aboard, sir."

"Estimated repair time, Scotty?"

"Admiral, I haven't even looked at 'er yet," Scott protested in his best put-upon voice. "How would the end o' the day be, sir?"

Kirk kept a straight face, but his eyes crinkled with amusement. *"That would be fine. I'll come down for an inspection as soon as I can. Don't forget to take before and after pictures."*

Scott allowed himself a half-smile. "Aye, sir. Scott out."

"Sir," said Ensign Greenberger from the bridge science station, "I think you may want to see this." Her fingers two-stepped across her keyboard, and the small viewscreen above the science console flickered as it sought to filter some heavy interference. "There!"

The signal cleared, presenting a distinct but distant image of a Chorymi harvest convoy over Akkallan seas, poised in descent formation.

"Where did they come from?"

"I was just checking the atmospheric probe to see if it was still working, and there they were."

Kirk frowned. "Why didn't they trip our deflectors, Mr. Sulu? Malfunction?"

Sulu ran a test from his own board. "Negative, sir—no malfunction. Judging by their location, I'd say they approached while we were one-eighty degrees away."

"Used the planet as a shield," Kirk mused.

"Good thing we kept the probe out there, sir," Greenberger said.

"Give us a closer look, ensign."

"Aye, sir." She adjusted magnification on the mother ship

just as its scoop-front was locking into open position. The diamond-shaped fighters flitted away, as if they feared being sucked into the mouth of the harvest vessel.

"Main viewer, ensign. And let's see if there're any Akkallan surface craft engaging the harvest fleet."

As Greenberger switched the video feed to the central screen, members of the bridge crew couldn't help splitting their attention between their own jobs and the images from the planet. The young science officer manipulated the probe's cameras, revealing Kirk's concern to be well founded—a trio of small Akkallan boats scudded across the waves, bent on converging in the heart of the harvest zone.

The convoy and the boats played out the same death-daring ballet as the starship crew had witnessed once before. As the giant vessel dipped down toward the swirling ocean, the escort fighters wheeled, banked, and dove, trying to scare off the interfering boats—to no avail. The fighters regrouped for a second pass—their last, judging by the leveling off of the mother ship at extremely low altitude. The waves were already forming into the heaving wall of water that would soon surge up toward the harvest vessel's great mouth. This time, the fighters fired their cannons, spitting blue flame from ventral ports, carving an artful warning arc around the struggling boats. But the boats refused to yield. The fighters spiraled away, and the harvest ship lumbered forward. The boiling vortex of seawater rose into the air, and the three Akkallan surface craft heeled hard over and sped toward the center of the cyclone.

Kirk's knuckles whitened as he gripped the arms of his seat. "Veer off," he whispered, urging the boats to safety.

At what must have been the last possible instant, two of the boats did just that. But the third wouldn't, or couldn't. It gyrated wildly, bouncing completely out of the water like a stone skipping off the waves, then tumbled end over end. It began to break up, then stood on its bow as it was irretrievably caught in the frothing waterspout, finally splintering like a fragile toy. Some pieces spun away, hurled by centrifugal force, but the mechanized leviathan swallowed most of the debris.

The horrific scene stunned the *Enterprise* bridge crew into total silence, broken only by the pinging of automatic electronic gear and the chatter of status reports issuing from the rest of the starship, from personnel who hadn't watched what they had.

Time itself seemed to stand still until the Chorymi harvest ship slowly closed its maw and rose into the funereal clouds hanging low in Akkalla's sky, joining its escorts for the journey home. Down below, the remaining pair of boats circled gingerly back to the calming waters like stricken animals searching for a companion stolen from the herd. They nosed about in aimless patterns for a while, then limped away.

Kirk let out a long-held breath, and all around the subdued bridge, his crew returned to work, trying to shake off what they'd seen, moving as if still dazed. But Uhura sat up with a start and clutched her earpiece tightly in place.

"Admiral." Her voice came out hoarse, unbelieving, and she had to clear her throat before she could continue. "Message from—from Mr. Spock!"

Kirk's eyes opened wide, and he sucked in a sharp breath. "What?"

"Message from Mr. Spock," the communications officer repeated, more smoothly this time. She extended one graceful finger and ceremoniously switched the signal to external bridge speakers. "On audio, sir. Go ahead, Mr. Spock."

"Admiral, we are alive and undamaged." The Vulcan sounded as impassive as ever.

Kirk laughed out his relief and gave the intercom button on his armrest a jaunty jab. "We're mighty glad to hear that, Spock. But where the hell have you been for the past week? And where are you now?"

"A long and complicated tale which I look forward to relating from the comfort of the Enterprise."

"The least you could've done was send us a postcard."

"Pardon me, sir?"

"Never mind, Spock, never mind. Uhura, are we locked on to their signal?"

"Coordinates already transferred to the transporter room."

"Admiral." It was Chekov, sounding incredibly overjoyed. *"Would you like us to bring you some fish?"*

"Fish, lieutenant?"

"Yes, sir—we're in the middle of the ocean."

"No fish, Chekov. Are you ready to beam up?"

"We are, sir," Spock answered. *"But we are a party of three."*

"I suppose we'll get the explanation once you're aboard."

Kirk switched to an intraship channel. "Transporter room, beam up three from Mr. Spock's coordinates. When they're aboard, tell them to report to sickbay." He switched to another channel. "Kirk to sickbay—Bones, I've got some customers for you."

"Who?"

"Spock and Chekov."

"Hallelujah!"

"They're beaming up now and heading directly for sickbay. Give 'em a thorough exam. And have Llissa meet us there—I want to get started debriefing them right away."

"I'm already here, Jim," Llissa's voice replied. *"That's great news about your officers. How did you find them?"*

"We didn't—somehow, they found us. Anyway, we'll get the whole story from Spock and Chekov. On my way. Kirk out."

When he popped out near sickbay, he could hear shouting from McCoy's office and wondered what the hell was going on. He could make out Llissa on one end of the battle, but who was she arguing with? The sickbay doors whooshed open, and he saw McCoy and Chapel standing with Spock and Chekov, both looking a bit tattered but otherwise healthy. They were all spectators as Llissa and an older man quarreled in voices rapidly reaching a crescendo. The man had the raw-boned stance of an outdoorsman, with close-cropped hair the color of burnished steel and a weathered face.

The bickering couldn't have been going on for long—*they just beamed up, for godsakes*—but it was already way past the point of communicating, well along toward coming to blows. Kirk couldn't make out more than an occasional word, so he waded in and physically shoved Llissa and the newcomer to opposite sides of the room.

"That's enough!" he thundered, and found himself surrounded by sudden and profound silence.

McCoy leaned close to Spock. "I didn't know he could yell that loud."

"Quiet!" Kirk barked, making McCoy snap to mock-attention. "Spock, Chekov, good to have you back. Now who is this?" He stabbed a finger toward the stranger.

"He is one of the leaders of the Cape Alliance, Admiral," said Spock. "We thought his presence might be useful in dealing with the problems on Akkalla."

"Uh-huh. And does he have a name, Mr. Spock?"

"Yes, sir. Zzev—"

"Kkayn," Llissa finished, standing with hostile arms folded across her chest.

The captain and the doctor did double-takes and wound up staring at Llissa. Spock and Chekov simply looked confused. "Wha—?" was all Kirk could manage to say.

"Zzev Kkayn," Llissa replied in a brittle tone. "My father."

CAPTAIN'S LOG—STARDATE 7828.8:

Lieutenant Chekov and First Officer Spock have been certified physically fit by Dr. McCoy and have returned to duty. By combining our information, we have a much more complete picture of the situation on Akkalla, though it remains to be seen whether that helps us ascertain the fates of Dr. McPhillips and her missing science team. Chief Engineer Scott continues repair work on the shuttle *Cousteau,* a vessel we're going to need in perfect working order if we're to explore the Akkallan ocean for evidence to support the existence of the legendary Wwafida. We now have aboard the Akkallan scientist who's been the driving force behind efforts to prove these mysterious sea creatures are still alive. That means we have Zzev Kkayn's knowledge and guidance. Unfortunately, we also find ourselves in the middle of a bitter and long-standing feud between Dr. Kkayn and his daughter Llissa.

Kirk hated to lecture anyone about anything, but on rare occasions he could be driven to it—a classic, finger-wagging, square-jawed, no-counterpoints-allowed lecture. This was one of those times. He sat Zzev and Llissa Kkayn down in none-too-soft sickbay lab chairs, right next to each other. He chased McCoy, Chapel, Spock, and Chekov out of the medical office and locked the door. He warned Uhura in the tersest of terms that she wasn't to disturb him with any messages or calls from anyone until further notice, unless said messages dealt with the imminent end of the universe. In that unlikely circumstance, he would allow a note slipped under the door.

For a full half-hour, he remained closeted with the Kkayns, informing them of the rules of life on the starship *Enterprise* and making damn certain they understood what was at stake now. He honestly didn't care what personal and familial animosities they'd nursed for the past thirty years. At this moment, they had a common cause. Distasteful as it might be, they were on the same team; and, frankly, they needed Kirk's help to accomplish anything. They might have to compromise with each other, something they'd evidently never been able to do in the past.

"I've got no time or energy to run a family counseling service," Kirk snapped. "We have a job to do. We all have something to gain by success. We all pull together, or I'll beam you both down and let the Publican deal with you. Is all this crystal clear to both of you?"

Father and daughter reacted with silence and the same downcast eyes, looking more like a couple of chastened schoolchildren than two eminent scientists. Kirk noticed a fleeting family resemblance, and he almost laughed. Almost. He called security to escort Zzev and Llissa to their quarters —separate quarters, different decks in fact—and when they'd gone, he found Spock and McCoy waiting in the sickbay examining room.

"I'm impressed, Jim," McCoy said with a grin. "You ever thought of being a psychologist or a hellfire an' damnation preacher?"

Kirk felt drained. "How do you know what I said?"

"Cross-circuited the intercom and patched into my office. Heard every word."

Kirk looked mildly annoyed. "I thought you were a doctor, not a communications engineer."

"A man of many talents," McCoy answered modestly.

"Spock—didn't you stop him?"

"He couldn't, Jim," said McCoy. "I threatened to use my medical authority and prolong his next physical."

The first thing Kirk noticed upon entering the briefing room was that the Doctors Kkayn had chosen seats at opposite ends of the table. Spock, McCoy, and Scott sat on one side, leaving a chair empty for Kirk. Maybri and Greenberger sat together across from the senior officers. The two youngsters had done such good jobs in Spock's absence that Kirk decided to let them continue working on the Akkallan situation.

"Computer—"

"Working."

"Display Akkallan topography charts."

The main viewer on the wall lit up with a computer-generated relief map of the entire planet, including the floor of the seas. The underwater mountain range that Zzev had wanted to explore rose up like a sawtooth spine from the bottom of the Boreal Ocean up north. The mountains were a third of the way around the globe from the mainland continent, with only a few insignificant islands dotting the water's surface anywhere nearby. Past the northernmost tip of the mountain chain were two groupings of larger islands, up near Akkalla's arctic circle.

"How does our chart compare with what you mapped?" asked Kirk.

"Looks like home," Llissa said. "Everything's right where it should be."

"And that's where you found your fossils?"

"My fossils, Kirk," Zzev said.

Kirk ignored the provocation. "All right—does it make sense to center the search in the same area?" Both Llissa and Zzev nodded. "Zzev, show us exactly where you were." Kirk picked up a penlight laser, clicked it on, and aimed the red pinpoint beam at the viewscreen. Then he handed it to Kkayn, who zeroed in on a widening of the range, on the west face, a quarter of the way down from the north tip.

"Right there, Kirk."

"Mr. Scott, are repairs on the *Cousteau* completed?"

"Aye, sir. M'crew is just completin' tests on 'er now."

"Computer," Kirk said, "rotational view."

The image on the viewer changed from sectional relief maps to a three-dimensional depiction of Akkalla spinning on its axis but stripped bare of its watery cloak. Kirk gazed at the screen as the simulated planet began at the mainland, then rotated from west to east. The western seaboard of the continent, with Havensbay and the capital of Tyvol, slid by,

184

then out of sight. For a long time, a third of a revolution, there was nothing but the irregular pocks and rilles of the ocean basin. Finally, they reached the mountain range that was their target.

"Those mountains sure are a long way from land," Kirk said softly.

"That's one reason nobody knew they were there," Zzev said. "Nobody had any real reason to look."

Kirk folded his hands on the table. "Okay, if we find more fossils, where does that leave us?"

"With proof," Zzev said, "that the Wwafida are real."

"*Were* real," McCoy pointed out.

"If we can match any new fossils to the contemporary bones McPhillips found," Llissa said, "that'll prove they're still alive today—somewhere."

Kirk shook his head. "We've got to have enough ammunition on our side to shoot down all doubts. We're going to have to find a living specimen."

Maybri's ear tips twitched. "Matching the fossils and the recent bones has to come first, sir. If we can do that, we'll know we're actually looking for something that exists."

"*May* exist," McCoy said. "Those bones we've got date from ten years ago. If they really are from one of these Wwafida, how do we know it wasn't the last of its kind?"

"Leonard McCoy, optimist," Llissa said with a scowl.

"I'm just trying to keep things in scientific perspective here. The best hypothesis in the world isn't worth beans without irrefutable, reproducible evidence."

Llissa shrugged. "Leonard's right. We're getting all excited over possibilities. It's a good thing you're so logical, McCoy."

Spock's eyebrow rose sharply. He looked at Kirk. "Has Dr. McCoy undergone some sort of metamorphosis, Admiral?"

"Well," Kirk shrugged. "You have been gone a whole week, Mr. Spock."

"I should have doubted that an entire lifetime would be sufficient for a modification of such magnitude."

McCoy fixed Spock with an unflinching look. "Somebody had to fill those Vulcan shoes while you were missing, Spock. Wasn't too difficult, I might add."

Kirk stifled a snicker. "Let's go explore Dr. Kkayn's mountains. Scotty, please prepare the shuttle for launching. Zzev, Llissa, and Spock will go with me."

Maybri's face darkened by several shades, betraying her disappointment. But before she could decide whether to protest, Spock spoke up.

"Admiral, Lieutenant Maybri is more familiar with Akkalla's undersea topography than I. I suggest you take her instead. In order to be most effective, I believe I can use the time aboard to review events that transpired during my absence."

Kirk frowned. "I haven't piloted a marine shuttle before."

"Mr. Chekov proved to be a skilled pilot."

"All right, Spock. Recommendation accepted. Maybri, pack up whatever you think we'll need." Kirk switched on the intercom. "Mr. Chekov, report to the hangar deck in twenty minutes."

Kirk, Greenberger, and Spock returned to the bridge.

"Mr. Sulu," the admiral asked, "any sign of Chorymi ships since their last appearance?"

"Negative, sir. And they won't sneak up on us again using the planet as a shield—we've had long-range sensors sweeping intrasystem space between Akkalla and Chorym."

Spock clasped his hands behind his back. "Admiral, a few recommendations, based on assessments of Akkallan military technology. They have a moderately effective detection system for tracking air vehicles. Originally intended to help the Chorymi harvest convoys, it is now directed at repelling them. And as we have seen, they do have surface-to-air missiles with which to attack. You will be unescorted and will be at much greater risk than the Chorymi harvest craft was. Minimize your low-altitude flying."

"We should use the shuttle submarine capacities?"

"Affirmative. We can attempt to cloak your approach to some degree by sweeping the area with our own sensors. It will confuse the Akkallan defense scanners. But it will also interfere with your sensors aboard the shuttle."

"What about radio contact, Spock? Can they detect signals?"

The science officer nodded. "Yes. Contacts should be kept

186

to a minimum, decreasing the chances that your presence will be noticed."

"Very well. You have the conn, Mr. Spock."

"Jim, in the event of severe interference with your mission—" Spock began.

"I see what you're getting at. Use minimal force. I don't want us killing any Akkallans. I trust you to come up with nonlethal alternatives. From our standpoint, I don't want to lose the *Cousteau* again. She's the most valuable tool we've got to find out what we need to know." He stood. "Do what seems . . . logical."

The turbolift doors hissed open and McCoy came onto the bridge.

"You'll have McCoy to help," Kirk said with a grin.

The *Cousteau* vibrated slightly as it sliced into Akkalla's increasingly dense atmosphere. Friction heated the shuttle's skin, and a pink glow curled up around the craft, fogging the viewscreen and windows with a fiery haze.

Kirk gave the sensors a cursory look, and ship's functions registered normally. Chekov throttled back, and the shuttle jittered for a few seconds as it passed through the cloud cover. The viewers cleared, and though the sea was still another five kilometers beneath them, it loomed up quickly.

"All right, Mr. Chekov, how does this shuttle submerge?"

"Theoretically," Chekov began.

"What do you mean, theoretically?"

"Well, we never got to do any actual diving, sir."

"All right then," Kirk said. "Theoretically."

"It can dive straight into the ocean, or it can land first."

"I'd prefer landing first."

Chekov nodded. "Aye, sir." He reduced the shuttle's angle of descent and rate of speed, settling into a soft touchdown on top of a calm sea. Gentle swells rolled the craft from side to side.

The Russian flipped a trio of switches, inducing a hydraulic throb deep within the ship. Then they began to sink, with waves splashing over the windows and viewer.

Kirk swallowed, popping his ears to adjust to the increased pressure. He looked at the viewer as the last sliver of sky disappeared, and he felt a sudden hush envelop them. Since the craft was sealed against all outside environments, this new feeling was probably psychological, but that didn't make it any less tangible. Kirk hadn't been underwater like this in years, and the experience brought on a mixed batch of sensations: fear at being completely enfolded in an alien environment, surrounded by dangers unseen and unheard; isolation; and yet, at the same time, a security perhaps akin to floating in a womb, surrounded by wonders, being one with life never before encountered.

The melodic pinging of the shuttle's sensors drew Kirk back from his reflections. "Course laid in, Mr. Chekov?"

"Aye, sir."

"Ahead, full."

Chekov eased the throttle up, and the shuttle responded with a smooth surge. Kirk felt a tap on his shoulder and turned to find Maybri in the hatchway.

"Permission to open observation ports and start recording, sir?"

"Affirmative, lieutenant." Then he lowered his voice to a whisper. "Keeping the peace back there?"

"So far, so good, sir." She ducked under the cross-beam and returned to the rear cabin, finding a small control panel protected by a smoked-plexiglass screen. With a touch of a button, it slid up. She threw a set of toggles, and the port covers retracted, converting much of the side walls into clear windows. In addition, four video screens displayed images from dorsal and ventral cameras, so they could see what was going on above and below the shuttle. Maybri reacted with delight, scurrying from side to side and screen to screen, trying to see everything at once. The Akkallan ocean teemed with life darting between beams of light knifing down through the shallows, first racing toward this intruder in their world, then veering off an instant before collision.

A mist of microscopic creatures sifted through the light rays, drifting with the current's eddies. Schools of thousands of streamlined fish moved as if linked together, following the clouds of tiny creatures that made up their food, light from above strobing off their sides as the mass undulated through their silent cosmos.

As the *Cousteau* descended, the watery world outside rapidly darkened. All around the craft's hull, powerful beams turned the perpetual night of the deep into midday, and what they revealed in their blaze astonished the starship officers. If anything, there was more life in this darker, colder realm than in the shallows still served by the sun—

—ornate shells powered by water jets thrusting out a rear orifice, like living armored warships—

—gelatinous bags with propellerlike appendages at both ends, capable of spinning so fast they became blurs as the sack creatures sped after prey—

—fluttery tendrils attached to what looked like a hunk of drifting flotsam. When an unsuspecting fish nosed up to try to eat the plantlike tendrils, a jagged pincer flashed out, clamped onto the fish, and yanked it inside for digestion—

—bulbous fish with outsized tusks jutting from their lower jaws—

—a creature that looked like a comical pair of floating lips, decorated in brilliant multicolored stripes. When a gelatinous sack stopped spinning its propellers near the lips, they parted and spat an inky, viscous stream that surrounded the sack and paralyzed it. The lips sucked their victim inside—

—and a diaphanous net, shimmering like silver strands in the shuttle's floodlights.

Chekov dropped the craft down, trying to go under the net. But it extended deeper and deeper; the lower the ship's light beams went, the more of the endless net came into view.

"Is that net alive?" Kirk called to the scientists in the back.

"Yes, Jim," Llissa said. "You don't want to run into it if you can avoid it."

"That may not be possible. It seems to go on forever. Is it dangerous?"

"It cranks out quite an electromagnetic charge. I don't know what it might do to the ship if it traps us."

"Chekov, deflectors?"

"They won't work under water, Admiral."

"Then keep diving. And stop forward motion. Don't get any closer to it."

"Forward motion is stopped, sir. It's coming toward us."

Llissa watched on one of the viewers. "It looks like it's decided to see if we're edible."

"Are we?" Kirk asked warily.

"Not edible, exactly, but it might be able to hurt us."

"Can we hurt it first?"

Before Kirk could get an answer, the net creature reached the shuttlecraft and folded around the nose cone, making little scraping sounds on the hull as thousands of suckers sealed onto the metal. Kirk looked out the side port and saw some of them pucker for a grip. A second later, main power sputtered and winked off, taking cabin lights, all major systems, and instruments with it. Batteries kicked in, powering up emergency life-support pumps and lights. A smattering of gauges glowed in the dim cockpit.

"Anybody have any ideas?" Kirk asked. "What if we channel some sort of charge through the hull?"

"Won't work, Kirk," Zzev replied. "It likes energy."

"Then what doesn't it like?"

"Shallower depths and lower pressures. You've got to get us closer to the surface."

Kirk huddled with Chekov. "Can we do it?"

"We've got no power for the engines."

"Batteries?"

"They'd be drained so much so fast, we might lose life support before we hit the surface. The only other choice is filling ballast tanks with oxygen. Once we do that, we'll have no way of refilling them, so we'll lose that option in case anything goes wrong later on."

"Mr. Chekov, if we don't get this net thing off us in a hurry, we won't have any later on to worry about. Hit the ballast tanks."

Chekov hunted for the valve controls, found them, and opened the tanks. The shuttle began to rise immediately, staggering like a punchy prizefighter. Kirk watched anxiously for signs of the suction cups letting go. With the *Cousteau*'s external lights off, they were engulfed in darkness again, limiting visibility to nothing. Those suckers on the windows were their only guide.

"We have risen five hundred meters, sir," Chekov said, his face inches from the green digital depth meter. "Is it working?"

"Not yet. Zzev, are you sure—" One sucker popped off, then another. "It's leaving!"

Suddenly the net creature released its grip all at once, as if being ripped away. Shuttle systems flickered back on, and

Chekov monitored all the vital readouts. "Admiral, full power is restored."

"Cut off the ballast tanks, Chekov," Kirk said quickly. "Hold our position here."

"Aye, sir."

The ship groaned as it stopped its rapid ascent, and Kirk poked his head into the rear cabin. "Zzev, you sure were right about it not liking shallower depths. That thing took off in a hurry."

"Uhh, Jim," Llissa said, "it was pulled off."

"By what? That net stretched forever. What could be big enough to—" Kirk's voice trailed off as he became aware of something gigantic swimming past the side observation ports. The external lights were back on, and Kirk carefully approached the window, not certain he wanted to be introduced to any more Akkallan sea life. By the time he looked out, whatever he thought he'd glimpsed was gone. "Did I or did I not see something extremely large?"

"You bet you did," said Maybri quietly. She turned to the Kkayns. "What was it?"

"A triteera," Zzev said. "The way that ganiphage got yanked off, I'd say it was more than one."

Kirk squinted. "What's a triteera?"

Llissa pointed over his shoulder, out the opposite observation window. *"That's* a triteera."

Kirk whirled in time to see a mottled dark-gray mass filling the entire port as it passed no more than five meters from the shuttlecraft. "That thing must've been thirty meters long."

"At least," Llissa said. She joined Kirk at the port, and he got his first full view of the triteera as it turned gracefully away from them. Kirk saw it was shaped something like a terran whale in profile, but with a bony beak at its front end, four flippers protruding from its side, a jagged spine running the length of its back, and a towering, triple-fluked tail propelling it effortlessly with powerful swishes.

"Awesome animals, aren't they?" said Llissa.

The one that brushed by the shuttle joined a herd containing more triteera than Kirk could count, extending out in their deep domain, well past the reach of the *Cousteau's* illumination. "Are they dangerous?"

Llissa shook her head. "Just the opposite. They're gentle

giants. They go out of their way to avoid small boats, and there are stories of them saving people from drowning by pushing them to the surface. We don't really know too much about them because they usually swim far offshore. But that rescue behavior in those stories coincides with what they do to aid babies or sick individuals in the herd."

Maybri's ear tips perked. "Why did they pull off the net thing?"

"The ganiphage," Llissa prompted. "Triteera eat ganiphages. They love them, in fact. We probably would've gotten it off just by surfacing, but this was a lot faster. And we managed to save some of the ballast air supply in case we need it later."

"Well," Kirk said, "we owe one to the triteera."

"We'll probably see them again," Zzev added. "It's spring, and they're heading north to their favorite feeding grounds. It's where the equatorial currents meet arctic waters. The temperature difference churns up the best nutrients from the bottom, causes an incredible soup of microorganisms, and that in turn attracts all sorts of other creatures. To top it off, the water's pretty shallow up there. There's a plateau that rises close enough to the surface to get some sunlight. Makes it even more fertile. All the triteera have to do is swim with their beaks open, and they gorge themselves."

One of the giant beasts swept by the shuttle as if on cue, and Kirk grinned. "Sounds like triteera paradise."

Llissa frowned. "Except for one thing, Jim. They've got no real predators, so they just sort of lumber along in herds that stretch for kilometers. That makes them perfect targets."

"I thought you said they had no natural predators," Maybri interrupted.

"They didn't—until the harvest ships came along. Triteera are their favorite catch. Once they start feeding, they don't like to pay attention to anything but that. By the time they realize a harvest ship's bearing down on them, it's too late for a lot of them."

"That's right," Zzev said. "Their only escape route is diving. But the harvest ships might take a couple of hundred in a single sweep. Lots of return for very little effort."

"Does that mean we're going to be in a target area, too?" Kirk asked with concern.

"Anywhere there're triteera," Zzev growled, "is a target area. But we'll be safe as long as we stay deep."

Kirk turned to the cockpit. "Any damage, lieutenant?"

"No, sir. All systems nominal. We're ready to go."

"Llissa, any suggestions for avoiding those ganiphage net things?" Kirk asked.

She nodded. "Dive deep right here. They tend to congregate at middle depths. Once we're below that, we shouldn't run into any more of them."

"You heard her, Chekov. Take us 'way down."

"Aye, sir."

As they started descending, Kirk leaned against the viewing port and watched the triteera playing and nuzzling, and he recalled the fate of so many of Earth's cetacean species, hunted to extinction in the twentieth and twenty-first centuries. He hoped these Akkallan creatures would fare better. He and the others aboard the *Cousteau* already owed their lives to the giant animals. If he possibly could, Kirk was determined to return the favor.

Chapter Nine

As THE *COUSTEAU* sailed through silent depths, Kirk marveled at how much the ocean floor resembled the land, with mountains and valleys, troughs and channels, craters, and featureless plains of mud and silt. Many of the mountain summits wore a coat of white powder, almost like snow, consisting of skeletons of tiny organisms from above, drifting down once they died. Other mountains in Zzev's range were steep-sided cones, never subject to erosion by frost or the cutting force of patient rivers. Some stretches of the flat sea floor were humped with huge dunes, shifting like desert dunes on dry land as strong currents scoured the bottom like gales.

And even at these great depths, there was life—less numerous, less colorful, but even stranger than the forms they'd seen at midlevels. Many were bioluminescent, their bodies producing the only light in this realm of perpetual darkness. Still other creatures lived not only without light but without sight as well, using tentacles, oscillating cilia, and other organs to sense their environment.

They were eight kilometers below sea level, where the crushing pressure came close to testing the structural limits of the *Cousteau.* Zzev crouched in the cockpit hatch, silently watching the viewers, the ports, and the navigational chart projected on a computer grid. In the short time he'd known Zzev Kkayn, Kirk had learned that this Akkallan wouldn't hesitate to speak up if he thought something was wrong—another characteristic father shared with daughter, although neither would admit it. The fact that

Zzev was quiet as Chekov piloted the ship was taken as an indication that they were on the correct bearing.

But to Kirk, all the exotic scenery had taken on a disconcerting sameness. "Zzev, are you sure you'll be able to find the caves?"

"We'll find them. And I'll finally get to see what's inside."

"You mean you never went in?"

"Our exploration was cut short last time." He flashed a brief glare at Llissa, who was too busy huddling with Maybri over a computer terminal to notice.

"Then where did you find the fossils?"

"On a higher plateau. And I think we're coming up on the spot."

They watched the sidescan sensors, probing the range's craggy flanks. The computer instantaneously digested the scanners' data and drew a three-dimensional depiction. At every point where the sensors detected an opening in the rock facade, they fired a measuring beam to chart the depth of the fissure. Then the screen displayed a three-hundred-sixty-degree cross-sectional image of the inside of the opening, spinning it around to show off all angles. So far, nothing qualified as a cave.

Not far ahead, the floodlights played across a flat outcropping beetling out from the slope.

"Slow down," Zzev ordered. He tilted the forelights down to reveal the squared contours of a mesa dropping off toward the ocean floor. Then he cross-referenced with the navigational chart. "This is it," he said with certainty.

"Where's this cave of yours?" Kirk asked.

"A little farther ahead. Go slow, Chekov. And deeper."

The Russian nudged the shuttlecraft forward at a crawl, and Zzev and Kirk stared at the sensor readout, which continued to show only the smooth slope. Then the image changed. The computer raced to analyze anomalous data and flashed the rotating view of the interior of an opening big enough to be a cave.

"That's it!" Zzev crowed.

Kirk rested a hand on Chekov's shoulder. "Let's take a closer look."

With a nod, Chekov steered the shuttle to starboard, examining the mountain's dark face with roving beams. Zzev and Kirk watched expectantly through the front ports.

"Not so fast," Zzev reprimanded. "Let me do it." He edged Chekov off the illumination remote and guided the beams with a deliberate hand. Finally, he found what he sought—a distinct entrance to a cleft in the stone side of the mountain.

"This vessel won't fit through that opening."

"Maybri tells me you've got two diving suits aboard that can withstand the pressures at this depth. I'm volunteering to go."

"I'm not accepting volunteers. We'll move a safe distance away from the mountains and send a remote probe in to take a look around. Maybri."

"Aye, sir," she said, turning right to the computer to call up the probe-control program.

Zzev looked displeased as he retreated to the rear cabin to watch Maybri at work. With arms crossed, Llissa gave her father a sidelong stare.

"Don't give Jim a hard time," she scolded. "You're finally getting to do what you've wanted for years."

"I'd like a little more cooperation."

"You're getting more cooperation than you deserve. And you'd better remember, this isn't being done for you. It's being done for the whole planet."

The ship vibrated as the probe popped out of a storage compartment in the shuttle's belly and floated free. One video screen at Maybri's console showed the view from the probe's camera, while the other showed the probe itself, a fat torpedo with three jointed arms tipped with four-fingered grippers. Zzev hovered over Maybri's shoulder, feigning casual disinterest.

"Uh, what can that thing do?"

Maybri smirked. "Anything we can. Probe's on its way, Admiral." The hand-held remote device had a simple joystick for all directional control, with side levers to manipulate the arms and claws.

Up front, Chekov maneuvered the *Cousteau* to its position of safety. Kirk bent low and left the cockpit to see how Maybri was doing. Onscreen, they watched the probe's-eye view as it approached the rift opening, powerful broadbeam lights shining in all directions from its stubby hull. Maybri deftly guided it through the opening and zoomed the lens to the widest possible angle. After advancing through the narrow passageway, the probe revealed an interior that abruptly broadened to form a wide but low burrow cutting into the heart of the mountain, its walls a jumble of curves and angles hinting at the violent natural forces that shaped it. The probe nosed into corners and niches, beams invading places that had never known light before.

Maybri spotted several stalks rooted in the sand, swaying with the flow of the water. Stopping the probe, she used the camera lens for a closer look and found each stalk had a mouth and a writhing bouquet of feelers around its head. "Are those animals?"

"Mm-hmm," said Zzev. "Canth eels."

"They live in caves?"

"Yeah. They filter microorganisms that float in on the current."

"Not a very interesting existence," Maybri sniffed. "Just sitting there."

"They display a more active behavior pattern, given the right stimulus," Zzev said.

The lieutenant edged the probe forward. Without warning, the canth eels erupted out of the sand, turning from swaying stalks into long snakes, thrashing like whips as they flung themselves at the mechanical intruder. The startling attack lasted less than a minute, and when they were satisfied that the probe was neither edible nor dangerous, they daintily reinserted their bodies into the sand and resumed their passive wobbling, leaving Maybri in open-mouthed amazement.

"I told you they could be more active," Zzev said with an impish smile. "They bury ninety percent of their length in the sand for camouflage. When they sense something bigger than micro-life, something that they either want to eat or that poses a threat, they do what we just saw."

"How dangerous are they?" Kirk asked.

Llissa considered. "Well, they've got tiny razor-sharp teeth, and they're constrictors, too."

"Are they aggressive?"

"If you steer clear of them, they won't come out chasing you," Zzev said.

"Admiral," Maybri said, her voice rising, "I think we've found something."

Everyone turned to a screen displaying the probe's view, watching with anticipation as the remote arm and hand carefully picked through silt on the cave floor, stirring up a veil of particles that obscured the picture. Maybri operated by feel, clamped onto a firm object, and backed the probe away from the murky cloud. Once in clearer water, she directed the sensitive claw to hold up its prize, *a fossilized bone.*

Zzev Kkayn clapped his hands in triumph. "I knew we'd find bones here."

"Bone," Kirk corrected, emphasizing the singular.

"No, sir," Maybri said. "Bones." The probe's second claw held two more bones, and all three were different sizes.

At Kirk's order, she told the little robot to stow the fossils and return to the *Cousteau.* Once aboard, they brought the bones up to the main deck for a closer look and decided they would need the facilities on the *Enterprise* to date and analyze them. Kirk opted for returning to space right away.

"There's a treasure trove in there," Zzev argued. "We're already here. It's stupid to turn back now."

"Calling the mission commander stupid isn't the best way to get what you want," Kirk said dryly.

"Admiral," Maybri said softly, "I think Dr. Kkayn is right."

Kirk's brow wrinkled. "Go on, lieutenant."

"The probe is a useful tool, sir, but it's no replacement for human hands and eyes and brains. If I don't have the camera and lights pointed just right, we could be missing the find of a lifetime. I'm volunteering to go in myself, if you'll let me. With two people, I think we'll be able to explore that cave twice as fast and be done with it, whatever we find."

Kirk pursed his lips. "You've made some good points, lieutenant. All right, two people will go into the cave—"

"That's more like it," Zzev growled.

"—and you're not one of them," Kirk continued, ignoring the outrage on Zzev's face. "I don't trust your judgment, Dr. Kkayn. Thorough exploration is important, but so is caution, and I don't think that word's in your vocabulary. Llissa, you and I will go in, if you want to."

"I'll go. A long time ago, my father called me a hothouse flower, devoted to books and theories," Llissa said. She

198

cocked her head at Zzev. "This seems like a good time for a little hands-on experience."

Down in the cramped air-lock, Kirk and Llissa prepared for their excursion, climbing into contoured, hard-shell diving suits with flexible joints and clear helmets that allowed an unobstructed view. Each suit had a small power and propulsion unit fastened to the back and lights attached to both arms, as well as an omnidirectional beacon on top of the helmet.

"The suit's so light, Jim. How does it work?"

"It's what we call a gill suit. It filters breathable oxygen right out of the water. Same principle on a larger scale provides the air for this shuttle when it's underwater. As for the specifics—" He shrugged, then indicated a stem coming up from inside the suit and curving across his chin. "This is your communications pickup. It's voice-actuated. Just press this"—he flipped a rocker switch on his suit's left forearm —"and it's on." He handed her a helmet and made sure she locked it properly on her neck ring. Then he put his own helmet on, activated both their communicators, and checked the pressure-seal safety light. "How do you feel?"

"Claustrophobic, but reasonably comfortable."

"Then let's go exploring. Mr. Chekov?"

"*Aye, sir,*" came the reply in his earpiece. They both heard it on the open-channel system.

"We're leaving the ship now." He hefted a flexible-mesh carrier containing some long-handled tools for poking, digging, and sifting. Llissa toted an empty one for carrying back whatever they might find.

"Good luck, Admiral. We'll be monitoring you. The homing beam is locked onto your suits in case of bad visibility."

Kirk waddled down the short ladder from the dressing shelf and stepped off into the water in the lower part of the air-lock. Climbing carefully, Llissa plunged in next to him. He pressed the release, and the external hatch slid open, allowing them to float out into the sea, where he hooked them together with a variable-length safety tether.

They swam purposefully toward the mountainside. Once they'd left the bubble of artificial brightness around the *Cousteau,* Kirk slowed and craned his neck to behold the darkness stretching in all directions like a permanently starless night. His eyes adjusted, and he could make out the peak above them, looming up beyond his vision. Knowing that the mountain's base was at least a kilometer beneath their position and that its pinnacle was kilometers over their heads—with kilometers more to the surface—made Kirk feel astoundingly insignificant.

"What is it, Jim?"

"Just waxing philosophical. Let's go." They moved ahead with powerful jets from the air-thrusters on their backs. Kirk did a forward flip, just for the hell of it.

"Pretty fancy. And here I was just worrying you were having second thoughts."

He grinned. "I was, for a second. I'd forgotten the feeling of freedom you get when you just float."

"Is this what it's like being in space?"

"Almost. In fact, before we had orbital stations for training old-time astronauts, they used to simulate weightlessness in water tanks. I've spent most of my adult life in spaceships, but I'm almost always *in* the ship, not actually out in space, floating free. That's why I'm enjoying this."

Their helmets lit up the face of the mountainside with a ghostly glow, and they found themselves facing the cave entrance. Shutting down their air-jets, Kirk swam in first, with Llissa following closely enough to touch his flipper tips. Ghostly shadows flickered and danced as the beams from the divers' arm lights moved with their strokes. Llissa tugged on the tether, guiding him away from the bobbing heads of the canth eels and toward the side where Maybri's probe uncovered the first three bones. She took one of the long sand probes and gently poked the sediment on the floor, taking care not to stir up too much and cut their visibility. Almost immediately, she turned up several more bones.

"Jim, I hate to say this, but my father might be right about this place."

She continued picking up large bones while Kirk took a sieve and strained for smaller fossils. Their combined effort had the collection bag filling up rapidly, and Llissa drifted off to the end of the safety cord. "Jim, look!"

Using the tether as a guide, he found her under a sharp

overhang, wedged into a space barely big enough for her to search without getting stuck. "What've you got?"

When she backed out of the crawlspace, she whirled quickly, hands thrusting toward him with a large round object clutched in her fingers. Before his brain could even pin a label to the thing, Kirk's reflexes made him start. Backlit by her sleeve lights, an intact skull grinned spectrally at him.

Llissa gave him a matching smile from within her helmet. "Sure do scare easily, Admiral Kirk."

He repressed a shudder. "This place is getting spookier by the second. And I can't help but feel we're grave-robbing."

"It's for a good cause." She placed the skull securely in the carrier. "Let's see what's back here——" With a graceful somersault, she swam toward recesses of the cavern the robot probe hadn't reached. Kirk hurried to keep her in sight as the passage grew increasingly twisty and tapered to the point where they could scarcely fit single file.

His shoulders were broader than hers, and he kept scraping the rocks. Though he knew the gill suit was sturdily armored, it was a sound that made him nervous nonetheless. Llissa darted around another bend.

"Oh, my seas, look at this," she whispered, her voice breathless with excitement.

Arms straight out because of the close confines, Kirk relied on a few extra-strong kicks to reach Llissa quickly, and he understood her thrill. The tiny corridor opened suddenly into a magnificent domed grotto. At the center was a structure that seemed to be some sort of altar, made of stones fit together like bricks, stones that had to be both hand-hewn and intentionally arranged. Hands fluttering, Kirk turned several times to take in the whole chamber. Around the outside wall were a dozen nooks. He went to one while Llissa swam to another. Before him, on shelves cut right into the rock, were casks that seemed to be made out of bones as big around as his biceps. Each was about as high as his forearm, and rows of symbols were etched around the outside of every cask. They were all sealed.

"Llissa, I found . . . containers of some sort."

"And I found more bones, but these are whole skeletons, and they—well, you've gotta see for yourself."

Putting the cask back on its ledge, Kirk swung around and found Llissa in an adjacent nook. There he saw five complete skeletons laid out on slabs in ritual fashion, with hammered metal jewelry clinging around their neck vertebrae. Momentarily stunned into silence, it took him an extra effort to find his voice. "Chekov, send the probe in here."

"Is something wrong, Admiral?" Maybri's voice broke in.

"On the contrary, lieutenant. I think we have your find of a lifetime here."

As commanding officer, Kirk had long ago made intellectual peace with the concept of delegation of responsibilities. On a vessel the size of a starship, he obviously couldn't do everything himself. He couldn't even oversee everything personally. He had the best crew a commander could want—talented, bright, eager—and senior officers who'd earned his trust over ten years of service together. But there were times he still wanted to be everywhere at once, doing most things himself or at least looking over the shoulders of the people to whom he'd been forced to leave certain tasks.

This was one of those times. But as he reclined on his bunk, he was proud of the restraint he'd shown on the hangar deck. From the instant the seashuttle touched down, he'd wanted to stay with those bones, casks and assorted samples every step of the way. Instead, he let McCoy and Spock cart the artifacts off to the medical and science labs, and he went to his cabin to clean up and rest up.

Now, two hours later, he was clean—but he wasn't resting. He was thinking, wondering what repercussions were about to spring from the load of bones and rocks and tricorder data being scrutinized without him.

"I know you're gonna want to sneak in," McCoy had warned, "and ask all sorts of incisive questions, thinking you see something we're overlooking, but *I* know everything, Jim. And anything I don't know, Spock knows. So stay out, don't bug us, and we'll call you when we're damn good and ready."

The bedside intercom whistled, and he stabbed the button. "Kirk here." He rolled to a sitting position and saw McCoy's poker face on the screen. "Ah, Bones. Am I permitted to leave my quarters yet?" he asked dryly.

McCoy scratched his neck. *"Speaking of bones, Jim, these had quite a story to tell. I don't mind tellin' you we're actually getting somewhere."*

"On my way."

He met Llissa and her father at the door of McCoy's office, and they entered together, finding the doctor at his desk, feet up, chair tilted comfortably back. Spock leaned on the edge of a cabinet, arms folded, his face as composed as ever—except for a definite cerebral fervor twinkling in those usually inscrutable eyes. Those who didn't know Spock well wouldn't have even noticed. Kirk noticed. He spread his hands in anxious invitation. "Well?"

McCoy tipped forward and ambled toward the lab next door. "Right this way, folks."

He led the group to a shallow trough atop one of the examining tables, where a complete skeleton was laid out.

"It certainly looks humanoid," Kirk said.

"Mm-hmmm." McCoy puckered his mouth non-committally. "Any other observations, Dr. Kirk—?"

"Sorry," Kirk surrendered. "Your patient, doctor."

"Thanks. You're right, it is definitely humanoid. In fact, a lot like this humanoid," McCoy said with a wave at Llissa, "but with some very interesting variations on standard Akkallan structure and musculature."

"Such as?"

"Such as lengthening of the femur late in life."

"Like a growth spurt in an adult?" Kirk interrupted.

"Right."

"Is that normal?"

McCoy deferred to Llissa, who shook her head. "Not for Akkallans it isn't."

"That's what I figured," McCoy said. He fingered the brown thighbone on the lab table. "But for this particular Akkallan—if that's what he was—it happened." He circled the skeleton. "Other niceties include evidence of webbing between fingers and toes, something Llissa seems to be missing, and changes in the size and shape of muscles."

"What else?"

"Well, judging from analysis of the bones themselves, this individual went through some sort of major physiological upheaval late in life."

Zzev's brows shot up. "The senescence!"

"Maybe, but we can't prove it, not from bones alone."

Kirk began to pace. "So what, if anything, *can* we prove? Is this the skeleton of an Akkallan?"

"There're a lot of similarities between this fella and a modern-day Akkallan, and there're also a lot of differences. These bones might very well've belonged to a creature that lived in the ocean. And wherever he lived, he's seven thousand years old."

Kirk's eyes opened wide. "And do these bones match the ten-year-old ones we found in McPhillips's lab?"

"I knew that'd be your next question, Jim. The answer is yes. Is this one of those mythological Wwafida? Beats the hell outta me. But if it is, then those new bones are from a Wwafida that died a decade ago."

"I knew it!" said Zzev. "I knew they still existed."

McCoy waggled a finger. "Now, we don't know that for sure. And we won't unless we find one that's alive."

"What do you think the chances are they're still out there, Spock?"

"Impossible to be specific, Admiral. There are any number of scenarios to support either possibility. Based solely on the meager information now in our possession, we have no way of extrapolating the condition of the population of these creatures over the past seven thousand years. Were their numbers increasing, decreasing, or remaining steady? Without additional facts, no logical conclusion is reachable."

Zzev turned surly. "Oh, c'mon, Spock. What's the likelihood that McPhillips just happened to find the bones of the last Wwafida to die?"

"Unknown. But in every case of extinction, one individual of a species was indeed the last of its kind, and the more recently that final specimen has expired, the greater the odds it may be found, before natural forces have had a chance to conceal or destroy it."

"And even if those new bones aren't from the last one," McCoy added, "if the population was down to almost nothing by then, it could be all the way to zero by now."

Kirk didn't really want to waste any more time arguing about a moot point. "Spock, what about the other artifacts we brought back?"

"A fascinating collection. We opened one of the casks. It contained a scroll, the substance of which was resistant to the deleterious effects of extended submersion in salt water." He rolled a small, clear tank over to the group. The scroll lay on the bottom, flattening out in the center but still partially curled toward the ends. "We have duplicated the chemical composition of Akkallan seawater to avoid any detrimental effects of a sudden change in environment. As you can see, it is in remarkably good condition, considering its age."

"How old is it?" Kirk asked.

"The same as the fossils—on the order of seven thousand years. We are still analyzing composition of the ink. The beings who manufactured it developed an ingenious compound that could withstand both the ravages of time and seawater."

Zzev and Llissa both hunched over the tank, studying the neatly scribed symbols, a precise fusion of blocky angles and compact loops. "It looks like Maic," Llissa mumbled absently.

"What's Maic?" Kirk asked.

"The first real language on Akkalla. I can't read it myself. One of the Guides on my Council is the expert." She straightened; her expression turned melancholy. "Was the expert—are they still alive?"

Kirk tried to be reassuring. "We've got no reason to think they're not. Could your expert translate this?"

"Probably. Let's hope she'll have a chance to try."

"What about the geological samples, Spock?"

"The mountains themselves are one billion years old, formed by normal geological processes. The rock samples from inside the cave indicate that the cave has been under the ocean for ten thousand years."

"Then this skeleton has to be from a sea-dwelling creature," said Kirk. "Land-dwellers obviously couldn't live in caves submerged for three thousand years. Isn't that logical?"

"It would appear to be, Admiral—barring totally unpredictable circumstances such as land-dwellers interring their dead in sea caves."

"Then what we've got," Kirk said, "is a ton of circumstantial evidence that Wwafida were real creatures in the past, evidently were intelligent and had a true culture, and they really *did* live in the ocean. We have a lot less evidence that the senescence actually took place, changing land-dwellers into sea creatures, right, Bones?"

"I'd say that's a fair statement, Jim. Medically speaking, I can't verify this senescence phase just by examining the remains of one individual."

Kirk started pacing again. "Okay, where does this leave us? We could go to your government with what we've got—"

Llissa shook her head. "Not enough, Jim."

"I agree, Kirk," said Zzev.

"We could go right to the Federation—"

"Without conclusive proof," Spock said, "I do not think the Federation would be able to act decisively. Politicians and diplomats are not noted for their bold actions."

Zzev chortled at the Vulcan's sarcasm. "I knew I liked you, Spock."

"All right," Kirk said. "Then we've got to find ourselves a living Wwafida."

McCoy crossed his arms. "Fine," he challenged, "but there's an awful lot of ocean down there. Now, if nobody's seen a live Wwafida in longer than anybody can remember, what makes you think we'll suddenly turn one up? I'd rather look for a needle in a haystack. At least the haystack's finite and the needle doesn't swim."

"Good point." Kirk's mouth tightened into a grim line. "If anybody's got any ideas, now's the time to speak up."

"I've got one," Zzev said in a subdued tone. "Can you have your computer cough up a map of Akkalla?"

"Sure." Kirk stepped over to the terminal on McCoy's lab desk. "Computer—"

"Working—"

"Display surface map of Akkalla."

With a flurry of blinking memory lights, the map appeared on the small screen. Zzev ran his fingertip on a line from the mainland's western seaboard to the underwater mountains they'd just visited, then northwest to some islands nearly on the other side of the world from the continent and at a latitude just below Akkalla's arctic zone.

"There," Zzev stated.

Llissa narrowed her eyes dubiously. "There what?"

"After we scrapped the cooperative project, I went off on my own again."

"Is that when you stopped publishing and started cutting your ties with everyone you ever knew?"

"I didn't have any choice."

Llissa shook her head. "A lot of your former close friends were sure you were dead. So was I."

"Did you care?"

She chewed on the question for an extra moment. "At that point," she bristled, "no, I didn't."

"At that point, Kirk, I was obsessed with these islands," Zzev said, jabbing at the viewscreen. "I had a theory, and I started to check it out. I tried to grab a few allies, but my *colleagues*"—he spat the word bitterly—"didn't want anything to do with this theory. According to every record I could find, nobody'd ever gone to these islands. They were so isolated, they didn't even have names. So I asked the government for permission to explore them."

"You didn't get it," Kirk concluded.

"I didn't get it. They told me these islands *had* been visited by the government a hundred years or so ago. In the days before we started getting Chorymi rhipileum, they were doing all sorts of experiments, trying to come up with ways of producing clean energy that also happened to be readily available and cheap."

"Every industrialized planet goes through that," Kirk sympathized.

"So they told me these islands were used for testing, and they wound up lethally contaminated by chemicals and radiation. That's why they were off limits to everyone."

"I never heard about this," Llissa said.

Zzev shook his head. "Nobody did. I figured I had enough enemies at Collegium."

"Whose fault is that?" Llissa snapped.

Her father ignored the dig. "I wanted inarguable facts on my side before I made anything public. So I kept pressing, trying every back-door route I could think of for getting more information about those islands."

"What did you think you would find there?" Spock asked.

"I didn't really have any idea. But they were old and

isolated. And they seemed like a good place to look for evidence of something that'd disappeared from the rest of the world, if it ever existed at all."

"Reasonable course of action," Spock approved.

Zzev snorted a short laugh. "I even tried sneaking up there for a look. I got caught, and that was about when the Cape Alliance got started. I'd done enough talking and writing about the possible existence of the Wwafida—even if Llissa didn't let me have my fossils—and people started to listen. Some of 'em were scientists, some were just people who didn't believe everything the government said."

"*We* didn't believe everything they said," Llissa protested. "But we thought there were better ways of changing things."

"Well, now you know there weren't," Zzev said, his voice suddenly weary, looking deeply into his daughter's eyes.

She returned the searching gaze. "I don't know if I can agree with that."

"Anyway, Kirk, once the Alliance started, I wasn't exactly in position to keep up the research and exploration. We just wanted to survive and keep up the fight. All we had some days was the hope that, sooner or later, more Akkallans would join us."

"Well," said Kirk, "you've got your allies now. What makes you so sure there's something being kept secret at these islands?"

"If you're looking for an orderly procession of facts, I can't give it to you. What I've got is a feeling, based not only on the government telling me I couldn't visit the islands, but the *way* they told me. I'm sure they're hiding something, as sure as I've ever been about anything."

Llissa cleared her throat nervously. "Jim, my father and I obviously don't see eye to eye about most things. But even his worst critics'll admit he's got a knack for making intuitive decisions based on evidence about as tangible as mist."

The grizzled scientist stared at his daughter, surprised at her testimonial.

"If he thinks those islands might hold the key," she continued, "I wouldn't bet against it."

"All right," Kirk said. "But before we go take a look, I'd like to see Akkalla's government records on the islands,

208

whatever they've got on those alleged energy tests and the contamination they left behind."

McCoy scowled. "Do you expect 'em to give us free access to top-secret files out of the goodness of their hearts? Does anybody even know where to find this stuff?"

"I do," Llissa volunteered. "There's a new archive complex they just built a couple of years ago, all the latest computer equipment. But security is so tight, it's impossible to break in, especially under current circumstances."

"It may be impossible to break in," Kirk said, smiling, "but not to *beam* in."

It was the middle of planet night when Spock and Llissa materialized in a deserted office at the Akkallan government archives. According to Llissa there was some nocturnal activity there, so it wouldn't attract undue attention to have a computer terminal in use at that hour. And all archive terminals had full access to the entire file memory, so they'd be able to do their snooping without ever leaving the office into which they'd transported.

"Which file next?" Llissa glanced up at Spock as he stood over her shoulder.

"I am most curious about the actual energy tests."

"Okay, energy tests it is." Llissa entered the proper code number, and the screen blanked out, flashing an advisory: OBSOLETE FILE SUPERSEDED BY ENTRIES 3-Z-403 AND 5-D-624. REPEAT REQUEST IF ORIGINAL FILE STILL WANTED FOR REVIEW.

Spock's eyebrow arched. "Obsolete?"

"I guess the data in the original entry's been split up and re-sorted under other headings. The original report dates back a century. Don't bureaucrats protect their jobs by shuffling the same information over and over?"

"That has often been my observation as well."

"Let's try again." She retyped her request, and the advisory was quickly replaced with the old file.

Spock recorded it, and when the map appeared, his eyes narrowed. "There is a discrepancy."

"Where?"

Before he could answer, the Vulcan suddenly stiffened, head cocked like an alert spaniel. "We must leave at once."

"Why?"

"Someone is coming."

"I don't hear anything."

"I do." Spock already had his communicator out and tricorder in hand. "Spock to *Enterprise*—two to beam up—energize immediately."

Llissa shut down the computer terminal, and out of the corner of her eye she spotted a shaft of light intruding into the dim office as an unseen hand opened the door from outside—

"There." Spock stopped the tricorder playback at the map of the seven islands contained in the file of quarantined territory. "Note that all seven are included in the sequestered zone."

The image hung on one screen above the science console while Spock called up the second Akkallan file on an adjacent screen. When the second map came up, he froze that one, too.

Elbows braced on the back of the science officer's chair, Kirk glanced from one display to the other. Both showed a string of seven bits of land in a vast ocean, with the largest island at the north tip, slightly apart from the others in its chain, shaped like a bloated kidney. Five more, little bigger than cays, stretched in a fairly straight line down to the seventh at the southern tip, which was vaguely fish-shaped. "They look the same.

"The depictions are in fact identical. The discrepancy comes in the appended data." On each viewscreen, he punched up the pertinent details. "The modern quarantine file lists all seven islands as having been used in the energy tests and thus contaminated. But the original energy-test file indicates that tests took place only on the southernmost island, with dangerous pollutants spreading only to the five small islands closest to it—not to the large island farthest to the north."

Zzev swore under his breath. "I'll bet when they did those tests a hundred years ago, they found something on that northern island that they didn't want anybody else to ever know about."

Kirk maintained some doubt. "Is it possible that seventh island was found to be contaminated later on and properly added to the quarantine list?"

Spock swiveled his chair to face the group gathered

around the science station. "The prevailing winds and currents in Akkalla's arctic and subarctic regions are northerly."

"Which would tend to sweep any pollutants to the south rather than the north. But there's a hole in your logic, Spock. You said the tests took place on the southernmost piece of land in the chain, but those five little islands just to the north of it got polluted anyway. Explanation?"

"There is no flaw in my logic," Spock said. "You interrupted before I completed my statement."

"Oh." Kirk looked chagrined. "I should've known."

"As I was about to say, there is a local current that circulates among those six islands in closest proximity. The island at the north tip is separated from the others by some eighty kilometers, enough to render it unaffected by that internal current. Before we began reviewing the data from the Akkallan archives, I had our sensors scan the islands in question. The six originally condemned as dangerous still show a residual level of radiation and chemical contamination. The northern island came up negative."

"What about life-form readings?" Kirk asked.

"The island where the testing actually took place is barren of animal life, though some plant life has returned. The five connecting islands have a normal complement of both plant and animal forms."

Zzev leaned close over the bridge railing. "And the northern island?"

"Life flourishes there, including, I believe, humanoid life."

"Are you convinced yet, Kirk?" Zzev growled.

"I'm convinced we should take a look at that island, but I'm not convinced what we'll find there."

"You will be."

The landing party convened in the transporter room—Kirk, Spock, McCoy, Maybri, Zzev, and Llissa. Everyone was issued a white hooded parka from ship's stores, and the starship officers all carried phaser pistols and tricorders.

"So we're off on our mermaid hunt," McCoy said as they received equipment and coats from the supply officer.

Spock raised a disdainful eyebrow. "Mermaids, doctor?"

"Mythical creatures that were half-woman and half-fish."

"I am familiar with the term. I am also constrained to point out that inappropriate romanticism is hardly a constructive addition to our search for useful data."

"How the hell would a Vulcan know when romanticism is appropriate?" McCoy shot back.

"One does not have to be something in order to be knowledgeable about it."

"Gentlemen," Kirk said as he mounted the steps to the transporter platform, "I hate to interrupt, but we do have business on Akkalla."

Llissa stepped up to the pod next to him. "Are they always like this?"

"Frequently," Kirk answered. He nodded to the transporter chief. "Energize."

They materialized on a frigid fringe of beach at the bottom of a fjord. Kirk took a step, and his boots crunched into a mosaic of ice, gravel, and sand. Shading his eyes against midday glare, he surveyed their surroundings. The water in the fjord was no more than thirty meters across and partially frozen, with chunks of ice bobbing unevenly as the tide rippled beneath them.

At first glance, this great cleft in the island seemed to have been cut by a single stroke of some colossal ax, so clean were the edges of its top rim and sheer marbled walls. But a closer look revealed snow-filled hollows in the shadows of craggy rocks and icicles clinging to outcroppings where trickles of water had melted under the sun's occasional appearances.

"You've got the map, Spock," Kirk said. "Any easy way of getting up there?"

McCoy stared at him. "You mean we've got to scale these cliffs?"

"Mm-hmm."

"Wouldn't it have made more sense to beam down up there instead of down here?"

Spock looked up from his tricorder's tiny screen. "It was necessary to transport to a point that would be secluded."

"Mission accomplished," McCoy grumbled. "What do we do now—flap our wings and fly up?"

"You may make the attempt, Dr. McCoy," Spock said, "while the rest of us climb that trail." He pointed to a rough-hewn path, hidden by shade deeper inside the fjord.

Kirk led the way, wondering if the trail was natural, chiseled from the rocky face of the cliff by local inhabitants, or some of both. It wasn't an easy climb. The landing party moved slowly, picking over rugged hand- and toe-holds, gloves and boots slipping on hidden patches of ice and treacherously unsteady stones.

McCoy was the last to clamber over the top, with a helping wrist grip from Kirk. As the surgeon caught his breath, he realized what the others were already gaping at, and he gave a low whistle. "This must be what they meant by a cold day in hell."

The landscape spread before them fit McCoy's description—a broad plain of ice and snow mingled with bubbling pools of viscous muck. Sulfurous vapors vented from craters and cracks in ground that was alternately moss-fuzzed bog, hardscrabble lava, and knee-deep snow. Looming over this jumbled terrain was a steep-shouldered volcano with its summit swaddled in a cloak of fog.

"Fascinating geology," Spock murmured as he swept his tricorder across the land.

"Just tell me that volcano's resting comfortably," McCoy said.

"Spock," Kirk said, "how far to that village?"

"I would hesitate to use the word *village,* Admiral. All our scanners indicated was a concentration of life forms that may be humanoid. And it is point seven-nine kilometers east."

Kirk determined their direction, and they began the hike, headed for round-topped hills that resembled the interlaced knuckles of folded hands.

Along the route, it became apparent that this island was home to a healthy abundance of life forms. Coarse green bushes and moss grew on patches of ground warmed by subterranean heat sources, and small white fur balls scurried to and from the bushes when the landing party passed by, unsure of whether to stay and eat the greenery or dive back into burrows under the snow. On the hillsides, slender trees grew straight and tall, with stubby branches, a generous coat of short, stiff fronds, and bulbous seed pouches hanging down. Llissa called them rikkekka trees, common even in the colder sections of the northern mainland, primitive but stalwart and perfectly adapted to their harsh environment. The rikkekka fronds were a waxy black-green, the better to absorb and retain a maximum amount of warmth from Akkalla's sun.

At the crest of the next hill, Kirk signaled a halt to reconnoiter the valley spreading below, with quite a bit of land free of snow and a flock of large, woolly animals engaged in lazy grazing.

"What are those things?" asked McCoy. "They look like a cross between hippos and sheep."

"What they are," Zzev said, his voice fired with anticipation, "are musk vinx."

"But musk vinx are extinct," Llissa said pedantically.

"On the continent they are, but those look just like old cave paintings."

The animals were stocky and barrel-shaped with stout kegs for legs. They were covered with thick white fleece, except for their bare hindquarters (which Zzev explained helped them lose excess body heat). The vinx had domed heads with tiny buds for ears; large, soulful eyes; and long snouts that ended in a single short horn. A few minutes of observation made it obvious the nose horn was used as a digging extension, perfect for gouging through snow and ice and frozen tundra to get at plants, roots, and small creatures believing themselves safe in tunnels and holes. Clawed hooves made them sure-footed in slippery terrain. Like the rikkekkas, musk vinx seemed well suited for their harsh island home.

"The ones with the antlers," McCoy said, looking at herd members with short, three-pronged growths on their heads, "those are the males?"

Llissa chuckled. "Matter of fact, those are the females. It's not uncommon with Akkallan animal species for the females to be bigger and more aggressive. They pick the males they want, and they dominate the group. The males function pretty much as stud stock and babysitters."

Maybri pointed out at some movement on the snowy fringe of the valley. "What're those?"

Zzev aimed his *Enterprise* mag viewer and saw a pack of four smaller animals with muscular haunches, thin waists, and massive shoulders and chests. They had coats of gray-white fur, with puffy ruffs around their necks. Their heads were dominated by ears that unfurled like fans, saber-tooth fangs in both upper and lower jaws, and broad flaring noses developed for detecting the faintest of scents. They skulked about the edges of the vinx herd, bodies flattened, noses twitching as they sought to single out a target that might be too young, too old, or too sick to flee or fight.

"Corotans," Zzev finally said in a hushed tone. "They're also extinct on the mainland. They're predators, probably the only thing on this island that's dangerous to the vinx."

He watched as a pair of females swung ponderously to face the corotan pack, snorting and lowering their antlered heads in a warning stance. Two of the corotans darted forward, as if to bracket the larger beasts, but when the vinx females turned rump to rump to protect in all directions, the corotans halted abruptly and slunk back to the waiting pair. Then all four of them wheeled and trotted away. The hunt would have to wait for another time, and for female musk vinx that were less vigilant.

"This is fabulous, Kirk," Zzev cackled. "There's no telling what we'll find here."

"I think," Kirk said, peering through his viewer toward the east, "we've found our village, and I think the term definitely fits. Take a look."

What they saw through their mag viewers was a sprawling cluster of fifty or so tents made of animal hides, with humanoid residents moving around them. Zzev could barely contain his excitement.

"We've discovered a completely unknown population of people. This is incredible!" he bubbled as they observed from behind a stand of rikkekka trees on a knoll.

"Before we go down there," Kirk said, "let's get a few things straight. We don't know anything about these inhabitants or how they'll react to strangers. We don't even know if they've ever seen outsiders. We don't know how primitive they are, and we don't know how hostile they might be. Obviously, they outnumber us. I don't want anybody hurt —us or them. We'll go in, but we stay together. Set phasers on stun. Keep 'em in your pockets, but keep your hands on them, just in case. If they turn out to be hostile, we withdraw. Understood?" He looked straight at Zzev, who met his glare briefly before nodding. "Okay, let's go."

The landing party made its way down the last hillside and

headed directly for the heart of the village, taking an open approach to preempt any fears that might be roused by the appearance of sneaking into the settlement. As they passed one of the structures at the edge of the village, Spock stopped to look at it. From a distance, all the dwellings had looked like standard, inverted-vee tents made of animal hides. Closer examination revealed this one and others to be tent-shaped but constructed of logs laid over a frame, with hides and blankets pegged to the slanted roof surfaces as insulation. They varied in size, but all were high enough to permit the tall natives to stand straight inside.

"Fascinating," Spock said. "This shows a high degree of ingenuity and skill."

They heard sounds of wood being chopped and scraped coming from the other side of the lodge, and they peeked carefully around the corner. A trio of natives smiled back at them, quite unconcerned at the sight of strangers. The natives were blond, fair-skinned males, young and tall, dressed in coats and leggings made of hides, fur, and heavy cloth, probably woven from vinx fleece. Their outfits were decorated with brightly colored designs, both stitched on and dyed. They worked with axes, knives, and other tools made of stone and bone. Two of them were busily hollowing out a log split lengthwise in half. The third native, considerably smaller and younger than the others, seemed to be an apprentice, alternately watching and helping by scooping up wood chips and adding them to a large pile and by fetching different tools as needed. Other hollowed half-logs, already finished, were piled in neat stacks to one side of the outdoor work area, with raw logs in another pile and odd-sized chunks of wood in a rail-and-rope bin behind the three young carpenters.

One of them bent low and whispered in the apprentice's ear, and he skipped over to the group of strangers, his face beaming and friendly. He chattered off a fast sentence and waited for a reply. Zzev and Llissa conferred quickly, then turned to Kirk.

"The language is a blend of old Akkallan and more modern," Llissa said, "dating from about a hundred years ago."

"Can you understand it?"

"Some of it."

Kirk's jaw tightened. "That's not enough. Spock, tie in the universal translator."

The science officer pulled a small cylindrical device out of his shoulder bag and twisted a control ring to activate it. A set of lights blinked in sequence. "Llissa, engage the boy in conversation in his language as best you can."

She nodded gamely and turned back to the young native, speaking in a halting way that made his face crinkle in amusement. When he answered, he spoke more slowly and distinctly, as if conversing with a dim-witted child. Llissa knew it and couldn't help feeling embarrassed. As they chatted, Spock watched the translator's indicator lights, then touched a switch and held it up between Llissa and the boy. As they continued talking, the device's circuits instantaneously translated his words into Standard and hers into native island Akkallan.

When the boy realized what was happening, he stared wide-eyed at the silvery cylinder in Spock's hand. *"Is amazing!"* he said. *"Can understand!"*

The Vulcan shrugged. "The syntax is less than perfect, but we should have no difficulty with essential communication."

As Spock's words were also translated into old Akkallan, the boy giggled in delight.

"We've come from very far away," Kirk said to the boy. "We would like to visit with someone in charge of your village. Can you take us?"

The boy nodded eagerly, then looked chagrined as he turned back to his elders. *"Is all right to show them?"*

The chief carpenter nodded. *"Go, Seif. But long do not take—for work you are needed."*

Kirk whispered to Spock, "Will the syntax improve?"

"The more accumulated data, the more accurate the translation."

They followed the woodworking apprentice through the bustling heart of the settlement, taking them past residents engaged in a variety of jobs and commerce:

—a butcher carving a musk vinx carcass while helpers cooked some chunks, cured others, and packed some raw slabs in wooden chests filled with ice blocks—

—a blade-maker using specialized tools to chip ax and knife blades out of stones—

217

—weavers spinning wisps of vinx fleece into long strands of yarn, making cloth, and stitching garments together—

—and females cooking and tending to family dwellings, some of them even repairing roofs.

The village was laid out in two concentric circles, with newer structures evidently added outside the inner ring. The original circle was tightly packed, but the secondary one still had gaps in many places. As the boy took them toward a larger dwelling at the top of the inside ring, Kirk pointed out the chimneys rising out of every tent and lodge.

"They're made out of those hollow half-logs we saw at the woodworker's. It looks like they bind the hollow halves together to form tubes."

Spock pointed to other half-logs used as pipes and aqueducts. "Creative use of naturally occurring materials, Admiral—indicates a high level of preindustrial development."

When they reached the dominant lodge, Seif picked up a stick hanging on a leather thong from the door frame. *"This where the Avi lives,"* he said via the translator. *"That is our chief."* He rapped the stick twice across one of the door posts, and the heavy woven doorflap opened. A woman of imposing bearing and height stepped out and straightened, standing a head taller than the men from the *Enterprise*.

"Sure do grow 'em big up here," McCoy murmured to the captain.

Kirk was a little surprised to find that the Avi didn't look much older than the young men running the woodworking hut. She looked down at Seif and rattled off a complex-sounding question. In midsentence, she became aware of the shiny cylinder in the hands of the stranger with the pointed ears.

She extended a hesitant finger toward the translator, and Spock looked quickly to Kirk, who nodded his approval.

"It's okay, Spock. Let her touch it."

The translator repeated Kirk's words in old Akkallan, and the Avi smiled in wonderment. *"Is there a small magician inside the silver log?"*

Kirk returned the smile. "No, it's just one of our tools. It lets us talk to people we'd like to meet and learn from, even if we don't know their language."

"That is a very useful tool," the Avi said. *"But I think you*

218

are telling me a tiny lie and there is *a tiny magician inside the log."* Her eyes twinkled as she said it. *"So, you have come to learn from us?"*

"Yes, we have. I'm Admiral Kirk."

"I am Keema, Avi of the Galeaya, the People. Welcome to Suberein."

"Thank you, Keema. Suberein is the name of this island?"

"Yes, Admiral. Is admiral your name or your title?"

"That's my title. It's similar to Avi. It means I'm the leader of my people."

"Fine. Then if we are to learn from each other, we should be friends. And friends should use names, not titles. So I shall call you Kirk. Where are you from, the big land on the other side of the world?"

Kirk glanced at Zzev and Llissa. "You know about the, uh, big land?"

"Yes. Many cycles ago, before I was alive, visitors came here from the big land. The storytellers have tales about it. Would you like to hear them?"

"Yes, we would."

"Then you are *from the big land?"*

"Well, some of us are, and some of us are from much farther away."

Keema narrowed her eyes. *"How much farther away? Is there another big land? The visitors who came before didn't have such tiny logs with magicians inside."*

"Yes, there's another big land," Kirk said. "That's where the rest of us are from. Those visitors who came here, did they leave anyone behind to learn more about Suberein?"

"No. They just came for a little while, then left. It seems it is not as cold as this on the big land," she chuckled. *"What would you like to learn from us?"*

"Everything about your people and how you live. Would you mind if we walked around your village and just observed?"

"If that is what you wish, Kirk." She grinned broadly. *"We Galeaya are very friendly, although sometimes we do not know when to stop talking. If that happens, just say 'Enough!' and walk away. This is a good way for you to meet us and see how we live. Then if you have more questions, come back and I will answer."*

"Thank you, Keema."

Keema bowed her head and ducked back inside her lodge.

Seif, the woodworking apprentice, fidgeted by the door. *"I must go back to work now."*

"You go right ahead," Kirk said. "We don't want you to get into trouble. Thank you for helping us."

Seif grinned. *"I had fun talking to the magician in the shiny log."* He waved, turned, and trotted across the open center of the village.

"It's like we've gone back in time eleven thousand years to the Culian Ice Age," Zzev said. "This must be what life was like when glaciers covered half the mainland."

"The question is, have these people been living like this for the past eleven thousand years?" McCoy wondered. "And if they have, how come nobody knew they were here?"

"Evidently," Kirk said, "somebody *did* know they were here—if those tales of visitors from the 'big land' are true and not some tall tales made up by their storytellers. Those visitors sound like agents of the Akkallan government at the time of the energy tests."

Zzev loosened the parka fastening below his chin. "What're you getting at, Kirk? That the government stumbled on these people by accident a hundred years ago?"

"Yes. And when they did, they discovered something they decided had to be kept secret from the rest of the planet. Isn't that your thesis?"

"Sure it is. I just didn't expect to hear it from you."

McCoy made a sour face. "I don't know, Jim. Maybe they just had no reason for coming back. I mean, this isn't exactly a vacation wonderland."

"But there is no logic in subsequent government actions, doctor," Spock noted. "Not returning here and blocking anyone *else* from coming are two entirely different matters."

"Let's split into two teams, walk around, learn what we can. Maybe some more facts will help us unravel this mystery. Let's draw a line—Spock, you, Maybri, and Llissa take that half of the circle. Zzev, McCoy, and I can take this side."

"Jim," Llissa said, "I can handle the language enough to

keep us out of trouble. Why don't you take the, uh, the shiny log with the magician inside?"

The Galeaya, all pink-cheeked and blond, were nothing short of completely hospitable, pleased to tell the strangers whatever they wanted to know, to demonstrate their skills and crafts, and to invite them into their shops and homes. Village society seemed completely self-contained, and everyone contributed something to the welfare of the community. There were no freeloaders here.

They saw a school, a large tent with a dozen youngsters gathered inside as a young woman taught them, reading from books made of animal skins, writing by scratching charred wood chunks on boards cut from rikkekka trees, and basic arithmetic. They saw vinx tenders, who cared for the all-important herd of a thousand placid beasts, whose responsibilities included chasing off hungry corotan packs, tackling and shaving the vinx come springtime, draining the musk sacs under the animals' hind legs to obtain a valuable liquid used as food seasoning and perfume (McCoy took a single whiff and pronounced it vile), and milking the females which weren't raising sucklings.

They saw hunters, who culled the corotan packs to provide extra meat and skins and trapped smaller creatures living in the trees and fields, and fishers, who rowed out to sea in longboats made of rikkekka frames and stretched skins to catch whatever came up in their nets, and to hunt triteera when the huge creatures swam north to feed in springtime.

And perhaps the most unusual indigenous profession belonged to the diggers, who knew how to find natural hot-spots underground. They would tunnel down and tap the subsurface heat, then pipe it up to warm tents and lodges. They also built ovens for cooking by carving out a hole, lining it with flat stones, then capping it tightly with a perfectly shaped slab to contain the heat inside. Spock measured the temperature at two hundred degrees Celsius at the bottom of one oven shaft, cooling as his probe came closer to ground level. The variation in heat allowed cooking of different foods at different levels in the shaft.

The exploratory hour passed quickly, and the two teams

met near Avi Keema's log dwelling and compared notes, providing ample testimony of the vitality and inventiveness of this small community. But Spock came to a darker conclusion.

"Though their culture is a model of efficient and creative use of social and physical resources, the population may be too small to sustain itself."

Kirk looked at him. "What're you saying, that they're dying out?"

Spock's eyes betrayed a tinge of regret. "They may indeed be headed toward extinction, Admiral. One concern is the danger of inbreeding. With a population of somewhat less than one thousand individuals, the gene pool is obviously limited."

"Bones, what about that? Is Spock right?"

"He could be, Jim. But as far as I could see, they don't show any of the dangerous effects of inbreeding—no high incidence of genetic diseases or anything like that. In fact, I don't think I've ever seen a healthier bunch of people, anywhere, anytime. But I did notice some other strange things. For instance, no old people. Nobody much older than Keema."

"Is it possible they have a shorter life span?" Kirk asked.

"Sure, anything's possible, but they're so healthy, I've got no idea what they die from. And we didn't see any burial grounds. Assuming they haven't discovered the fountain of youth here, when they do die, what do they do with their dearly departed?"

"Did anybody see any evidence of outside visitors being here?" Llissa asked.

No one had—no tools or materials more modern than the ice-age artifacts the natives had evidently been making themselves by the same methods for thousands of years.

"Well," Kirk said, "the government obviously didn't come here to help, then."

"The opposite may be true," said Spock. "If these primitive people harbor some important secret, the government may have isolated them in the hope they would in fact die out, taking their secret with them."

"And I'd wager," Zzev said, "that secret has something to do with Wwafida. I think it's time we asked some direct questions, Kirk."

"I concur," said Spock.

Reaching for the knocking stick, Kirk tapped on Keema's doorpost. The blond woman drew the flap aside and came outside, stooping to fit through the door. *"You have questions now, Kirk?"*

"Yes, we do, if you don't mind."

"You have come to learn, so I'm happy to be able to teach. What would you like to know?"

"Well, we didn't see any old people in your village."

Keema looked perplexed. *"Old? I am old."*

"Compared to children, maybe. But nobody is much older than you. What happens when Galeaya get old? Do they die?"

"Everything living dies."

"Well," McCoy said, "what do you do with people, with their remains, after they die?"

"There are no remains, as you call them, not unless someone dies in a fall or is attacked by a corotan."

McCoy shook his head as if to clear it of confusion. "But you said everything living dies—and remains are left behind . . ." His voice trailed off as an idea lit his eyes. "Unless your people go someplace special to die away from the village. Is that what happens?"

"In a way, that is right. When we reach sens, we return to Mother Sea and become wafta. When Mother Sea is ready, she takes wafta back where all life comes from at the beginning."

"Sens is senescence," Zzev blurted, "and wafta is Wwafida! They go through it all here on this island. That *has* to be the secret the government didn't want anyone to know!"

"Spock," Kirk said, "could the translator be misinterpreting other words to sound like senescence and Wwafida?"

"Unlikely. They are specific nouns, and their contextual usage matches that of the modern words. It is more likely that the words as Keema pronounces them are simply local corruptions of original forms."

"Jim," McCoy said, "we've gotta see one—"

Kirk held his hands near his chin, fingers interlaced, mouth set in a pensive line. "Keema, could you show us a Wwafida?"

The Avi shook her head. *"They are all far out in Mother Sea."*

"Do they ever come ashore?" Zzev asked.

"No. Once they change, their lives are not with us, except for encounters at sea. They may bless our fishers and cast spells to lure food into our nets."

"What happens when someone goes through sens?" asked McCoy.

Keema thought for a moment. *"The body alters. The sens-one spends long hours at the shore and in the sea. Then, one day the sens-one is wafta and does not come back. It is a quiet thing—we make no ceremony."*

"How long does it take?"

"Six tidal cycles."

"Akkallan months, Admiral," Spock said.

"This is it, Kirk," Zzev insisted. "This is all the evidence we could've prayed for."

"Not all, Dr. Kkayn," Spock said. "Without a living Wwafida, or a Galeayan in the process of senescence, the evidence is purely anecdotal."

"And that's not enough to get your government to stop the crackdown on your scientists," Kirk said.

"Have you forgotten you're a scientist?" Llissa goaded her father. "This time, there's no one else to fill in the holes in one of your brilliantly intuitive theories, nobody else to do the work you're too damn impatient to do yourself."

"Impatient?" Zzev flared. "Who did all the work that pointed us in this direction, and where do you—"

"That wasn't work," she cut in, "it was scratching an itch. If you were about to ask where I thought we'd be without you, well, I don't know. But where would you be without *them?*" she said, circling a hand toward the starship officers. "We're a team, and we're here because of a once-in-a-lifetime confluence of people and events. We're the ones who can take advantage of that and do this thing right—or we can do it wrong and lose not only the chance, but maybe the whole planet, too!"

Kirk picked that moment to break into the private bout. "Whatever we've discovered here, we've got to be able to convince the rest of Akkalla and maybe the Federation, too. Keema, are any of your people going through senescence now?"

224

"No, Kirk. I am sorry. It is a thing that just happens when it happens. We have no way of knowing when. Is this the thing you came to learn about, the most important thing?"

"Yes . . . yes, it is."

"We can help you learn more. We have the storytellers and the paintings in the caves."

"Admiral," Spock said, "the cave paintings could provide a useful reference point in two ways. First, a visual record, independent of previously known depictions, and additional chronological data for comparison purposes."

"Agreed. Keema, can you show us the cave paintings?"

"Yes. Come with me."

The caves were a half-kilometer from the village, down by the ocean shore along a desolate stretch of gray sand scoured eternally by the strong hand of nature, by force of wind and waves. Back in the village, Kirk found he'd forgotten how cold the island climate was, countered as it was by the industrious warmth of the Galeaya going about their lives. But here on the beach, with only the rolling, rhythmic thunder of the surf and the stinging whip of the wind, he felt chilled to the bone.

Keema led them over stones rounded and smoothed by the seething sea through millennia of high tides, to the head-high overhang that sheltered the cave's entrance. She was the only one who had to duck to enter, and once inside she lit a torch that flickered brightly and filled the cave with a dancing radiance. The flame revealed a vaulted ceiling rising up to create an almost perfect natural dome. And the slanted cave walls, from floor to ceiling, were covered with primitive but elaborate tableaux of islanders' encounters with the wonders of their beloved Mother Sea—fishers in longboats spreading nets and hurling spears, majestic tri-teera with their distinctive triple-fluked tails, and, more than any other thing, Wwafida—swimming, leaping over crested waves, haloed by heavenly light, gathered in a group beneath a crag lined with people, and all essentially similar to the Wwafida that appeared in Akkallan books, art, and religion much later in the planet's history.

As most of the group moved through the cave, inspecting the paintings in the sort of hush usually reserved for holy shrines, Spock scanned the walls with his tricorder.

"Admiral—" His voice echoed, jarring the silence.

"Found something?"

Kirk came over to him, and the Vulcan checked his tricorder. "Readings indicate these paintings were done approximately ten thousand years ago. This adds to the likelihood that the Wwafida myth is no myth at all, but firmly based in ancient reality."

"Sure was real to the people who did these pictures. Look at the detail."

"Yes, and the colors are surprisingly vibrant considering the age of the pigments."

The two Starfleet officers stood before one panoramic painting that included triteera, Wwafida, and an ancient longboat, taking it all in like admiring gallery patrons. The artist had used the textures and contours of the rock to give the mural a three-dimensional essence, and Kirk could almost feel himself a part of it.

"You have found my favorite," Keema said through the translator as she and the others joined Kirk and Spock. *"I discovered this cave when I was a child—even though the elders warned me to stay away from here. They said it was too dangerous."*

Maybri's ear tips twitched with interest. "What made you disobey?"

Keema smiled at the memory. *"I always liked adventures, going where no one went before me. I reasoned that younglings had been told forever to stay away from these caves— and continued to stay away when they were grown. Which meant this place was untouched. I had all manner of dreams about what I might find."*

"How did this measure up to your dreams?" asked Maybri.

"It exceeded my dreams many times over." The Galeayan leader chuckled. *"Strange how I grew up defying authority, only to become the top authority."*

"Do your own children abide by authority?" said Maybri. "Or are they like you?"

"Oh, I have no younglings of my own. Once appointed to become the Avi, a Galeayan must devote all energy to governing the village. To have your own children would distract." Keema sighed. *"At times, now and again, I wonder which would have been more satisfying."*

"Well, thank you for showing us your cave, Keema," Kirk said. "We're glad you didn't obey your elders when you were small. But we'd better be getting back to our ship. You've given us a lot to think about."

She led them out onto the windswept beach, and they saw a fishing boat jumping the ebbing waves as it was rowed to shore by eight powerful Galeaya. Even before it was securely beached, two of the fishers leaped out and splashed through the breakers toward their leader, both shouting at the same time and bedeviling the universal translator. By the time they reached Keema, one was out of breath and couldn't talk, and the landing party listened closely to the second fisher's gibbering.

"Avi, Avi—we could not help what happened—just hauling in the net—saw it—tried to cut it loose—too late—already dead!"

Keema clamped her hands on the young fisher's shoulders and steadied him. *"Be calm, Frae. Tell me slowly. What was already dead?"*

"The wafta," Frae gasped as he whirled and jabbed a frantic finger toward the longboat, where the other fishers were lifting something with a net wrapped around it.

"Admiral," Spock murmured, "the fisherman seems to be terror-stricken. It could be that inadvertent interference with a Wwafida violates one of their taboos. I suggest we tread extremely carefully, or we could find Keema's hospitality withdrawn."

Zzev poked Kirk's shoulder. "We've got to get a look at it."

Kirk spun on him. "Didn't you just hear what Mr. Spock said? We'll examine it if the Galeaya let us, and this very moment isn't the time to ask." Following at a respectful distance, he led the landing party toward the surf as Keema went to meet the fishermen carrying the limp form in their net like pallbearers.

With infinite care, they laid the body down on the sand and unrolled the net. Kirk edged forward, tugging Zzev's parka to keep him from lurching ahead. Keema's gentle hand peeled back the last sheet of netting as if it were a funeral shroud, revealing a creature that looked exactly like the Wwafida painted on the cavern wall.

"Jim," McCoy said quietly, "I feel like all those old-time

227

crazies who spent their lives hunting unicorns and dinosaurs in the Amazon."

"Your analogy is askew, doctor," Spock said. "Those creatures never proved anything other than mythological. A more apt comparison would be with the plesiosaurs eventually found in lakes in the Scottish province of old Britain, if I recall correctly, rather unimaginatively dubbed the Loch Ness Monsters."

"Keema," Kirk began slowly, "we could learn a great deal if you would let us examine the Wwafida—but only if it's permitted by your laws and religion."

She gestured at the corpse. *"This is a very bad omen. This wafta was on its way to return to Mother Sea forever, and these fishers have prevented that. If we don't make this right and help the wafta go where destiny has sent it, Mother Sea will punish us."*

"How?" Zzev wanted to know.

Kirk wished he had a muzzle to slap over Zzev's mouth.

"Bad waves, no fish to catch, taking fishers to their deaths before they can become wafta—"

Kirk shouldered in front of Zzev. "We don't want to interfere with your customs. But it would only take our doctor a few minutes to examine the Wwafida."

"He would not harm it, Kirk?"

"No. He doesn't even have to touch it."

"We have to send these fishers right back out to Mother Sea from here—there can be no delay."

"There won't be any delay," Kirk assured her. "He can look at the Wwafida right where it is now. But if you decide it's not allowed, we'll accept that."

Keema took a deep breath. *"The laws are not exact. You can have your few minutes, Kirk."*

"Thank you," Kirk said with grateful relief. "Bones—"

Chapter Ten

CAPTAIN'S LOG—SUPPLEMENTAL:

Following Dr. McCoy's examination of the dead Wwafida, the landing party has returned to the ship to analyze all the new data collected on the island called Suberein by the native inhabitants. As soon as Dr. McCoy and Science Officer Spock present their conclusions, I will have to decide if we have enough evidence to confront the Akkallan government—or to make a formal recommendation to the Federation for quick mediation.

KIRK, SPOCK, ZZEV and Llissa Kkayn, Maybri, and Greenberger sat around the table in the darkened briefing room while McCoy delivered his summary, complete with exhaustive illustrations from his tricorder scans of the deceased creature and subsequent computer-graphic diagrams and charts, all projected on the main viewscreen.

"—and there's the blowhole that's opened in the back of the neck," he said, using the laser-pointer. "That would be the dorsal surface of an animal that swims. Internally, a preexisting branch of the trachea opens and connects the blowhole with the lungs. Next, you can see how membranes have developed between fingers and toes, with a corresponding growth of cartilage between finger and toe bones, giving the extremities extra length and flexibility, making hands into fins, and feet and legs into powerful flippers. Most body hair is shed, since that'd just cause aquadynamic drag—and on this cross-section, we see where an extra layer of insulating blubber develops, and the musculature is reshaped."

"How old is it, Leonard?" Llissa asked.

"Well, based on interviews, the oldest people on the island are around forty, and I'd estimate this dead Wwafida is about twenty-five to thirty years older than that."

"Bones," Kirk said slowly, "is all this possible?"

"Ask me three days ago and I'd've said no. But now? Well, you've seen what I've seen. It's hard to argue with it."

"There are scientific precedents for such a metamorphosis," Spock said. "In the standard model of evolution, indigenous life generally develops in planetary seas and migrates to land, with efficacious mutations enabling the transition. On earth, cetaceans—whales and dolphins—reversed the process and readapted to aquatic existence after millions of years as land-dwelling mammals."

"Basic biology, Jim," McCoy said helpfully. "In the course of prenatal development, the humanoid fetus goes through stages that resemble more primitive species, heading progressively toward the final birth stage. Just shows that any given creature can go through an awful lot of changes during its life span."

"But Spock said it himself—it took whales millions of years to return to the sea and readapt. According to what we've been told, it takes these island people a matter of *months.*"

McCoy shrugged. "Well, it only takes nine months for a human fetus to go from conception to birth, and that's makin' a whole baby from scratch. There's nothing in the rule book that says this Akkallan senescence can't happen. Rare, yes—but impossible, no."

Kirk thumped his elbows onto the table. "Then what causes this senescence—and why don't all Akkallans go through it?"

"Computer," McCoy said, "comparative diagrams of standard Akkallan physiology and Galeayan."

The appropriate graphics were traced on the screen, and McCoy picked up the pointer again, flashing its pinpoint beam onto the images. "The only difference between one of Keema's people and Llissa, other than increased height, is this—a small gland I found under the right arm of every person on Suberein. But Llissa doesn't have it."

"But we do," she said. "It's called the dgynt gland, and it's removed at birth."

McCoy looked at her. "It is? Why?"

"Custom. We name our infants in a ceremony a few days after birth, and that's when the gland's removed. It's a simple, painless process—and up till now, our medical community believed the gland had no real function."

"It goes back at least three thousand years," Zzev added. "It started as a religious ceremony. When it's removed, the gland is thrown into the ocean, kind of a symbolic sacrifice that sanctifies the new life by showing its devotion to Mother Sea."

"Everybody on Akkalla has this gland removed?" Kirk asked.

Zzev nodded. "Even back when the mainland was run by a bunch of warlords always fighting each other, religion was never the issue. Because our continent is relatively small, we have only a single religion. The naming ceremony was something from the scriptures that became secular."

"So—" Kirk asked, looking around the table, "*does* the dgynt gland cause the senescence?"

"I did some tests on the older Galeaya, and now the results make more sense," McCoy replied. "Those still in their reproductive years have no dgynt hormone in their bloodstreams. But once they're past the reproductive phase, they've got varying traces of it. And the farther they get past the end of the fertile cycle, the higher the level."

"Indeed," Spock said. "Then that would appear to be medical confirmation of our hypothesis."

Kirk sat back. "You mean the simple act of removing this gland is what makes the difference?"

"That's what it looks like," McCoy said.

"If it wasn't removed, then all Akkallans would change into Wwafida?" The question was rhetorical, and no one bothered to state the self-evident reply. "That means in prehistoric times, before the Akkallan religion started the naming ceremony, the seas must have been full of Wwafida."

"And that must've been going on for at least a hundred thousand years," Llissa said in numb tones.

"But why change a biological fact of life?" McCoy wondered. "Why did your religious leaders decide to do that? They must've had a reason."

Llissa shook her head. "If they did, it's been lost in time.

231

Maybe they decided it was advantageous for civilization to have us live our whole lives on land. Maybe those scrolls we found'll tell us something once we translate them."

"So now," Maybri said, "the only people who still go through the senescence are these stone-age islanders. The Akkallan government must've stumbled across them when they did those energy tests."

"But why keep 'em a secret all these years?" Greenberger said. "If I suddenly found a whole new population of people who turned into sea creatures, I'd sure want to study 'em."

"Maybe not," Kirk dissented. "Not if you were a planetary ruler looking to protect the status quo. Think of the cultural implications of learning you've got a race of intelligent beings living in your ocean somewhere. *And* you've got a fresh new treaty with your neighboring world, supplying unlimited fuel for industrialization in exchange for unlimited fishing in those oceans."

"Right," said McCoy. "You couldn't very well tell the Akkallan public, 'Oh, by the way, those harvest ships are scooping up people who've changed into those legendary Wwafida you thought never really existed.' I don't think it would go over very well."

"So, what do we do next, Jim?" said Llissa. "Take on the Publican?"

"If we could've preserved that dead Wwafida, we'd be able to. But we've still got no tangible proof."

"We've got all our medical records," McCoy protested. "I finally get somewhere, and you don't even want to use it?"

"It's not enough, Bones. Not for the Publican and Vvox. It might stand up in a fair court hearing, but I don't think we can expect that here. If we could get one of Keema's people going through the change—"

McCoy shook his head. "By my estimates, it'll be at least five months before any of 'em are changed enough to prove all this."

"There's another problem, Kirk," Zzev said. "The triteera migration is pretty much complete, and they're not far from Suberein. This is the first time since the Chorymi broke the treaty that they're going to have a crack at all those huge creatures."

"How come they never harvested this far north before?"

"Because triteera not only feed here, they mate here too.

232

Our government didn't want the harvests to disrupt the triteera's reproduction. So the treaty stated no harvesting of northern herds. Now with the treaty inoperative . . ."

"Admiral," Spock said, "that answers a question I had as to why the harvest ships never found the Galeaya. Their paths never crossed. This is the season for the Galeaya to hunt triteera themselves. If, as we suspect, the Chorymi fleet raids these northern waters, the Galeaya are in grave danger. They stand not only to lose their annual catch of triteera, but should they be caught in a harvest zone, they may also lose the lives of their most accomplished fishermen. For a precarious population, those combined results could prove disastrous."

"Jim," McCoy said, "we've gotta do something."

"What do you suggest, doctor?" Spock inquired.

"I don't give a damn about the Akkallan government, but we have to at least help those people on the island. We've gotta stop the Chorymi raids."

"Dr. McCoy," Spock said gravely, "are you advocating a military confrontation?"

"If that's what it takes, dammit, then yes. The Chorymi wouldn't have the nerve to take on a starship."

"Upon what do you base that assumption? To the Chorymi, the situation is desperate. Although it is unlikely they could inflict serious damage on the *Enterprise,* there is a more perilous possibility."

"And what's that, Spock?"

"We may be forced to fire on *them,* to disable their vessels, or even destroy one or more."

"Action," Kirk said, "that would cripple any chance the Federation has to mediate some sort of peaceful solution to the mess in this star system. A military confrontation must be avoided."

"At all costs, Kirk?" Zzev demanded. "What good is power if you never use it?"

"I didn't say at all costs, Dr. Kkayn. Whenever possible, the power of this starship is to be used as a deterrent and a persuasive prod, not a bludgeon."

McCoy spread his hands in frustration. "Then what the hell are we gonna do—sit by and wait till this whole thing explodes?"

"We must construct an impregnable case," Spock said

calmly, "one that cannot be ignored by Federation authorities."

"And the only way to do that," McCoy said, his voice sapped by resignation, "is to find a living Wwafida, which we may never do."

Zzev pounded a fist on the table. "Then let's make one." Questioning gazes turned his way, and he met them without flinching. "McCoy, your medical reports say the only physiological difference between mainland Akkallans and the Galeaya from Suberein is the dgynt gland. Can you synthesize the hormone?"

"I—I suppose so. What kind of question is that?"

"If there's nothing else that keeps the rest of us from going through senescence, then I'm willing to take the dgynt hormone in concentrated doses and change myself into a Wwafida. Then you'll have your living proof, and we can get on with toppling this slimy government and halting the harvests once and for all. And on top of all that, I'd be able to make contact with other Wwafida, and warn them about the harvest raid."

McCoy stared at him. "Are you out of your waterlogged mind?"

"I'm offering you the solution to this quandary. I don't hear anyone else coming up with a better one."

"Kkayn," McCoy argued, "you don't have the slightest idea what this hormone could do to you."

"Sure I do—turn me into a Wwafida."

"Your body may not be prepared to accept the hormone. That gland may not be dormant all during presenescence. The fact that the islanders are taller practically proves there's something going on before they change completely. We fool with this stuff and it could kill you."

"It's my life, and I'm willing to take that risk. Instead of arguing with me, you should be going over all your medical data and learning everything you can to make sure you *don't* kill me."

"Bones." Kirk's tone was solemn. "Is it possible?"

Incredulous, McCoy spun to face the Admiral. "Jim, I've never treated a garden-variety, air-breathin' Akkallan, let alone one who's turning into a fish!"

"You sell yourself short," Zzev said casually. "Your briefings prove you're already pretty familiar with basic

234

Akkallan physiology. Kirk obviously thinks you're a competent physician. And Llissa can help you."

She glared at her father. "What makes you think I agree with this idea of yours?"

"All right, Llissa," said Kirk. "What do you think?"

"I agree with Leonard. It's a crazy idea, and it's likely that Zzev is going to wind up dead if we go through with it."

"But if it could be done without putting your father's life in danger, would you help?"

With her mouth twisted into a disapproving scowl, Llissa gave a nod distinctly lacking in enthusiasm.

"All right then," Kirk said. "Bones, I won't order you to do this. If you judge it's an unsafe procedure, we'll forget about it. All I ask is that you evaluate the idea with an open mind. Then give me your recommendation."

"Evaluate," McCoy grumbled sarcastically. "Then it's up to me?"

"It's up to you." Jim smiled. "Aren't you the one who used to claim you could cure a rainy day?"

McCoy snorted. "Damned lousy time to start quoting the gospel according to me . . ."

An hour later, Kirk sat in his quarters munching an apple, trying to relax. It wasn't working. If McCoy found Zzev's proposal unworkable, what options did they have? Not a hell of a lot. And even if the doctor said yes, was it still medical insanity?

Kirk's door tone chimed. "Come."

The door slid aside, and McCoy came in, looking hunched and grumpy. He plowed a hand through his hair and slumped into the recliner facing Kirk's desk.

"I checked everything I could think of. Did computer simulations. God help me, I even asked Spock for his input."

"And—"

"And it looks like the hormone treatment might work. By that I mean the treatment itself probably won't kill him. But whether the creature he becomes'll really be able to function as a completely adapted sea-dweller, I just don't know. I—I wish we had another choice."

"Do we?"

McCoy shrugged. "No. But I don't mind telling you, I'm

235

not comfortable with this plan, Jim. I feel like I'm some sort of Dr. Frankenstein, going against nature."

"I wouldn't say that, Bones." Kirk paused. "In fact, I think you're doing the opposite. The Akkallans've been going against nature ever since they started removing those glands thousands of years ago. You're just using some genetic engineering tricks to help nature do what it used to do perfectly well on its own."

McCoy chewed on that for a few seconds. "Hmm. Maybe you're right. But I still don't like it."

"You don't have to like it. All you have to do is—do it."

"I guess. Well, I already have Dr. Chapel workin' on manufacturing the required quantity of the hormone. We're gonna need a big water tank in sickbay. I want Zzev Kkayn in there while we're doing this. I want him close to emergency equipment, in case anything goes wrong."

"I've got faith in you, Bones."

McCoy's eyebrows scrunched into a frown. "Well, I'm glad somebody does."

"Okay. We'll get on that water tank. Anything else you need?"

McCoy got up and headed for the door. "Anything else I need—" he muttered. "I need my head examined for getting into this."

By McCoy's best estimate, it would take seven days for Zzev Kkayn to change into a being minimally capable of physical survival in the open ocean—a timetable about which Zzev was not pleased. He insisted on an accelerated pace, claiming the Galeaya might not have seven days, certain that a massive Chorymi harvest fleet would strike well before that.

With Kirk's backing, McCoy refused any course changes. As much as the ship's surgeon wanted to help the friendly island people, this whole procedure still gave him a belly full of tension-churned acid. Sailing waters this uncharted, he wouldn't abandon his instinct for caution when a life was at risk, even when the life belonged to someone as surly as Zzev.

By the end of the first day, McCoy was cursing himself for having such a well-developed sense of ethics. He'd ruled that, from the instant the treatments began, Zzev would have to be confined to sickbay. And McCoy was so nervous about the entire experiment, he barely left the medical section himself, despite the fact that this relentless proximity exposed him to the Akkallan's constant carping. When McCoy retreated from the wardroom to his office to escape, Zzev promptly disregarded the doctor's prescription for total bedrest until they could gauge the hormone's effects, hopped off his bed, and padded after his quarry to continue the abusive barrage of criticism.

It was nearly dinnertime. Zzev had been quiet for the past twenty minutes, and McCoy took the opportunity to tug his boots off and put his feet up on the desktop. He'd just closed his eyes when the intercom whistled. For an instant, he thought of ignoring it, then reconsidered. "Sickbay."

"That you, Bones?" Kirk's face appeared on the desk screen.

"Who wants to know?"

Kirk grinned. *"Tough day?"*

"You don't know how tough."

"Tell me over dinner."

"Thanks, Jim. But no thanks."

"Just what do you think you're doing?" said a new and accusatory voice from behind him.

McCoy clunked his feet to the floor as he spun around to see Christine Chapel glaring at him. "What d'you mean, what am I doing? I'm being an antisocial curmudgeon. You're allowed once you reach my age."

"Admiral," Chapel said, addressing the intercom screen over McCoy's shoulder, "he'll be there."

"Says who?" McCoy stood and found himself nose to nose with his associate.

"Says me. You've been cooped up here with that—*patient* —all day. You need a change of scenery. Go to dinner with the admiral."

"Okay, okay," McCoy sniffed. "But don't expect me to be great company."

Chapel shoved him toward the door. "Leonard, he's known you too long to expect miracles."

Kirk and McCoy sat alone in an isolated corner of the mess lounge, enjoying dessert and coffee.

"I've been good, haven't I?" McCoy said around a mouthful of apple pie. "Haven't talked about you-know-who for the whole meal."

"Do you want to?"

"Sure. Why should I suffer alone?"

"Go ahead, doctor."

"I will. That Akkallan is impossible. Nothing we do is right—or so he thinks—and he still hasn't given up the idea of speeding up the treatments."

"How's it going so far, medically speaking?"

"Medically speaking, he's a pain in my rear end. But the treatment seems to be working. Why don't you come on down and take a look?"

When they were done with dinner, Kirk did just that, finding Zzev Kkayn sitting up in a sickbay bed, reading a book on the bedside library viewer. The diagnostic panel above him showed his body functions to be steady and strong.

"Where's the water tank?" Kirk asked.

"That comes up here tomorrow," said McCoy. "He's not ready for it yet."

Kirk looked the Akkallan over from head to toe. The changes, if any, weren't yet apparent. "How're you feeling?"

"Like a prisoner, Kirk."

"This whole thing was your idea," McCoy snapped. "But now that we're doing it, we're doing it *my* way. He's feeling fine, Jim."

"What's happening to him? He looks the same to me."

"Ahh, someone agrees with me!" Zzev said.

"Shut up. The changes aren't visible yet, for the most part." McCoy raked his fingers through Zzev's hair, and several strands came out. "He's starting to shed body hair. Hold up your hand, Zzev. Look—he's starting to grow the membranes between digits. Toes, too. And there're lots of internal things going on—buildup of blubber, alteration of muscles. It's not instant, y'know."

The sickbay door whooshed open, and Llissa entered from the corridor, a little surprised to see the crowd gathered. "Is he all right?"

"I'm fine. Everybody else get out of here. I want some privacy with my daughter."

"You do?" McCoy brows arched suspiciously. "Since when?"

"Since now!" Zzev thundered. "Leave us alone."

The others filed out, and Llissa stood a pace away, arms akimbo. "Well?" she said.

Zzev looked away. "Llissa—I know we haven't had much of a family connection all these years, and—well, this may be our last chance. Once I've changed over, I'm not going to be dropping by for dinner on holidays, y'know."

Llissa's eyes narrowed. "That never bothered you before."

"That was when it was voluntary. And maybe I was wrong and thick-headed. A man's entitled to admit his mistakes, isn't he?"

"Do you mean that?" Llissa asked.

"Partly."

She snorted. "Which part?"

"Why does everything have to be an argument with you?"

She could see her father was having difficulty moving, and she came to the bedside. "Are you sure you're all right? Are you in any pain?"

"I'm fine. It's not pain exactly. It's just that if I don't move for a while, the next time I try to, my body isn't the same as it was. I never get a chance to get used to the way everything feels."

"Then maybe we're going too fast. Once you're out in the ocean, you'd better be functional, Zzev."

"Don't worry."

"Did you really mean what you said?" she repeated. "Are you *really* sorry for all those years we didn't have together?"

He didn't answer right away. "Yes and no."

"What's that supposed to mean?"

"If we're talking about what I've done with my life, then no, I'm not sorry. If leaving Collegium and my family and friends behind was what I had to do to get certain things done, and done in my own way, then I've got no regrets."

Llissa felt like dashing from the room, but she held her ground, and her dusky eyes bore into his. "That sounds pretty all-encompassing," she said bitterly. "Where does the sorry part come in?" Her defensive tone of voice made it clear she didn't expect much from his response.

"It's all-encompassing because I don't regret very much of my life. If I'd stayed, I'd've killed one of my so-called colleagues, or they'd have killed me."

239

"Are we done here?" Her ire heated by several degrees.

"No, we're not done. The part I do regret—deeply—is knowing that you became what you are—and that's pretty damn impressive—without any help from me. Maybe even in spite of me. You're my flesh and blood, Llissa, but that's all we share."

"You were there for fifteen years of my life. That counts for something."

"But they weren't good years. I don't think I contributed much to you those years."

"I don't know. I was a pretty observant child."

"So you observed me and learned what not to do, is that what you were going to say?"

She nodded. "Partly. But I also learned some positive things. Mother Sea, I *can't* believe I'm about to say this—"

"Say what? Is this going to be some deep, dark revelation?"

She laughed. "Mm-hmm. I worshipped you when I was growing up."

"You did?" He was genuinely stunned. "Why?"

"Oh, I don't know. I've wondered about that a lot over the years. Maybe it's because you were this angry whirlwind that other people were terrified of. But that didn't keep them from looking to you for leadership."

"I didn't *want* to be their leader. I was never accused of being the most cooperative person in the place."

"I knew that. Maybe I learned that a leader didn't have to be loved to be a leader, and sometimes coercion was at least as important as cooperation."

"Sounds strange coming from you, the queen of consensus," he said, half-mocking, half-admiring.

"The trick I learned—but you never seemed to—was how to coerce people into going along with what I thought was best and get them to think it was their idea all the time. How come you never figured that out, Zzev?"

"Not in my nature."

"It wasn't in mine, either. But sometimes you've got to learn to go against your nature to reach your goals."

"Not everyone's capable of that. Lucky for you, you are."

They were quiet for a few awkward moments, until Zzev cleared his throat.

"There's something I need you to do for me—"

240

"I don't think I like the sound of that."

"Do we agree that we have to do something to stop the harvest raids?"

"And we are, thanks to your being crazy enough to try this."

"We have to save the Wwafida and the people on Suberein."

"Yes, yes—what are you getting at?"

"If the Chorymi come back and raid the north Boreal before I'm ready, then all of this won't do a damn bit of good. We'll be too late to save anybody or anything. The treatment is safe. I'm going through the senescence the same way Akkallans did for thousands of years."

"So?"

"I want the treatment speeded up, but McCoy won't do it."

"And I'm sure he's got good reasons."

"He doesn't. I'd do it myself—"

"You can't," Llissa said sharply. "If you had a strong negative reaction, you might die before anyone could get here to help you."

"That's why I want *you* to give me a more concentrated dose."

"Oh, no, Zzev."

"Yes, you've gotta do it! You're taking a turn on monitor watch, right?"

"Yes, but I'm not—"

"That's when you can do it. By the time someone comes to relieve you, the speed-up in adaptation will be done with, and we'll have proved we can accelerate the treatment safely."

"You're asking me to—"

"I'm asking you to do what's right, what we have to do. Kirk and the others don't have to do this. Akkalla's not their world. They're doing this because it's their job, and maybe they're going beyond the call of duty, but it's still *not their world*. They don't have the stakes we do, Llissa. It's our home—we *have* to do more. We *have* to be willing to make the ultimate sacrifice!"

"Not if that sacrifice destroys whatever chances we have of accomplishing what we set out to do."

"It won't."

241

"How do you *know* that? Nobody's ever done this before. If you're wrong—"

"I'm not wrong," he said, his voice suddenly serene.

"What is this, another one of your infamous hunches?" she said with irony.

He nodded. "Is that enough for you?"

She spread her hands helplessly. "I don't know. I—I can't give you an answer yet. *That's* going to have to be enough for *you,* at least for now."

"But you haven't ruled it out."

"I guess not."

"We don't have much time, Llissa. You've got to make up your mind soon. If we don't take the risk, we may be dooming ourselves to failure—and that could finish Akkalla."

Without another word, Llissa hurried out of sickbay.

Kirk was startled to see Zzev Kkayn the following morning. The effects of the artificially induced senescence were readily apparent, and even McCoy seemed shaken after they examined the altered Akkallan.

"This is spooky, Jim. I've never done anything like this before."

"Oh, come on, you did genetic modification."

"That was different. With genetic modification, we knew what the results were gonna be. But this—"

"I know what you mean. It's—weird—watching him change. It's—it's like peeking inside a cocoon."

"But that's all preordained by Mother Nature. *We're* making *this* happen, and I—I've got no idea if we're doing it right."

Kirk's forehead furrowed as he looked into his friend's eyes, glimpsing the turmoil there. It was no secret that McCoy was an emotional man, but those emotions were usually used for particular effect, like tools for psychic surgery. For all his moods and outbursts, Kirk had always believed McCoy to be as soundly anchored and sure of himself as any being he'd ever known. It bothered him to see the doctor in this muddle of uncertainty, bothered him even more to know he'd brought it on by prodding McCoy into approving the experimental treatment.

242

"I'm sorry, Bones. I don't know what to say."

McCoy shrugged. "That makes two of us."

Later in the day, they placed Zzev in the two-meter-high water tank constructed in the sickbay ward. To everyone's great relief, he seemed perfectly at home, even pleased to be out of the diagnostic bed. Though not large, the tank gave him enough room to swim a bit and limber up his re-formed muscles. There were no noticeable complications, although, as McCoy phrased it in conversation with Kirk, "he's still kind of like a tadpole."

"Neither fish nor fowl?" Jim offered.

McCoy scowled at him. "You're mangling my metaphor."

Llissa volunteered for the overnight monitor shift, taking over from Dr. Chapel, who rubbed her sleepy eyes as she surrendered the chair at the medical console in McCoy's office.

"No problems at all," Chapel said brightly.

Llissa's mouth twitched. "What?" she said in a distracted tone.

"I said no problems. He's been fine all day."

"Oh. That's—that's good."

"Are you okay, Dr. Kkayn?"

Llissa stiffened, sitting straight-backed at the monitor panel. "Yes. I'm—I'm fine. Why do you ask?"

"You just seemed a little—I don't know—jumpy."

"Just tired, Dr. Chapel."

"You don't have to take this shift. We can get one of the staff to do it."

"No, that's okay. I'm fine." She stretched her arms over her head. "I'm just not used to spending so much time in a spaceship."

"Well, all right. If you need anything, you know how to use the intercom. Dr. McCoy and I can be back to sickbay in a few seconds. Call us anytime."

Llissa watched Chapel leave and the door slide closed.

The glowing digital clockface confirmed for McCoy what his weary bones already knew. He'd been tossing and turning for four hours, with hardly a moment of actual rest. No matter how he tried to trick his mind into shutting down and not worrying about this crazy project being conducted in his sickbay, nothing worked. In fact, now that he gave it some thought, he must've fallen asleep for a while—since he could recall a nightmare about sharp-fanged fishmen ramming and capsizing his rowboat during an innocent fishing trip.

"Better to stay awake than go through that again," he muttered.

The bedside intercom whistled and he heard Chapel's urgent voice. "Dr. McCoy to sickbay—emergency!"

He punched the switch. "Coming." Leaping out of a tangled blanket, he stripped off his sweaty nightclothes, yanked on a pair of pants, jammed his feet into slippers, threw his robe over his shoulders, and ran for sickbay.

The doors snapped open, and he skidded to a halt in the ward. Chapel and an aide were trying to hoist Zzev out of the tank—the Akkallan was in some sort of distress. "Get him out of there! I can't work on a dying man in an aquarium!" McCoy joined the others on the catwalk rimming the tank and added his hand to the effort. "Where the hell is Llissa?" He spun around and saw her cowering across the room. "Get over here and help us."

They got Zzev out of the tank, holding his dripping body in their arms as they lowered him to the floor, and carrying him to the nearest diagnostic bed. The indicators quivered erratically, and McCoy stared at them, trying to figure out what was happening to this creature turning ever more alien, ever more out of the surgeon's realm of experience. "Llissa, get over here! Help me!"

She hurried over, her face pale, eyes hollow.

"What happened? What did you see on the monitors?"

"Nothing—nothing on the monitors," she whispered.

"There must've been something. Dammit, he may be dying. I need something to go on!"

"It—it had nothing to do with the monitors. I know what happened. I—I gave him a double-concentration dose of the hormone."

McCoy wheeled furiously on her. "Are you insane?"

Llissa's composure returned; now that she'd made the terrible admission, it seemed easier to talk. "Zzev asked me to do it."

244

"And you agreed?" Complete disbelief distorted McCoy's face.

"Not right away."

"Great. That'll make this premeditated murder."

"Leonard, do something—help him!"

"I don't *know* what to do—" He grabbed a medi-scanner as much out of reflex as with any real idea of what to do, automatically thumbing the mode selector to tie the hand-held device into the bedside display screen. He made several rapid passes over Zzev's heaving, shivering body, then watched the charts, graphs, and numbers that flashed on the viewscreen.

"Dr. McCoy," Chapel said in amazement, "his respiration and cardio rates are settling back to predicted levels. His system may be absorbing the extra dosage."

McCoy looked down at Zzev's face, now substantially changed by the middle stages of senescence. His mouth had elongated on the sides, and his upper lip and nose had extended into a slightly beaked formation. His neck had widened, giving the appearance that his head was mounted directly on increasingly sloped shoulders, forming a stream-lined shape that could flow easily through water. The beaked mouth opened and closed, as if he was trying to speak, but eerie hisses and creaks were all that came out. Zzev rolled slightly onto his side, clearing the nearly complete blowhole on his back just below his head. The blow-hole pulsed, and he tried to talk again. This time his words were understandable.

"Not her fault . . . did as I asked . . . best thing . . . dry . . . back in tank . . . sea creature now . . ."

"Dr. McCoy," Chapel said, "his body tissues are becoming dehydrated. Look at the mottling on his skin."

"Mmm—looks like he's reached the point where he has to be in the water most of the time. That means if anything else goes wrong, I've gotta go in there with him, or we've gotta keep pouring water over him to keep him wet. Put him back in the tank, Christine. Get a couple of aides down here to help."

McCoy clamped his hand roughly around Llissa's wrist and dragged her out to his office. "That was a damn stupid thing to do."

She tried to square her shoulders in defiance, but the ploy failed. "Maybe it was," she said, dejected and bleary-eyed, "but it's done."

"Why did you do it? What could you've been thinking, after everything we said about needing to be cautious if we didn't want to kill him?"

"I don't know, Leonard."

"Did he talk you into it?"

She stiffened. *"No.* He just articulated some things I guess I was already considering. Maybe there's more of my father in me than I ever cared to admit."

The door slid open, and an angry Jim Kirk stormed into the office, wearing his uniform pants and a black T-shirt pulled on over hair he hadn't bothered to comb. "Chapel called me down. What in God's name were you trying to do, Llissa?"

"Trying to save my planet, Jim," she stated, summoning all her tattered dignity.

"By sabotaging McCoy's treatment schedule?"

"No, of course not. But I started to think my father was right, that we couldn't wait. If we did, it might be too late to help. I decided it's our world, so it was our decision."

"How is he, Bones?"

"How the hell am I supposed to know? For the moment, he seems to be stable. But I don't have the slightest idea what the overdose'll do to him in the long run."

"Look," Llissa said, "we knew from the outset that there was no control in this experiment, no sacred protocol. In the end, it was his life, and he wanted to take the added risk. I decided to go along."

Kirk shook his head, not quite comprehending. "Well, what's done is done. We're stuck with the consequences, whatever they may be."

"You all can go on back to sleep," McCoy said. "I wasn't sleeping anyway—I'll spend the night in sickbay, just in case."

"Okay," said Kirk. "Call me if anything happens." He started for the door, but Llissa lingered.

"I can't sleep either, and besides, I'm the one who's supposed to be on monitor duty."

McCoy's dirty look made her pause. But he held his tongue.

"So, unless I'm barred from sickbay, I'll stay and keep you company. Hmm?"

He glowered at her. "Fine, as long as you don't do anything I'll want to strangle you for."

"Promise."

"Which I suppose isn't binding."

"Right."

Kirk rubbed his bloodshot eyes. "I want you both alive in the morning—which, unfortunately, is only a couple of hours from now. Good night."

The whistle of the intercom made Jim wince and tug the blanket over his face. His hand fumbled for the switch on the audio terminal. He emphatically did not want to face the bright light from the viewscreen right now. "Kirk here," he mumbled.

"Good morning," said McCoy's voice. *"Are you in the closet? I can barely hear you."*

Kirk slipped the blanket beneath his chin. "Is that better?"

"Yeah. Just thought I'd pass along some good news. Llissa's damn fool meddling appears to have done no damage. In fact, the pace of senescence has speeded up quite a bit. I'd guess Zzev'll be ready for the open seas by tomorrow."

That made Jim sit up. "That's three days early."

"Yep. That means we'd better figure out exactly what we're gonna do with him."

"I'll meet you in sickbay in a half-hour. Kirk out."

"I'm worried about the glycoprotein level," McCoy said. He, Kirk, Spock, and Llissa sat at the briefing-room table.

"The what—?" Kirk said, feeling ignorant.

"They're proteins that act like a sort of biological antifreeze in animals that live in cold climates or cold water. They keep the cells from freezing solid. Otherwise, they'd rupture and destroy the tissue. Now, I'm not sure what the right level should be in a Wwafida, but I can't help but feel that Zzev's body's been sluggish in building 'em up."

"Well, we've still got a little time."

"We've discovered another unforeseen development, Jim," said Llissa.

247

It was difficult to tell from her tone just how serious this was, but Kirk braced himself. "What's that?"

"My father's lost the ability to communicate vocally."

"It has to do with the rerouting of his respiratory system," McCoy pitched in. "See, in making the dorsal blowhole the primary external breathing organ, air doesn't pass over the vocal cords in the larynx anymore. Without that, he can't speak the way humanoids like us normally do."

"How much of a problem is that going to be? How do we communicate with him?"

"Evidently," Spock said, "the Wwafida counteract the loss of vocalization in two ways. They are capable of producing a variety of whistles and clicks, which actually travel underwater with considerably greater efficiency than the sounds produced by our larynxes—"

"And the second way?" Kirk asked impatiently.

"They are able to communicate telepathically," Spock replied. "I have already ascertained that I am able to establish contact with Dr. Kkayn over some distance."

"We experimented," McCoy said.

Kirk raised his eyebrows. "I see you all were busy before I got my wake-up call. All right, Spock. Present your plan."

"We will utilize the *Cousteau* to transport Zzev directly to the seas off the island of Suberein. He will attempt to make contact with other Wwafida and inform them of the impending harvest raid."

"Dammit," Kirk growled, "why is he so set on risking his life to warn them of a raid that may not take place? And he may not even find any Wwafida. If anything happens to him, we're back to square one. Llissa, can't you try again to talk him out of this?"

"No, Jim, I can't talk him out of it. He didn't go through this just to become an exhibit. Contacting the Wwafida is very important to him. It's the breakthrough he's been working for." She paused, then continued more quietly but just as passionately. "And he's not the only one."

"Then you agree with him? Even knowing how dangerous this is?"

"Yes, I do. There are lives at stake, Jim—the lives of the Wwafida are just as important as the lives of the people on Suberein and the lives of my friends at Collegium. And if contacting those Wwafida to warn them about the harvest can make a difference, then I think we should do it. As far as being back to square one, you've still got me. If my father dies, I'd be willing to undergo the same treatment. We'll still have proof that senescence takes place and Wwafida are real."

With a frustrated sigh, Kirk turned back to his science officer. "Recommendations on shuttle personnel."

"Dr. McCoy, Llissa, Chekov, and myself. I will serve as our communications link with Zzev."

"Approved," Kirk said grudgingly. "But make sure Zzev understands we don't want him searching the entire ocean for Wwafida. I don't want you and the shuttle getting caught up in a Chorymi raid."

"I will impress upon him the need for caution, Admiral."

"We'll be scanning, so we'll be able to give you plenty of warning if a harvest fleet's spotted, but that won't do you any good if you've got to wait hours for him to get back to the ship. He'd better understand that if it's necessary to save the shuttle and its crew, you'll leave Akkalla without him."

From his balcony at the Cloistered Tower, Publican Abben Ffaridor watched as an armada of thirty military cutters idled in the smooth water of Havensbay, gathered across the harbor at the base of the Citadel cliffs. It was dusk, and a veil of clouds turned the sky dark and melancholy. The fleet, built of the most heavily armed craft on Akkalla and commanded personally by Brigadier Jjenna Vvox, would be leaving port soon, bearing northwest. With no harvest raiders hitting the planet for nearly a week, Vvox had become convinced the enemy was waiting for the massing of the giant triteera in their northern feeding and mating grounds. She argued that this would be the time and place to make a convincing stand. If her combined force could turn back the hunting convoy, it would prove to the Chorymi that they couldn't continue to raid Akkallan seas with impunity.

Ffaridor had timidly voiced doubt that the oceangoing vessels could turn away Chorymi spacecraft, but Vvox was certain previous defensive forays had failed because they'd lacked the firepower. This armada would write a different outcome altogether. With the Chorymi thus warned, she promised, she and Ffaridor would buy themselves the reprieve they needed to deal with the chaos caused by martial law and the imprisonment of legislators, scientists, and educators—and by the curfews, disruptions, and unrest still spreading like concentric shock waves from the radical actions they'd initiated.

This military mission, Vvox swore, would end the nightmare and bring on a new morning of light and progress by ridding them of the shadow and threat of more Chorymi raids.

Had he been able to foresee the consequences of what he'd done in recent weeks, Ffaridor might not have gone through with the grand plan to mold Akkalla's government to fit the vision he and Vvox had nurtured and shared together. Together? Or had he been maneuvered by his brigadier? He could no longer separate fact from perception, no longer be sure of who'd been responsible for strategies that once seemed so promising and now had his rule teetering on the brink of a precipice no less perilous than the craggy bluffs that protected the harbor entrance below his balcony.

But it was too late for regrets. Nothing they'd done could be undone. Was it too late for prayers? As he watched the cutters glide in silence through the strait of Havensbay toward the open waters of the ocean, Ffaridor wondered if the nightmare was truly about to end—or if it had yet to begin.

Chapter Eleven

THE SEASHUTTLE *COUSTEAU* emerged from the starship's hangar bay and streaked across black, starlit space toward Akkalla. Inside its fiery cocoon, the shuttle pierced the planet's wreath of atmosphere, then traversed a dawn sky that was sullen and overcast.

McCoy pressed his nose to one of the aft-cabin viewports. "What the devil are those things?"

Llissa joined him at the port. They were alone in the compartment, with Chekov and Spock in the cockpit and Zzev in the water-filled air-lock belowdeck. Even at an altitude of two miles, they could make out the jagged backs of thousands of triteera, gleaming as they plunged through the waves in an endless procession. These were the stragglers, still on their migratory journey north.

"Triteera—the biggest, most magnificent creatures on Akkalla—and sure to be endangered as a species if the harvest raids keep going. Might not happen tomorrow, but it will eventually."

McCoy turned pensive. "I've read that's what happened to whales on earth—hunted near to extinction before whaling finally stopped. Some species came back, but it was too late for a lot of 'em."

"Probably no species is indispensable, but nature put them here for some good reason, I think," Llissa mused. "You'll never know when one that's gone turns out to be the one you need someday."

With surgical precision, Chekov piloted the shuttle down, decelerating and skimming the waves, incidentally giving a closer view of the triteera continuing with their voyage and their dining.

"They don't even notice us," McCoy marveled. "Then again, if I was their size, I guess I wouldn't care much about a little ship like this either. Are they intelligent?"

"We don't know—haven't been able to study them close-up. Now that we've opened up this part of the world, maybe we'll be able to. Especially if my father can make contact with Wwafida and cooperate with them."

Up front, Spock and Chekov consulted the navigational chart displayed on a computer screen. They were about forty kilometers off the southeast tip of Suberein, perhaps a kilometer or less from the fringe of the triteera herd. "Set us down here, Mr. Chekov."

With a sure touch on the thrusters, the Russian stopped their forward motion and lowered the craft gently down onto the rolling surface of the sea.

The Akkallan cutters fanned out in a wedge, with Vvox on the bridge of the lead vessel. She and three of her officers crowded around the scanning console, staring at the small visual display screen with its vector lines and locational grid. A barrel-chested trooper named Ttoom sat with his hands on the scanner controls.

"It's off the grid, brigadier," Ttoom said with assurance. "And that means it either crashed or it landed on the ocean exactly where it gave us our last reading."

"Then it couldn't be a Chorymi convoy," Vvox said. "And if it's not a harvest raid, then it has to be from the starship. Whatever they're doing, I want to catch them at it. Pilot," she called across the bridge cabin, "change course to intercept!"

Kirk rested his elbows on the railing circling the elevated outer bridge level, standing below the science station where Ensign Greenberger sat peering into the sensor viewer. Her deft fingers bounced lightly across the science computer console, and the sensor image flashed on the screen above her. "Positive I.D., Admiral. Thirty Akkallan ships, military cutters by configuration and size, heading dead-on for where the *Cousteau* just landed."

252

"Damn." Kirk balled his fingers into fists. "What about spacescans—any activity between Akkalla and Chorym?"

Greenberger whisked a blond forelock off her cheek and punched up an outbound view of the solar system. "Nothing, sir."

Kirk started to turn toward Uhura at communications when the young science officer abruptly spun in her seat.

"Hold on—they're out there! Just came within range." She stared into the viewer again, reciting the readout as it came up. "I'm picking up three of those monster harvest ships and ten escort fighters."

Kirk's jaw tightened. "Shields up, Sulu—full power. Greenberger—distance from Akkallan surface boats to the shuttle."

"Ten kilometers."

"Okay, they're not in immediate danger. Uhura, open a channel to the Chorymi harvest convoy."

Spock and Llissa knelt on the rim of the air-lock platform. Zzev Kkayn—or the being he'd become in the past four days—bobbed in the water, waiting for them to open the hatch and set him free to roam the domain that would be his home for the rest of his life. Spock's hand was poised at the hatch control.

"Are you ready, Dr. Kkayn?" Spock said aloud, since Zzev could still hear even though he could no longer speak.

Ready, Spock, Zzev thought back. *Let's get this over with.*

"Wait," Llissa blurted. "I want to—to say something to him."

"We have little time to spare," Spock said.

"I know. Zzev—Father—I don't even know what to call you. We might not ever see each other again. I never thought about what to say to you until this instant, and now there's more than I have time to say."

Spock, Zzev thought, *tell her she doesn't have to say anything.*

"I can *hear* him," Llissa said, startled. "I mean, I can *sense* him. At least some of what he's thinking at us. How come I couldn't back on the *Enterprise?*"

"Perhaps because he has become more adept at transmitting. Fascinating. This means that it is possible for land-

253

dwelling Akkallans to communicate with Wwafida. Now, please hurry. We must release him."

Llissa, Zzev thought, *glad we worked together . . . wasn't perfect . . . some of . . . old arguments . . . better than we might've . . . when I come back . . . Now, open the damn hatch!*

"That last part I got loud and clear. Open the hatch, Spock." She reached down, and Zzev lifted a webbed fin-hand out of the water to brush her fingers.

With a muffled rumble, the hatch slid aside. Zzev flipped, feet up, and dove through the opening out into the ocean.

Spock and Llissa clambered up the ladder to the aft compartment, hurrying to the science console. Chekov and McCoy were already there.

"The transponder is functioning perfectly," said Chekov with a firm nod.

They all watched the telemetry being beamed back to the shuttle, displaying his depth, direction, and distance from the ship. "Good, good," Spock murmured. "He is proceeding with caution and appears to be attempting to get accustomed to his new surroundings before diving to greater depths."

"This is Admiral James T. Kirk of the Federation starship *Enterprise*—I repeat—do not approach Akkalla. If that's your intention, we will be forced to intervene. Please acknowledge."

Uhura shook her head. "No response, sir."

"Greenberger—?"

"They're still coming, Admiral. No deviation in course or speed. If they heard us—"

"They heard us."

"Then they don't give a damn—sir."

"Enterprise to *Cousteau*—come in, Spock."

"Spock here."

"We've got problems on two fronts. There's a Chorymi harvest convoy on its way—and a fleet of thirty Akkallan military boats. I suspect the Akkallan force was on its way to defend against an anticipated raid, but they spotted you, and they're headed in your direction."

"Indeed. Those are distressing developments."

254

"Yeah, and we're going to have our hands full up here. We may not be able to cover you from two directions. Better not release Zzev. Just get out of there and return to the *Enterprise.*"

"*We have already released Zzev.*"

"Then get him back aboard, on the double."

"*I shall attempt to recall him.*"

"Make it fast, Spock. Let us know as soon as he's aboard. We'll do what we can to give you some breathing room. Kirk out."

Spock shut off the comm system, then turned to face the direction in which Zzev was swimming. He closed his eyes and concentrated all his considerable mental powers on reaching out through the watery distance between them. In silent anxiety, Chekov, McCoy, and Llissa watched him.

Zzev, Spock thought, trying to infuse his signal with as much urgency as possible, *you must return to the shuttle. We must leave Akkalla at once. We are endangered by both a Chorymi harvest convoy and a group of Akkallan military boats.*

Spock waited. Nothing.

Zzev, are you sensing my thoughts?

Still nothing.

Then—

Spock's eyes opened wide as he absorbed a burst of euphoric mental energy.

Amazing! Amazing! Swimming free isn't like anything I've ever experienced! It's like a religious revelation—seeing the true face of Mother Sea for the very first time in my life. The colors—the feeling of being part of a whole.

Zzev, Spock tried to interrupt, *you must come back—*

But either Zzev didn't hear, or he simply wasn't listening as he swam and pirouetted in a joyous ballet. *The freedom,* he exulted. *There's nothing like it on the land. Maybe flying is like this—no limits, no bonds or chains—I'm going to try diving deeper now. There are some triteera not too far away. I wonder what they'll think of me? But no Wwafida so far.*

No, Zzev, Spock called out with his mind. *You must not—*

* * *

255

The sleek Akkallan military cutters skipped over the whitecaps, riding high on their hydrofoil outriggers. In the lead craft, Trooper Ttoom pressed his earphone tightly to his head.

"Brigadier Vvox, Defense Control reports a Chorymi raiding convoy approaching the planet. It's a big one."

Vvox crossed the bridge cabin and leaned close. "How big?"

"Three mother ships, ten fighters."

The brigadier gave him a flinty glare. "Are they in the atmosphere yet?"

Ttoom shook his head.

"Then we take care of these starship interlopers first. We're going to even a few scores today, Ttoom. You keep in touch with Central. Keep updating the position of the Chorymi."

Ensign Greenberger pivoted in her seat. "The Akkallan boats're still closing, Admiral."

Kirk leaned forward in the command chair. "Mr. Sulu, are you ready for some precision phaser surgery?"

The helmsman looked back over his shoulder with clear-eyed confidence. "Aye, sir."

"Set power at minimum—fire a couple of bursts just off the bows of the lead boats in their wedge."

"Herd them away from the shuttle, sir?"

"Exactly. I'm hoping this'll be enough to buy Spock some time. I don't want to have to use stun force. If we knock out those cutter crews, the vessels'll be out of control. I want to avoid loss of Akkallan lives if at all possible."

"Understood." Sulu keyed his weaponry controls to implement Kirk's orders, priming phaser banks at minimum power, and engaged the tracking system on target. "Phasers locked and ready, sir."

"Tactical display on main viewer," said Kirk.

Sulu obliged, and the image of the planet was replaced with a green sensor grid of lines and concentric circles. At the center of the grid, a winking red spot marked the sea shuttle, sitting motionless in the ocean. From the lower right corner, thirty yellow blips made up the advancing wedge of Akkallan cutters, cruising inexorably toward the *Cousteau*.

"Fire at will, Mr. Sulu."

"Aye, sir." Sulu peered at his targeting scope. The cross-hairs leveled, centered—and he hit the trigger.

Three needle-sharp beams of energy spiked through the Akkallan atmosphere and struck the surface of the ocean in a triangle exactly ten meters from the bow of Brigadier Vvox's cutter. Even at their lowest setting, the fire-orange bolts boiled the water into a blinding screen of steaming vapor. It happened so quickly that the only reactions possible on the sea vessels were those springing out of pure reflex, including an instantaneous yank on the steering wheel by the pilot, sending people sprawling all over the boat. The cutter swerved into the path of the next boat over, forcing it in turn to cut suddenly. Within seconds, the entire right half of the formation had sundered into fifteen pieces, like a badly cut gem shattering into shards. The other half of the delta fell into chaos too, as those pilots tried to figure out what was going on.

At the bottom of a pile of fallen bodies, Vvox spluttered as she shoved Ttoom and three other troopers off her and scrambled to her feet. The pilot had also been forced to slam the throttle back to lower speed, causing the hydro-foils to retract. They were now subject to both the toss-ing of the waves and the spasmodic pitching of crossed wakes.

Ttoom hauled himself up. "What was that?"

"The starship," Vvox growled. "Signal every cutter—get back into formation—*now!*"

"Right away," said Ttoom as he stumbled across the heaving deck to the radio console.

The yellow blips jostled erratically on the *Enterprise* viewscreen, their forward progress halted for the moment.

"Nice shooting, Mr. Sulu."

"My pleasure, Admiral. We don't want to let them regroup."

Kirk stretched an approving hand. "At your discretion, commander."

Sulu grinned and turned back to the targeting display on

his panel. "Now that we've got 'em stopped, let's get 'em corralled." His fingers flashed across the buttons on his console—

—and six pillars of fire sizzled into the sea around the scattering surface vessels, driving them farther off course and farther toward complete confusion.

Llissa sat across from Spock in the shuttle's rear cabin, her hands clasped at her chin, searching the Vulcan's face for some sign that he was getting through to her father, getting him to come back before they had to leave without him.

"Chekov," said Spock, "prepare for liftoff."

"Spock," McCoy began, then muzzled his dissent. There was no choice.

Spock closed his eyes again, head bowed, centering his concentration once more on communicating with Zzev. Llissa could no longer sit, and she jumped up, opening all the viewports and pacing from one to the other, hoping for a glimpse of her father swimming toward the shuttle.

Suddenly, Spock's head snapped up, eyes clamped shut. *Zzev! Where have you been?*

I can't come back, Spock, Zzev thought back to him. *I know they're here, very, very near—I feel it. I have to warn them. Don't worry about me. If you have to leave, go. Protect yourselves. I'll dive deeper than the raiders can reach. I'll be safe.*

Zzev, Zzev—you are not yet acclimated for great depths. Surface for a breath first.

I'll be fine. It feels like I've been doing this all my life. In case Llissa can't receive my thoughts, tell her—tell her I'll be safe. I'm going down now—much darker just a few meters farther down. Colder, too. Tell McCoy I seem to have enough glycoproteins.

Zzev, if you must dive, do it slowly.

Can't see the light above anymore. Like night here—hard to tell directions—

With Sulu keeping an eye on the Akkallan cutters, firing another phaser salvo when needed to hold them at bay, the main viewscreen again showed outer space, and by now the

Chorymi convoy was close enough to appear as a collection of specks in the center of the starfield.

"Anything, Uhura?" said Kirk.

"Negative, sir."

"All right." Kirk's jaw took on a belligerent set. "New message."

Kirk thumbed the comm button on his armrest. "This is Admiral Kirk of the U.S.S. *Enterprise*. If you cross the plane of this vessel's orbit, we will have no choice but to fire on you. This is your only warning."

Getting short of breath—got to get to surface—need air . . . Not sure which direction—

Then there was a long silence. Spock waited.

Zzev, respond—

More silence. Llissa didn't know exactly what was happening, but she knew she didn't like the creases deepening around Spock's eyes.

Spock—can't find it—can't get to—can't—

The Vulcan wrenched his eyelids open and tried to stand but slumped back into the seat, completely drained. Llissa dropped to her knees in front of him and shook him by the shoulders. "Spock, *where is he?*"

His parched lips opened, but no sound came out. He gazed at her with hollow eyes. "I—lost contact," he finally whispered.

Chekov looked back from the cockpit. "The transponder is still working."

"But that doesn't mean he's still alive," Llissa said, her voice numb.

"Do something," McCoy urged. "I don't care if it's logical—just make it fast!"

"I shall continue trying to contact him," Spock said, regaining his orientation. "He is a sea creature now. He may have capabilities of which we are not aware."

"Is that the best you can do?"

The science officer raised a rueful eyebrow. "Yes."

Under maximum tension, the *Enterprise* bridge crew tended strictly to business, with no extraneous conversation, just an undercurrent of job-related murmurings from the outer ring of work stations. At times like this, when Kirk had little to do but wait for something to happen, the comparative quiet could be unnerving, and he was glad to hear Greenberger's voice out loud.

"Admiral, some of the Chorymi ships're changing course."

He pivoted toward the science station. "Which ones?"

"Four of the fighters, sir."

"Heading?"

"Right at us."

Kirk leaned back in his chair and crossed his arms. "Evidently, a word to the wise wasn't sufficient. Sulu, status of the Akkallan surface fleet?"

He smiled. "They'll never win any awards for choreography, sir."

"Good. Keep two phaser banks aimed at the planet. Lock the others onto the Chorymi fighters."

"Power level, sir?"

"Make it one-quarter power, Sulu. That should be enough to shake 'em up."

On the viewscreen, the diamond-shaped fighters were clearly discernible now, growing larger as they bore down on the *Enterprise*. Without warning, all four fired their weapons, licks of blue flame spitting from their cannons, energy pellets streaking across black space. The pellets exploded harmlessly against the starship's deflector field, with only a slight shudder reaching the bridge deck. The tiny fighters split into pairs, two peeling off to the right, two to the left, wheeling around for another pass.

"Shields solid, Admiral," Sulu reported. "Phasers tracking."

"Hold your fire, Mr. Sulu. Is the mother ship within range?"

"Yes, sir."

"Lock onto it. When I give the word, fire across its bow."

"Aye, sir." Sulu adjusted his target controls, then flexed his fingers above the trigger buttons, waiting.

Out in space, the quartet of Chorymi fighters regrouped and charged toward the *Enterprise* again.

Kirk leaned forward, one elbow resting on his knee, chin propped on that hand. "Stand by, Sulu." He paused. "Fire!"

Without even a split second's delay, the helmsman pressed the trigger button, and an angry orange bolt lanced out from the starship and sizzled across the harvest ship's blunt nose.

"Mr. Sulu, fire again."

The second phaser beam slashed past, missing by a hair's breadth.

Without a return shot, the four fighters veered sharply and retreated to the relative security of their convoy.

"Admiral," Greenberger said, "they've stopped their engines, holding their position."

"Message from the Chorymi fleet commander," Uhura said. She patched the signal to the bridge speaker, and the voice that came out was a flustered mixture of fury and fear. *"—won't stand for this unwarranted hostility. We demand an apology and your assurance of safe passage to our destination. Reply now!"*

Kirk's index finger jabbed the comm button on his chair. "This is Admiral Kirk of the *Enterprise*. You fired first, commander. You are violating Akkallan space, and you've ignored the valid request of a Federation vessel that you stop. You'll get no apology for initiating hostile action. And as for safe passage, you've already arrived at your destination. You'll hold your present position until I give you permission to depart. If you don't do as I say, we'll be forced to pursue and disable your ship. Is that understood, commander—" Kirk's tone made it clear he wasn't asking a question.

"Yes," the Chorymi growled.

"Good. *Enterprise* out."

All eyes remained on Spock—Chekov looking back from the pilot's seat, Llissa and McCoy huddled around the Vulcan in the cramped aft compartment. Spock's own eyes were still closed as he listened for the vaguest hint of a telepathic sign from Zzev Kkayn. The transponder signal continued to wink on the computer screen.

"Dammit, it's been forever," McCoy finally blurted.

Spock's eyes opened. "It has been two minutes, fifty-three seconds, doctor."

"What're we gonna do, Spock? We can't keep waiting here."

"No, we cannot. Mr. Chekov, prepare to submerge the shuttle."

"Submerge? What for?" said McCoy.

"To follow the transponder signal and ascertain Zzev's condition."

"But, sir," Chekov said, "Admiral Kirk ordered us to—"

"I am well aware of the admiral's orders, lieutenant," Spock said. "Submerge immediately, and head directly for the location of the transponder beacon."

"Yes, Mr. Spock," said Chekov.

The shuttle dipped below the waves, enveloped by the sea. As they went deeper into darkness, Llissa glanced at the directional locator display on the screen and sucked in an astonished breath. "Look! He's coming back to the surface."

"Continue closing, Mr. Chekov," Spock said as he and McCoy turned to the screen.

"Can those numbers be wrong?" McCoy asked, his voice apprehensive.

Spock ran the sensing system through a quick check. "It appears to be functioning."

"Then he must be all right."

"Not necessarily, Dr. McCoy. There could be any number of reasons why the transponder is surfacing, including—"

"Dammit, Spock, this is no time for lists of—"

"He's right, Leonard," Llissa interrupted. "Let's wait and see what we find."

"Mr. Spock, look out there," Chekov called back through the midship hatch, turning the craft slightly so they could all see a three-quarter view through the starboard observation ports. They were already deeper than the reach of daylight, down in a twilight world of shadows and shimmers and darting shapes, where human vision could not always be trusted. But there was no mistaking the sight rising up from even murkier depths—the vast bulk of a full-grown triteera.

In the first seconds of watching the creature, Spock was struck by an impression he knew to be illogical, unprovable, but there nonetheless. This massive animal seemed to be swimming with a conscious yet conflicting sense of tender urgency. The Vulcan hit the switches for two starboard floodlights. As the beams flashed on, the triteera's three tail-flukes lost their rhythm and quivered uncertainly, though for just a couple of beats.

Spock panned the light toward the animal's head and found confirmation for his perception of purposeful tenderness in the way it swam. It was balancing something on its flat rostrum, nudging it toward the world of air and light above. Coming a little closer, they got a better look at the object of the triteera's attention. It appeared to be a Wwafida.

McCoy leaned over the science officer's shoulder, squinting through the port. "Could that be Zzev?"

"Possibly. Mr. Chekov, do not get any closer to the triteera. Head directly for the surface."

"Spock, is that such a good idea?" McCoy asked.

Llissa answered first. "If that is my father, and if he's still alive, that triteera's his best chance."

They felt the deck tip back slightly as Chekov let the shuttle rise as quickly as possible. As the *Cousteau* broke through, water pouring off its nose and sides, the triteera came up about fifty meters away, exhaling a plume of steamy breath that swirled in the breeze. Only the creature's angular head and a short portion of its back were out of the water, and it rolled slightly to its right, allowing its primary side flipper—four meters of shiny, mottled black skin—to support the Wwafida and keep it floating where it could breathe.

Spock closed his eyes and sent a pulse of mental energy out toward the Wwafida and the triteera. *Zzev, is that you? Are you able to communicate?*

"Well? Anything?" McCoy prodded.

Spock opened his mouth to answer, then stopped in midbreath.

Spock—? I thought . . . was going to die—

"It is Zzev," the science officer announced formally.

Llissa and McCoy stood stunned for a moment. McCoy found his voice first as joy and relief burst across their faces. "It *is?* Then he's alive?"

"Obviously," said Spock, arching a critical brow. "And I am going to take an emergency raft and retrieve him. Mr. Chekov, while I prepare the raft, take us closer—but do so with great care. I do not want to alarm the triteera."

"Aye, sir," Chekov grinned. "Very, very carefully." He eased the throttle forward and steered toward Zzev and the proprietary creature that had saved his life.

With McCoy's help, Spock released a rescue raft from its storage locker in the shuttle ceiling. Then he opened the side hatch, letting the tangy salt-sea breeze in, popped the raft's auto-inflation valve, and tossed it down to the water, where it unfolded and filled to its completed shape. He handed the mooring line to McCoy, then climbed down the access ladder.

"Spock," Llissa called down to him. "Look what's out there."

He paused at the bottom rung and turned to see what she was pointing at. From all around, small sea creatures were joining the triteera, at least a score of them. It wasn't until a pair swimming together leaped all the way out of the water, diving playfully, that he could be sure of what they were. Now there was no doubt—about a lot of things.

"I don't believe it, Spock!" McCoy shouted. "They're Wwafida!"

"So they are, doctor," Spock said as he stepped into the bobbing raft. "Now release the line so I can get our own Wwafida back to safety."

McCoy threw the cord down. Spock caught it, then found the control stick for the compact engine mounted at the raft's stern. He started it and drove the inflatable through the swells.

Faces still spread into wide grins, McCoy and Llissa stood in the open hatchway, hanging on as the shuttle rolled with the waves.

"Dr. McCoy," Chekov yelled from the cockpit, "the ship is calling."

McCoy ducked back inside and pressed the comm button on the computer console. "Jim?"

"Bones—what's going on down there?"

"It's a long story. Zzev's okay. Spock's gone out to get him. And we found Wwafida—lots of them!"

Kirk slapped his armrest gleefully. "That's great, Bones. Tell Spock to get back up here as quickly as possible."

"What happened with the Chorymi raid and the Akkallan military flotilla?"

"We've got them both on hold. Now, I've got one more

piece of business to take care of. We'll see you in a little while. Kirk out.''

Kirk turned toward the communications station. "Uhura, contact the Publican. And this time, we don't take no for an answer.''

Abben Ffaridor took a half-step back and regarded his painting with a critical eye. In direct contrast to his mood, he'd created a sunny landscape with blossom-dappled hillsides and a crystal-blue sky—not a cloud or drop of water to be seen. Now that the painting was finished, he felt a curious sense of tranquillity come over him, accompanied by a fatalistic acceptance of the real world outside his fantasy work of art. He'd been closeted in his suite since Brigadier Vvox and her armada sailed from Havensbay, wrestling with decisions made in recent weeks. He still didn't think they'd been bad decisions, but the events they'd set into motion hadn't gone at all according to plan.

He was mildly surprised that the crumbling of his would-be empire hadn't driven him to despair. Whatever finally transpired, he believed in his heart that the people of Akkalla would understand the extraordinary circumstances that had forced him to seek radical solutions to grave problems, and they wouldn't blame him. When it all came out, and he was certain it would, they would see that he did his best.

His best, as it turned out, hadn't been good enough. He thought they would forgive him for that.

What good is order without freedom, freedom without truth?

The old maxim had been running through his mind all day. Freedom and truth were truly important. That's what his whole term of office had been about—preserving freedom and truth. He hadn't forgotten them, not ever. But without order, they would wither and die. *They know that, don't they? They understand . . .*

They'll forgive me.

The Publican heard a tap on his door. "Come in.''

A young female trooper with bright eyes and short curls entered diffidently. She looked barely out of childhood.

265

Ffaridor knew all the more experienced troopers were out trying to quell civil demonstrations and riots.

"I'm sorry to bother you, sir."

"Quite all right, quite all right. What is it?"

"Admiral Kirk is calling from the *Enterprise*. Should I tell him you're too busy to—"

"No, no. I'll talk to him." He went slowly to his desk and switched on the communications console. The screen lit, and Kirk's stern face appeared. Ffaridor sat down. "Yes, Admiral."

"We've collected evidence to prove the existence of large numbers of Wwafida, sir, more than enough to convince the Federation Council and prompt an investigation into your actions. You know as well as I do what the results will be."

"Yes." Ffaridor paused. "What would you like me to do?"

Surprise overtook Kirk's severe manner, and he hesitated for a second as he found himself forced to change gears. It seemed there wouldn't *be* any confrontation. *"Recall your fleet of military cutters from the northern Boreal Ocean."*

"I can't, Admiral. They're out of radio range."

"We can take care of that. Uhura, set up a signal relay, please."

With her usual competence, she had the circuitry arranged in a matter of seconds. *"Ready, sir. Publican Ffaridor, you can contact your fleet any time."*

"Thank you. Brigadier Vvox, this is the Publican. I'm reaching you with the help of the *Enterprise*."

"The Enterprise?*"* Her voice came over the bridge audio system. *"What's going on? They've been interfering with our mission, Publican, and they—"*

"You're being recalled to port, Jjenna," Ffaridor said in a voice devoid of rancor. "It's over."

"No! They don't have the right—"

"But they have the power. That's something you should understand."

"We've got to take on the Chorymi raiders."

"There'll be no raid," said Kirk. *"We've stopped the convoy in space. They've got you outgunned, brigadier."*

"That's impossible."

"Are you that anxious to shed Akkallan blood?" Ffaridor asked, shaking his head in regret.

* * *

"What's happened to you?" Vvox shouted, her fury and frustration boiling over as she pounded her fists on the control panel of her cutter. "We *rule* Akkalla. We don't take orders from Federation intruders!" With bulging eyes, she fixed her stare at the radio speaker, as if she could see through it all the way to Ffaridor, hoping her power over him could force him to rescind his decision to cower before Kirk's threats.

"If you'd prefer, brigadier, we'll let the convoy through. I'll collect all Federation personnel on Akkalla, as well as Akkallans wishing political asylum, and leave the mess to you," Kirk said evenly.

"We'll fight, Kirk, and we'll win. This is our world—we can't give up." She whirled to search the faces of her officers, expecting to find rabid support. Instead, she saw defeat in their hollow eyes, the same defeat she heard in Ffaridor's voice.

"Brigadier." It was Kirk on the speaker again. *"You can agree to these terms—immediate release of the Synod and all political prisoners, stop the purge directed at your scientists, and observe a ceasefire with Chorym if they halt their raids on your oceans. The Federation will be glad to mediate— Akkalla is a Federation member, after all. Your choice, Publican Ffaridor."*

"No! Don't take it, Abben," Vvox hissed, spinning back to the radio panel. "Let us fight for what Mother Sea has to offer us—all the power in—"

Trooper Ttoom bashed the butt of his pistol across the back of Vvox's head, and she slumped to the deck. "I declare a mutiny," he announced, without much spirit. "Anybody want to argue with me?" None of the other officers in the bridge cabin moved a muscle. "That's what I thought. Publican Ffaridor, we'll abide by your decision."

Ffaridor sat sadly at his communications station. He folded his hands with great dignity. "We accept your terms, Admiral Kirk."

Chapter Twelve

CAPTAIN'S LOG—STARDATE 7835.8:

A Federation mediation team has arrived, and talks between Akkalla and Chorym are already underway. Meanwhile, on Akkalla itself, order has been reestablished after a tense standoff between military units loyal to Brigadier Vvox and units agreeing to accept the constitutional authority of the Continental Synod. The Synod is once again in charge, with Lord Magister Ddenazay Mmord appointed temporary Publican until new elections can take place. Ffaridor and Vvox have been arrested and face trial for treason. Dr. McPhillips and her staff have been released unharmed.

As to the cultural ramifications for Akkalians of rediscovering their past, that could take a while to sort out. Llissa Kkayn is back at her Collegium post, and she's asked the McPhillips team to stay on and assist with creation of a whole new research program. Llissa has some extra help. Her father, now a fully adapted Wwafida, will work as a Collegium consultant and liaison with Wwafida living in the wild.

At Mr. Spock's suggestion, the Federation will help Akkalla become energy-independent by using the ocean's thermal layers to produce unlimited, clean power. And Chorym has accepted the Federation's offer to apply terraforming techniques to help them turn their deserts back into productive land.

JIM KIRK SAT alone in his quarters, conversing with Llissa on the desktop intercom screen. "Sounds like you've got plenty to keep you busy."

"That's for sure." She smiled. *"And I plan to be right in the middle of everything, hands-on. These past couple of weeks working with your people convinced me I'm at my worst when I get bogged down in administration."*

"I think that's a good decision. How do you feel about working with your father?"

"Not sure. We still don't agree on much, and he's still a terror. But I'm not a child anymore. And we do agree on some basics."

"Like?"

"Wanting to learn everything there is to know about Akkalla. Y'know, it's strange. For thousands of years, we've had two groups of intelligent beings inhabiting the same planet, but in totally separate worlds. Maybe now we can share it as a single world. Oh—I almost forgot—we've got a plan."

"What kind of plan?"

"When things settle down a little, we're going to propose that Akkallans stop removing the dgynt gland. That means the next generation'll get back to the life cycle nature gave us. Maybe that'll give us some real unity."

"I hope so."

"Thanks for getting involved, Jim. You didn't have to."

"That's what they pay us for." He grinned.

"Oh, it's more than that. Good-bye."

"Good-bye, Llissa." Kirk touched a button, and the screen went dark. Then he called the bridge. "Mr. Sulu, as soon as we're ready, take us out of orbit."

Sulu's face appeared on the viewer. *"Heading, sir?"*

Kirk hesitated only a moment. "Home."

"Home, sir? As in earth?"

"That's right. Warp five." Kirk noticed Sulu's open-mouthed confusion. "I'll explain later, Hikaru. I promise."

It didn't take long for word to spread. Within twenty minutes, McCoy was at Kirk's door. "Mind if I come in?"

"Making a house call?"

"Don't worry—it won't cost extra. I didn't know we got orders to go back to earth." McCoy sat at Kirk's desk.

"We didn't."

"Then why're we going there?"

"Brandy?"

"We're going home for brandy?" McCoy gestured at the decanter on Kirk's shelf. "You down to your last bottle? Seems like a waste of antimatter to drive a whole starship home for a trip to the liquor store."

Kirk's lips curled into a sardonic half-grin. "I meant, would you like some brandy?"

"As long as it's medicinal." Kirk poured, and the surgeon took the proffered shot glass. "Now, would you like to answer my question? Or are you hoping I'll get soused and forget I asked."

"What was the question?" Kirk asked, eyes wide with innocence.

McCoy glared as if interrogating an intentionally obstreperous child. "Why are we headed home?"

"I'm tired."

"Why do I have the feeling you're *not* talking R and R?"

"Because you're unusually perceptive," Kirk joshed, then turned serious. "I just decided it was time to wake up in a bed that wasn't moving at warp-speed."

"You're giving up *Enterprise?*" McCoy asked, spacing the words carefully.

"Mm-hmm."

"I don't believe it."

"Believe it."

"Wait just a damn minute. What's Starfleet gonna say about this?"

Kirk sipped his brandy. "They had their say. I talked it over with Admiral Morrow last month. The decision was left to my discretion. We were scheduled for shore leave anyway after this mission—we won't be leaving any holes in Starfleet coverage." His sentence was punctuated by the door chime. "Come."

The door slid open, and Spock entered. "You wished to see me, Admiral?"

"Have a seat, Spock."

McCoy looked from one to the other. "Jim, does he know?"

"Not yet. You want to tell him?"

"Not on your life, but I wouldn't miss *you* telling him."

"Tell me what, Admiral?"

"You can't put it off by offering *him* brandy," McCoy challenged.

"Actually, I would enjoy a drink, if I may."

McCoy did a double-take. "Spock drinking? You giving up the *Enterprise?* When did I fall through the looking glass?"

Kirk chuckled.

"Admiral," Spock said, "did I hear Dr. McCoy correctly?"

"You did," Jim said.

"He's decided it's time for a change," McCoy announced, obviously disapproving of the notion.

"Indeed." Spock's voice betrayed genuine surprise—for a Vulcan. "What prompted this decision?"

"Lots of things. Do you know the myth of Sisyphus?"

"A king of Corinth condemned for an eternity in Hell to roll a large boulder up a hill, only to have it roll down again," said Spock.

"That's what I feel like."

"But we just saved two planets from destroying each other," McCoy protested.

"But Bones—for every place we succeed, how many times does it turn the other way? How many times when there's nobody there to put out the fire?"

"You're not makin' sense, Jim. We need *more* people like you out here, not one *less.*"

Kirk took a sip, savoring the taste on his tongue. "You're right. That's why I've decided to go back to Starfleet Academy and teach. Time to pass on what I know to the next generation—make sure they're better than we were."

"Better than us?" McCoy scoffed. "That won't take a teacher—that'll take a miracle worker."

"Then there's the challenge," Kirk said brightly.

"Jim, don't you remember what happened last time you took a shore assignment?"

"This'll be different. I won't be chief of operations. I'll be with young cadets, where the action is."

McCoy shook his head. "You may not feel that way when *they* sail off on the *Enterprise*—and you're not with 'em."

"I think you're wrong, Bones. I've been considering this for a while. Maybe it was visiting Llissa and her Collegium that crystallized it for me. Morrow also promised me some special assignments. I won't get stale." He put a hand on McCoy's shoulder. "I appreciate your input—"

"But your mind's made up. Spock, don't be so damn quiet. Talk him out of this."

"That is not my place, doctor—nor yours."

McCoy gulped down the dregs of his brandy. "The hell it isn't. You haven't heard the last from me on this, Jim. We're not home yet. I'm a doctor, and I'll try to save you till the second we hit Spacedock." With that, he clunked his glass down and swept out of the cabin.

Spock started to get up. "If there is nothing further—"

"Actually, there is." Kirk waited till Spock sat again. "It's about the ship." He gazed solemnly at his first officer. "She's yours if you want her."

"Jim . . . you know I have no wish to command."

"There's nobody else I'd trust with the *Enterprise*. Can't I—persuade you?"

Spock was silent for a moment. "If the ship were to be used for cadet training, I would be willing to assume temporary command. But only as a teacher."

"After a while, you might change your mind and want regular command. It grows on you."

Spock shook his head. "My hope would be that, after a while, you should wish to *resume* command. In which case, I would be pleased to relinquish the center seat."

Kirk spread his hands plaintively. "Why can't I just be a teacher?"

"Because you were meant to lead, Jim. I do not believe you will be content to remain a teacher. Shall I calculate the odds—?" The slightest hint of a smile played at the corners of his mouth.

"You drive a hard bargain, Spock. But if that's what it takes, I'll ask Starfleet to assign the *Enterprise* to training duty." He refilled his glass and raised it. "Deal?"

One slanted eyebrow elevated. "A quaint human custom, this confirmation of agreement by consuming a ceremonial beverage. If I recall, the proper response is—deal."

Their glasses clinked together.

Backlit by reflected moonglow, Starfleet Spacedock rode high in earth orbit. The *Enterprise* floated inside the cavernous docking bay, moored alongside one of the wedge-shaped service wings jutting from the central core structure.

Most of her crew was on leave now, resting before

272

embarking on new assignments. Only a skeleton maintenance staff remained, along with senior officers taking care of final details. One of those details was a farewell dinner in a private corner of the mess lounge. In issuing the invitations, Kirk indicated that casual attire would be perfectly appropriate. It didn't surprise him to see his senior staff show up in their dress best.

As appetizers were served, the mood was subdued, but drinks and camaraderie soon took care of that. Kirk didn't want this gathering to be funereal, and he was glad to see smiling faces and hear boisterous voices by the time a huge cake baked in the shape of the starship was brought out for dessert. Things quieted down a bit as Kirk stood to cut the first slice.

"Actually, you should be doing this, McCoy," he said. "You're the surgeon."

"Yeah, but I'm off duty—and I've had too much to drink."

Kirk laughed, then made a careful incision around the bridge. "This is for Mr. Spock," he said with a grin. "By the way, I'd like to thank you all for accepting his request that you be part of his teaching staff."

"After all these years of taking orders," Uhura said, "it should be fun to boss other people around—for a while, anyway."

"Besides," said Scotty, "we'll just be keepin' her in good shape f'r when y' decide to take 'er back, sir."

Kirk brandished the knife in mock anger. "Nobody believes me. I won't be back. Not to stay, anyway. But I will be grading *you* at the same time as *you're* grading those cadets, so you all better watch your step."

"Admiral," Spock said, "are you forgetting something?"

"Forgetting? That's right, I do have an announcement. One of you won't be staying with the ship under Mr. Spock." He paused as his officers glanced around the table at each other, seeking a hint. But they were all equally in the dark. "Mr. Chekov, your new assignment will be as first officer of the starship *Reliant*. Starfleet told me Captain Terrell was looking for a top young officer with wide-ranging experience. I suggested you, and since you already happened to be at the top of his list, he was more than happy to accept my recommendation. Congratulations."

While everyone broke into applause, Chekov sat stunned, a forkful of cake frozen in midflight.

The empty corridor rang with the sound of boot heels coming around the curve as Uhura, Sulu, and Chekov headed for the docking port on the starship's flank, where a shuttle pod was waiting to take them over to Spacedock.

"But I don't want to go off alone," Chekov said with unstinting glumness. "I was looking forward to being with the rest of the crew."

"C'mon, Pavel, it's a good assignment," Uhura said. "It's not everybody who gets asked for."

"I guess it will be good experience." They reached a corridor intersection and stopped to look down the silent passageways. "It's hard to believe so many years have gone by."

"Sure is. Funny how those kids at Starfleet Academy keep getting younger and younger, and we haven't aged a day," Sulu said seriously, then burst out with his staccato laugh.

"Do you remember how old I was when I first came aboard?" asked Chekov.

"Twenty-two," Uhura said, "and green as grass."

Chekov grinned. "I was so nervous I could hardly speak to the Admiral. And Mr. Spock—? Forget it."

"As I remember it," Uhura said, "you couldn't even talk to me."

"That's because I thought you were the loveliest creature I'd ever met—"

"What about me?" Sulu pouted.

"You were not so lovely, even back then. And once I saw you playing with a sword, I thought you were one of the *strangest* creatures I'd ever met. All these years later, I know I was right."

As they approached the docking port, Chekov's grin faded and his expression darkened. "I'm going to miss everybody," he said, swallowing the catch in his voice.

"Oh, Pavel," Uhura huffed, "don't get all weepy on us."

"Besides," said Sulu, "I have a feeling we'll all be together again."

Chekov gave his friend a sidelong glance. "Are you getting spiritual, Sulu?" he asked suspiciously.

"Maybe. Call it karma, but there's something about

serving on this ship. I don't know if it's a blessing or a curse—I guess a little of both—but I *know* we'll all be back aboard her someday."

They tossed their duffels through the open pod hatch, then folded into a three-way hug.

"You take care of yourself out there, Pavel," Sulu warned.

"Yeah, kid," Uhura said playfully. "You won't have us to look out for you anymore."

"I will be careful. I promise. And you two take good care of this ship. I don't want to come back to a rusted hulk."

"Don't worry," Sulu said. "Admiral Kirk wouldn't ever let that happen."

Chekov laughed. "Neither would Mr. Scott."

They linked arms and filed into the waiting pod. With a hydraulic whine, the hatch shut and sealed behind them. Sulu powered up the thrusters and released the docking ring, and the tiny shuttle moved away. Chekov stood at the window for a last look at the *Enterprise* floating in repose, her curves highlighted by spotlight beams that made her look alive and sensuous.

"*Dosvedanya, lubima,*" he whispered. "Good-bye, lady . . ."

STAR TREK

THE NEXT GENERATION

THE STAR TREK PHENOMENON

___ ENTROPY EFFECT 66499/$3.95
___ KLINGON GAMBIT 66342/$3.95
___ PROMETHEUS DESIGN 67435/$3.95
___ ABODE OF LIFE 66149/$3.95
___ BLACK FIRE 70548/$4.50
___ TRIANGLE 66251/$3.95
___ WEB OF THE ROMULANS 70093/$4.50
___ YESTERDAY'S SON 66110/$3.95
___ WOUNDED SKY 66735/$3.95
___ CORONA 66341/$3.95
___ MY ENEMY, MY ALLY 70421/$4.50
___ VULCAN ACADEMY MURDERS 64744/$3.95
___ UHURA'S SONG 65227/$3.95
___ SHADOW LORD 66087/$3.95
___ ISHMAEL 66089/$3.95
___ KILLING TIME 65921/$3.95
___ DWELLERS IN THE CRUCIBLE 66088/$3.95
___ PAWNS AND SYMBOLS 66497/$3.95
___ THE FINAL REFLECTION 67075/$3.95
___ MINDSHADOW 70420/$4.50
___ DOUBLE, DOUBLE 66130/$3.95
___ CRISIS ON CENTAURUS 65753/$3.95
___ DREADNOUGHT 66500/$3.95
___ DEMONS 66150/$3.95
___ BATTLESTATIONS! 70183/$4.50
___ CHAIN OF ATTACK 66658/$3.95
___ DEEP DOMAIN 70549/$4.50
___ DREAMS OF THE RAVEN 70281/$4.50
___ ROMULAN WAY 70169/$4.50
___ HOW MUCH FOR JUST THE PLANET? 62998/$3.95
___ BLOODTHIRST 64489/$3.95
___ ENTERPRISE 65912/$4.50
___ STRANGERS FROM THE SKY 65913/$4.50
___ FINAL FRONTIER 69655/$4.95
___ IDIC EPIDEMIC 63574/$3.95
___ THE TEARS OF THE SINGERS 69654/$4.50
___ THE COVENANT OF THE CROWN 67072/$3.95
___ MUTINY ON THE ENTERPRISE 67073/$3.95
___ THE TRELLISANE CONFRONTATION 70095/$4.50
___ VULCAN'S GLORY 65667/$3.95

more on next page...

THE
STAR TREK
PHENOMENON

____ **THE KOBAYASHI MARU**
65817/$4.50

____ **SPOCK'S WORLD**
66773/$4.95

____ **TIME FOR YESTERDAY**
70094/$4.50

• •

____ **STAR TREK– THE MOTION PICTURE**
67795/$3.95

____ **STAR TREK II– THE WRATH OF KHAN**
67426/$3.95

____ **STAR TREK III–THE SEARCH FOR SPOCK**
67198/$3.95

____ **STAR TREK IV– THE VOYAGE HOME**
70283/$4.50

____ **STAR TREK V– THE FINAL FRONTIER**
68008/$4.50

____ **STAR TREK: THE KLINGON DICTIONARY**
66648/$4.95

____ **STAR TREK COMPENDIUM REVISED**
62726/$9.95

____ **MR. SCOTT'S GUIDE TO
THE ENTERPRISE**
70498/$12.95

____ **THE STAR TREK INTERVIEW BOOK**
61794/$7.95

**POCKET
BOOKS**

Simon & Schuster Mail Order Dept. STP
200 Old Tappan Rd., Old Tappan, N.J. 07675

Please send me the books I have checked above. I am enclosing $_____ (please add 75¢ to cover postage and handling for each order. N.Y.S. and N.Y.C. residents please add appropriate sales tax). Send check or money order—no cash or C.O.D.'s please. Allow up to six weeks for delivery. For purchases over $10.00 you may use VISA: card number, expiration date and customer signature must be included.

Name_____

Address_____

City_____ State/Zip_____

VISA Card No._____ Exp. Date_____

Signature_____ 118-23

THE LEGEND OF <u>STAR TREK</u>® ON AUDIO!

Plug in your headphones and take a trip to another world. The STAR TREK series on audio is your ticket to exciting adventures! Six titles to choose from! All STAR TREK audio adventures feature dramatic readings by LEONARD NIMOY and GEORGE TAKEI and/or JAMES DOOHAN and feature SPECIAL SOUND EFFECTS and the STAR TREK television series theme or an original score!

ORDER YOUR STAR TREK AUDIO ADVENTURE TODAY!

☐ 62951-4 STAR TREK: ENTERPRISE,™ The First Adventure (McIntyre) $9.95

☐ 66864-1 STAR TREK: The Entropy Effect (McIntyre) $9.95

☐ 64718-0 STAR TREK: Strangers From the Sky (Bonanno)$8.95

☐ 64629-X STAR TREK: STAR TREK IV—The Voyage Home (McIntyre)
$8.95 –**A Grammy Award Nominee!**

☐ 64719-9 STAR TREK: Web of the Romulans (Murdock) $9.95

☐ 66865-X STAR TREK: Yesterday's Son (Crispin) $9.95

Please send me the audiocassette(s) I have checked above. I am enclosing $_____(please include $1.50 to cover shipping and handling for each tape ordered. N.Y.S. and N.Y.C. residents please add appropriate sales tax.) Send check or money order only—NO CASH OR C.O.D.'s PLEASE. Allow up to six weeks for delivery. VISA and Mastercard accepted.

Send Order To:
Simon & Schuster Audio Division
1230 Avenue of the Americas
New York, NY 10020
Attn: STAR TREK Audio Offer (B.A.D.)

NAME_____

ADDRESS_____

CITY_____STATE_____ZIP_____

VISA NUMBER_____EXP. DATE____

MASTERCARD NUMBER_____EXP. DATE____

SIGNATURE_____

Copyright © 1987, 1988 Paramount Pictures Corporation. All Rights Reserved.
STAR TREK is a Registered Trademark of Paramount Pictures Corporation.

For more information regarding

STAR TREK®
THE OFFICIAL FAN CLUB

please call or write to:
STAR TREK: THE OFFICIAL FAN CLUB
P.O. Box 111000
Aurora, CO 80011